OLIVE AND THE BLUE DRAGON

A STEM College Romance

&

Later-in-Life Love Story

C.M. Clark

For my dad, George Clark, and my mom, Laura Ryan Clark, and for the marine biologists who work to preserve our oceans and the engineers developing inventions to help combat climate change.

See Page 241 for Book Club Group Discussion Questions
See Page 223 for Extended Author's Notes
See Page 211 for the Bibliography

"Hannah's" Texas Hill Country Photography

Photos by C.M. Clark

One

Kiera falls asleep that night, feeling hopeful once more about growing closer to Ryan during their group excursion in two days. Her mind whisks her away to the waters around the Great Barrier Reef, where they splash and share a laugh. This image fades and becomes a dream she has experienced countless times before.

It is not her own father and brothers but another woman's father and brothers she sees sitting in a small wooden fishing boat holding nets. A fish leaps out of the water, going straight up and straight back down, with little splash. The youngest boy howls with laughter.

"Hush," scolds his much older brother.

Another fish comes up, turns on its side, and makes a bigger splash. As the child attempts to prevent another outburst, his pop points into the distance. A dolphin has its sizable, round head and lengthy snout partially above water, and then disappears.

In silence, they search the cove intently, waiting for the mammal to resurface.

Water churning at the stern causes them to turn around, where they are greeted with clicking sounds and an apparent grin. The father slowly and carefully moves across the last bench seat to reach out and touch the dolphin's head as the creature squeals with approval.

She awakens with a smile on her face. This is her favorite recurring dream, one of many she believes connect her to a woman who lived on the island over 100 years ago. Most of what Kiera encounters in these visions reveals a painful past.

NINE YEARS EARLIER

Twelve-year-old Kiera is at the shore on Swaggerty Island in Queensland, Australia. The sand is white, and the water is a brilliant turquoise. The waves are strong today. There are not many people around.

She is searching for seashells with her two younger brothers, Kian and Kevin, for their mother, who has a small business making jewelry mainly for tourists. The boys are goofing around. Usually here by herself, she becomes aggravated straight away.

The littlest brother, Kevin, runs up to his big sister and opens his hand.

"What about this one?"

"No. Conch shells like that are homes for crabs. Put it back. We want one-sided clam and scallop shells in excellent condition. Two-sided shells mean something could be living inside. In order to leave nature alone as much as possible, we are only going to take nine or ten."

In the past, Kiera collected empty conch shells until she learned how crabs need unoccupied ones to move into after they outgrow their current home.

Several times during her searches, she has stumbled upon spiral shells with a sea snail inside and returned them to the ocean where they belong because the snails can dry out and die. Now she knows that even if you cannot see a snail, a very tiny one could be in there. Unlike crabs, the snails never leave their homes and add on spirals as they grow. She convinced her mum not to use spiral shells anymore for her creations.

Kiera walks along with head held down. All of a sudden, she is staring at a small sea turtle on its back. The reptile's eyes are barely open, and the mouth is turned down like a frown. A piece is missing from the left front flipper. She picks up the critter and yells to her brothers, "Quick! We need to take this turtle to the marine station."

From the beach to the station is about 950 meters. The kids move along swiftly and arrive in under 15 minutes.

The Marine Life and Weather Study Center is a three-story tan brick building with metal statues of anchors in the courtyard and a 10-foot solar-powered red and white wooden lighthouse for decoration. Mounted on the rooftop are large, stationary binoculars for viewing the ocean, popular during whale migrations, along with weather monitoring equipment.

Kiera has always wanted to go inside. She was immensely jealous of her neighbor, who is older and got to attend a high school camp at the center the previous summer.

The boys follow their sister into the facility. People turn to look at them as she speaks a little too loudly, "Help, I found a sick sea turtle."

A woman in her late 20s rushes over. They are escorted back to a lab area.

"What is wrong with him?"

The scientist examines the turtle. "She is a girl sea turtle, an olive ridley. We see this often. The turtle has eaten a plastic bag, and her belly is swollen. We will nurse her back to health and release this beautiful girl at the beach when she is ready. You saved her. She would have died if you had not found her, but next time, don't touch them or pick one up yourself. Come and tell us so we can do that, OK?"

"OK."

As the marine life specialist continues to probe the turtle, Kiera drills her with questions. They talk about the fact that climate change is affecting sea turtles and their migration paths, making it harder for them to survive, and how plastics are making the oceans warmer as well.

Because she was so focused on the turtle when they first entered, Kiera did not notice the substantial room surrounding her. Across from the lab area, she sees giant tubs of water and aquariums lining the walls. Pipes run above their heads. There are people on the other side looking into microscopes, and someone is standing in front of the largest tub holding one device in the water and another in their other hand, as if taking some reading.

In awe of this setting, she cannot wait for high school and college to be able to study the ocean and all the creatures in it.

"Why are there plants in here?" she asks after spotting an area of plants on bright orange scaffolding.

"Marine botanists research how to improve plant survival."

"I never think about plants, just the critters."

"It is an important field. Many marine species rely on aquatic plants for food and shelter, and the plants in the ocean produce a large percentage of oxygen for the entire Earth. They even combat climate change. We need them. In a few years, you will learn all about this in school. Let me walk you out. I need to get back to work."

"One last question. Can I name the turtle Olive?"

"That would be great, and my name is Amelia."

"I am Kiera."

"It was nice to meet you," says Amelia, amused by the enthusiasm of the young girl who is obviously very intelligent and will be a good steward of the Earth.

"Let's go," she announces to her brothers, who were surprisingly quiet and good the entire time.

On the way out of the building, she again catches sight of things unnoticed. Marine life artwork hangs in the hallways and open spaces. An aquarium near the front door features the cutest round yellow fish with enormous eyes for its small body, and it looks as if it is smiling at her. Kiera knows she will be back here someday to work with the scientists.

The kids start their trek back home. As they approach a building that local teenagers say is haunted, the boys begin making ghostly sounds. Sis does not think it is the least bit funny and directs her attention elsewhere.

Precisely when foot pain sets in from running all around in tattered thongs two sizes too small for her, the holiday resort comes into view, consisting of many individual wooden bungalows in various earth-tone colors with thatch roofs and welcoming porches.

Turning right at the mustard yellow bungalow where the pebbled path ends, the siblings make their way to the back of the property, out of sight from resort guests, and enter a narrow two-story house. Stilts keep the structure off the ground in case of high waters. The first story is aqua blue, while the second is a fading green color in desperate need of a new and matching coat of paint.

Creaky, decrepit steps lead to the enclosed front porch, where a vintage cast-iron BBQ grill stands and a shabby couch previously kept inside. Buckets and coolers sit piled in a corner for when the men go fishing. White lattice and mesh surround the area. Underneath are all kinds of items being stored, such as tools and bicycles.

The boys throw the door open and proceed to jabber a mile a minute to their mother about the turtle, but she is not interested at the moment. With an annoyed look, she hands her daughter an outfit.

"We are going to be late for dance practice for the festival. Get dressed now, please."

Holding up the small spaghetti-strap scarlet red top and bright yellow skirt, Kiera makes a displeased face. She hates dresses, skirts, and clothing that attracts attention. Her mother teaches dance and creates a routine each year for the annual performance.

Like every summer, she loses the argument of why her participation is required, just because Mum loves to dance. Dread comes over her at the thought of being up on stage in full view of an audience in only six days.

FOUR MONTHS LATER
CORPUS CHRISTI, TEXAS, USA
The Laren family is in Corpus Christi, driving to the coast from their home in Fort Worth. They pass the ship channel, where several oil tankers are docked. Smoke billows out from chemical plants. The channel is busy with tug boats, cargo ships, and constant activity.

Upon arriving at a local public beach, people and cars are everywhere, along with a sea of umbrellas. Jack and Hannah's 15-year-old son, Ryan, does not seem to mind. He is entirely about being at the shore and cannot wait to get in the water. They squeeze in between others to put up an umbrella. The teenager starts to run off. "Wait," his mother calls out. "You need sun lotion first."

Seeing her son's excitement pleases Hannah, but she secretly worries about him swimming in the Gulf. With climate change making the water warmer, he is more at risk of coming in contact with bad bacteria. In the interest of family fun, however, she keeps these thoughts to herself, tossing aside the spine-chilling idea of a flesh-eating bacterial infection and deciding to trust in his immune system.

Jack plays in the water with Ryan for a while, but sitting under the umbrella is more appealing, so he leaves the boy to enjoy the ocean.

On the way to lounge, a seagull walks behind him in the sand.

"Looks like you made a friend," his wife laughs. "I think we have some crackers left."

"I know it is tempting to feed them, but it is better not to. It can lead to aggressive behavior and even make them sick."

Another Laughing Gull about twenty feet away begins to make its signature laughing call.

Jack repeats the sound, prompting the gull beside him to do the same.

The seabird leaves to find someone else to feed it.

"Bye, Gerald," he calls out.

Their son floats on his boogie board, allowing the waves to propel him almost to shore. He kicks and paddles back out. After doing this repeatedly for probably an hour, he finally stands up. Looking down at the seaweed beneath his feet, a tiny blue organism clings to part of it. Somehow, knowing not to touch the life form, he gently pushes it onto his board, carefully maneuvering up the beach to yell, "Mom, look what I found. Bring my phone."

Hannah meets him halfway.

"What *is* this?" he asks, not believing his eyes.

"I have no idea. I've never seen such a thing. Don't touch it."

Ryan gives her the boogie board to hold while he takes pictures and a video. She stares at the little creature that resembles one of those squishy rubber insect toys. It has webbed arms, fanning out at the ends to look more like feathers than fingers. The legs are much shorter than the arms but have the same featherlike appearance. It is only about one inch long and has the most beautiful shiny blue-colored body. She would not believe it was real if it weren't moving.

"I better return him to the ocean so he doesn't die."

"That is smart," she acknowledges. "When we go to tour the university tomorrow, we can stop by the Marine Biology Department and show them the video and pictures. I have a feeling others will find this fascinating as well."

The Larens leave their hotel and drive on a road that curves around Oso Bay, ending at the gulf. They turn right onto Ocean Drive to Texas A&M University Corpus Christi. The campus entrance faces the ocean with the bay surrounding the other sides. For someone who loves the seashore, Hannah could not imagine a better college to go to.

"A university on its own island. How cool is that?"

Her remark gets no response.

Ryan had developed quite a negative attitude about education during his first year of high school, after making nothing but A's his first eight years of school. He was starting to question the need to even go to college.

Hannah points to the long beige-colored brick wall bearing the university's name with a sculpture on top. "There is the *Momentum* sculpture in the shape of a wave. I want to get your picture in front of it on the way out."

"Is that really necessary?"

She ignores her son's comment and irritated tone of voice. "The Wave shape is 30 feet in diameter and is meant to give you the feeling of wind and water and movement, and the possibilities that exist by studying here."

He shakes his head and rolls his eyes.

The family parks and begins their stroll across the modern-looking campus, where towering palm trees and light tan buildings with abundant windows give the grounds a nice feel.

A Laughing Gull perched on a sign laughs out loud while appearing to stare directly at Jack.

"It's Gerald," his wife teases.

They reach the Life Sciences Building and enter the three-story glass-covered atrium, which houses the staircase. This arrangement allows for a splendid view on the way up.

Hannah pushes open the door of the Marine Biology Department and greets the receptionist. "Hello. My son caught a curious ocean creature on camera and wants to show it to someone here."

"Dr. Clarke, come here for a minute," the older woman practically yells.

An attractive man in his mid-30s appears from an office. He does not look like the professors Hannah had when she was in college.

Jack nudges his shy son, indicating he should pull up the images.

"I found this blue creature at the beach yesterday and took a video and pictures," Ryan explains as he holds his phone out and shows the professor the video first.

"It's a blue dragon. Outstanding. They are poisonous with a painful sting, you know?"

"I didn't know, but I never touched it. I put him right back in the ocean."

Dr. Clarke goes on to explain about the species. "The scientific name is *Glaucus atlanticus*. They are sea slugs that float upside down and have countershading to protect against predators from above and from below. The part of their body in blue faces upwards, merging with the water to anything above, and the opposite silver side faces down to mix with the sunlight reflecting on the water when viewed by underwater predators."

The professor grabs a business card from the desk. "Can you send me the pictures to this email so I can include them in one of my lectures?"

"And I'm Professor Mark Clarke by the way," extending his hand to the young man. "You should apply to our Marine Science program in a few years."

The enthusiasm at these words is written all over the boy's face.

"Here, let me get you a copy of my book about how climate change is affecting our oceans." Dr. Clarke returns and begins a discussion on the topic while Ryan asks some smart questions.

Hannah and Jack grin at one another as their son converses with the professor. "I think we need to put more money aside for college," she whispers.

Two

EIGHT YEARS, THREE MONTHS LATER
Hannah leaves her house to get some exercise. She loves being able to walk and walk and still be on her own property. Initially, moving to the Texas Hill Country after their son went away to college was something she did for her spouse, but she has grown to treasure it.

Jack already worked remotely with his cybersecurity job. Fortunately, the internet functions well enough for him to continue to do so from "no man's land," as her sister-in-law calls it. The closest town is only 30 minutes away. It isn't as if they are in the middle of nowhere.

Her husband enjoys having a tractor and doing projects on their land. They both share an interest in photography, constantly taking pictures of the wildlife around them, such as deer, rabbits, bobcats, coyotes, Mexican wolves, and a variety of birds.

Hannah has numerous photos of wildflowers and even bugs, making a picture collage of butterflies, dragonflies, grasshoppers, and katydids. Amazed with the quality of images their new camera captures that bring the striking colors of butterfly wings and the complex designs of the veins and membranes of dragonfly wings into absolute focus, she is considering making greeting cards out of them to sell online.

This place is perfect for Jack. Animals and birds have always been drawn to him, but out here, it is a heartwarming sight to watch. The day before, he sat on a bench he made while "Sally" the deer stood nearby. A Greater Roadrunner ran past just as a Golden-cheeked Warbler landed, followed by a Painted Bunting. Three rabbits were also hopping around. Wishing she could take a picture, Hannah knew they would all scatter if she were to step outside.

For a daily walk, she chooses one of many paths created by the utility vehicle's constant use. The route today takes her alongside a fenced-in field of goats. Jack built a website for her to sell goat milk soap, but business is slow. They had no idea owning goats would be so much work.

While raising their son, she ran a solo medical transcription business from home for a number of years. Within a short period, the doctors she provided the service to either retired or sold their practices to become part of large healthcare organizations. Her self-published books for children were done as a hobby. She did the drawings herself, even though they could definitely use the aid of graphic design software.

From a distance, the property is similar in appearance to a Lincoln Log playset. The main home is a log cabin. Everything is wooden: the floors, walls, doors, cabinets, and furniture. There is a smaller log cabin a short walk from the central house constructed for Jack's then 90-year-old father, but when it came time to pack him up and sell his own home, he refused. Next to this cabin is a one-room guest house. A fourth log structure is Jack's workshop.

They are surrounded by hills in close range, but their own property is flat. There are 20 level acres in front, another 29 in back, and one acre in between, a little higher up than the rest, which made the perfect spot to build. Mesquite trees surround their home and the edges of the property, while the rest of the land is open pasture. The view is amazing from the living room and off the back porch. The hills are covered in dark green junipers. However, the land turns brown for months in the sweltering summers, finally transforming back to green with some good October rains.

As Hannah returns from her outing, she hears the phone ringing. It is her stepdaughter, Allison.

Allison is five years older than Ryan but began college a few years after high school, and it took six years for her to finish after changing majors twice before settling on Environmental Science. Using her college graduation money to renovate a small school bus and turn it into a livable RV, she moved to Oregon four months ago to live in a community of school bus homes. While currently working at a local coffee shop, the goal is to get on with the forest service eventually. Entry level positions in the field are hard to come by. She did her best to fix up the bus with limited funds. The neighbors in her community have done impressive renovations with their buses, including all modern appliances, stylish furniture, and elaborate porches. Her new home has solar power, something Allison is especially proud of.

Both siblings are deeply concerned about the environment and climate change, engaging in role reversal with their parents over the years. Hannah has been lectured to for buying products from companies that do not practice sustainability, being caught with a plastic water bottle from time to time, and using plasticware at family parties. Now she makes it a point to always use reusable bottles and research companies and their environmental policies. Ryan volunteers to do dishes to prevent the use of plastics, and Allison sends her website links from which to order eco-friendly, recyclable, and biodegradable products.

Hannah did have to draw the line at her son's request to begin hanging clothes to dry instead of using the energy-consuming dryer. While her husband could not be convinced by his daughter to purchase an electric car, they know both kids will purchase EVs when in a position to do so. At Ryan's urging, they finally agreed to have a solar power company come in two weeks to speak about how panels would work for their own home.

She picks up the phone. "Hi Allison."

"Hi. Is my dad there?"

"He is at Aunt Tracy's political rally in Austin today. Tomorrow, they will be in San Antonio, and then on the third day, it's Houston."

Allison forgot all about how her aunt was running for Congress. She senses a tone in her stepmother's voice. "You don't like Aunt Tracy, do you? I know she doesn't like my views, which are very liberal in her mind."

"It is politics I don't like. And I love your aunt, at least as much as you can love someone who thinks you are going to hell." Hannah laughs, but then feels guilty. "I'm sorry. I shouldn't talk that way. I didn't go to the rally because someone has to take care of these goats."

"So, Tracy believes we are going to hell for not going to church?" her stepdaughter asks with curiosity.

Regretting her flippant remark, she makes an attempt to explain.

"Your aunt voiced her disapproval years ago on how we only show up to church for Easter and Christmas services. And a concern for our souls was mentioned. I do feel bad that we did not set a good example for you and your brother."

Going on to chat longer than they have in many years, she shares stories about how funny her sister-in-law can be when discussing topics related to her bible study group.

"Some members thought it was sinful for your aunt and cousin Tiffany to watch *Friends* reruns with all of the premarital sex. One time, Tracy suggested the group see a movie, and several people became upset over her choice of film because they had a big problem with an actor's bare bottom being shown."

She had laughed so hard at that, and now Allison was laughing too.

Meanwhile, at the political rally, Tracy is being humorous, telling jokes, some at the expense of her brother Jack, and making everyone laugh. She is a great speaker and has enjoyed a large support base in the Texas legislature, as well as during her run for Congresswoman in the United States House of Representatives.

Hannah hangs up with her stepdaughter and examines a nearby picture of Allison and Ryan taken years ago at the beach. The contrast between the two of them standing side by side is amusing. Allison was six feet tall by ninth grade. She was 14 in the picture, and absolutely gorgeous, with her olive skin and long, flowing, honey-brown hair. Ryan was nine and the skinniest little thing, pale as could be with her Irish skin. He also has his mother's green eyes and dark brown hair.

Thankfully, her son got his height from his father and was taller than Hannah by the time he turned 13, not that passing 5 feet 3 is hard to do. Still, for her side of the family having no man over 5 feet 6, it is astonishing to look up at this 6-feet-2-inch person she gave birth to, who is filling out more and more each time they see him, thanks to all the weights he lifts. You have to be careful where you step in his college apartment with dumbbells of various sizes all over the floor. The weight rack Mom and Dad purchased never seems to get used.

She hopes Ryan is doing well at school. The stresses of finishing up a Master's in Marine Biology and facing a PhD program have been getting to him. He completed his bachelor's in three years with the help of dual-credit high school courses. The 18 months of graduate school have flown by, but it has been an entirely different ball game at this level.

Most of Hannah's friends stay in contact with their college-aged and adult children on a daily basis. This is not the case with her son. She sends a weekly text: *How was your week?* Only to receive a reply of *Good*, even when she knows that isn't true. And occasionally there is no response, prompting a follow-up message. Communication is sparse, but that is how it was for her as a young person. During college, she would pretty much say goodbye to her parents until Thanksgiving, and again till the spring and summer breaks, something she would later regret. Of course, that was well before the days of cell phones and texting. The dorms had a community phone down the hall.

TEXAS A&M UNIVERSITY - CORPUS CHRISTI, TEXAS, USA

Ryan is sitting at a computer in an office inside the Marine Biology Department. Professor Clarke, whom he first met eight years ago, walks in. Being hired as Dr. Clarke's Graduate Research Assistant was big news for the Laren family.

"This is a superb report. The computer program you wrote to do this analysis is just what I needed for my ocean pollution research."

Ryan appreciates the praise. "Programming in Python is awesome. I will have the data analysis on ocean dead zones by the end of the week."

"It can wait until after midterms. You should go and study."

MACDERMID UNIVERSITY - QUEENSLAND, AUSTRALIA

She is running through the mangroves, zigzagging around the trees. It is a pitch-black night. The moon is behind the clouds. She falls but swiftly picks herself up off the ground, knowing she must get back home. She runs and runs but feels as if she is no closer. A door slams. Kiera opens her eyes.

It's only a dream, she tells herself. *Another dream. Go back to sleep.*

After trying to fall asleep on her back, she rolls over onto her side, but her heart is pounding so hard she hears it beating through her ear pressed against the pillow. This sensation has bothered her since she was a little girl. Continuing to change positions for almost an hour, somehow, she manages to fall back to sleep. She is thankful to have her own room now at the university residence hall.

Despite being tired, Kiera finds herself able to focus all day. In Ocean Science class, the professor is finishing a lecture with her last two slides. One slide shows small particles of different colors.

"These are nurdles. They are the building blocks for all of our plastic products. During the manufacturing and shipping processes, the particles get released into the environment and end up in our rivers and oceans. Their color is usually white or clear, but some are black, green, or blue."

Kiera listens intently. Ocean pollution and what it does to marine life upsets her greatly. She was shocked to learn how microscopic plastic particles washing up on the shore can make the sand hotter, affecting sea turtles and their eggs.

The last slide is of a dead fish with a mouthful of nurdles. The professor explains how these fragments are often mistaken for food by fish, seabirds, and other wildlife.

"Next Saturday, you can earn extra credit by participating in a nurdle cleanup on the Sunshine Coast. That's it for today, and remember, your reports are due on Friday."

Rushing out to get to her last class on the other side of campus, she overdoes it and has to duck into a bathroom to use her inhaler. Growing up, her asthma was mild, but it worsened while in college, resulting in more frequent flare-ups. She keeps her condition to herself as much as she can. It makes her feel different and weak, and the possibility of being more at risk as the effects of climate change intensify makes her angry.

MACDERMID UNIVERSITY - HISTORY CLASS

"I know you all must have done your assigned readings," probes Professor Cillian Colin Ryan, who goes by his middle name of Colin. Several students smirk. A university cricket player named Cooper is looking down.

"Cooper, please tell the class how the New Zealand Māori leader Hongi Hika's actions led to 20% of the Māori population being killed and also to New Zealand being annexed by Britain."

The young man raises his head. "Why does learning about New Zealand matter to us? This is Australia."

"New Zealand *was* part of Australia according to the British until the 1841 annexation made it a separate colony. Today, about 20% of all Māori, over 170,000, now live in Australia. It is all part of history."

The professor begins his slide show. At first, the female students appear to pay close attention, while many of the guys look bored.

Colin is closing in on 50, but his muscular physique, blondish wavy hair, and attractive short-trimmed beard make him look younger. He has a year-round tan from surfing, hiking, and rock climbing. Well-known for his published works, he also receives media attention for attending events with beautiful women, including actresses and a professional tennis player. He supports theatre groups in Queensland, and a movie is rumored to be made next year based on his book about Hongi Hika.

The second slide depicts the Māori chief with a tattooed face. "From the beginning, Hongi Hika was focused on building relationships with the Europeans, becoming interested in their muskets. He made trips to Sydney in order to trade and acquire muskets from them. Hongi also traveled all the way to England in 1820."

Dr. Ryan knows he is losing the attention of the room instead of gaining it. Admittedly, he lacks his usual enthusiasm today, tired from a trip to New Zealand with Jerry Spiner from the marine biology department. His colleague invited him to attend a conference on the effects of climate change on the Māori. The invitation was for the company and to pick his brain on the culture and history of this group that refers to themselves as tangata whenua, "people of the land."

Spending time with a professor from a different discipline was refreshing. Within his own department, competition runs rampant over who has the most prestigious published work, awards, and recognition. Snide comments are often directed at him, and the lack of collaboration is disheartening. Several years ago, his peers had a blast mocking the historical play developed from his writings. They will not be laughing when one of his books becomes an award-winning film, an endeavor he has been toiling away to make happen.

Despite the students' apathy, he continues on, pulling up a slide with a drawing of the King of England standing beside the chief. "Hongi Hika went to England with Thomas Kendall, a missionary and New Zealand's first Justice of the Peace, to meet a professor at Cambridge to assist in compiling a Māori language dictionary. King George invited the indigenous leader to meet, giving him gifts, which Hongi exchanged for muskets by stopping in Sydney on the way home. He did keep the helmet and chainmail armor the King gave him to wear in battle."

Colin proceeds with a picture of a Brown Bess Musket. "Hongi started an arms race for muskets amongst all the native tribes, lasting over 20 years. Their battles came to be known as the Musket Wars. Before they were introduced to guns, the Māori tribal conflicts were ritualistic events during the autumn months, resulting in only a small percentage of deaths. The carnage from guns was unlike anything they had ever experienced."

POLITICAL RALLY IN HOUSTON, TEXAS, USA

Gunshots sound off at a rapid pace. People are screaming. Jack falls to the floor. Several others on stage go down as well. Tracy is surrounded by security guards guiding her to safety as gunfire continues in the direction of the fleeing audience.

Hannah receives the call thirty minutes later. She lets out a wail and drops the phone with word of Jack's death.

Following one hour of absolute sobbing and a second hour of lying down, completely in shock, she picks up the phone and calls Allison. While concerned at first about the girl being alone, a new boyfriend is revealed during the conversation, a fact her stepdaughter chose not to mention before.

After hanging up, she packs a small suitcase. Given that telling Ryan in person is a priority, a decision is made to drive to Corpus Christi. One of the ranch hands Jack befriended on the next county road is available to come around daily and take care of her goats. Under normal circumstances, she would not bother Luke with this request.

Ten minutes into the journey is this quirky little town, which would be the perfect spot to film a hillbilly movie. At the foot of the hills, there is a row of 100-year-old homes in bad shape with boards covering windows, patch jobs on roofs, and falling down porches. Many residents use the property as their own personal junkyards. Animals are always running around everywhere, from cats and dogs to chickens, goats, and pigs.

When she and her husband first drove through the area, they could not believe their eyes. It felt so strange, coming from the suburbs where the community association will knock on your door if you leave anything in your yard that isn't allowed.

Driving past, two goats with long curved horns are fighting on top of a small car. They both stand upright to appear larger to their opponent, ram their horns into each other, and repeat the process, over and over. She bursts out laughing. Jack would have found this to be the funniest sight. "Only in the country!" he'd say.

Alternating between crying and laughing about old memories, the three hours pass quickly. Knowing her son does not watch TV or even look at news reports regularly, she takes deep breaths, trying to compose herself before knocking on his door.

"What are you doing here?" Ryan asks, totally surprised.

His apartment is a disaster. It is a one-room studio with only enough space for a bed, desk, and a small table and chairs. The bed is unmade, and stuff is scattered everywhere. She peers into his almost empty closet. Apparently, every item of clothing he owns is on the floor, except for two pairs of slacks and two dress shirts that were bought for him in case there was ever an occasion to look nice. The kitchen is filthy. Dirty dishes fill the sink and line the countertop. On a positive note, the dumbbells are where they belong on the weight rack.

Why she is giving a second thought to the state of his living conditions under the circumstances is beyond her. Finally, she sits down on the bed to answer his question, motioning for him to take a seat beside her.

He bursts into tears at the news.

FOUR WEEKS LATER

Out on the balcony of a charming beachfront condo in Corpus Christi, Hannah is enjoying the ocean view with a cup of coffee. Even though this is the first week in November, it is 70 degrees. She pulls up Ryan's number on her phone and calls. It rings and rings.

Her son is taking his father's death terribly hard and shortly after stated he should drop out of school. She decided to rent a place nearby to ensure he finished his master's degree for the December graduation. Because he was way behind schedule on his thesis, she is helping out to serve as a research assistant and editor. The paper is now back on track and will be ready to submit before the deadline. Of course, taking a break from school for the funeral contributed to his falling behind.

Unlike herself, Ryan seemed to find no consolation in mourning with others. He barely said a word to his sister Allison, his cousin Tiffany, Aunt Tracy, Uncle Alex, or other relatives who came to the Celebration of Life service.

Tracy managed all of the service arrangements and burial at the family plot where their parents were already resting. She also gave the eulogy. Hannah, Ryan, and Allison all felt unable to get up in front of everyone without becoming a complete mess.

The days after the tragedy became a blur. Being alone at the condo and staring out at the ocean is exactly the therapy she needed. It breaks her heart how Jack only had a handful of years to enjoy the property. They were very much in harmony there and feeling great about being empty-nesters. Finding any sort of comfort in the hill country now with all of her husband's belongings was not going to happen.

If only she could help their son with his grief. Being five minutes away from Ryan has improved the situation for her, if not for him, despite how the two mostly communicate through texts and emails from their separate dwellings and only about school. He eats at odd hours and prefers eating alone.

Not being able to reach him gets to her. Paranoia and anxiety set in, and her hands begin to shake. Coffee spills as she tries to raise her arm to take a drink. She closes her eyes, opening them moments later at the sound of wings flapping.

A seagull sits on the railing. "Hi Gerald," she laughs through tears forming. Even though Jack would disapprove, the bird is offered muffin crumbs. During a search for information on the species, a surprising fact is found. They can live up to 20 years. There is no need to change the name to Gerald, Jr.

Moving on with the morning, she drives to Ryan's. A great sense of relief comes over her when the door opens. He pivots and walks away.

With hands in his hair, pacing the floor, the young man declares, "I'm never going to get through a PhD program. I just can't do it."

"You *can* do it, but right now you need to finish your master's next month. I think you should consider working for a year or two and then decide if you really want to pursue a PhD."

She continues. "It doesn't hurt to explore other paths. I have been researching Data Analyst positions, and you have all the skills they are looking for because of your university job and your natural ability with computer programming. Thousands of opportunities exist. We can try to find a position related to marine biology or at least science. Can I begin a job search to give you options?"

Ryan is silent, surveying the room with posters, pictures, and knickknacks of marine life.

Hesitantly, he agrees. "OK, but I want to do meaningful work involving the oceans and marine life and climate change."

"It will be my first priority to find that."

Her son became passionate about fighting global warming when one of his undergrad professors had a leg amputated after being in the Gulf water for a research project with a wound on his leg. Dr. Gilmore developed a Vibrio infection. Ryan was horrified to learn how this type of bacteria, resistant to most antibiotics, is becoming more common in warmer waters due to climate change.

She was particularly distressed over him that summer when he appeared to struggle mentally with his thoughts on the future of us all. Fortunately, he decided to become part of the solution for a better Earth, rather than being overwhelmed by the problem. Now, it is clear his data analysis skills can be put to good use in this field. It is just a matter of in what capacity.

Back at the condo, Hannah hopes she is steering him in the right direction. While not wanting to squash his dreams, she has read about the extreme rigors of PhD curricula and how one can get all the way to the end, only to have their dissertation rejected. Writing and research have not been his strongest qualities.

He is incredible with databases, computer programming, and data analysis, constantly being praised by the professors he works with. Pursuing a technology career makes sense to her, but she doesn't want there to be any regrets. On the one hand, he can always go back for a doctorate, but on the other hand, life might get in the way, making it difficult to return.

She decides the job hunt can wait another day and turns on the TV. A local reporter explains about a new assault rifle now available in the civilian market that is even more powerful than the one used in Jack's shooting.

Hannah is outraged. *What is wrong with this country? How can we sell weapons like this to the general population?* She doesn't understand why a line is not drawn between military guns and guns appropriate for regular people for self-defense and shooting sports, such as skeet, trap, and sporting clays.

The television goes right back off. She opens her laptop and types the following: Marine Biology and Environmental Science Data Analyst jobs in Australia.

TWO WEEKS LATER

Ryan is on a video conference job interview with several professors from the Department of Biological Sciences at MacDermid University in Queensland.

"Tell us, Ryan, why do you want to work here?" inquires Dr. Spiner, head of the Marine Biology graduate program.

"I am fascinated by your projects at the Great Barrier Reef. I believe my computer programming and data analysis skills will make me an asset to your department."

From the other side of the room, Hannah smiles as her son provides details on ocean pollution and climate change research.

SEVEN WEEKS LATER

Ryan's apprehension towards relocating to Australia has his mother concerned. He is not showing any enthusiasm and keeps pointing out reasons not to go. She counters with talk about the remarkable work of the university's science professors. Once in his new role, she is certain he will be content with the decision.

They board the plane, and Ryan takes the window seat. He stares out from the time of take-off and for the next 30 minutes. Finally, he turns to her and speaks.

"I can't believe we are moving to Australia. Do you really think it is right to leave the country? Isn't that unpatriotic?"

Hannah shrugs. "I have always liked the idea of living somewhere else. Since I was young, I have been interested in Ireland and Australia, reading novels by their authors."

He leans his head back and closes his eyes.

"Did you know that it snows in Australia?"

"No," he responds with eyes still shut.

"There is an area called the Snowy Mountains with ski resorts and everything." She mistakenly thought this fact would perk him up since he had asked a few years back if they could go on a family snow ski trip, but the idea was rejected by his father.

"Did you know that it is required for citizens to vote in Australia, or they will be fined?"

His eyes open. "Well, that is one way to get everyone to participate in democracy."

"And did you know Australia is still under the British monarchy with the King of England as their King?"

"No, I didn't. Why do I not know that?"

"I don't know. Maybe you were asleep in history class, but it is a formality only. Australia governs itself and no longer pays taxes to the British. My great-grandfather, William Ryan, came to America from Ireland while his two brothers chose to go to Australia instead, so we do have relatives there somewhere. Maybe we can track them down."

Ryan exhibits excitement for the first time in months. "Yes, that would certainly be interesting."

They chat for a while about family history and Australia. She is relieved to see him coming back to life. To her, it was not a hard choice at all to leave. Living in the hill country alone was not something she wanted to do. It was Jack's dream, and something that worked for them to do together. She did not hesitate to sell the property to the local ranch owner, who made a good offer. The man was pleased to be able to move his ranch hands to a new location instead of them living in campers outside his place.

Hannah hopes she and Ryan can make Australia their home and stay.

Three

THREE WEEKS LATER

Running across a dark street, the man with a gun is chasing her again. He is going to catch up. She turns down an alley, and out of the corner of her eye, sees a porch light turn on. The sound of his boots hitting the ground stops for a few seconds, allowing her to run farther, climbing over a short chain link fence and into a backyard to hide behind a doghouse. The canine comes out. Thankfully, it is a friendly German Shepherd like the one she had as a child. She stays out of sight, hugging and petting this beautiful animal, but then freezes upon hearing the rattle of the fence as the man goes over it. He is only feet away.

Hannah's eyes fly open. With hands in tight fists gripping the top sheet, she lets go. This must be at least the twentieth nightmare she has endured in the last four months about being pursued by a faceless man. Sometimes he has a gun, and sometimes he doesn't.

Luckily, she is able to roll over and get right back to sleep, this time dreaming about her mom, who died many years ago. It is always enjoyable to see her parents in her dreams. Normally, only one or the other is present, not both of them together, but it brings her comfort. They passed away during her 20s, her mom when she was 25, and her dad when she was 29. Hannah is an only child.

Ryan was too young to have memories of her wonderful, caring father. Jack lost his mother when their son was in high school, but his father only recently passed at the age of 94.

She remembers her son's last exchange with Gramps well. It was a debate over climate change. The elderly man drove a 40-year-old diesel truck with black smoke spewing out. A favorite topic of his "grumpy old men's" breakfast group was their fear of the government outlawing gas vehicles and forcing them all to buy electric ones.

His grandson tried to explain that making everyone get rid of their older cars and trucks was not going to happen, but requiring manufacturers to move exclusively to eco-friendly automobiles by a future date would be beneficial to the environment. Gramps refused to acknowledge the reality of human activities contributing to climate change.

Hannah sleeps in later than usual. The morning disappears in no time, and the only thing she accomplishes is to email some friends back home.

Her girlfriends have not been acting like themselves. She knows they are going out of their way to not complain about their lives, their husbands, or their families at all because of what she has been through. It is good to be grateful and not disagreeable, but at the same time, it is beneficial for some to be real and say what they are feeling. She has met people who never want to complain. While admirable, it is not how Hannah and her girls operate. In her messages, she lets them know it is OK to vent as they have always done. She understands and wants to hear their woes.

After a late lunch, she walks down the stairs from her apartment above a garage in the mid-sized college town of Kirkdam, Queensland. Two boys are playing with toy construction trucks in the front yard. Their Golden Retriever is watching them. Bailey barks at her like he always does but then calms down when she pets him.

"Hi, guys."

The brothers act as if she isn't there. Evidently, they had just returned from the beach with partially wet hair and sand stuck to them, and now dirt from the yard.

Before she can knock on the main house door, it opens. "Hi. Come on in," says Marci, the homeowner and landlord, a woman quite a bit younger than herself.

A very handsome man around Hannah's age is inside. He is in great shape and has thick blondish-brown wavy hair with a short beard.

"This is Colin, Simon and Sam's father." Marci had already mentioned the father of her twin autistic nine-year-olds, who, according to her, "comes around every weekend in the summer, but not regularly the rest of the year."

The boys have their dad's bright blue eyes and wavy hair, but theirs is much more blond like his was at their age.

Colin extends his hand. "Hi, nice to meet you. Marci tells me you are from Texas. I am, too." He has a strong Australian accent.

Confused, she replies, "You are?"

"Texas, Australia," he laughs.

"I didn't know there was one."

He goes on to tell her about the town, but Hannah isn't really listening, focusing instead on how attracted she is to him.

After some time, she becomes embarrassed by this, and the flush of her cheeks turning red makes her want to escape.

First looking at Marci, then Colin, she says, "Here is the check for next month's rent, and it was nice to meet you."

"You too." He is eager to keep talking. "What do you think of Australia?"

"I think it is very nice. This is a beautiful area."

"Is it what you expected?"

"I thought there would be kangaroos hopping all around." She laughs nervously. "Just kidding. I love having the ocean a short drive away."

"Yes. I can't imagine not living by water." He thinks she is the cutest lady. His eyes move down to her navy-blue shirt with a white star.

"What is this shirt you are wearing?"

With a big smile, she announces, "Dallas Cowboys football."

"Oh no. Not *American* *football*." He shakes his head, saying the word American with disdain.

"I know. Isn't it great? I had no idea Australians watched it. I wasn't expecting it to be on here."

"Well, it shouldn't be. That is *not* our sport."

He has her grinning from ear to ear, but she still wants to leave. "Well, I'd better get going."

As she moves towards the door, the professor catches himself eyeing her, with Marci watching him. Directing his attention back to his ex, he mumbles, "I should go too."

Meeting this man literally made Hannah's head spin.

What is wrong with me?

The odd dizziness fades as she gets to the end of the driveway. She definitely needs to go for a brisk walk and stop this absurd behavior.

Sam's screams can be heard in the distance. He obviously does not want his dad to leave.

A few minutes later, the sound of hurried footsteps approaching makes her turn around. Running to catch up to her is an out-of-breath Colin. He had pretended to leave but parked around the corner.

"Can I join you?" he asks.

"That's fine. I'm only going around the block."

"I hope the boys don't get too loud for you. I know Sam yells a lot."

She shrugs. "Just a few times. It isn't a problem."

"Marci told me how Simon had the longest conversation with you that he has ever had with anyone. Even us."

"Right," she chuckles, beginning to feel her normal self again. "We spoke at great length about *Pikmin*."

He rolls his eyes. "Yes. One of those video games he is obsessed with."

"The game has been around for over 20 years with different versions. My son loved it. When he was probably six or seven, he would draw very elaborate, detailed pictures of the characters in various settings. My only concern was I felt he thought they were real. I think he wanted there to really be Pikmin characters, which are part plant, part animal. He acted like he was searching for them in the backyard."

"I don't understand it at all. I hate how Marci lets him play them. Sam mostly watches, except with racing games. Simon is much higher functioning."

She nods. "The game teaches the player to be a leader. It is goal-oriented, with many puzzles and challenges, and is non-violent. Some say it is a commentary on climate change as the Pikmin deal with environmental issues and weather conditions."

In the past, she had many debates with her sister-in-law over the subject of video games, so the details of her pro-game arguments have not been forgotten.

"You sound like a gamer yourself."

"No, I am not. Not for me. But when my son was in elementary school, he played good games that taught him skills. He also read many of the guidebooks, which were written at an advanced level. Now, when he was older, there were zombies and wars and a lot of blood."

Colin grimaces. "I am definitely going to put my foot down on that."

"Well, there were many positive goal-oriented games when he was a teenager, too. I have read how video games can foster the development of analytical abilities. And not once during his childhood do I recall him saying the words 'I'm bored.' He always had something to do with those games."

"Maybe I should reconsider my stance, but I like to get them outside and away from the games. A love of the ocean is what I share with them. I have read research on autistic children confirming their love of water, but I knew this from day one. Marci got mad at me for giving them too many baths when they were babies. She said it wasn't good for their skin, but putting them in the water stopped them from crying. We couldn't even agree on that. I did try to live with her as a family, but it just didn't work."

Hannah immediately feels ill at ease with Colin sharing things about his relationship with Marci. She gets tongue-tied, and there is a moment of silence.

Then she tells him, "My son is the same way. Water has always had a good effect on him. Ryan isn't exactly the happy-go-lucky type."

"Ryan. Does this mean you are of Irish descent?" he guesses.

"Yes. Ryan is my maiden name."

"Your son's disposition is probably the curse of being Irish and from the starvation by our ancestors during the potato famine which affected our genes, making us more likely to be depressed."

"You know, I read something about that on the internet."

"I know. I published an article on the subject. And since my last name is Ryan, I was curious about the history of Ryans in Australia. I compiled my research into a book called *The Ryans Down Under*."

She is impressed. "I told my son recently how we have relatives here somewhere and should check into it."

"The book includes a multitude of family trees and resources for tracing ancestry. I will bring you a copy."

"OK. Great."

Satisfied to have a reason to pay her a visit soon, he tries to think of a way to broach the subject of her husband's passing.

"I'm sorry for your loss, by the way. Marci told me about your husband. How long were you married?"

"26 years."

He shakes his head, unable to imagine being with one person for so many years. "Wow, I guess after *that* long, you become just good friends."

She grows irritated, almost infuriated. Marci had informed Hannah of her ex being a bigshot professor and ladies' man, always dating different women.

"What does *that* mean? Are you talking about sex?"

He grins slightly, indicating this *is* what he is referring to.

"We were very busy all those years, and I am proud of it, thank you very much."

"Sorry. It's just my married friends always complain about the topic. I thought kids and work and day-to-day routines and problems got in the way," he explains.

"Not for us. There was only one kid in our house most of the time, and he was frequently in his room playing video games. We both worked from home with relaxed schedules, making us well-rested, and we were smart about not allowing irritations or disagreements to interfere with that part of our lives. Often, in the middle of the day when our son was at school, and we should have been working, there was a bit of a thrill in doing something we weren't supposed to."

"All I have to say is your husband was a lucky man." As Colin makes this statement, the expression on his face leads her to believe he is getting all kinds of ideas in his head.

"I think so, and I think I'm glad we are almost back because this discussion is a little too much. See you later." She picks up the pace to a fast jog when the house comes into view and leaves him behind.

He watches her run away. She is shorter and more petite than he is usually captivated by, but he is attracted to her. Very attracted.

After returning home, Colin does an internet search on Hannah. An article about the shooting shows up first. He reads the details of the horrific day when twenty-three people were shot, six fatally, before the shooter took his own life.

Next, he sees the news on her sister-in-law who won the election for the US House of Representatives. This is followed by her husband's obituary. Last in the results are Hannah's children's books, *Walter and the Magic Carrot* and *The Blue Dragon*. He orders them online.

Back at her place, Hannah pours herself a glass of wine and reaches for the laptop. She also does a search. There are many articles about Dr. Colin Ryan. Pictures of him appear with beautiful women. In addition to the publication about The Ryans, she finds four of his other books and orders them all, telling herself that she isn't interested in him but in his work and writing.

She moves to the couch and flips through the printed photographs from her excursion with Ryan during their first weekend in Australia.

They found their respective residences within three days of arriving, both fully furnished already. Purchasing two used cars was done in one hour. Of course, her son insisted on electric vehicles, already researching how to run an extension cord from his apartment. Marci gives Hannah the use of her garage for charging.

Elated about his new/used car, Ryan was in good spirits for the drive to the Australia Zoo. They reminisced about *The Crocodile Hunter* as he remembered watching re-runs of the show with his dad, a big fan of Steve Irwin. Years ago, the family discussed a trip to Australia, but it never happened. While mother and son had a wonderful time seeing the animals, Jack's absence weighed heavily on their minds.

Ryan had one week to settle in before it was time to start work. Normally, he is shy around new people, but Professor Spiner immediately assigned him a project involving computer programming, and the two had endless topics to discuss. Their field has many talking points, such as possible solutions to reducing plastic fragments in the oceans. Other research involves ocean acidification caused by climate change, as carbon dioxide emissions from human activity end up being absorbed by the oceans, decreasing pH levels and harming marine life.

On this particular day, two and a half weeks into his new role, a professor from the chemistry department arrives to show the group a documentary he was involved with. The film begins by explaining how microplastics are extremely small plastic particles found in the environment as a result of industrial processes and the breakdown of bigger plastics. Nurdles are a type of microplastic. Then Ryan learns something he has never heard of before.

A significant amount of this plastic debris in our oceans comes from the simple act of machine-washing clothes made of polyester, acrylic, and nylon. Most of what he wears is quick-drying athletic clothing. These items are exactly what the problem is about. He has always made it a point to use as little plastic as possible, but overlooked the fact that his clothes *are* a form of plastic.

Another alarming piece of information is revealed. Microplastics are in our blood and organs and could damage veins and cells. *Absolutely frightening.* The documentary goes on to describe how scientists are developing ways to remove microscopic plastic pieces and pollutants from water. Dr. Moore is collaborating on this research, so he is interviewed for the show. Everyone claps when he appears on the screen.

Ryan leaves the office for the day energized about the contributions he can potentially make with this job. The month before, he came close to calling the whole thing off and telling his mom he didn't want to move. Deep in thought, he is unaware of two young ladies watching him.

"Who is that?"

Her friend is silent.

"You are blushing. Do you know him?"

She shakes her head.

"You need to find a way to get to know him. I can feel you crushing over him."

"Don't be silly. Let's go."

She would never admit her heart skipped a beat at the sight of him. Not at any time has she felt so drawn to someone. Of course, he does not notice her at all, yet she has this feeling that he is part of her future. She must be mistaken. Just a silly thought.

Four

Hannah and Ryan embark on another Saturday adventure, this time to Mount Coot-tha in Brisbane, a 40-minute drive from Kirkdam. The mountain was the first thing they saw when approaching the area by plane.

Along the way, Ryan talks nonstop. He tells his mom what he has read lately about possible technologies that could cool the oceans and reduce atmospheric carbon dioxide. She is curious about these developments but struggles to concentrate. How did the boy who had a hard time learning to tie his shoes and the teenager who cursed up a storm trying to understand Algebra turn into this man speaking so eloquently about climate engineering methods to save the Earth?

The scenic drive loop ends at the parking area for the restaurant and lookout point. As they journey on foot to their destination, he points to the left. "Over there, we can rent mountain bikes."

"Ryan. That just isn't my thing. You can come back another time, OK? You will meet lots of people who will want to ride with you."

Her son rolls his eyes. He has had the same two friends since childhood. She is not aware of him making friends at college. Not a word about girls or going on a date. Nothing. Dating isn't always a good thing for young people, so maybe it has been for the best.

They go up to the observation deck. He is impressed.

"Wow, what a view! I don't recall ever being where I could see a city this way, and I didn't realize there was such a big river going through Brisbane. Can we swim in it?"

"Actually, no. I read the river is full of bull sharks. There is a Streets Beach in the middle of the city with a man-made beach and lagoon for swimming."

"Can we go when we are done here?"

"Another day."

It is hard to keep up with younger people, she thinks to herself as he lets out a semi-irritated groan. Vacations were challenging because her husband would tire easily, but her son wanted to do one activity after another.

The pair has an early lunch followed by a picturesque hike. They will end the day trip with a Cosmic Skydome show.

Walking through the botanical gardens to get to the Sir Thomas Brisbane Planetarium, a white circular building appears with a small dome in front and a bigger one at the back. Hannah could spend an hour on the trails of the gardens. Ryan, however, is not the least bit interested in the greenery, beautiful flowers, or smelling the roses, so to speak. She decides to come back alone.

While waiting for the film to begin, there are fascinating displays to examine. They arrive at the *Skylore* exhibit about Aboriginal and Torres Strait Islander Astronomy, where elders share their knowledge for the first time. Ryan sees a quote on the wall: "Everything on the land is reflected in the sky."

"I wonder what that means," he utters out loud and begins reading the entire wall.

He notices his mom off to the side with her phone. "Why aren't you looking at this?"

"Sorry. My friend's daughter had a baby the other day, so I was messaging her."

"This is an awesome exhibit on how Indigenous Australians made decisions on the best paths to travel, when to travel, and how to make use of food sources, all by viewing the night sky to predict weather changes and animal behavior."

"That is certainly interesting, but it is time for the space show. We had better go." She places her hand on his arm, gently pulling him away from the display.

Hannah has always loved the atmosphere of a dome theater with the big panoramic screen and the feeling of being surrounded by outer space. The show takes the audience on a journey through the universe. About twenty minutes into it, she finally glances over at her son, who is sound asleep. So much for youthful energy!

Marci and her sons come outside as she pulls into the driveway. "I hate to ask this of you, but I need to leave for a wedding, and Colin is running late. He is taking the boys out for a couple of hours and should be here in thirty minutes. Can they stay with you?"

"Of course. Come on up." The brothers follow Hannah. She isn't sure what to do with them.

"Where are your games?" asks Simon.

"I don't have any."

He appears disappointed.

"Do you guys like music?" Her question goes unanswered. She turns the radio to an 80s station and sits with them on the couch.

The twins are uninterested at first.

A song called "You Spin Me Round" by Dead or Alive plays, bringing back memories of junior high school dances.

Jumping to her feet, she enthusiastically exclaims, "Let's dance."

They look at her as if she is crazy, eye one another, and then get up and begin spinning in circles. Sam whirls around too fast and drops to the ground. The three of them laugh hysterically.

Their dad arrives earlier than expected and witnesses this comical scene through the living room window of the garage suite. His knock on the door cannot be heard over the music, so he lets himself in.

At the same time, Hannah loses her balance and starts to fall backward. He reaches out to keep her from falling. The sound of her shriek at the surprise of unfamiliar arms wrapped around her has Simon and Sam howling. She promptly moves away and out of his embrace. The song ends, and the boys run out the door.

Another 80s favorite immediately follows, the Australian band AC/DC's "You Shook Me All Night Long." A mischievous grin comes across his face at the thought of her American thighs. She turns the music off.

"Thanks for watching them. Do you want to come to the bounce house place with us?"

"I have been gone all day. I'll pass. You guys have fun."

Colin is in high spirits all evening, thinking about Hannah dancing with his sons and trying not to think too much about that figure of hers. Ordinarily, being in a room with screaming kids would bother him to no end, but he is in too good of a mood.

While the day was enjoyable for Hannah, nighttime is another story. For years, around the 4 am hour, she often wakes to feelings of intense anxiety and bad dreams. This has gotten worse since her husband's shooting.

The pre-dawn hours bring nightmares about her college boyfriend. Not once before, during, or right after the outing, did she think about the planetarium at her university, where she and Jason spent their first date.

The two met as freshmen and dated for two years. She got the idea from him to apply for internships. The letter arrived two weeks before the second semester of junior year, offering a position at a Dallas oil company.

On the bus to the downtown location, a man got on at the next stop. Hannah caught him staring directly at her and had a feeling he was going to sit with her intentionally. She quickly buried her head back in the Maeve Binchy novel she was reading, her favorite Irish author. The man did, in fact, take a seat beside her. Despite the plan to not look up and avoid all conversations, he started one anyway.

Giving in and putting her book down, she went on to chat with him for the entire hour-long ride. She thought he was the most charming person she had ever spoken with. Jack had just turned 30. She was 21. In her eyes, he was a man, not a college boy. He asked her out, and she couldn't resist.

On their third date, Jack let her know about his four-month-old daughter, who lived with her mother several hours away in the town where he grew up. Five weeks following the signing of the divorce decree, his ex-wife, Susan, took a pregnancy test. Hannah never questioned the timeline of events, but her parents did and were wary of this new relationship.

Several weeks after she learned about Allison, Jack and Susan agreed to meet halfway once a month for him to bring the baby girl to his home for the weekend. The arrangement continued throughout her childhood. When Allison turned one, Susan began dating an old friend from their high school who became a doctor and moved back to town. They married the following year and went on to have three boys.

While Hannah was enthralled with her new man, the college boyfriend took the breakup hard. Eight months later, she bumped into a good friend of his on campus, who told her Jason was not doing well. Another eight months went by, and right after she graduated and became engaged in the same week, she found out he had committed suicide. *Was this my fault?* She sometimes asks herself.

Surely, Jason had already moved on to another girlfriend after almost one and a half years. She remembered his name was not in the graduation booklet. Maybe he failed courses and felt he had no future. He struggled with his Computer Science program. Whatever the reasons, thoughts of his suicide had her up many times in the wee morning hours for the next 27 years and counting.

The following Saturday, Colin arrives to pick up his sons for the beach. Marci comes out in a flash with the boys and their bags, interrupting his plan to go upstairs first. She sees him holding a book.

"What's that?"

"This is for Hannah since her maiden name is Ryan." As he speaks her name, she steps out of the apartment, also dressed for a day at the shore.

Marci looks over to her tenant and then back at her ex, realizing the two have been talking and thinking they are going on an outing together.

"Spending the day at the beach, Hannah?" she inquires.

"Yes. I am picking up my son to drive down to the Sunshine Coast to nurdle hunt first and then swim."

"Very nice. Have fun," Marci replies, relieved since she knows this isn't what Colin has planned. She glances back at him.

"Bring them home by five. They have a birthday party to go to." With that, she goes inside.

"Here is the book I mentioned."

"OK. Thanks." Hannah grabs it and hurries to her car.

Many people are gathered on the sand. A cute girl approaches, who is assisting with the event.

"Hi. My name is Kiera. I see you brought your own sieves. Have you done this before?"

The girl has her eyes on the young man, but he is already looking away, expecting his mother to handle the interaction.

"I haven't, but Ryan here did in Corpus Christi, Texas, where he went to school. My name is Hannah."

Kiera smiles at the pleasant woman and then turns her head to the son.

"I've seen you around the university."

Silence.

Embarrassed by his lack of social graces, Hannah speaks up. "Ryan works as a Data Analyst for the Department of Biology, mainly working on marine biology projects. Are you a student there?"

"Yes. I am taking summer classes and studying to be a high school teacher in biology and ocean science. I considered marine biology, but staying for a PhD would be a long road. My calling is to work with younger people."

"That's great. Good science teachers are important. Ryan has a master's in marine biology, and his specialty is working with the data professors need for their studies and published work."

While the two women talk, Ryan finds himself admiring Kiera's pretty face. Since she has her eyes on his mom, he feels it is safe to study her. After noticing the seashell earrings and necklace she is wearing, he impulsively says, "I like your shell jewelry. Did you make that?" He immediately feels self-conscious about interrupting them.

"My mum did a long time ago. She made jewelry to sell to tourists. For years, she used real shells like my earrings. I convinced her to buy molds and paint the plaster to make the shell shapes for necklaces, such as this one. When I was younger, I didn't realize how seashells are utilized by marine life, not only as homes for living inside, but also for camouflage and habitat-building material. Corals, sea grasses, and anemones anchor themselves to the ocean floor with shells. And, of course, leaving them on the beach is best to prevent erosion."

"Right," he responds, and then averts his eyes.

"How did your last nurdle hunt go?" Kiera asks him.

Ryan finally matches her gaze with a little more confidence, at least temporarily.

"It was good. In Texas, my friend is studying marine environmental law. He was upset about a plastics company responsible for countless nurdles in a bay. I went there to be part of the clean-up. An environmental group sued and won. The company had to put millions into a trust for earth-friendly efforts."

"Excellent how they were held accountable." She is about to say something else, but realizes new people have arrived. "Nice meeting you both. You can start over there."

Mother and son get halfway to the area where Kiera pointed to when Hannah hears the familiar sound of a boy screaming in the distance. She whirls around to see the twins and their father.

"Those are my neighbors," she lets Ryan know, not bothering to explain the situation between Colin and Marci or the fact that he doesn't actually live there. "Come with me. I will introduce you."

Kiera had already greeted the professor by the time they reached the check-in tent.

"What are you guys doing here?" asks Hannah.

He tries to appear innocent in his intentions. "I have read about these hunts in the university newspaper. Teaching the boys about nurdles and volunteer work before having fun seemed like a good plan. You have no idea what I went through driving over here."

"Ryan, this is Colin and his sons, Simon and Sam."

He nods at the man who begins to extend his hand, but Sam is pulling on his dad's arm and getting upset.

Kiera brings over a perfect sea star specimen.

The boy's demeanor changes. He giggles and yells, "Patrick!"

"It is a velvet sea star," she explains

"Patrick! Patrick!" Sam insists.

She seems confused, so Ryan helps her out. "He is referring to the character Patrick from the cartoon *SpongeBob*. Even divers call velvet sea stars 'Patricks.' Where did you find it?"

"My great uncle gave it to me years ago. I didn't watch much TV growing up. I am not familiar with the different *SpongeBob* characters."

Ryan laughs. "How can this be?"

They continue the conversation, and even Simon joins in. Sam holds the sea star with the biggest grin on his face.

Hannah and Colin step away from the group.

"You have no idea how shy Ryan is and how happy I am right now."

"Tell me you aren't one of these mothers who wants to marry off her son by 25 so he can start producing grandbabies."

"No, but I haven't heard a word about a girlfriend since the first grade, when he came out of school holding a girl's hand. A week later, he told me how Savannah broke up with him. He let out a big sigh and said, 'I guess I need to find a new girlfriend.' I told him he didn't need to worry about girls until college, and he has held me to that and beyond. I'm sure he doesn't even remember any of it."

"Trust me. He doesn't need to worry about girls. There are plenty of years for that."

As he gives his thoughts on the subject, two ladies in their early 30s walk by in bikinis. They flash him their big white smiles. Hannah finds this so annoying. In her opinion, men can often age without losing any attractiveness, even if they have gray hair, wrinkles, or a bigger gut. Of course, Colin has gorgeous wavy hair with hardly any gray and a great body.

He watches them go past for only a moment before turning back to her, catching those beautiful green eyes rolling. "Where is *your* bikini?" he teases.

"Not only do I not *do* bikinis, I don't do bathing suits altogether. These jogging shorts and shirt are my beach attire."

He scans her up and down. "You know, you look fantastic. Can I give you a surfing lesson sometime?"

"Ha. No way. I am boring. Trust me. I only go in the water halfway. I don't even like to get my hair wet."

"Are you serious?"

"Yes. I am."

"Surfing for me is necessary. I forget about everything else, and a calm comes over me, allowing my mind to focus on work for days afterwards. It also helps me to be more patient with the boys. The waves and the ocean are my life's blood."

She can't relate but tries to understand.

"And I am a member of an organization called Surfers for Climate. I donate and volunteer at sessions with a contractor mate of mine to educate local tradespeople on greener building, and I help promote environmental campaigns throughout the year." He goes on to give her some details and then asks, "What do you like to do outdoors?"

"Just walk mainly. I do enjoy sitting on a beach for a couple of hours, as long as I am under an umbrella. I am willing to occasionally go on a two-hour hike or kayak outing on moderate waters. That is the extent of my adventurous side."

"I don't think you are challenging yourself enough. There is a group of people I rock climb with. You should join us."

"I'd rather remain on solid ground, thanks."

After observing how Kiera had to leave Ryan to greet other people, she begins to walk away from Colin. "It is time to do what we are here to do, nurdle hunt. Bye."

Some other children show up, and Kiera groups them with Professor Ryan, Simon, and Sam.

Following an hour of collecting nurdles, most everyone gets in the water. Colin joins his sons while Hannah sits in the sand watching. Ryan stays behind for a while to organize the plastic pellets into buckets before taking a swim.

Back at her dorm room that night, Kiera is exhausted from her day. She falls asleep in a matter of minutes.

The pain is excruciating. She screams and screams. The older women of the colony surround her as she lies on a bed of rags. "It's coming," one of the women yells. The pain is over. It is such a relief. She props herself up on her elbows. The woman holds the lifeless baby in her arms and shakes her head.

Kiera awakens from this disturbing dream. She had fallen asleep thinking about Ryan. *Why couldn't she have dreamt about him?*

TWO DAYS LATER, out on the Pacific Ocean, a marine research vessel is anchored near the Great Barrier Reef. Several scuba divers from the university go under, heading towards the reef for a new project. Kim, a master's student, is following a PhD candidate named Michael. Something makes Kim look behind her, and she sees Dr. Taylor floating off. She alerts the others, and they swim over to the professor, bringing him back up to the surface. Everyone works together to get him on the boat. Michael performs CPR, but his efforts are unsuccessful.

Five

LAW OFFICE IN SYDNEY, AUSTRALIA
Clay Ryan and two of his engineering friends from university, James and Theresa, are sitting in the waiting room. Today is the big day. They are forming their own company.

James designed an innovative type of electricity transformer with the potential to reduce the energy needed to power homes and businesses by up to 50%. The transformer will work regardless of the power source, so it can also be used in the near future with clean energy methods such as hydropower, solar, and wind, improving the efficiency of delivery.

In the meantime, widespread use should facilitate the reduction of fossil fuel emissions until, hopefully, someday, all power will be clean. The transformer units can be installed in neighborhoods, supporting between 30 and 40 homes per unit. Commercial business areas can benefit as well.

Clay and Theresa joined James to further develop the process he invented and create a prototype. Clay also has ideas for carbon capture devices on vehicles since the transition to electric vehicles is not happening fast enough. The group needs to file for a patent, obtain permits, and make their partnership legal before securing funding. Theresa will take charge of finding investors, a task James and Clay are overjoyed to hand over to her.

Ten days after his passing, a memorial service for Dr. Taylor is held in the university's largest auditorium. As Ryan enters, Kiera sees him and hurries over. They say hello and take seats in the second-to-last row. He feels anxious but does not understand why.

Many speakers get up to express their fondness for the professor and describe his love of the ocean and his accomplishments. When the ceremony ends, the young acquaintances exit the building in silence.

Kiera takes a deep breath, determined to present him with an idea she thought of during the service. "Professor Taylor's work is displayed at the museum. Do you want to go?"

Very slowly, he says, "Now? I mean, sure."

"It will be a good way to honor and remember him. Do you have a car to drive us?"

"Yes."

They are awkwardly quiet on the drive to the museum.

After parking to begin their tour, they follow the map to the professor's exhibit.

"I can't believe he is gone," Kiera comments, still emotional. She was in Dr. Taylor's class the previous year. Ryan had only met the man once, briefly, during a department meeting.

"There is always a risk with scuba diving. Forty percent of deaths have to do with the heart because the elevated levels of oxygen increase your blood pressure, narrow your blood vessels, and reduce your cardiac output."

She stares at him.

Not wanting to sound insensitive, he apologizes. "I'm sorry. I don't mean to sound so matter-of-fact."

"I know what you are saying. It is true. Part of the reason why I decided not to become a marine biologist is that I have a fear of diving."

His eyes widen with surprise. "I do, too. I could have taken free lessons to go on an expedition in graduate school, but I chose not to."

She nods, leaving out the fact that her asthma condition is a contributing factor. "Not everyone appreciates how marine biologists sometimes put themselves at risk for their research by being exposed to dangerous environmental conditions, toxins, carcinogens, and can be stung, bitten, and attacked by marine life."

"So true." He does not want to share any details on his haunting nightmares at the bottom of the ocean, unable to breathe and frantically trying to get the oxygen regulator to work.

The two continue their stroll, stopping as they reach a marine life photography display with some remarkable pictures of dugongs. The exhibit explains that there are two families of sea cows: dugongs and manatees.

A sad expression comes over her face. "My mum died from cancer when I was 14."

"That must have been awful."

"It was. My biology teacher helped me to get through it and focus on the future. She got me involved in the Biology Club and local marine science and environmental events. But the thought of something happening to my dad gets me down."

"My dad is gone, and my mom's side has a bad family history of heart disease. I can't imagine both my parents being gone."

Her eyes meet his with complete understanding. "I don't know how I'll survive it. I've been trying to get my dad to go to the doctor. It is strange how out of breath he gets, and I've seen him clutching his chest. He says it is just heartburn, which seems more likely since he is only 40, but I'm not convinced."

They turn their heads back at the glass showcase.

"Do you believe in reincarnation?" she inquires.

"I'm not sure."

"I do. I saw a dugong once, a few years ago. The way it looked at me made me believe it was my mother reincarnated."

"Why do you think she would come back as a dugong?"

"She liked them. And dugongs can live 70 years, so Mum could live much longer as a dugong than she did as a person."

"True."

"If your dad was reincarnated, what do you think he would be?"

"I don't know. We had a cat named Sammie who followed my dad wherever he went. My mom said the cat was my grandmother reincarnated. She would sit for hours and watch him do projects in the garage. I thought my mom was joking. Maybe she wasn't."

The pair resumes the tour. Kiera's mood lightens, and she shares her favorite memories.

"I feel like I can't talk about Mum with my dad and brothers because it makes them sad, but I like talking about her. It means a lot how I have been able to do that with you."

"I enjoy hearing about her. I guess I'm not the same way, though. I don't want to talk about my dad too much, but someday, I'm sure this will change."

"Can I ask if you dream about him?"

"Yes, I do. It makes me feel close to him."

"I think loved ones who have passed come to us in our dreams to let us know they are still with us. I, too, dream about Mum except I believe she is making herself known to me and not that my subconscious is coming up with the dream."

"I definitely never thought about it that way."

Their last stop is a section on the fragility of marine ecosystems due to climate change. Gravitating to the aquarium, they begin a discussion about how the more carbon dioxide the oceans absorb from the atmosphere, the less calcium carbonate ocean life has for making their shells.

After seeing everything ocean-related in the museum, they drive to campus, and she directs him where to drop her off for the shortest walk back to the dorm.

"That was a good idea to go to the museum," he offers.

"Yes. It was nice."

Silence.

Kiera wants Ryan to say or do something, although she isn't sure what.

He doesn't.

"Well, good luck on your exams next week."

"Yes. Thanks." And she gets out of the car.

Ryan locates Kiera on social media, seeing posts dedicated to her mother. He finds articles from years back about her mom and the jewelry business. Her jewelry is beautiful, impressive, and works of art.

Kiera does a search on Ryan to check out past girlfriends, but she only finds a LinkedIn page describing his education and career skills.

An outing to the local swimming pool is the plan for the afternoon. Colin's hair and swim trunks are already partially damp from a morning surf. When getting out of his car, he notices Hannah jumping up and down in front of her living room window. He decides to knock on the door and see what she is up to.

"Hi. I saw you at your window and wanted to make sure you didn't need help with something."

She points to the top of the curtain rod. A kitten is walking across. It peers at him, becomes frightened, and proceeds to fly through the air onto the couch and then runs up a tower made of carpet. The feline tree condo has three levels of platforms and a cubby hole. The cat disappears into the hole.

"A cat, huh?"

Reaching in, Hannah pulls out the kitten. "This is Rosie. Isn't she beautiful?"

She sits back on the couch and puts a pillow on her lap. The tabby kitten kneads her paws into the pillow.

"I'm a dog person." As he says this, his sons' dog begins barking loudly outside.

"I love dogs, but cats are quieter and easier. See how sweet she is?"

"Very sweet. Well, I guess I'll go. I am taking the boys swimming."

As Colin begins to leave, he spots two Tim Winton books on her table. *The Riders* and *Breath*. "I see you have discovered one of Australia's best authors."

"I've been reading his books for years. I've read all of his novels and even his short stories. Because I am trying my hand at writing a novel, I start the day re-reading parts of my favorite books of his for inspiration. Winton is so good at describing surroundings in great detail, while I struggle with that."

He picks up *Breath*. "Have you seen the film?"

"Of course. It was really good."

"It was."

Curiously, he asks, "What is your story about?"

"It's a secret."

"O…K… On that note, I will go."

When he returns, Colin pretends to leave but parks around the corner and walks up the steps to the garage suite. Marci makes him uneasy each time she uncovers their interactions.

Hannah yells, "Come in," when he knocks. She is typing with her laptop on a pillow, and the kitten is asleep across her stomach.

"I see you are busy, but I have a quick question. Will you go to the university gala with me next Friday?" He inquires this with excitement in his voice.

"No. I'm not a gala type of gal. I don't do dresses. If you can't show up in jeans, I don't go." She resumes typing.

His face falls. "Really?"

"Really."

"What about dinner sometime when you can wear jeans?"

She stops what she is doing and looks directly at him. "Colin, that isn't a good idea. There is no reason for us to date."

They stare at one another for a moment.

Making his way to the door, he sees his book about the New Zealand Māori leader, Hongi Hiki. He picks it up. There are sticky notes on a number of the pages with her handwriting.

"Did you read this?" he asks, surprised she found the book on her own and made the effort to purchase it.

"Yes. I wrote down some things that I wanted to learn more about."

"I'd love to discuss it. Can I stop by tomorrow at about the same time? Simon and Sam talked me into going to the pool again."

Half-smiling at his disappointment over her turning down his date request, she responds, "I'll be here."

After he walks out the door, Hannah realizes she is being mean-spirited but knows he isn't used to rejection. She definitely does not want to be involved with him other than as a friend. Given her situation, dating does not sound like something she would ever do after all these years. The idea of it is strange. And honestly, she feels insecure about the pictures of him with long-legged beautiful ladies in skimpy dresses and bikinis.

Colin meets old mates from his undergrad days at a pub that night. He enjoys hanging out with them several times a year, but gets the impression they see him as having this charmed life with no right to complain. They never ask about his sons, almost as if they forget the twins exist. Their own children range in age from 16 to 22.

"Have you met any enchanting ladies lately?" teases Tim, who has been married for over 25 years and enjoys living vicariously through Colin.

"No."

Tim is not buying it, determined to get more information. He sometimes finds himself envious of his buddy's lifestyle and money. The know-it-all scholar privately offered to pay for his daughter's tuition. Insulted by this, he turned the proposal down, but is drowning in debt. The situation is growing more depressing.

"I can tell you are lying, mate."

"Well, there is this woman, but she won't go out with me. Her husband died around five months ago, I think. Maybe she just needs more time."

They pry him for details. He tells them all about Hannah, concluding with how she and her spouse had been a couple for probably 30 years.

"You really like her, don't you?" asks Tim.

"I do." Colin sighs and takes another sip of beer.

After a few drinks, Tim makes a comment he probably shouldn't have.

"Her husband will always be the love of her life."

A second day of swimming proves to be a mistake. Delivering two crying boys to the doorstep, the drained father perks up, looking forward to spending some time with Hannah. They discuss his books on Hongi Hika and The Ryans, going over information on how to search for long-lost Ryan relatives in Australia.

Out of the blue, he states, "I know you think I am awful and should have married Marci."

She is taken aback by his declaration. "That is not true. I don't think you should have married her because she got pregnant."

"I guess I wasn't willing to put in the work," he confesses.

"I have never understood that phrase about 'relationships being a lot of work.' To me, it is more about keeping your damn mouth shut. I don't call that work. I call it restraint. It took me years to learn not to speak in anger or point out everything I disagreed with my husband on. My strategy became to think things over first. Most of the time, I decided to let whatever I was mad or annoyed about go and move on to the next thing, often sharing my opinion later when it would be better received. Relationships can be suffocating when it isn't the right person. I don't blame you for wanting to live as you want and do what you want."

"I'm surprised to hear you say these things."

"People worry about me being lonely," she continues. "Believe me, I'm not lonely. I had a lifetime with someone already, or at least what felt like a lifetime. I would not be good for anyone. I only want to think of what is best for me and my son. I don't have it in me to make someone else part of my life. Love is patient. Love is kind. Well, my patience is gone, and frankly, I don't know how I'd ever muster up enough emotion."

He is very skeptical of this. "When I first spoke with you, you made it sound like you had this great marriage."

"We did. Jack and I had a good life. But there was a long learning curve to be able to communicate. I'm not interested in going through that with someone else. And I want to do what *I* want to do, and when I want to do it."

Colin is unsure of what else to say. He glances at the clock, surprised to realize they have been chatting for almost two hours already. "I had better go."

On the drive home, he smiles to himself, impressed with Hannah's interest in Hongi Hika and their conversations about his research. The surprise on her face was priceless upon revealing that he read her children's books to Simon and Sam. He did, however, leave out one small detail about how the boys were not the slightest bit interested in the stories.

Attributing her tirade on relationships to having a little too much of the beer he brought over, he dismisses what she said. One topic he won't abandon is Hannah mentioning how his books and the internet videos of his public lectures will live on after he is gone. He has always lived in the here and now, not ever thinking about his legacy. She has definitely given him something to ponder.

On Friday night, Colin is getting ready for his date to the gala with Sophie. The two have attended quite a few parties and events over the last year and a half. Sophie is trying to make a career of playing tennis professionally and is often out of town. While he has enjoyed her attitude of having a casual physical relationship since she is usually preoccupied with her tennis training, he feels differently now.

He cannot stop thinking about Hannah and wants to show her that while she will always love her husband, she can be with someone else without it taking away from the marriage she had and without compromising her freedom.

The more he thinks about it, Colin is confident she wants to be wanted and desired. He sees how she gazes at him before catching herself and pretending to be indifferent. It is only a matter of him being patient, gaining her confidence, and breaking down her barriers.

Of course, going on a date with someone else isn't exactly the way to earn her trust, but he hopes to make her jealous. He is worried, though, that she will see waiting a year as an appropriate amount of time. If that is what it takes, he will bide his time.

Throughout the evening, he is distracted by these thoughts. Afterward, he declines Sophie's invitation to go back to her flat.

Three days later, Hannah sees pictures online of Colin with his gorgeous date at the gala. The woman is wearing a turquoise blue mini dress and has the sexiest long tan legs.

For herself, she would never feel right in such an outfit with her short pale legs, and has never been one for dresses anyway. Her mom had trouble getting her to wear them as a girl. Jeans, t-shirts, and athletic wear have always been her preferred clothing, unless she absolutely has to wear a dress for a wedding or other event.

Viewing these images leads to thoughts of him being with this Sophie. Such thinking makes her uncomfortable. She is relieved to have her writing to focus on.

Hannah had been considering trying her hand at creating a romance novel for a couple of years before she finally started one after moving to Australia. For over ten years, she read Debbie Macomber books while waiting in carpool lanes and at the city pool every day in the summers while her son swam. Impressed with learning how Debbie has written somewhere around 200 novels, she decided to attempt to write just one.

After going back and forth on what her story should be about, she decides to make the love interest an Australian English professor who writes historical fiction novels that always have a love story in them. A woman from America moves to Australia, and they meet.

Sounds a little too familiar, huh? They say to write what you know.

The idea of Colin finding out about this and seeing the English professor as himself and the American character as her is embarrassing.

On the off chance her writing gets published, she will have the story set in Melbourne to support the argument that the main character is not based on the Dr. Ryan she knows. Her professor will be of Italian descent, like her own maternal grandmother's side of the family, the Biggios. Alessandro Biggio will be his name, Alex for short. She had read how many Italians immigrated to Australia after World War II.

Hannah gets the idea to visit Melbourne next month to encourage and support her writing about the city. Going on a vacation by herself is definitely new territory, but this is how it should be: a writing and self-exploration trip. She is beginning to get enthusiastic about things.

Colin starts the new semester and suddenly finds himself with a great deal to do. Hannah takes him up on his offer to attend one of his lectures about Irish Australians. She drives to the university, finds the History building, and walks up the stairs to sit in the back of the large lecture hall.

Waiting for him to arrive, she hopes he will understand that her desire to be present is from an appreciation of a good lecture, not because she has a thing for him.

A young man moves to sit beside her.

"Hi. I'm Cooper."

"Hello. I'm Hannah. Nice to meet you."

"I haven't seen you around before."

"I am just visiting today."

Dr. Ryan enters and prepares for his lecture, pulling up a slide show. The first slide has a picture of the Irish-Australian flag.

Students are visiting amongst themselves. Cooper is chatting away to Hannah and annoying her.

The professor clears his throat. "Time to begin. Everyone, take a seat. According to the National Museum of Australia's Irish in Australia exhibit 'Not Just Ned,' Australia is the most Irish country in the world outside Ireland. I know you all read the assigned readings about Irish Australians."

Surveying the room, he spots Hannah and grins. Then he sees Cooper talking to her, and this irritates him. The wannabe athlete ended up in his class again after previously failing the course.

A girl in the front row raises her hand enthusiastically. He points to her. "Stacy, what did you find noteworthy about the readings?"

"I always thought the Irish were good to the Aboriginal Australians because they were both oppressed by the British, but now I understand this wasn't always the case. My question is, were the Irish Catholics good to them because they experienced so much more oppression themselves, and was it the Irish Protestants who were more likely to be cruel?"

Trying not to keep looking up at his special guest, he explains, "I have not found enough historical accounts to address your question."

Another young lady close to the front wants to speak.

"I think it interesting how Australian Irish Catholics did so well in a short period of time to achieve equal income levels with both British descendants and Protestants. They also rose to political positions much faster than in other countries. While they may have been oppressed in the early colonial years, this was not long-lasting like it was for Aboriginal Australians."

He nods and starts to respond but finds the young man disturbing Hannah again.

"What about you, Cooper? What do you think about Sarah's comments?"

Silence. He obviously was not listening and most likely did not read the assignment.

"Did you learn anything from the readings?"

Teacher and student practically glare at one another.

"Let's get to the main lecture." Dr. Ryan goes on to show a slide of Australia with Irish ancestry demographics and talks about Irish Australians and Aboriginal Australians for almost an hour.

Hannah is amazed at how well he speaks and cannot take her eyes off him. She finally makes it clear to Cooper to leave her alone, as she wants to listen to the lecture undisturbed. He moves over a few seats to bother a girl his own age.

"In conclusion, many Aboriginal Australian groups are still fighting for native title rights. See you next week. Your term paper topics are due Tuesday."

She lets the masses leave first and then descends the stairs to the front of the room.

Colin can't stop smiling as she approaches. "I can't believe you took me up on my invitation to come to my lecture."

"It was interesting."

"I noticed you made a new friend."

"Very funny."

Without thinking about the previous rejection, he asks, "Why don't you have dinner with me? Somewhere casual. We will both wear jeans."

"Colin, we are both Ryans. We could be related."

"Right. We could be eighth cousins twice removed."

With a controlled smile, she continues to think of reasons to turn him down. "You are too fancy for me."

"Fancy? Me?? You clearly do not know me."

"I am not your type. Trust me. But I enjoyed the lecture. It brought back good memories of my college days. See you around."

After returning to her apartment, she studies the research information on finding Irish ancestors in Australia. Having an extended family for Ryan in case something happens to her makes this pursuit particularly worthwhile. However, she has definite reservations about contacting people out of the blue.

Six

Hannah is at her son's place, dropping off some things she bought for him.

"I'm excited about our plans for tomorrow. Why don't we invite Kiera?"

Suspiciously, he asks, "Why are you suggesting that?"

"It seemed like you two really got along at the nurdle hunt."

"So?"

"So… I think she would enjoy touring Swaggerty Island with us."

"That is where Kiera grew up, where her family lives."

"Well then, she can be our tour guide since she knows the island."

"No, Mom."

Unaware that the two young people had already spent more time in each other's company, she tries to think of a way to bring Ryan and this wonderful girl together.

Mother and son take a water taxi to the island. She loves boat rides and finds the 45-minute trip enjoyable. The island is magnificent. A kayak outfitter van delivers them to the launch point.

"The tour starts in 15 minutes. We are waiting on a few others to get here," announces the guide.

"Look, they have SUP." Ryan points to some men in the distance standing on what he thinks are boards.

"What is that?"

"S-U-P. Standup paddleboarding."

She makes a face. "I don't get it at all. How can that be relaxing? Sitting down in a kayak is relaxing. That's what we are doing."

Shaking her head, she begins to move towards the water. A guide goes over to Ryan. "Those are not paddle boards. They are standing up in their kayaks holding spears to catch fish."

"Do we get spears?"

"That isn't the trip you are booked on, mate."

Rushing over to his mom, she cuts him off before he can speak. "You don't need a spear! And like me, you don't even eat fish."

She turns her attention back to the crystal-clear sea. "The water and shore aren't like this in Texas." Sitting down in the soft white sand, he joins her.

Hannah is full of questions about Kiera. He explains that her parents moved here right before she was born. Her father performs the maintenance and groundskeeping at a resort.

"Kiera's Great Uncle Aidan brought her parents over from Ireland to live and work with him. He passed away five years ago. The uncle was worried because the young parents-to-be were only nineteen. Kiera's mom was raised by her grandparents, who kicked her out of the house when they found out she was pregnant. Her dad never had a good relationship with his own parents. Uncle Aidan thought they would have a better life on the island."

"So sad for the families to not be supportive."

"A few years ago, there was a wildfire here that burned down part of the resort, but thankfully not all of it, and not their house."

Loudly, the tour guide calls out, "OK, we are ready to go now."

As they get up, she remarks, "You sure have gotten to know Kiera well."

The comment receives no reply.

Their leader takes them in and out of the mangroves, staying close to shore. "Keep your eyes open. Some have spotted stingrays, eagle rays, shovelnose rays, dugongs, dolphins, and turtles on these trips." The knowledgeable man in his early 30s speaks about climate change and other environmental issues and management efforts.

Ryan listens attentively and asks several questions, which is not how he used to be.

They had never been on a kayaking tour like this, always going out on a river or lake on their own in the past. When her son points to a mud crab, Hannah nods but then observes him squinting to see better. It has been way too long since he last visited an eye doctor.

The guide gives them a mud crab lesson. "We call them muddies. They are very good to eat, but you have to be careful when catching them and always wear thick gloves. Their claws are like a vice and even if you cut the claw off, it remains in a clamped down state. I have a mate who almost lost his thumb that way to a giant buck, a male. Curiously, they can shed their own claws to get away when needed and they usually grow back."

Gently using his paddle to give everyone a better view, he continues. "This one is a jennie, a female. Females have much smaller claws and a larger oval-shaped abdominal flap tucked in on their underside. Males have a smaller triangle flap."

Ryan mentions to the group an article he read based on the findings of a San Francisco State University study. "Porcelain crabs can go into survival mode to adapt to lower ocean water pH and warmer temperatures due to climate change, but this leaves them with less energy to grow and reproduce." This leads to many other discussions.

After kayaking, he directs his mother to the summer festival. Kiera is on stage dancing with five other girls.

"Look who it is!" Hannah says with surprise. "Did you know she would be here?"

He smiles with eyes fixed straight ahead.

When the performance is over, she suggests they find her.

"No, Mom. I didn't mention I would be here. I had no idea if we would actually see her. I came to kayak and hike."

"How did you know she was participating in the festival?"

"We bumped into one another in the university cafeteria and had lunch. Before that, we went to the museum in honor of the professor who died scuba diving. We are just friends."

They hike on a track with spectacular views and then decide it is time to return to the mainland. Steps lead down to an inside sitting area on the water taxi, where Ryan takes a seat next to one of the large windows.

She is uncertain of how to talk to her son about girls. "I saw how you were looking at Kiera. Why can't you admit you like her?"

Still staring out the window, he simply states, "She needs to concentrate on school, and I need to focus on my work."

In a soft tone, she carefully replies, "I think you are afraid and don't know how to deal with that. Everyone is insecure about new relationships."

"I am fine by myself. Besides, I'm a university employee, and she is a student."

Hannah wonders if this is a real issue. She intends to find out.

When her part of the festival is over, Kiera walks back to her family home. It is a mess. Her brothers are just sitting around. She shakes her head. "Why can't you two clean up after yourselves?"

Kevin giggles. "You know we hate to clean, Olive."

Family and friends nicknamed her "Olive" after she rescued the olive ridley sea turtle and became obsessed with saving all sea turtles. For years, she made it a point to search the beach every week in case other turtles needed rescuing. There were three more she saved while in high school.

As she begins cleaning up, even though she shouldn't, she asks, "Where's Dad?"

An anxious expression comes across Kian's face. "In bed. He has been sleeping more lately."

This deeply troubles her, but she does not know what to do about it. Before returning to the university, she takes the time to sit out at a favorite spot by the water. Breathing in the ocean air helps her immensely. Listening to the waves crash on the shore, she feels the built-up stress leave her body. Being here brought great comfort growing up, especially after her mother passed away. She had almost forgotten how this simple activity connects her to the island and the ocean, providing clarity and a sense of wholeness.

Hannah has not seen Colin for a couple of weeks. She is doing a good job moving along with her writing, committed to working on it daily. Developing the characters is relatively easy for her, and creating the dialogue between them comes naturally. The visit to Melbourne is almost planned out.

Late one afternoon, she decides to take a break and phone a friend in Texas. In the middle of their chat, she sees Colin trying to call. Reaching him later, she hears the enthusiasm in his voice.

"I have an offer you can't refuse."

Skeptically, she replies, "Oh yeah, what is that?"

"I am going to New Zealand. A film is in development about my book on Hongi Hika. You can come with me and be a production assistant on the set while I work as a consultant and assistant to the director. I received approval to hire you earlier today."

"Why would they hire me?"

"I told them you would be an asset. You will print and distribute scripts and coordinate messages among the director, producers, and everyone else, including me. The film will fail without teamwork and coordination. Doesn't that sound like you, helping everyone to communicate? Being a wonderful wife and mother gave you endless practice at that, right?"

He doesn't receive a response.

"Didn't you tell me you needed a job at some point? Don't you think you would be good at this?"

"Well, yes, that does sound like something I could do."

"I learned two weeks ago that we finally received full funding, so I have been drowning in phone calls and emails ever since. I am very involved in the pre-production process. If you are able, you can start work tomorrow. Then in three weeks, we leave for New Zealand, where we are scheduled for 2 ½ weeks of shooting and another 2 ½ weeks in Australia."

She is quiet, trying to take it all in.

"Do you have any plans over the next two months or so that this would interfere with?"

"I had planned a trip to Melbourne, but I can do that when we get back."

"Is this a holiday with your son?"

"No, just by myself. It is for research for my book."

"Right, your secret novel. Well, I don't want to interfere with your creative endeavor."

"No one is paying me for that," she laughs.

"So, you will take the job?"

"Yes, I will. I can start tomorrow."

"Great!"

"What about your classes?"

"Another professor is taking over for me. I had not mentioned this to you before because there was a chance the project could fall through, and I didn't want to jinx it by talking about it. Now, there is a big rush because we need to film in New Zealand before winter arrives. Kerikeri doesn't get too cold, but Rotorua does. It would not be good in winter with partially dressed Māori warrior actors. People there have been preparing for this, but many parts of the Sydney shoot still need to be coordinated, which I need your assistance on. When we are done filming, I will also be part of the editing process."

"Congratulations on having your book made into a movie. This is a big deal. And I understand all about not wanting to jinx something by telling others."

"I have many other Irish superstitions, but we will chat about that another time. Can I come over tomorrow morning around 10 to get you started on what needs to be done?"

"Yes. See you then."

She calls Ryan to give him the news.

"What a great opportunity for you, Mom."

"I will be gone for about five weeks, first in New Zealand and then in different places in Australia. I will try to call when I can."

"That's fine. Don't worry about me."

"Did you know that New Zealand is made up of two main islands, North and South?" she asks.

"I did."

"Well, I didn't."

"Sounds like someone wasn't paying attention in Geography class," he teases.

"I probably was, but the problem is that it was over 30 years ago. My memory of geography doesn't go back that far. I thought it was one big island."

Hesitating at first, she continues. "So, changing subjects, I checked out the university website. Their policy states that employee/student relationships are only a problem if the employee has, and I quote, 'academic, supervisory, or other authority or influence over the student.' This is not the case. The fact that you work there is *not* an issue for getting to know Kiera, OK?"

"OK. But again, she needs to concentrate on school, and I need to concentrate on work." As he reiterates this, his phone indicates another call coming in.

"Guess who is calling?"

"I'm so excited! Have a good talk."

"We are just friends. There is nothing to be excited about."

"You are no fun."

Hanging up with his mom, Ryan says "Hello" to Kiera, who sounds distraught.

"What's going on?"

"I am having a hard time with a paper and presentation involving statistics and data analysis. I thought it would be fascinating to do my ocean science project on low-oxygen areas or dead zones in the ocean and how this relates to climate change. I already have the topic approved, but now that I am finding articles on the subject, I can't make sense of all the formulas and statistical concepts. Do you think you can help me?"

"Of course," he assures her. "For my research assistant position, I supported professors on dead zone projects and became good at understanding the research publications. They are complicated, that's for sure."

"Why don't you email me the articles and what you have so far, and I will get back with you about it."

He spends the rest of the evening reading over everything and constructs a lengthy email to her with detailed explanations. Smiling, he thinks to himself, *Kiera is an incredible writer. She and I together would make the perfect PhD student, but that is not a joint endeavor.*

Hannah speaks on the phone with Colin frequently to make sure they have all the bases covered for the film production. She has made countless calls and emails to coordinate the parties involved. Now it is time to think through what needs to be done before leaving town.

She goes downstairs and knocks on Marci's door. When it opens, she tells her landlord, "This is for the next two months' rent."

Marci stares at the check. "Why are you paying in advance?"

"Oh, for some reason, I thought Colin would have told you. I am going to be working on the movie about his book."

"No. He didn't tell me".

"I have been so busy getting ready, I didn't think about mentioning it."

"That's fine." After a moment of silence, Marci hesitantly asks, "Are you two seeing each other?"

"No. Definitely not. It is just a job."

"It sounds like a way for him to get closer to you."

"It isn't like that."

"I see how he admires you."

Hannah becomes nervous and finds herself chatting away.

"My Uncle Paddy was a history professor. His last name was Ryan, and I began to think about how I didn't even know what books he published. He died when I was young. I did a search and found a book he wrote about Native Americans, and then I saw this book of Colin's on the Māori and bought them both. After asking him some questions about his research and mentioning how, at some point, I will need to get a job, that led to working on the film."

For some reason, she is attempting to justify the situation to Marci by awkwardly throwing her uncle into the conversation. While it is true she ordered her uncle's book, doing so came as an afterthought and a distant second to the priority of Colin and reading his works.

Marci nods, trying not to let on how it bothers her deeply that the two of them have been collaborating and are now going away together. She had never shared the details with her tenant of how she fell in love with Dr. Ryan, 18 years her senior, when he was her history professor. After graduating two years later, she attended one of his public lectures for the purpose of seeing him again.

The new graduate went up on stage to greet her former instructor at the end of his presentation, thrilled to learn he remembered her. Colin asked Marci if she wanted to grab a bite to eat, and three months later, she found out she was pregnant. It has not been easy juggling the twins and her job as a high school English teacher. She has not dated since.

"I almost forgot," Hannah continues. "If something were to ever happen to me, there is a book upstairs in the desk drawer that I need you to give to my son. It is basically a 'What to do when I die book.' I want Ryan to have it written down, step by step, what to take care of, and I included personal messages, pictures, and memories."

"O...K...," Marci responds slowly. "Why are you saying this? Are you afraid to fly?"

"No, I'm not, but with my husband gone, the idea of something happening to me and what it would do to my son is disturbing. I completed the book a couple of months ago."

"Of course, I would give it to him, but you will be fine. Have a good trip."

The following day, it is time to leave. Hannah drives to Ryan's to drop off Rosie.

He reaches out for the cat condo/play tower. "Is this necessary?"

"Yes, she loves this thing. And you need to watch her. I have caught her chewing on electric cords. Don't let her do that. When you are at work, put the tower in your bathroom with the litter box, food, and water bowl, and close the door. Keep the toilet lid down. Small cats can drown in the water."

"I didn't know cat-sitting would get this involved," he sighs.

She holds the kitten so they are face-to-face. "Goodbye, Sweetie. Ryan will take good care of you."

"I'm sorry I will be gone for your birthday."

He shrugs, "Birthdays are for children. It does not matter."

She steps forward for a big hug. "It matters to me, and I will make it up to you when I get back."

"Bye, Mom."

Observing the cat explore his space, he looks up at the ocean and marine life posters on his walls and begins to make plans to set up a saltwater aquarium with sea snails, urchins, and various fish.

She is with several other women collecting water at the river when a koala appears, prompting her to wander away from the others. Suddenly, she is grabbed from behind. A big hand placed firmly over her mouth prevents her from screaming. The man's sizeable arms press her body against his so tight she can barely breathe. Another man runs in front of them. He is wearing a uniform. The man holding her follows the other. She is taken farther and farther away from her group. Between being so scared and being held so tight, the trees and sky above her begin to spin around.

After awakening in a room that is clearly not in her colony, she hears men speaking but cannot make out what they are saying. Wait. They are female. She listens intently and hears the words "such a cool party." The voices come closer. "I danced with Robert three times," says a girl. "Randy actually came over to talk to me. I couldn't believe it," says another.

Kiera's eyes open, realizing the girls down the hall had just walked by. They are always chatting about the parties they go to. It is a relief to be free from that dream. That is, until it happens again.

Seven

KERIKERI, NORTHLAND, NEW ZEALAND

Hannah and Colin land after a 5 ½ hour flight. They did not talk much on the trip. He was heads down, going over and over the script and the schedule while she sent yet another round of emails.

Content to relax in the taxi, Hannah enjoys the landscape of rolling hills with various shades of vivid greenery. He shares some knowledge of the area.

"Kerikeri is called the Cradle of the Nation by some because of its historic buildings, and this is where the missionaries first set up a site. We will be filming near that spot. Hongi Hika facilitated the mission and protected them so that more Europeans would come to trade tools and weapons."

The cab pulls up to a quaint place nestled in palm trees.

"Wow, this is beautiful."

Colin hesitantly brings up an undiscussed subject. "There is something I didn't tell you."

Eyeing him suspiciously, "What?"

"The local hotels are completely booked. The crew and Māori actors filled up the vacancies they had, so some of us are staying here. These are short-term rental units, and we are sharing a flat because that is all they have available unless you would rather room with Hal, the director."

"Very funny."

"The bedroom has two beds. If you insist, I will sleep on the living room couch."

No response is given.

They retrieve their bags and proceed to the apartment, opening the door to a nice kitchen, living room, and balcony. She finds the bedroom with two beds, a twin and a queen, and shakes her head.

He peers in. "Should I keep my stuff in the living room?"

Without looking at him, she answers, "No. You can have the twin bed."

Biting his lip and trying not to smile, he tells her, "In thirty minutes, we have a reservation at the best restaurant in town. Are you game?"

"I am starving, so I guess I don't have a choice."

At dinner, he orders a bottle of wine. As Hannah reviews the menu, she asks, "What is kumara?"

"They are sweet potatoes," he explains. "I have given entire lectures about potatoes."

"Why is that?"

"Growing kumara required religious rituals by the whole Māori tribe, as it is a sacred plant. This kept the men home, not off fighting. Battles among the tribes were only done for part of the year. The British changed this when they introduced regular potatoes to New Zealand. It did not matter who grew regular potatoes because no rituals were required, and they were easier to grow. This meant the men were free to go to war with the new muskets they were acquiring from the British."

As the waiter brings their wine, she catches herself staring at Colin, engrossed in the way he speaks and how handsome he is.

He offers a toast. "To finally have the honor of dining with you."

With a skeptical expression, she also raises her glass.

They go on to talk nonstop about the upcoming shoot.

Upon returning to the hotel, she decides against sleeping in the same room. "There is enough space to move the mattress from the twin bed onto the floor in the living room. That is the best option for us both to get a good night's sleep."

"Whatever makes you comfortable," he says, hiding his disappointment.

SYDNEY, AUSTRALIA

After receiving notification that the patent was granted, Theresa reached out to the investors who had told her previously of their interest. There are numerous venture capital firms ready to invest in new technologies addressing climate change, so it was not nearly as hard as she thought to find people willing to fund them. The first round of money should be in the company account on Monday.

However, the group must set up shop, find a facility to rent, and prove progress every step of the way to receive continued support. They are all anxious about failing in this endeavor and letting their investors down. Overriding this fear is the motivation to contribute to Australia reaching a balance between the amount of greenhouse gas produced and the amount that is removed from the atmosphere. Net-zero emissions by 2050 is a worldwide goal, but the trio hopes to help achieve this sooner. They are optimistic about a brighter future and being part of making that happen.

Ryan and Kiera find themselves coming from opposite directions in the hall.

She observes a mark on his face and the fact that he is wearing glasses.

"What's this?"

"Yeah, I know. I hate wearing glasses, but I hate putting in contacts more."

"I like your glasses. I mean the scratch on your face."

"Oh. Right. My mom is on a trip, so her kitten, Rosie, is with me. She got me good with those sharp claws."

"I love kittens!" Kiera says enthusiastically.

With a sigh, he replies, "I guess. She gets into everything. So, how is your analysis and dead zone paper coming along?"

"Not too good," she confesses.

"Do you want me to take another look?"

"That would be great, but I know you are busy. I didn't want to bother you."

"Don't be silly. Do you want to meet at the library or do you want to come over and see the kitten?"

"I'd love to see Rosie."

They agree to meet at 5:15, picking up a pizza on their way to his apartment. As they enter, the cat races to the door, immediately rubbing herself against Kiera's legs.

"I guess she likes you."

"I'm glad."

He puts the pizza in the oven to keep it warm for later. "Let me see your work."

Ryan reads what Kiera has written so far as she plays with the kitten, placing her on the tower and watching the animal move to each level.

While checking out his belongings, she spots a book about saltwater aquariums.

"Are you getting a fish tank?"

"Yes, but I want to become knowledgeable first. I don't want to kill the marine life."

"Good idea." She wants to ask to accompany him for the purchase, but decides not to.

He motions for her to sit with him. Rosie darts over to take a position on the couch above Kiera's shoulder. The cat kneads her paws into the side of their guest's neck and purrs.

"Looks like you have a new friend."

"She is so cute. It's like getting a neck massage. My dad wouldn't let us have a cat inside. He is allergic and didn't even like us feeding stray cats outside. We did anyway. Occasionally, he would catch us and get mad. But enough about that…we should get started."

In the middle of explaining some errors he has found in her analysis, his phone buzzes.

"It's my sister."

"Answer it."

"I guess I should. She never calls me."

"Hi, Allison."

"Hi. I left a message and text for your mom yesterday and haven't heard back, so I was concerned."

He informs her about his mother's temporary job on a film shoot.

"How exciting! Well, I wanted you both to know that I can't come to visit in June as planned. I got a job with the forest department, working with land owners on compliance and forest sustainability, conservation, and soil erosion issues. I have six weeks of training and can't take a vacation until after six months."

"Congratulations. That is great."

"Yes. I am thrilled about the opportunity to use my environmental science degree. My boyfriend got me the interview since he already works there."

He is unsure of what else to say, and so is she.

"I need to go now," says Allison.

"OK. Bye."

Kiera sits back down. "You could have talked longer."

"It's fine."

"I heard some of what she was saying. We should have asked her about Oregon and climate change measures there."

Realizing he could have had Allison on speakerphone and introduced the two, Ryan hopes Kiera doesn't think he is rude. While he would present her as a friend, there would still be the risk of taunting from his sister. Many remarks have been made over the years about why there is no girlfriend in the picture. He has always felt that he isn't what girls want. And now he feels even more unappealing with his glasses. Maybe he should give the contacts another chance.

"Are you OK?" she asks after he has gone silent.

"Yes. Let's go over the data on low-oxygen ocean dead zones from the computer model you found. It supports your statements on how the projected outcome of climate change will result in warmer waters not only holding less oxygen but also increasing the metabolism of some marine life, which in turn makes their need for oxygen even greater."

He begins clarifying the results, but she has trouble concentrating. Her thoughts are about how handsome and clever he is, and she ponders why she is even more attracted to him with the glasses.

Colin and Hannah spend the next five days filming scenes around Kerikeri. Before their arrival, a mock Māori tribe village was constructed. Scenes from the beginning and the end of the film are shot here. They want to show what life was like in Hongi Hika's settlement. The set contains rectangular sleeping houses built from wood and tree ferns with thatch roofs. Separate structures are for cooking, storing, and meeting. The thatch hangs over the buildings to create covered porches.

On the first day, he introduces her to the lovely woman in charge of costumes and makeup.

"Thanks for getting me on this project," says Kristen.

Hannah wonders how they know one another and gets vibes that they used to date. She will ask him these things tonight. Not that it matters to her, of course.

They shoot footage of the villagers starting their day by singing and praying as the sun rises. Then a group performs a *Haka*, or traditional war dance, involving facial expressions of fear and sticking out their tongues while chanting loudly and stamping their feet.

On a break from shooting, one of the Māori actors approaches Hannah.

"I am Rawiri."

She nods. "I'm Hannah."

The man moves closer and begins to lean his face into hers. Her reaction is to step back.

Colin laughs. "He wants to give you a *hongi*. It is the Māori greeting of touching noses and sometimes foreheads, too. It is their way of showing unity by exchanging the breath of life, called the *ha*."

"Oh, OK. That is fine." She steps towards Rawiri. They touch noses and foreheads. He is a handsome man.

Dr. Ryan speaks in broken Māori with one of the actors. The indigenous people of New Zealand call their language Te Reo. The actors all speak English, but they know the professor can at least partially converse in their language.

Later, he explains to Hannah how Aboriginal Australians have hundreds of languages. Unfortunately, most are dying out because so few speak their native language today. The Māori have higher numbers of native speakers due to a unified language among them. Still, the percentage is low.

Another Māori actor, Mahuta, says to him, "Kei te pehea koe?" to ask how Colin is doing. A number of the other Māori actors gather around.

He replies, "Pai" to indicate he is "good."

Slowly and deliberately, he sounds out, "Kua reri koe ki te timata?" to ask if they are ready to get started.

A man much smaller than the others inquires, "Ka roa te ra. Ae?"

"Ae," Dr. Ryan confirms. Then in English to others standing around, he explains, "Yes. It is going to be a long day."

They resume filming. Hongi is shown with his first wife who was blind. He is being very kind to her. In another scene, he is taking advice from his spouse.

As the group moves to a more wooded area, mosquitoes are all around them. Hannah brings out bug spray from her bag.

"You think of everything, don't you?" remarks Colin.

"I am always armed with sun lotion and bug spray when spending time outside." She passes the bottle around after spraying herself.

They go on to film the battle depicting how Hongi's two brothers died. The segments are extensive and require many retakes.

When the day is finally over, they return to their shared flat. It is late, and dinner consists of eating in silence during the drive back to the hotel.

Colin plops down on the couch and puts his hands on his head, obviously in pain.

"I have some aspirin if you want it."

"I don't like to take drugs."

"O.K...Well, have you ever tried massaging your temples?"

"What do you mean?"

Hannah proceeds to stand in front of him, placing three fingers on either side of his forehead to massage in a circular motion.

"That feels good. It didn't get rid of my headache, though."

"Sometimes the pain in your head comes from somewhere else. Come sit in this chair." He takes a seat. She pushes down on his trapezius muscles at the bottom of his neck above the shoulders.

"Ouch!"

"There is a knot on this right side. That is a trigger point. It needs to be massaged out."

She kneads his neck for a spell.

When she stops, he opens his eyes. "That made a big difference. Are you a massage therapist or something?"

"No. My husband had a lot of aches and pains."

"Do you do backs also?"

"I can," she replies hesitantly. "Let me get the coconut oil."

"Why do you have coconut oil?"

"Because I use it all over, literally. It is great stuff."

"Literally, huh??"

"Yes, but I guess I shouldn't have said it that way. Fatigue is setting in, so let's make this fast."

He takes his shirt off, moves to the twin mattress in the middle of the living room floor, and lies down.

First, she works the oil into his back.

"I don't think I can do this properly without sitting on your bum."

Laughing, he heartily affirms, "Fine with me."

"I'm sure it is." Not thinking through her suggestion, she sits on him. Giving the massage isn't easy for her as her hands and fingers tire quickly.

After a while, he turns his head to her with obvious desire.

"That's enough. Time for bed. Goodnight." She retreats to the bedroom, shutting the door with a little too much force.

He reminds himself not to make any moves on her while they are working together, but when they get back home, all bets are off!

Hannah gets in bed. Closing her eyes, she keeps seeing him lying there, his muscular, tan back ingrained in her mind. She should have made it clear that her arms were too short to reach over and apply the necessary pressure. Her husband had a large back and shoulders, so she knew this from experience. Realizing now it was a mistake to be on top of him, she is embarrassed. *I hope he doesn't think I was hitting on him.*

She finds herself listening to his movements and wondering if he will come into her room. He doesn't.

In the morning, she has trouble looking at Colin after the dreams she had about him during the night.

He speaks first. "I had the weirdest dream about my teeth breaking and falling out."

"That means you are feeling a loss of control over a situation or over your life in general."

"Are you a dream expert now?" he teases.

"Recently, I have read about what certain dreams mean. I have been dreaming for months about my purse being stolen. That has to do with emotional loss."

He often forgets what she has been through, but doesn't know what to say.

She continues. "I used to have crumbling teeth dreams. Then it was bugs in my room, which represent one's worries. Now it is the purse dream and dreams about being chased, which has to do with anxiety."

"I usually don't remember my dreams."

"I definitely think women are more likely to remember their dreams than men. Since we are more aware of our dreams, we want to attribute meaning to them. Well, anyway, we need to get going. How is your back and head?"

"You healed me. I feel fine."

"Right."

On the drive to the set, she casually comments, "Kristen sure is friendly."

"Yes. She used to act in local plays and also do the costumes and makeup. She and I used to date."

"That's nice." *So, they have slept together.*

A part of Colin wants to make her jealous, but at the same time, he wants Hannah to know there is nothing between him and this woman. "Kristen has a serious boyfriend. They are making plans for marriage and children."

She intentionally attempts to appear indifferent to this information.

The following few days are long and tiring. Each night, they return and go straight to sleep. On the last day in Kerikeri, they film the conflict in which Hongi is shot with a musket. The bullet penetrates his lungs. He is shown being treated for his wound.

Additional scenes during his final year of life convey Hongi's hope. He visits with people and makes plans for the future. However, they can all see how weak he is becoming, and it is obvious he does not have much longer to live. The sound of air passing through the hole in his chest is heard.

With the depiction of the main character's death, the filming around Kerikeri is now complete.

"Great work. See everyone in Rotorua tomorrow," says the director.

"Kia ora." The professor gives thanks and nods to several of the actors.

Rawiri speaks to Hannah. "Po marie."

She turns to Colin. "He is saying Good Night."

"Goodnight."

After Rawiri walks away, Colin chuckles. "I think he likes you."

She gives him an annoyed look.

"I saw you two making eyes at one another."

"No one was making eyes. He told me about being forced to move away from his hometown because of flooding due to climate change. The flood waters brought debris flows down on part of the town. We went on to discuss that, in addition to intensified storms, rising sea levels will have many others facing evacuation along the coast in the future, and the dilemma of when to move and where to build."

Before he can respond, she continues. "And I let him know what Ryan told me about how the angle of the moon's orbit will alter in the 2030s, leading to significant increases in high tide flooding when combined with the sea level rise. Of course, this means it is all the more important to plan ahead."

Well aware of the issues facing New Zealand and Australia, Colin knows several people who lost their homes to flooding. But at that moment, he isn't in the mood for a serious conversation and wants to tease her instead.

"I see you trying to look through his little grass skirt to admire his strong thighs."

"Ha, yeah right."

"I know what it is, you are trying to picture me in a tiny see-through skirt."

"Give me a break!"

He finds having Hannah around to be a nice break from the pressures to make the film a success.

Eight

The movie production moves six hours south from Kerikeri to Rotorua. The crew is split up among three hotels. "This time, you will have your own room," Colin tells her on the ride there.

"Good!"

As they approach the city, Hannah observes clouds accumulating in one area on the ground.

"What's that?"

"Central North Island sits on a volcanic plateau, and Rotorua is built inside the crater of a dormant volcano at the heart of the area's geothermal belt. That is steam drifting up from the Pōhutu Geyser. It erupts up to 20 times a day," he explains.

Observing the city, it is larger than she thought it would be. All of a sudden, an offensive smell fills the car.

"P U!" What is that?"

He laughs. "Well, along with geothermal gases rising up comes hydrogen sulfide. Today is a cloudy day with low wind, making the odor stronger. Wind and clear skies dissipate it. You will get used to the smell."

"I don't think I can get used to *that*."

"You'll be surprised."

She points to a building with the word Aotearoa on it. "What does that mean? I keep seeing that word."

"It is the Māori name for New Zealand. Many want to officially change the country's name to Aotearoa. The building you pointed to is Te Wānanga o Aotearoa, a small university focused on a Māori learning environment."

Their high-rise hotel is located downtown. Impressed with the modern room, a row of windows gives her a stunning view of the lake.

They have a late dinner at the Pig & Whistle Historic Pub.

"I highly recommend the Steak, Ale & Mushroom Pot Pie," he suggests.

"I will eat any food with beer in it," she laughs. "I don't like to cook much, but I do make beer turkey chili a few times a year."

"Will you make it for me?"

"Maybe."

As they eat, he tells her about the upcoming shoots and the local landscape. "We will launch canoes in a few days from Tikitere, less than 15 minutes from here. It will take the actors and crew about 20 minutes to paddle to Mokoia Island, and there we will do the battle scenes. A group of us will go to the island ahead of them on a boat. Tikitere is also called Hell's Gate because it is the most active geothermal spot in this area. It has acidic lakes, mud pools, a small mud volcano, and a hot waterfall called Kakahi Falls."

"Interesting. I've never heard of a hot waterfall."

He goes on to speak of the forbidden love story between a young man named Tūtānekai, who lived on Mokoia Island, and his sweetheart, Hinemoa. The girl's father forbade her to marry him, ordering his daughter not to canoe over to the island. She decided to swim instead, listening to the sound of Tūtānekai playing the flute to direct her where to go.

"The things we do for love," he expresses, expecting her to say what a sweet story or something to that effect.

"Yeah, right. She should have just moved on to someone else."

"Aren't you a cynic?"

She rolls her eyes.

The next morning, Hannah reviews the schedule for the day. She notes the date: April 22nd. "Oh no, I forgot Ryan's birthday. It was yesterday. I can't believe I forgot."

"He will understand."

"You don't get it. Most likely, no one even said Happy Birthday to him. I always message his sister to remind her. I don't think the guy friends he plays games with online think about each other's birthdays."

"True. I never remember the dates for my mates."

"Right. That's what men are like. You have no idea how it worries me that my son doesn't have other people in his life."

She sends a text. *Happy Birthday! Whenever you are ready to pick out an aquarium it will be your gift from me. We can go to the pet store when I get back.*

Once on location, discussions are held about the various Māori skirmishes that they will film. There are many run-throughs and costume changes.

Things move along smoothly, to their surprise. It becomes apparent that the shooting day will end early for a change. Lastly, the actors representing

Hongi Hika's Māori tribe, the Ngāpuhi, are filmed assembling at a spot before they trek to attack another enemy tribe, the Te Arawa.

Colin explains to the cast and crew how the goal is to stick to as much of what is known about the real historical events. "The Te Arawa tribe believed they were safe from attack because they gathered up all the canoes in the area to retreat to Mokoia Island. They did not foresee that an enemy tribe would supply Hongi with additional canoes or that his warriors would have hundreds of muskets. The Te Arawa fought with traditional weapons and had only a musket or two."

He holds up a poster with a map, pointing out the trail the Ngāpuhi, led by Hongi, took to drag the canoes to Lake Rotorua, where Mokoia Island is located.

Amiri, the largest Māori actor, asks, "How far do we have to drag and carry the canoes?"

"The trail is about 2.7 kilometers, but we will only film at the beginning and the end. The trail has many fallen trees that have been cut to pass through, but it will still be tricky with the canoes. We have extra crew members to assist. See everyone tomorrow."

To Hannah, he says, "I thought you and I could scout out the area for tomorrow's shoot. Are you up for a hike?"

"I am."

Along the way, he notices her checking her phone. "Have you heard from Ryan?"

"No. I am worried he is mad at me. I will text again and ask if he got my message, and tell him cell service is kind of spotty. I know this isn't true, and my phone has been working fine, but I want to give a reason why he did not hear from me on his actual birthday without an outright lie."

"You are sneaky," he laughs.

She pretends to be irritated.

They park the car and amble towards the trail, taking in the scenery. The dirt path disappears into a thicket of trees. The sign says Hinehopu Scenic Reserve: Hongi's Track.

Colin shares some history of the area as they walk.

"This trail is referred to by two names: Hongi's Track because of the attack we are filming, and Hinehopu's Track. Hinehopu was a Māori chieftainess who lived in this region over 400 years ago. She traveled along this trail between her two homes. When Hinehopu was a baby, her princess mother took her down this path. After realizing a warring Māori tribe was approaching, the princess used the hollow base of a tree to hide with her baby as the warriors unknowingly walked past them. We will get to this tree later."

With the sun disappearing from the expansive shade created by the crowns of mature evergreens, they cross a bridge and go through the downed trees cut to keep the path accessible. She can imagine people here hundreds of years ago.

It is an unusually warm day for April in this region, the type of day snakes in Texas like.

"Are there snakes in the area?"

He laughs. "There are no snakes in New Zealand, at least not on land."

"Good to know because I'm used to seeing rattlesnakes."

"How common are they where you are from?"

"I saw probably 13 or 14 during the 4 ½ years we lived there. Only one was huge. What about other predators?"

"Actually, there are no dangerous animals at all. Bats are the only native mammals. There are a few types of biting spiders, but there is nothing poisonous and nothing that can gobble you up. You are safe."

Grinning, he puts his arm around her for a minute as they carry on down the path.

Reaching an enormous tree covered in moss, Colin studies it.

"This is a Pukatea tree. The Māori used this timber for the figureheads on their canoes because it is soft but strong. An extract from the bark was used in traditional Māori medicine for pain. The extract has a chemical structure similar to morphine."

Continuing their walk, they arrive at another towering tree.

"And this is the famous Wishing Tree. It is a Black Pine, also called a Matai. It is about 28 meters tall, or 90 feet to you Americans. When Hinehopu grew up, she met her future husband here, and the tree became sacred to them. Her husband's group was the Ngāti Pikiao, one of three tribes making up the Te Awara that were attacked 200 years later by Hongi and his tribe. People today come here and place gifts and money in the hollow trunk and make a wish. It is said these wishes come true."

She smiles at him.

"Do you have a wish you want to make?"

Grabbing an American one-dollar bill from her purse, she places it in the tree, closing her eyes momentarily. She still has not bothered to get Australian currency since using cards is more convenient.

"Is your wish about me?"

"No, definitely not."

"I have a wish to make, also." He pulls two bills out of his wallet. "This Lobster should be worth a very good wish."

"Lobster?"

"Yes. That is what a 20-dollar bill is called. See, it is red. Not sure I want to go as high as a Pineapple." After showing her the yellow 50-dollar bill, he puts the 20 in the opening, looking back at her with a big grin.

She shakes her head, not wanting his wish to have anything to do with her.

The day starts early at 4:30 am to shoot several scenes as the sun rises around 6:30. The director fell ill and asked Colin to step in.

The actors playing Hongi Hika and his Ngāpuhi army are hauling canoe-like wakas along the trail. The vessels are red with black poles running along the top and white rings evenly spaced down them. Each waka has a figurehead at one end, consisting of eyes, a nose, and a mouth displaying a protruding tongue.

As the trek progresses, the cinematographer indicates he did not get a good shot.

"Stop. Stop. Kati!" yells Dr. Ryan, motioning the actors to return to where he stands and start over.

Because his view was obstructed by the waka, a Māori man trips over a log and falls. "Awhina! Help!"

They begin to run behind schedule. Hannah notices Colin holding his head. She hands him a water bottle and two aspirin. He reluctantly takes the pills.

That afternoon, they reach Hell's Gate to shoot the scenes where Hongi and the Ngāpuhi paddle to Mokoia Island to fight the Te Arawa.

A helicopter lands to take two of the camera crew up for aerial shots and also to reach the island first, so the approach of the warriors in their wakas can be captured.

Hannah, Colin, and twelve others board a boat for transportation and to film alongside the Māori actors during their water journey. The weather had turned windy and cold.

Once all the men arrive by canoe, they take a break while the crew prepares for the battle scenes. Hannah approaches the actor who plays Hongi. She and Kristen adjust his costume. He is wearing what is supposed to be the armor and helmet given to Hongi by King George IV during his visit to England.

Afterward, a group returns to the shore to film Hongi being shot in the head by one of the only Te Arawa with a gun. The other Te Arawa actors pretend to attack with traditional weapons.

Before the next scene, "Hongi" is handed a helmet that appears the same but with a hole in it to reflect the historical account of the lead ball going through the protective hat, slowing down to hit his head without penetrating the skull. The man rubs his head and winces as if in pain. Kristen is skillful at creating fake injuries with makeup and artificial blood.

Many Te Arawa are shown trying to swim away while being pursued by Ngāpuhi in canoes. Some did escape, but the majority were either taken prisoner or shot. The outcome for the Te Arawa was a massacre.

The filming lasts until the sun begins to set. Most of the crew will be camping on the island overnight. Luckily for Hannah, she, Colin, and several others can get back on the boat to return to their hotel.

On what feels like a trudge to their rooms, he comments, "You sure are quiet tonight."

"I have never been so tired in my life. Making a movie is exhausting."

He laughs. "Get some sleep because it starts all over again at 5 am."

With a weary expression, she closes her door. About 30 minutes later, there is a knock. The necessity of discussing the schedule for tomorrow finally dawned on him.

After getting up to unlock the door, she falls backward on the couch. "I don't know how much longer I can keep going like this."

"You can do it. Tribal and war scenes are draining with so many people to coordinate. I think you will find our days in Australia to be much easier. The settings in Sydney involve only a handful of people when Hongi meets missionaries and learns about agricultural techniques."

Doubt is written all over her face, but he continues.

"As you know, I made the arrangements for shooting at Iandra Castle, four hours from Sydney, but I didn't explain the details. The mansion is where we will re-create the places Hongi visited in England. It has many different rooms, which will serve as the university where he and the professor worked on the first Māori-English dictionary, in addition to a royal location for the meeting with King George IV."

She sits up. "You told me to remind you to check the script for the Australia scenes and make sure it was revised to emphasize how Hongi Hika's motivation in developing good relations with missionaries was to have more trade opportunities and to acquire muskets. It was about personal goals of power and revenge, not religion."

"Right. Thanks. I will do that tonight."

He gazes at her with admiration. "You have been so helpful. You may be exhausted physically, but I am exhausted mentally and physically. It scares me how I keep forgetting things, but there you are to assist when I lose my train of thought in front of everyone. I am not used to that happening."

"I think you are just worn out and have too much to think about," she says reassuringly.

"I am thankful you agreed to do this project with me."

About ten minutes into going over things, Colin asks a question, but receives no response. He turns his head to find her fast asleep, sitting there beside him.

Kiera manages to listen carefully to six ocean science presentations without obsessing over her own. No matter how many speeches she gives, she always ends up overwhelmed with anxiety. It makes her wonder if teaching is right for her. However, she is self-assured when speaking to young teenagers, unlike with her peers, where she feels inadequate, resulting in shaking hands and sweating.

Finally, it is her turn. She moves to the podium. "My presentation is on low-oxygen areas called dead zones in our oceans where most marine life cannot survive."

With a wavering voice, she continues. "A major contributor to dead zones is the extra fertilizer from crops to grow our food that ends up in the ocean. The nutrients in the fertilizer lead to algae blooms, where bacteria decompose the algae and consume the oxygen in the water during that process."

Her hands shake even more as she observes students on their phones. The lack of interest is getting to her, but she thinks of Ryan and imagines giving the speech only to him. With more confidence, she explains the locations of dead zones in the world.

When class is over, she practically runs to Ryan's office, eager to tell him about her presentation and how Dr. Seaver said it was outstanding. The professor asked her several questions, as she does for everyone. Kiera answered them in detail, clearly having done her research. Not all students hold up well to the interrogation.

Approaching his office, Ryan comes into view. He is deep in conversation with a gorgeous blonde-haired girl, who is sitting side by side with him, touching shoulders and looking at his computer. Kiera moves on before they spot her. *What have I been thinking? He is not interested in me as a girlfriend.*

TWO DAYS LATER

She walks up the steps of the log structure with a porch surrounding all sides. As she enters, many women in the long room smile and call out to her. The ones who can get up without much effort come near. She greets each one with a hug and then tends to the bedridden women, checking on their sores and various ailments. Another attendant gives every patient a plate of chicken and vegetables for lunch.

After treating those in need, she leaves but does not get far before a man comes up and points to the adjacent building. The smell in the room is terrible. Men make crude remarks. She begins to examine an elderly male. Another man grabs her from behind. No one comes to her rescue. As he is about to throw her down on a cot, she takes a pair of scissors from her coat pocket, stabs him, and escapes.

A broken sequence of images shows her running, entering a different building, and crying to a man wearing a long black coat. He sits her down, and she regains her composure. The next scene is of her assisting the apparent doctor in a rudimentary exam room.

Finally, she is back home in the arms of a loving man who begs her to never return. This is not an option in her mind. The pay is in rations, allowing her to provide food and supplies for themselves and their extended family.

Kiera wakes to the clock displaying 7:30 am. Her first class is in thirty minutes. For some reason, the alarm did not go off. Trying to pace herself and not run, she is already feeling winded and worries about another asthma attack.

Being able to concentrate on ocean science eludes her. She keeps seeing the woman in her dreams, who appears to be a nursing assistant for the mentally ill and disabled at a facility on Swaggerty Island in the early 1900s. It is her understanding that terrible things happened there. Some of the original structures still stand. The dreams about the woman did not begin until Kiera turned 15. But as a child, she had nightmares from neighborhood kids telling ghost stories about the remaining buildings.

At the end of her lecture, Dr. Seaver motions for Kiera to come to the front. "Can you meet me at my office later, say around two?"

"Yes, of course." Kiera wonders what this is about. Surely there isn't anything wrong with her work. She was fastidious about citing sources and paraphrasing.

Right before 2 pm, she finds the professor's room listed on the syllabus.

Dr. Seaver raises her head. "Come in and shut the door."

The request is concerning, but she does so and takes a seat.

"I have read all the papers, and yours is, by far, the best. You are an exceptional writer and researcher. Have you thought about pursuing a PhD in Marine Biology?"

"I've thought about it, but didn't think it was for me."

"I see you are pursuing an education degree. You could pursue a master's, and if you decide not to continue on for a PhD, you can then teach as planned. Your salary will be higher because of the advanced degree. This dead zone project could be the start of your thesis, where you would greatly expand on it, especially with climate change data, and collaborate with PhD students and other professors. I could be your program supervisor. I would also write a recommendation letter to nominate you for a scholarship covering everything, including living expenses."

"I never thought about the possibility of all expenses being covered. Even with partial scholarships, financial aid, and loans, my bachelor's degree has been a struggle."

"Why don't you think about it for a week, and we'll talk again," Dr. Seaver suggests. "And to encourage your decision, can you come to the island science station this weekend to work on a project with me and some PhD students on the effects of plastic pollution on marine life?"

"Yes. That would be great."

Kiera is exceedingly excited about the invitation. In high school, she was devastated when it did not work out for her to attend summer camp there. She hoped for opportunities in college, but that had not happened until now.

The professor provides details, and then she leaves for her last class of the day, arriving early. She desperately wants to tell Ryan about this, knowing he will be happy for her since he contributed to the project. Even though she hates to bother him at work, she decides to send him a text.

My ocean science prof wants to supervise a masters/phd program for me because of the dead zone project - promised I would at least think about it

He responds right away. *Awesome, she must have really liked your paper*

Said it was the best one

She isn't sure what else to say and knows Ryan is busy.

He messages again. *Want to talk this over? can meet at cafeteria around 5:30*

Yes, see you then. She can't stop smiling. It is hard to focus her attention on Calculus, her least favorite subject.

A little before 5:30, Kiera is standing outside the cafeteria. As Ryan gets closer, he sees that she is wearing the shell necklace he noticed at the nurdle hunt. *She is so beautiful.*

Over dinner, they chat constantly. "My professor says she will write a letter of recommendation for me to apply for a full-ride scholarship with housing."

"Wow, that's amazing."

"I told her about the scuba diving issue, and she said that is not a requirement at all to pursue a Marine Biology PhD. There are always people willing to do the dives to support others in their research when needed."

He is surprised. "The professors I worked with in Texas were all divers, so I guess that is where I got the idea from. And I was teased in graduate school about not wanting to dive. I did like going out on the research vessels with them."

"I actually don't even like boats, which isn't good when you live on an island." She laughs and then becomes serious again. "Even though diving isn't a problem, I guess the truth is that I don't want to apply to the program and only feel excited about the professor thinking so much of me. Am I crazy?"

"No. You aren't crazy."

"The dead zone project was super stressful to me. I was beyond happy when it was over. The idea of making research and writing my life…Well, I don't see it."

"Just because you are naturally good at those things does not mean you need to pursue them. As a teacher, you can still do some research and writing on your own if you decide to, or you could go back to school later to pursue a master's or PhD."

"I agree."

"I feel like I should be encouraging you to go ahead with it, though."

"Why?"

"For one thing, research is the foundation for major advances. Marine biology studies are necessary to save our oceans. Contributing to research allows the university to grow and receive funding. Having a professor believe in you this much to want to mentor you says a lot. And you wouldn't know if you liked it until you did it. But you need to go with your instinct, so I am done with my speech." He nods, letting her know it is her turn.

"My instinct is that I am ready to be done with school! And teaching at the high school level is what I feel I was meant to do. Besides, if the professor knew how much you helped me on the paper, she might have a different opinion of me."

"That's not true. I assisted with the analysis, but it was totally your paper. It is OK to get help, you know? Professors collaborate on research, and that is why. Because everyone has their strengths and weaknesses. My entire job is to help researchers with data and analysis."

"I suppose you are right."

"Of course, I am," he teases.

Before she can respond, Kiera becomes aware of the girl from his office. As she nears, the girl stares at her as if saying, *He is mine!*

"Hi, Ryan," says Kim.

"Hi."

He does not introduce the two of them because Kim doesn't give him time to as she keeps walking.

Kiera wants to ask him about this girl, but decides not to.

After they eat, he suggests it is time to go. "I'm sure you have studying to do."

"Thanks for talking it over with me."

On the way out, she shares her invitation to be part of a project at the island station. "I can't believe I almost forgot to tell you that part."

Ryan is thrilled for her. "Congratulations!" he practically yells and throws his arms around her. Kiera is surprised at his affection. The hug is only a few seconds long, but this action sends her off the deep end, thinking about him for the rest of the night. At first, it amazed her how he found the news something to be congratulated on so vibrantly. But, of course, he recognizes this is a big deal for her. He knows her well enough to know that.

Nine

The film production wrapped things up in New Zealand and moved on to Australia. Hannah enjoys being in The Rocks area of Sydney and filming where Hongi trades with the Europeans and meets with missionaries. This is her first time in the city, and she is interested in the historical sites.

The hotel miles away, however, is not the best, and Hannah admits she is having trouble sleeping. Colin decides to book two rooms at a five-star hotel at his own expense for their last night, while the crew moves on to a motel fifteen minutes from the final shooting location at the castle.

Unfortunately, filming goes on longer than expected, and they are unable to have dinner at the hotel with a romantic view of the harbor as he had planned. Growing more confident every day that they should be together, he wanted to set the stage for when they return. Those thoughts are put on hold as exhaustion takes over, and they both go to their separate rooms and fall fast asleep.

The drive to Iandra Castle is at the crack of dawn.

As Colin navigates the winding road and enters the gates of the property, Hannah sees how the rolling green grasses, terraces, orchards, and gardens give it an English feel.

The sight of the castle gives her a sense of being somewhere long ago.

The structure is referred to as a castle versus a mansion because of the courtyards, granite arches, and columns, along with Medieval-period chimneys, towers, and turrets. The stained-glass windows in flower designs are amazing. The main house has over 50 rooms filled with elegant antique furniture. One room has a fireplace with people carved into the mantle, similar to miniature Greek sculptures. The dining room contains the longest table she has ever seen.

They spend a week at the local motel with the crew and shoot at the castle during the day. Working inside is a refreshing change. Despite her bug spray,

Hannah and everyone else ended up with mosquito and sandfly bites in New Zealand.

An insect called a Huhu beetle fell from a tree into her hair on Mokoia Island. Kristen saw the critter land and tried to remove it, but since the species' legs have tiny hooks, she had to cut it out and got bitten in the process. After the beetle bit Kristen, she shook her hand, making the four-inch bug fall onto Hannah's arm, where she was bitten as well after taking too long to brush it away out of shock at it being the largest beetle she had ever seen.

The men standing around were amused, roaring with laughter as the ladies each screamed at different points. The two women allied, making it a joint effort to interact with dozens of men.

Hannah's job does become easier at the castle, and Kristen has fun with the costumes of 1500s England.

On the last day, the cast and crew are ecstatic. The final scene is filmed.

"That's a wrap!" exclaims the director.

Colin turns to her. "We did it. Thank you so much for your help."

"It was tiring but entertaining. Thanks for the opportunity."

While driving back to Sydney, a severe thunderstorm develops, cancelling their flight to Brisbane. Colin suggests spending the night again at the elegant hotel and flying out the following day.

They find their rooms and change clothes. As they take the elevator downstairs for dinner, he gets a call from Marci's brother Frank. Hannah watches as his face goes white. He winces and pulls the phone away from his ear a little bit, allowing her to hear. The man's voice says, "I'm not going to tell them. You can do that when you return. I told them their mom had to go on a surprise trip, and you will be here tomorrow. You can come back tomorrow, right?"

The elevator reaches the ground floor. They both exit and step away from everyone.

"Yes, Frank. I will leave as soon as I can and will be there when the boys wake up. Call me if you have any trouble putting them to bed." He hangs up.

"What's wrong?"

"Marci was in a car accident. She's gone."

They stare at one another. Hannah is speechless. She thinks back to the last exchange with Marci for instructions in case something happened to her. A spell of dizziness hits, and she suggests they take a seat in the lobby.

His eyes well up with tears. She hands him a tissue and then needs one, also. Their chairs face away from the activity of the hotel's main floor, giving them some privacy.

After a few minutes of silence and tears, they decide to gather their belongings and get to the airport. Nothing is said in the elevator to the rooms.

As Colin begins to open his door, he stops. "What am I going to do? How can I raise these boys without Marci?"

"You don't have a choice. You have to. I will help. Others will lend a hand. You *can* get through this. It will take time, but Simon and Sam will be OK."

He looks at her with a glimmer of hope in his eyes. She moves closer and hugs him. Not wanting to let go, he wraps his arms tightly around her, feels her warmth, buries his nose in her hair, and takes in the wonderful scent of her shampoo, something he had wanted to do many times. He knows that she is right. With her a part of their lives, he can get through this.

A few hours later, after the storm passes, they board a plane. It is almost midnight. Somehow, they manage to sleep most of the flight and then drive in silence to Kirkdam. Colin enters Marci's house while Hannah goes upstairs.

She wakes up to the phone ringing. The bright sunlight shining through the windows hurts her already bloodshot eyes. In a hoarse voice, she accepts the call. "Hi. How are the boys?"

"I haven't told them yet," Colin discloses, sounding as if he never went to bed.

"I have no idea what the right thing to do is," she admits. "But to me, it makes sense not to tell them right away. Why don't we spend the day with them? We can play video games, watch movies, or whatever. And maybe do the same tomorrow, but by the next day, we should tell them. I know they love donuts, specifically chocolate-covered with sprinkles. I will go and get some and come over."

"OK. Sounds good."

They give Simon and Sam their full attention. Even Colin took to a fighter jet game, determined not to let two 9-year-olds shoot him down every time. He withdrew to his office to make phone calls as she watched a movie with them.

After an enjoyable day, the twins fully cooperate about going to bed at 8 pm, which is a welcome break for their dad and Hannah, who step out onto the porch with cups of coffee in hand to ensure conversations are not overheard.

"What's the plan?" she asks.

"I say let them enjoy their Sunday, and then on Monday morning, I will tell them, and they can stay home from school, of course. I already told the film's executive producer to count me out of the editing process. He almost sounded relieved. I think he was worried that I would be totally obsessive about it and slow the editing down."

She gives a half-smile, knowing him well enough to see perfectionistic, if not obsessive, characteristics in him. "I don't know about him being relieved, but I do think it is for the best. Your sons need you to be here as much as possible over the next few weeks. I can come around often and give you some breaks."

"Thanks. I couldn't do it without you." With a gloomy sigh, he continues. "I think Simon will take it the hardest, and Sam might keep asking for his mom as if he doesn't understand."

"I can see that, too."

"Marci's mum died when she was growing up. Her dad moved to New York City after she graduated from high school. He started a second career as a stockbroker and stayed there, remarrying and having two more children. Frank, her older brother, was in and out of drug and alcohol rehab for years. It is my understanding that he has been sober for at least five years. He works at a warehouse and lives with several other people in a small flat. I told him I would plan the service."

She reaches out to briefly place her hand on his. "I have planned many services. I can help."

"Thanks. And Marci's dad, Phil, hates me, so if he is rude to you because you are a friend of mine, I apologize in advance."

"Don't worry about me. I can take it."

"I know you can. I saw how tough you can be with people during the shoot. Being around Phil is something I dread. He makes a trip back here each year, timing it with the boys' birthday. We are all together for their parties, but he never brings his wife or kids, who are now teenagers, which is peculiar to me."

"You have to give him credit for making the trips a priority. It had to be hard on Marci with him so far away and having a new family."

She decides to speak up about an important topic. "I want to help your sons, but I need you to tell me if I am overstepping."

"What do you mean?"

"I know you aren't religious, but I personally think it is important to tell them how their mother is in heaven, and she will be an angel watching out for them. Is it OK for me to talk with them this way?"

"Yes. That is fine."

"I will go to the library. There are tons of children's books about heaven and angels to read to them. I did this for a neighbor's son who lost his mom at a young age, and it comforted him."

He explains to her his thoughts on Simon and Sam hearing the truth that someone made a terrible mistake and ran a stop sign, not following the rules of driving, and hit their mother.

"I think they can understand how disobeying rules has consequences. Marci told me the autistic school is very structured, which the boys have come to respond well to. She and I were frustrated about not being able to establish this model at home."

"I agree with explaining what really happened, and I will tell the twins how proud their mom, I mean mum, is of them about their behavior at school and let them know she wants them to do what they are supposed to do in school and at home, but also wants them to have fun and enjoy their lives."

"That will ease their grief. Thanks." He takes her hand and holds it for a while.

THREE WEEKS LATER

Hannah has spent a great deal of time playing video games with Simon and Sam. She played this same racing game with her son when he was seven because his best friends, two Scottish brothers named Lewis and Leo, had moved back to Scotland, and he was sad. To their surprise, the family ended up moving back to Texas two years later. Their leaving was devastating to Ryan for a while, and she played with him every day for two weeks. However, her wrists began to hurt as if she were developing carpal tunnel syndrome, so she stopped.

The pain is returning. She hates to disappoint the boys because they find it hilarious how bad she is at the game and how she can never beat them, but she can't go on doing this for much longer.

Colin enters, motioning with his head towards the hall.

"I need to make a phone call. You guys keep playing," she informs them.

The adults withdraw to the bedroom and shut the door. They kiss heatedly, as if for the first time, not the twentieth. The two didn't last long, spending so much time under the same roof, before he kissed her, and that was it. Game on. Whenever possible, they sneak away from the twins. At night, she returns to her place. Although he often comes up to visit after his sons are sound asleep.

The condo went up for sale right away, and Colin moved into Marci's house, which is actually his house that he bought for her and the boys to live in. He took over what had been the guest room, leaving Marci's room untouched for now. It was his idea for her to rent the garage suite for extra income to keep for herself.

A new semester for him begins in one month. Simon and Sam missed three weeks of school, and now their school is on a three-week break. They would not cooperate with going back to school after a week, as originally planned, so it was decided they could miss two more weeks and start fresh after the break.

It has become part of Hannah's routine to read to the brothers twice a day. She is pleased they enjoy it. After angel and heaven books, she checked out books about saving the earth, pollution, renewable energy, and climate change. It is surprising how intently they listen.

The three began recycling, replacing products in the home with biodegradable ones, and making it a point to conserve energy and water. Simon volunteered to only shower once a week to save water, but she gave him a big "No!" on the idea. "That doesn't work for boys who roll around in the dirt with their dog."

One night, Colin lets his sons stay up until 10 pm because they are all watching a movie. When it ends, Simon looks over at Hannah. "Can you spend the night?"

Not knowing how to respond, she doesn't.

His dad grins. "Yes. She can spend the night."

"OK, great," says Simon with a giant smile. "See you in the morning!" Running off, Sam follows him to their room.

In a whisper, she asks, "Is this what you want?"

"Of course. But I have to warn you, I snore and fart in my sleep."

She bursts out laughing. "Boy, am I used to that!"

Having trouble sleeping, Hannah gets up and goes into the master bedroom to use that bathroom instead of the one right next to the twins' room.

With the bright light of a full moon coming through the window, she can see Marci's knick-knacks, framed family pictures, and other personal things. Tears fill her eyes, and she sits on the bed. Overwhelmed with thoughts of the tragedy and how Simon and Sam will grow up without their mom, she begins to weep.

After a while, the tears shed over this sad event turn to sobbing for her husband. It has been eight months since she lost Jack. She begins to feel guilty about her physical relationship with Colin. The idea of one year being the appropriate amount of time to be in mourning hangs over her, but she does not know where that concept comes from.

Relocating to Australia felt therapeutic, allowing her to move forward. And not being in the States to see news reports of shootings improves her mental health as well.

When she cannot cry anymore, she decides that what happened to Marci is a good example of how people should enjoy their lives before it is too late. There is no question she is doing right by the boys, spending so much time with them. Simon talks to her about his mother, which is a very healthy thing for him to do. Having fun with Colin on the side is a definite benefit, but it is not like it's something serious.

Once she settles down and feels calm enough, she quietly walks back to the guest room and slips into bed.

In the morning, they awake to Simon and Sam in the room. She foresaw this scene and slept in her pajamas.

"Will you get us donuts, Hannah?" asks Simon.

Their dad answers first. "I will get the donuts. You two feed Bailey." They run to the kitchen.

"I will be right back. I need to check on Rosie," she explains, getting out from under the covers.

"Why don't you bring her back here with you? At some point, you will have to let Bailey and Rosie learn to get along, you know? Bailey won't gobble her up. I promise."

Her face indicates she obviously disagrees.

Ten

For the first time in Colin's life, work is not a priority. He never thought he could enjoy spending so much time with his sons, and he is blown away by his feelings for Hannah.

They all have another good day together. The following morning, he hands Hannah a cup of coffee. "I want to talk with you about something, but I hope it doesn't make you feel uncomfortable, and it is totally fine for you to say 'No.'"

"O...K..," she says hesitantly.

"Simon and Sam go back to school soon, and I will need a tremendous amount of assistance. I have looked into it, and you can get a work visa to remain in the country if you become a Disability Support Caregiver for them. If you agree, I will take the boys to school in the mornings, and you will pick them up. On weekends, we can hire a babysitter so you and I can go out. You will have the time they are at school to work on your book and do your own thing. What do you think?"

"I think that will work."

"But you have to promise me that if at any point you decide it isn't working for you, you will let me know, and it won't affect us. I can find someone else to be their caregiver."

"I promise."

"And I want you to promise that you will get back to writing your mystery book."

"I absolutely will."

"Also, the cleaning service and gourmet meal provider that came to my condo will start coming here instead. I have been taking care of those things, but I won't want to once I get back to work. I don't want you cleaning up after us or feeling responsible for all our meals. The food is wonderful in my opinion. I will send you the link to what they offer. We can do this three times a week, and then two nights a week, I will bring home food from the university."

"That sounds marvelous. Having a man cook and clean has been something new to me, and then to have the services will spoil me for sure."

"You deserve to be spoiled." He gives her a kiss. "And before things get busy, why don't we take a trip with the boys? My dad left me, my sister Anne, and my brothers Archie and Aaron a vacation home in Port Douglas near the Great Barrier Reef. We could all go there. In fact, you could even invite your son and his friend Kiera. I'd like for her to spend time with Simon and Sam and hopefully be able to babysit until she graduates."

"It is winter. Why would we go this time of year?"

"The water at the reef is warm year-round, and between June and October, water visibility is higher because it is much less likely to rain and be affected by river runoff. So, this is actually the best time to go for clear water for the semi-submersible sub that I know everyone will like. I think Ryan and Kiera would enjoy seeing the reef. Don't you? And they can go snorkeling also."

"I do think it would be fun for them, it's just that my son doesn't know about us, and I'd like to keep it this way for now. As far as he is concerned, we are friends, and I help you with the twins."

"The house has five bedrooms. Two downstairs. Three upstairs. Ryan and Kiera can have the ones downstairs in case they want to sneak into each other's rooms. We can all be upstairs. You, in your own bedroom, with me coming over to visit. I will make it clear to him that you have your own room."

"Sounds good." Then she laughs, "I don't think he will be sneaking into Kiera's room. He is one shy boy, but I will ask him about the trip."

Hannah calls her son later in the day, and he likes the Great Barrier Reef idea. He looks up information on the internet about the trip and decides to text Kiera, learning she is at the library already doing research for her last semester paper, which isn't due for months.

Can I come there? I want to ask you something.

Ryan parks and makes the long trek to the library. It is an odd building with no windows. He finds her and inquires, "What are you working on this time?"

"My final topic is on possible ways to remove carbon dioxide from the oceans themselves, not just from the atmosphere. One way is with electrochemical processes. I don't know enough yet to explain it. This is what I am reading about now."

"Amazing stuff. Well, I have a surprise for you. I thought we would go on a trip for a few days to the Great Barrier Reef next week with my mom, Dr. Ryan, and his sons. The professor has a nice house there for all of us to stay."

He does not get the expected response as she only stares at him.

"What's wrong?"

"I want to go, of course. It's just that my first thought is how we would be contributing to harming the reef by participating with all of the tourists."

"Actually, I investigated this. Some of the money from tourism goes towards conservation efforts. The tour guides preserve the reef by teaching others how to protect it. They discuss ocean absorption of carbon dioxide and how we can all reduce our carbon footprints to address this issue by recycling, composting, minimizing the use of plastics, and things like that. And when we go snorkeling, a Marine Biologist will be our guide."

"Only snorkeling, right? And not scuba diving."

"Right," he laughs. "I have not changed my position on that. Just by snorkeling, we can see amazing marine life. I found an area where we are most likely to see sea turtles. How does that sound, Olive?"

She gives him a big grin. Only her brothers and a few others she grew up with call her that.

"And to address your concerns about human impact on the environment," he continues, "people are not always the problem. Have you heard of Raine Island?"

"Of course. It is the largest green sea turtle nesting area in the world."

"Did you know that Raine Island was created from waves bringing sediments from the Great Barrier Reef, and they collected to form an island, so the island is always reshaping?"

"No."

"The cliffs expanded to where the turtles were having trouble climbing up them. The island was reshaped by people coming in with equipment to give the female turtles a smoother path to nest and spread out more because they were all trying to go to the same spots."

Ryan carries on with his speech, even though he feels like he is being a bit of a know-it-all. "So, sometimes human involvement is better than letting nature take its course. Climate change is the biggest threat to the Great Barrier Reef, not the people visiting it. Our trip will contribute to funding efforts for scientists to grow specific coral species that have a better tolerance to warmer ocean temperatures. Other money supports researchers with their computer programs to monitor the reef. If you want, we can join these reef protection groups."

"I would like that."

"Once you are making the big bucks as a teacher, you can donate."

"That is *not* nice! You are making fun of me!" exclaims Kiera a little too loudly, pretending to be mad.

"Well, you can afford a small donation each year."

"I know you will always make more than me." This time, she does feel annoyed to some degree.

"You never know. You might come up with a learning app idea or other science tool that I can code. We can make it a joint venture and become rich," he quietly laughs.

She shakes her head to indicate how unlikely this seems.

He stands up. "I should let you get back to your studies."

"That's OK. I was about to go back to my room anyway. Do you want to see where I live?"

"Sure."

As they stroll across the school grounds, Kiera remembers something she read.

"Speaking of Raine Island, did you know that 99% of the baby sea turtles hatching there are female because the area is the hardest hit by climate change and warmer temperatures, which females can withstand more than males?"

"No, I didn't."

"Yes, isn't that crazy? This is a problem for sea turtles all over, but like you said, humans can actually help by creating more shade on beaches, which increases the chances of the males hatching, so there is hope."

He asks about her "dorm," since he never lived in one. This was a requirement for Freshmen at his university, but dual-credit courses advanced him to Sophomore status.

She explains that residential facilities here are called colleges and are a community, not just a place to live. From the outside, her building is a basic two-story structure. They enter a hidden tunnel which opens into a courtyard full of plants, flowers, and fountains, transforming Ryan's thoughts of campus living.

A butterfly lands on his shoulder. "It's like an oasis in here."

"I love coming out to the garden to sit and read on a nice day."

Ascending the indoor staircase, she tells him how everyone gets their own room, but there are four girls for each bathroom. Her best friend Naomi works as the Resident Assistant on her floor. A friend of theirs, Jess, who moved into a flat with three other girls, had a bad experience, and her grades suffered. There were issues over paying rent, fairly dividing up food costs, distractions with boyfriends coming over, meal preparations, and everything else a residential facility takes care of.

Kiera's room is bright and cheery with a sizable window providing a panoramic view of the campus. A long desk runs the length of an entire wall.

"For my first two years, I was in another building and had to share a room. Having my own space is incredible."

He looks around but can't think of anything else to say. "I'd better be going now."

She is hopeful this holiday will bring them closer. While occasionally feeling like something is developing between them, more often than not, she thinks he sees her only as a friend.

Hannah is getting ready for the vacation in three days and watching the boys. Colin has meetings at the university. Their neighbor, Jane, knocks at the door. The two ladies have previously engaged in conversation a few times. Of course,

Jane came over to give her condolences about Marci when she first learned of the tragedy.

Marci had told Hannah early on about how her neighbor has five children and homeschools them all. Colin went to their house the day before to talk with Danny, the oldest son, about coming over to care for the boys' dog and her cat to earn money.

"I hate to ask you this," says Jane in a weary voice, "but I am in a bind. Can Ned, Jimmy, and Jacob come over for the afternoon? I need to take Mary to a couple of appointments. I guess Danny forgot he was supposed to be home by now from a friend's house. They are off on their bikes somewhere. I will leave him a note to come get them, but chances are he won't be back until dinner."

Despite dreading the idea, she hesitantly answers, "Sure." Once the boys arrive, she suggests they play video games, but Ned lets her know they aren't allowed to do that or watch TV.

Ned is eight, Jimmy is seven, and Jacob is five. They do not detect anything different about Simon and Sam and see them as kids to have fun with, which is good, except five children running around is not what Hannah is used to. She can't control them from running amok. They run in and out of the back door, chasing one another. The screen door slams over and over. She tells them to choose: play inside or outside, but they ignore her.

For a spell, the boys are quiet in the backyard. The door slams again, and Simon comes running into the living room. "Ned found a snake!" She gets up to find everyone in the kitchen.

"I dropped him," Ned confesses. The boy sees the fear on her face. "Don't worry. It is just a garden snake. I know about snakes. My dad taught me about which ones are poisonous. This one can't hurt anybody."

She feels relieved, at least a little. Ned and Simon look around the kitchen for the reptile.

"How big is it?" Hannah asks Jimmy.

The boy stretches his arms out as far as he can, proclaiming, "This big."

She gets a ruler. "How long is it compared to this?"

Sam places his hands on either side of the ruler and nods.

"Yeah, it's only about that size," admits Jimmy.

They move out into the living room to search. She continues with her questions. "Do you think it is a baby?"

"Yes, a baby. A mom or dad snake would be much bigger," Ned explains.

Then Jimmy announces, "Well, I guess it's gone. Let's find another one."

The boys all scream and run back outside.

Her head is throbbing. She is frustrated beyond belief dealing with the kids. Eyeing the clock, she cannot wait for their mom to pick them up. She begins to think back on how to entertain elementary school-aged boys. Looking around the kitchen, she finds what is needed to make volcanoes. They do this in the backyard. The boys end up covered in flour but have a great time making the volcanoes erupt over and over until they run out of baking soda and vinegar.

Jane finally returns for her sons, and twenty minutes later, Colin is home.

Hannah greets him at the door. "There is a snake in the house. Simon and Sam can tell you all about it. I am going to my apartment. See you tomorrow."

"Don't you want dinner? I brought Chinese food."

"I will get something upstairs."

Later in the evening, after somehow getting the twins to go to bed much earlier than usual, Colin goes up to Hannah's. He knocks and hears her say, "Come in."

"Are you OK?"

Drinking a glass of wine with Rosie in her lap, she replies, "I am doing much better now. I just needed some time to myself."

"Great news. We found the snake and put it back outside."

"Good to know, so I won't be wondering tomorrow."

He sits next to her on the couch. "I'm sorry you had to deal with them."

"I am the one who agreed to watch three extra boys. It isn't your fault."

"I hope we aren't driving you to drink already," he lets her know as she takes another sip of wine.

She laughs. "You don't need to worry about me. A glass and a half is about all I can handle."

The wine is obviously affecting her. In an animated voice, she articulates her views on children. "I mean, why anyone would have five kids in this day and age is beyond me. And she homeschools them. I can't tell you how thrilled I was to drop my son off at school every day. When Ryan was in first grade, he found out our neighbor was homeschooled and asked to do the same. I laughed and said, 'No way. You are going to school!' I like Jane, but I don't get her at all. And she doesn't let her kids play video games. I'm sure you agree with her, but boys need games if you ask me."

Smiling, he reveals, "You have changed my mind on that subject."

She puts her glass on the table and turns to him, eyes widening. "You don't want more children, do you?"

He bursts out in laughter. "No! Why do you ask?"

"I had never thought about it before. Just making sure that isn't the case because *that* won't be happening with me."

"I had a vasectomy seven years ago, so the decision has already been made."

"Good. And I didn't mean what I said about Jane. Everyone has the right to live their lives the way they want. I am selfish and need time to myself, which it seems would be impossible for her."

"You are not selfish. You are wonderful." He puts his left arm around her shoulders and stretches his right arm across her, running his hand up and down her arm. "You need to relax. Do you want a massage?"

"Oh, let me guess, now you want sex after the day I've had." The serious expression on her face gives way to a giggle. "Just kidding. Sounds good to me," and she pulls him closer to kiss him.

Ryan and Kiera meet for a one-time snorkeling lesson on the other side of town. First, they pick out their own snorkeling gear. He insists on buying equipment for the two of them to ensure a correct fit, rather than renting it at the reef. Leaving the store area, they move on to the indoor pool. Ryan decided to learn how to wear contact lenses after all, for swimming, snorkeling, and other activities.

With swimwear under their clothes, they undress. Kiera does not like being in a swimsuit in front of him. She has always been a little self-conscious about her body. At the nurdle hunt, she was in shorts and a t-shirt.

At least she likes her one-piece bathing suit and considers it somewhat flattering. A brilliant shade of royal blue, the suit has a high neckline, wide straps, and a generous lower portion to be minimally revealing. She would never wear a bikini, that's for sure.

They get in the water.

"Have you done this before?" she asks.

I went a couple of times in college."

"What about sharks?"

"No worries. The most common sharks near the Great Barrier Reef are reef sharks, which do not harm humans. They get scared easily and only eat fish. The water is too warm for great white sharks."

"I should know that, but in school, whenever sharks were mentioned, I didn't even want to hear about them. Watching *Jaws* gave me nightmares for weeks."

He laughs and starts to say something, but it is time for their lesson.

The instructor introduces herself and inspects the fit of their masks, making some adjustments. She goes over deep breathing methods.

"This is necessary because your lungs have to work harder when breathing through a snorkel. When you exhale, you rebreathe some of it, causing carbon dioxide to build up. These techniques will help you to be more efficient at exchanging air with a snorkel."

They also learn strategies for holding their breath longer in order to enjoy snorkeling more. The one-hour tutorial goes by fast.

While driving back to campus, he tells her more about the trip.

"Where we are going to snorkel, there is also something I've never heard of called ocean walking."

"What is that?"

"They place a big helmet on your head, and a tube goes into the top to constantly give you fresh air from the surface. You walk around underwater on a platform. There is still exciting marine life to see, even at only eight feet under. We can watch others do this and then decide if we want to."

"You could hold your breath much longer than I did. Not worrying about air would be a good thing."

"I also booked a helicopter tour of the reef."

She stares at him.

"Don't tell me that you are afraid of helicopters?"

Shrugging her shoulders, she affirms his statement with a certain look.

"It only lasts 30 minutes. They do this all day, every day, but I can cancel it if you want."

"No. I'm sure it will be breathtaking. I'll be fine. And you do realize I have never flown on a plane, either? So, I am a little concerned about the flight to Port Douglas, too."

"I didn't know. You have told me about all the places you want to visit someday, especially Ireland. It is time to get used to flying, right?"

"Yes. It is time."

Eleven

It takes a little over two hours to fly from Brisbane to Port Douglas. Hannah reads several storybooks to the boys and then turns on a *SpongeBob* movie. Colin works on his laptop, preparing for the new semester. Kiera studies while Ryan sleeps because, for the previous two nights, he was up late. One of the professors had a hard deadline for a paper submission to a prestigious journal, making a last-minute decision to add data points for him to assist with.

The plane lands, and the group rents two cars. As they pull up to Colin's family home, Hannah notices a pool through the palm trees. She has never seen one in a front yard before. The pool is similar in appearance to a natural lagoon. Boulders surround the edges, and pebbled brown concrete on the bottom and sides gives the water a greenish look.

The house is beige. With the landscaping, the apparent intention was to be natural, be one with nature. Then, once inside, it is all white and anything but natural. The floors are white tile, and the walls are bright white. Off-white modern furniture with metal legs on the chairs and stainless-steel tables and shelving clash with a natural-world concept.

Colin gives them a tour, first of the downstairs with the bedrooms for Ryan and Kiera. They all go upstairs, which looks like a completely different house with blue carpet and lots of color. The first room has yellow-painted walls, the second aqua-blue walls, and the one at the end of the hall has pink-orange coral walls. He mentions how the last room is Hannah's.

Ryan and Kiera are not at the house for long before it is time to leave for their helicopter ride and dinner. When the heliport comes into view, he practically shouts, "Wow, so cool!" while admiring the scarlet red helicopter. He has always wanted to learn to fly a helicopter, going up in one several times on family vacations.

"It has a Fenestron tail rotor. I have never been on one of these."

"A what?" she asks, trying her best to calm her nerves.

"Fenestron. It is an enclosed rotator tail similar to a plug-in fan instead of an open rotor like a ceiling fan. It comes from the Latin word fenestra for window."

After the pilot greets them, they hop in the back seat and put on headphones to talk with one another.

They fly around Port Douglas and over a neighborhood of expansive homes, all pearl white in color. The terrain is so green and beautiful. Then they reach the coast with a long stretch of beach and the most pristine sand and vivid blue waters. As they approach a reef, the water changes to a see-through bluish-green, allowing them to see straight to the bottom of the ocean with the corals and plants in view. Going further out, Kiera spots them first. "Look, dolphins!"

When the pilot mentions this is Batt Reef, it doesn't sink in right away, but then Ryan remembers, "Oh no, this is where Steve Irwin died from a stingray."

"Yes," the pilot confirms.

In a sad, barely audible voice, Kiera says, "I didn't realize that."

"I didn't know this was where we were going. My dad was a big fan. When I was little, he often said we would take a trip to Australia someday and visit the Irwin family zoo. But after Steve's incident, this was not mentioned again."

Back at the house, Colin swims with Simon and Sam. He can't convince Hannah to get in the water. She enjoys sitting by the fountain and watching them play.

At dinner, Ryan and Kiera discuss their ocean studies and scientific knowledge, but then turn quiet halfway through the meal. While hoping this would feel like a date, a romantic date, she isn't getting that vibe from him.

He goes straight to his room when they return. Getting so little sleep the previous two nights is weighing on him.

Simon and Sam come running up to Kiera. "Will you play with us?" pleads Simon.

Colin lets her off the hook. "I think she is tired tonight, but maybe another time. Go to the kitchen. Hannah just made cupcakes." The boys instantly leave.

"Would you be interested in earning money by watching them on weekends during your last semester?" he asks.

"Sure. That would be fine."

Hannah appears, full of questions for her about their outing.

At first, Kiera enjoys describing the helicopter ride, fancy waterfront restaurant, and delicious food. But then she begins to realize what is going on here. It was Professor Ryan and Hannah's idea for Ryan to invite her for the weekend. They want her to get to know all of them for the purpose of babysitting.

When the conversation ends, she closes her door, feeling down.

I've got to put the idea of a romance between us out of my mind.

Ryan and Kiera prepare for their snorkeling and semi-submersible reservation. He comes into the living room wearing only shorts. "Mom, you said you brought a new swim shirt for me?"

Colin, on his second cup of coffee, observes the young man's chiseled muscles and abs. It takes a lot of work to look like that, more than he has ever been willing to do at any age.

After they leave, he remarks to Hannah, "Your son is in exceptional shape."

"Yes. In the 5th grade, they were having arm wrestling contests. Something happened between him and another boy, and the next thing I knew, he was working out almost every day. It wasn't until college, though, that he really started building noticeable muscle and putting on weight."

"Boys can be over-the-top competitive," he laughs. "Even male kangaroos like to show off their forearm size. And of course, the bigger, stronger ones in nature get the females."

She rolls her eyes. "It is all a little obsessive if you ask me."

"I guess you would rather we buy you things."

"I don't need *you* to buy me anything, but my son should buy Kiera a little something, like a souvenir for this trip. On the news the other day, they said male dolphins will dive into the water and bring back sea sponges to the females they are interested in. Leave it to a dolphin to realize that being sweet is what works. They are so smart."

"Aren't *I* sweet?" he asks.

Before she can answer, the boys walk in. "We are ready to go!" Simon announces.

Colin, Hannah, Simon, and Sam go to another location on the reef for a semi-submersible tour with a different operator. They spend time at the underwater observatory until the sub ride begins. The water is extraordinarily clear, and the corals, giant clams, and colorful fish can be seen in all their brilliance. While the brothers make a game of counting the various types of fish, the adults are content to sit and watch marine life and the scuba divers descending down for their adventures.

The funniest fish Hannah has ever seen appears in front of the window closest to her. It is huge with a large blue-grey face and the biggest lips. Above the top lip and going back onto a lump at the top of its head are unique markings, almost as if they were painted on. The rest of the body is a light greenish color.

"Bonzer!" Colin exclaims with excitement as she scrunches up her face at the word he used, which is so peculiar to her. "That is a Māori wrasse. I have never come across one before. It is one of the world's largest reef fish. This big bloke is a male because males are blue and green. Females are bronze. Of course, the name comes from the pattern on its head, similar to Māori warrior facial markings. It is a protected species."

"Come look, boys," he tells Simon and Sam, who finally stop counting fish and go over to look at the unfamiliar creature. They burst out laughing at its unusual appearance.

Ryan and Kiera approach the catamaran to take them out to the floating activity pontoon. He is impressed with the large, modern vessel. The guests listen to a combined marine biology presentation and snorkeling demonstration.

At the pontoon, a guide gives them a tour.

They board the semi-submersible, sitting along the row of wide windows. The sub takes off.

"Look, a parrotfish!" Kiera points to the colorful fish with blue around its mouth, a pink body, and a yellow tail.

He studies it. "They actually do have a mouth like a parrot."

A group of yellow and white striped fish goes by. "I know those are called butterflyfish, but I don't see why," she mentions.

"Me either." His eyes scan the water. "Look, a nudibranch."

"That's the same as a sea slug, right?"

"Basically, yes. I have read all about them because the blue dragon I found is part of that animal family. There are several thousand species of nudibranchs. Odd, aren't they?"

The creature appears as a small pink blob with a white fringe around its body. It has two orange horn-like projections called cerata coming out of its head where you would expect eyes to be. The tail has eight more poking out. It looks like something a child would make up.

"Unlike most nudibranchs, the blue dragon has wing-like cerata instead of ones sticking straight up out of its body." He holds Kiera's gaze, thinking about how he would never have met her or be living in Australia if he had not found that blue dragon years ago. Studying marine biology was not a consideration until then.

The sub moves slowly through the coral gardens. The tour guide explains how over 1500 species of fish can be found around the reef, and there are 2900 different reef systems making up the Great Barrier Reef. There are also 600 types of coral.

Several orange and white fish go by.

"I knew we would see Nemo," Ryan laughs.

"What's that?"

"You really didn't watch much TV or see movies as a child, did you?"

"I preferred to read or be outside most of the time, instead, thank you very much."

"Nemo was a clownfish they made a movie about. It was one of the first movies I remember seeing."

After the sub returns to the pontoon, they go to the dining hall for lunch. In the middle of a discussion about a documentary they had both seen called *Chasing Coral* about coral reefs vanishing around the world due to climate change, Kiera becomes aware of the two girls with bikini tops and short shorts eyeballing Ryan. She saw them earlier up on deck. They were watching him then and now, but he is oblivious to them.

The girls get their food from the buffet and proceed to sit on the other side of the long table.

"Hi. Where are you from?" asks the one in the blue bikini, directing her question to Ryan.

He turns his head to Kiera and then back at the girl who never wavers from focusing squarely on him. Hesitantly and slowly, he replies, "I moved here from the US this year. I work at Mac U as a Data Analyst. I assist marine biology professors mainly, but also help with other projects in the field of biology. My name is Ryan, and Kiera here is a student there."

"I am Addison, and this is my friend Summer," nodding to her companion. "We are students at Sydney University. I am studying marine biology, and Summer is an English major. Are you going to be a professor someday?"

"No. I don't think so."

"I haven't decided about that yet," Addison shares, going on to talk about her program.

"What are you doing after lunch?" inquires Summer.

He looks over at Kiera. "We are snorkeling."

Both girls act as if she isn't even there.

"Us too."

Kiera rolls her eyes without anyone noticing. *Great. These girls will be around for the next two hours.*

The melancholy feeling and thoughts of him only seeing her as a friend return. *Why would he see me otherwise? There are plenty of girls, much prettier than me, that he can date if he wants to.* Her negative self-talk gets the better of her.

The four young people go up on deck to retrieve their snorkeling gear. Ryan assists Kiera in getting ready. Summer and Addison ask for his help. He is uncomfortable interacting with them this way, but feels he has no choice. As he adjusts Summer's goggles around her head, she reaches up and touches his hand. "I think that is the right notch for them."

Kiera is watching this like a hawk with jealousy she has never felt before. While they are all busy, she puts on her waterproof waist pouch containing her inhaler. No one questions why she is wearing it.

The group gets in the water and goes under.

Kiera spots a sea turtle early on. She reaches out to touch Ryan's shoulder and points to it. He tries to get a good picture with a waterproof camera, but the turtle swims off in the other direction.

She had no idea they would get this close to the coral by snorkeling. It is so colorful. Pink and purple coral were expected, but not blue and green as well. Of course, they know better than to touch the reef. With organized tours, the guides make sure everyone knows the rules and abides by them.

They see many different kinds of fish. While watching a school of vivid blue and yellow angelfish go by, suddenly, the sea turtle is back and right in front of them. At least she thinks it is the same one. Instead of being scared, the creature looks at them out of curiosity. This time, he gets some excellent pictures and video footage. Despite its species being named the green sea turtle, this one has a mostly brown and tan shell with a mosaic pattern of black ovals outlined in whitish-gray covering its flippers and face.

A lionfish appears. Kiera starts to get too close, but Ryan puts his arms around her and pulls back. He shakes his head, later explaining how they are venomous.

It felt good to be in his arms, even though it was brief. *At least those girls can't talk to him underwater.* Summer and Addison gave up trying to interact with him when Addison motioned for Ryan to follow her, only to see him wave her off as he and Kiera went in a different direction.

After their snorkeling adventure, the girls seek him out, and he gets carried away speaking about his work, not realizing he is excluding Kiera. Addison comes up with a reason to ask for his contact information. Because he mentioned a project on a substance that takes microplastics out of water, Addison shared how one of her professors contributed to the research. She also wrote a paper on the subject, prompting an exchange of email addresses.

Finally turning to Kiera after they leave, he asks, "Do you want to do the ocean walking?" The expression on her face indicates she doesn't, so he adds, "It is fine not to."

"Are you sure? I don't want to spoil things for you." She had been eager for the activity, but then read how people with asthma shouldn't participate.

"You could never spoil things. We have had a full day. It is time to go."

He worries that she seems out of sorts, but doesn't know what to say. While they have had some great moments, he is confused about why she hasn't been as happy on this trip as he thought she would.

The two enjoy viewing the pictures and videos of their excursion until the catamaran departs. However, it is a quiet ride to the mainland.

Colin is in the living room to greet them. "How was your day?"

Ryan replies, "Good," and keeps going down the hall. Kiera stays to share some interesting facts about the marine life they saw on their adventure.

A little while later, he enters the kitchen to find the professor with his arm around his mother, whispering in her ear.

The older man notices him over his shoulder and takes a step back, announcing, "Dinner is almost ready."

Twisting around to see her son leave, she remarks under her breath, "Great. I think we are busted."

At dinner, he barely says a word. Hannah tries to keep the conversation going with Kiera, who also seems upset. She hopes he will not blow this first-ever relationship with a girl.

"Did you two get some good pictures and videos on your outing?" She purchased the underwater camera for this purpose.

"Yes!" Kiera perks up. "He got some super footage of a sea turtle. I will show you later."

"I love turtles. We rescued a turtle at our property in Texas. It had an injured leg. We took it to the vet and learned it was a girl. We named her Olive. When she was better, we released her by one of our ponds."

Coming out of his dark mood, Ryan says, "Olive? You're kidding."

"No. Why?"

He and Kiera look at one another and start laughing. "That is Kiera's nickname. Her family began calling her Olive after she rescued an olive ridley sea turtle."

"How funny. Since our turtle was olive green, that was the first name I thought of."

"Why didn't I know about this?"

"Because you were in college, and it was hard to get you to take the time to communicate with us."

He is clearly bothered by this comment.

"But you graduated with honors, so we understood."

Colin decides to let everyone else talk. Catching Ryan's eye during dinner, he can feel how irritated the young man is with his presence.

When the meal is over, Kiera shows the others their ocean images. Then Hannah hands her a movie called *Sea Fever*. "I thought you two would like this. It is about a marine biology student and an ocean creature that infects the crew of the ship she is on."

"Sounds good," she confirms while turning to Ryan, who shrugs, "Sure."

Hannah finds some board games in the house. She follows the boys upstairs to their room. Colin joins them after he does the dishes. The twins become distracted by dogs barking outside. They rush to the open window and watch the neighbor's pets.

Colin leans over and tells her in a low voice, "I don't think your son likes me."

"He realizes now that we aren't just friends. This is a weird concept to him. You can understand, right?"

"I get it, but I hope he will warm up to the idea."

"I feel like I should take him aside and say something, but I don't know what to say or how it would help. I think it might be best not to say anything at all."

She hears Ryan and Kiera reacting to the part of the film where people's eyes start popping out from the parasitic infection. They scream and laugh at the same time.

Simon and Sam resume the board game, staying entertained for another hour. Hannah knew better than to let them get one glimpse of a sci-fi horror movie.

Kiera suggests a walk around the neighborhood. Ryan is quiet, which isn't unusual, but he also seems glum. She finally speaks about the film they just watched. "I thought it was harsh how everyone on the ship gave the student a hard time because she has red hair and accused her of being bad luck."

"This is actually true. It is a boating myth that redheads bring bad luck."

"I've never thought about someone being singled out for their hair."

"Growing up, my friend Lewis was always teased about having red hair. They called him Ginger. His parents, brother, and sisters all have light brown hair, so people questioned where he came from, but they never saw his aunt with red hair."

"A friend of mine from the summer bible group in high school has red hair. Her parents have a second home on the island. Anyway, no one said anything to her."

"I would hope people are nicer at bible study," he teases.

"They were."

"Even my dad told me not to have a redheaded girlfriend because they have bad tempers. It is silly, I know."

"Have you ever had a redheaded girlfriend?"

"No. I have never had a girlfriend at all."

Surprised at this news and hoping to bring things to a deeper level, she confides, "I have never had a boyfriend."

He does not take the bait and only switches topics. "I forgot how big sea turtles can get until we were face to face with one today. Three years ago, I participated in a rescue mission to save a bunch of stranded loggerhead turtles near my university. The species averages 300 pounds, but these were dehydrated and underweight. We took them to a local aquarium, where they were nursed back to health and released. I'm surprised I had not mentioned it before."

While normally interested in such subjects, she is distracted by wishing he would make a move to show her that he wants to be more than friends.

"That's great," she weakly utters.

As soon as they return, Kiera tells him, "Goodnight," and retreats to her room.

Ryan hears his mom in the kitchen and confronts her. "I need to talk to you."

The two walk to his bedroom and shut the door.

"I don't want to go on this group train ride to the rainforest tomorrow."

"Please don't do this. I already bought the tickets, and Simon and Sam are looking forward to an outing with you and Kiera. Colin and I can sit in a different part of the train. We don't have to actually be together the entire time, but you have to accept him. I would never reject someone you were seeing."

"How can you do this to Dad?"

The comment takes her breath away for a second. She stammers, trying to find the right words. "I never thought I would be with anyone else, but it just happened. And it's not like we are going to get married or anything. If you think about it, I could live another 30 years or more. Do you think I should be alone for the rest of my life?"

He lets out a long sigh. "No, not when you put it that way."

"We will only be in the car for one hour. Please don't be rude."

"I still don't trust him."

"You don't have to worry about him hurting me. If it doesn't work out, I will be fine either way. It is different for younger people. I think you have been afraid to be in a relationship because the idea of it not working out feels devastating to you, but it isn't the same for me. Can you trust me that there is nothing to be concerned about?"

Silence.

"OK?"

"I guess."

She gives him a hug.

"Goodnight, Mom."

"Goodnight."

When she opens the door to leave, Colin is standing in the hallway.

"I was wondering where you were."

Ryan can't help but roll his eyes, which the professor sees, and his mother catches it also as she directs her attention back to him before exiting.

Twelve

Hannah has the most wonderful dream. They are all at a wedding ceremony for Ryan and Kiera right before sunset in a tent by the ocean. After exchanging vows, the wedding party and guests go down to the beach. The group releases baby sea turtles onto the sand, allowing them to make their way back to the ocean. To protect them from predators, the sea turtle eggs were safely incubated at a marine life hatchery.

The dream continues as they drive to another location for the celebration dinner. The decorations, even the napkins, read *Olive and the Blue Dragon: Ryan and Kiera*. A poster of the couple at the entrance details the story of how they met and their shared interest in marine biology.

Her eyes open. *Wow, what a dream.*

It is very early, and she tries to fall back to sleep, but her racing mind won't let her. She waits until a decent hour to get up and then prepares for their outing.

A little later, while putting some things in the car, a van pulls up. A man and a woman get out.

"Hello," Hannah says in a friendly voice.

"Who are you?" is the gruff response from the man.

"I am Hannah. I am here with Colin and his boys."

He rolls his eyes.

"Are you his brother?"

"No. Can I talk to him?"

Colin had just passed by the window and was already on his way outside. "Hi, Aaron. Looks like you have met Hannah. Hannah, this is my brother Aaron and his girlfriend Jill."

Jill gives a nod.

Confused as to why Aaron said that he isn't his brother, Hannah manages a partial smile.

"What are you doing here?" Aaron asks, unquestionably annoyed. "I told Anne we would be here this weekend. I left her a message."

"I left her a message also. She is visiting her daughter in England. But, no problem. We will be gone all day, and then we are leaving first thing in the morning. There is an extra bedroom for you both upstairs." He glances at Hannah to indicate she needs to give up her room.

"I guess we don't have a choice." Aaron gets their bags from the van.

Colin hurries everyone out of the house while Hannah goes upstairs to put fresh sheets from the closet on the bed and move her things into the other room. They all pile into the SUV with three rows of seats. Ryan takes the last row to himself and goes to sleep. Kiera sits in the middle and reads storybooks to Simon and Sam. The older adults do not say a word the entire trip.

They arrive at the station. The boys become excited at the sight of the train.

Simon lets it be known that he wants to sit at the front to see the engineer.

"See you guys later." Ryan motions to Kiera. "Let's sit towards the back," he says, apparently forgetting how the plan is for the brothers to spend time with them.

"Where are you going? I want you to sit with me," declares Simon.

Ryan looks over at Kiera. "We can't say 'No,'" she implores in a whisper.

They follow the twins to the lead train compartment, taking the first two rows of seats facing each other. Colin and Hannah decide they should be in the same section, but sit many rows behind them.

The train will go through the rainforest to Kuranda Village. It passes several waterfalls by way of the Barron Gorge, with astounding views of the canyon.

Colin appears upset.

She makes an effort at conversation. "I read this railway is 127 years old, and these carriages are 100 years old. The train passes over 37 bridges and through 15 hand-carved tunnels."

Realizing he should make the most of this time with her, he finally speaks. "These are the traditional lands of the Djabugay people. Bama was the name for the group specifically living in the rainforest. When European settlers came into the area for gold and tin mining, the original owners found themselves unable to move around and hunt and fish as they had for thousands of years. They referred to the white man as 'Gadja' or ghost spirit. Many of the Bama became farm laborers on the coffee plantations, which the settlers developed."

She had read some of this on the Kuranda Village website, but his memory is commendable. Her husband had an extraordinary recollection of American history, thanks, in part, to The History Channel. However, he never could remember how many years they had been married or the ages of his children once they became adults.

"Did you see the snake painted on the train engine?" he asks.

"No. I guess I wasn't paying attention."

"There is an Aboriginal Australian myth of a Rainbow Serpent in the form of a giant carpet snake which traveled through the country and created the landscape, the canyons, and waterfalls, and in this area, finally coming to rest at Double Island, not far from here. In addition to shaping the earth, the Rainbow Serpent was seen as the giver of life because of its connection with water. It could also be a destructive force if angered."

"Very interesting." She turns her head to begin taking pictures from the train window of the land he just described.

Once at the village, they venture over to the wildlife park. Hannah spots some picnic tables in the shade. "Do you want to sit and let them go ahead?" she asks Colin.

"Yes. Great idea."

She turns to Ryan, knowing this will make his day. "You guys go on. We are going to stay here. If there are any issues, text me."

They find an open table. Laughing, he says, "You guys? I thought Texans said 'Ya'll.'"

"My cousins in Utah made fun of me as a child for saying 'Ya'll,' so I have made it a point to not say that my whole life."

His comment leads to the theme of word differences between Americans and Australians. She can tell, however, that he is forcing himself to make small talk.

Ryan, Kiera, Simon, and Sam stroll through the park. The first stop is the koala enclosure. Simon watches a koala named Barnie. "I don't think Barnie wants to be in there," he remarks.

Kiera addresses his concerns. "Actually, Barnie is lucky. In nature, the koalas have a hard time with bushfires and warmer temperatures from climate change affecting their habitats and the eucalyptus trees they love so much. They are picky eaters, and eucalyptus leaves are their favorite. The problem is that those trees are in severe distress, dropping their leaves and often dying. Barnie is well taken care of. Don't worry."

They move on to the kangaroos and then the wallabies.

"Does anyone know the difference between a kangaroo and a wallaby?" she quizzes.

"Kangaroos are bigger," yells Simon.

"Yes."

"Short legs." Sam points to the wallaby closest to them.

"Yes!" She is delighted to hear Sam speak.

Ryan remembers something he read. "Wallabies live around 11 to 14 years in captivity, while kangaroos can live up to 25 years or more."

Simon reads out loud a sign on the wallaby enclosure. "This is Hank. He is 13 years old." Turning back to the others, "So he will die next year?" His voice indicates alarm at this idea.

"No. That is only an average," Ryan explains. "He could live a few more years."

"That *isn't* very long!"

"I know Simon, but that is how it is for many animals."

"You mean dogs?" he asks, becoming even more upset.

Ryan remembers how the brothers have a dog.

Kiera intervenes. "No one is going to die. Look, there are baby wallabies," and she pushes the boys on to the next cage, giving Ryan a look.

"I didn't mean to," he mumbles.

After the baby wallabies, the group approaches the quokka enclosure. One of the brown furry creatures, about the size of a cat, is standing upright, observing them with funny little eyes. It has a big black nose, rounded ears, long feet sticking out, pudgy hands clasped together, and what appears to be a smile on its face.

Sam's mouth is wide open. He points to it and looks back and forth from Kiera to Ryan.

She laughs. "He is cute, isn't he?"

"Yes, yes," agrees Sam. He looks at the Quokka sign and tries to sound it out. "Q-o-ka."

"It isn't an easy word. It is actually pronounced Kwaa-kuh. I said it wrong until I learned about them in school," she tells him. "They have been called the world's happiest animal because their mouths usually look like they are smiling."

Sam gives her a sweet smile, which warms Kiera's heart. They continue on their tour.

Hannah and Colin have mostly been sitting in silence. She has enjoyed watching all the families with young children, but decides to broach the subject that has him troubled.

"Is there anything you want to talk about? Your brother sure was mad. I know it is bothering you."

Before meeting Jill that morning, she already knew that Aaron had a girlfriend and Archie was married later in life, during his 40s, with two daughters, ages eight and ten. Both men are fishermen and surfed competitively in their younger years.

She met his sister Anne, the oldest of the siblings, at Marci's funeral. With everything going on, she did not think about how both brothers were missing from the service.

"I suppose I should tell you the truth. I am not really a Ryan. My mum was not married when she had me. My father worked at a factory in town, the town of Texas, like I told you. He moved on after finding out she was pregnant.

When I was two, my stepfather, John, visited the area for research work as an archaeology professor and met my mother. They married six months later. John's wife had died from cancer the year before. My step-siblings were six, four, and three when he married Mum."

"Wow. That was a lot for your mom to take on with three more children."

"Yes. She did a good job taking care of everyone. When she married and changed her last name to Ryan, she had my name legally changed also, but John never adopted me. He did pay more attention to me as I got older, which made his own boys jealous. Because my stepbrothers preferred surfing over studying, John took an interest in my education, encouraging me to take honors courses."

"You said they taught you to surf. That's good, right?"

"They did, but only because they were forced to spend time with me. They preferred to run off without me. But Dad, I mean John, put a stop to that. We did have some good times surfing. At least, I thought we did."

He takes a deep breath before carrying on with the painful discussion.

"John must have talked with them because growing up, everyone thought we were a family unit. We moved to a new suburb. It was never questioned by anyone that I wasn't one of them. My mum was Charlotte Martin. So, she gave me the last name Martin when I was born. I don't even know my father's name. He was not listed on my birth certificate. When I finally asked, she already had advanced Alzheimer's and only stared at me."

She knew his mom developed early-onset Alzheimer's by 60, and his father had a heart attack and died five years ago, but didn't realize the man was his stepfather.

"I always called John 'Dad,' but now it feels funny to refer to him as 'Dad.' To my step-siblings as kids, my mum was 'Mum.' As adults, knowing our family situation, we all feel differently. It has become clear that Archie and Aaron do not see me as a brother."

Colin pauses to collect his thoughts.

"When John died, he had already sold his home and moved to a retirement village. It was a shock to my stepbrothers that their dad did not leave them any money, only this Port Douglas house to all of us. His beneficiaries were environmental organizations, as he was concerned about climate change."

"Do they struggle financially?"

"Yes, they always have. Years ago, John was tired of them going from job to job and asking him for money. I remember him saying, 'I'm tired of them making a dog's breakfast out of their lives. I'm going to buy them a damn boat so maybe, just maybe, they can make a living fishing.' He hated boats and never went out, but I did and got seasick. They laughed their arses off."

"Anyway," he continues, "they did well for a number of years, but warming ocean water began changing the movement of fish and the timing that they and other fishermen were used to relying on to make their catch. Many fish species are moving southwards, away from the east and west Australian coasts. Climate change can also result in more fish disease outbreaks and algal blooms to deplete their oxygen. Fishing has become a tough occupation. Anne bought out their shares in the holiday home, but she still lets them stay whenever they want, of course. They don't seem to acknowledge my share."

It was Marci who told Hannah about Anne being married to a doctor and having two grown daughters. One daughter moved to the US, and the other to England. Marci also mentioned earlier in the year how Anne tried to be part of Simon and Sam's lives, but the boys would not talk to her and did not want to even be in the same room. Sam threw a gift from his aunt on the ground and jumped up and down, breaking it into pieces. Anne had not visited since this happened until news of the tragedy.

"Your mom and stepfather loved you, which is all that matters. Sibling relationships are often strained," she tells him, trying to be supportive.

"You are probably wondering why I wrote a book about The Ryans when I'm not even one of them."

With a sigh, "I don't think you should see it that way. You all were a family. Your stepdad must have been so proud of you and what you accomplished."

"He was. My brothers knew this and hated me for it, is what I think. John and I occasionally bonded over material related to history and archaeology, but that is all we ever discussed. I wouldn't say we were close."

She didn't have the heart to tell him how Aaron said he wasn't his brother.

Hannah spots them first. "Here they come," she reports as the group rounds the corner. Kiera and the boys each hold a stuffed animal. Sam has a stuffed quokka, Simon a stuffed snake, and she a stuffed koala.

Colin looks over at Ryan. "You didn't have to do that. Let me pay you back."

"It is fine. I was happy to do it."

Kiera shares how Sam was speaking and even tried to sound out the word quokka.

Hannah and Colin glance at one another with a pleased expression.

"We also learned that Sam does not like crocodiles," reveals Ryan, even though he shouldn't have mentioned it.

"*What* happened?" their dad inquires.

Kiera decides to interject. "He became upset when we got too close to the crocodile area. It wasn't a big deal. We quickly moved on to the reptile house. He likes lizards, frogs, and even snakes."

What was your favorite, Ryan?" asks Simon.

"I liked the glider. I had never heard of the animal."

His mother is interested. "Me either. What is it?"

"It is a rodent, kind of ugly like a possum, and this one has fur that looks green with a black stripe in the shape of a lightning bolt starting on its forehead and going down its back. I was impressed with how far it could glide."

"Dad, can we play?" Simon points to the playground area.

"Sure."

The brothers and their father go over to the slides.

Hannah seizes the opportunity to poke fun at her son in front of Kiera. "You could have gotten a stuffed animal also."

"Very funny, Mom."

"He slept with a teddy bear until he was 12. I thought he was too old for that and told him he couldn't sleep with it forever and couldn't bring it to college. He got upset and asked why not."

"I did *not* bring a teddy bear to college. I don't even know what happened to it."

"I put it up in the closet and eventually gave it away to Goodwill."

Kiera enjoys hearing stories about Ryan when he was young.

The weary travelers return to the house around 9 pm. Aaron and Jill had left and were out past when everyone else went to bed. In the morning, as Hannah showers, Colin goes downstairs. He is surprised to find his brother having coffee in the kitchen this early.

"Hannah is nice," comments Aaron, "but isn't she a little old for you?"

Doing his best to refrain from giving him a dirty look, the twins race in, saving them from further conversation.

They all pack up to leave, awkwardly saying "Goodbye" to Aaron and Jill.

On the return flight, Hannah sits with the boys. Her son and Kiera are behind them, but Colin has to sit many rows away, which he does not mind, and goes to sleep.

She gets an idea, pulling up the website for the World Wildlife Fund Australia with a list of animals to be "symbolically" adopted.

Simon chooses a koala. Since quokkas are not on the list, Sam picks a platypus, which is in danger of extinction. She lets them know that the monthly donation will contribute to saving the animals and their habitats.

While greatly disappointed about not being able to meet the actual critters as she tries to explain what symbolic means, they are excited to learn the adoptions include packets with a stuffed animal, a sticker, and a book.

"Kiera. I am going to adopt a sea turtle in your name, OK?

"I would love that."

"What about a penguin for you, Ryan? Adélie penguins are suffering from climate change with declining sea ice and less krill, food they rely on."

"I like penguins."

"But can I have the stuffed animal that comes with it?"

"Yes, Mom. You can have it."

"The adoption also comes with regular email updates on your selected creature and how they are being helped."

"Awesome," says her son, and Kiera agrees.

After turning around to see Colin asleep, she thinks about how fortunate she was to grow up with a strong sense of family connection, secure in her place in the world.

Of course, being an only child, she knew she was number one. Two childhood friends she still has today have always been honorary sisters in her mind. She has met many people with sibling issues, but never thought about what it is like for someone to feel like an outsider in their own home. For the first time, she understands his scars run deep.

That night, after the boys go to bed early, Colin still seems down. Sitting in his office, not working on anything, Hannah enters.

"I hope you don't regret telling me about your family."

"No. I don't. It isn't something I talk about, though."

"I understand. I'm sorry your stepbrothers feel the way they do. Jealousy can be a big issue between siblings, whether they are related by blood or not."

"True. Enough of that." He stands up and takes her in his arms. "I'm sorry I went to sleep on you last night. That was only the third time we spent the night in the same bed. I want to do more of that."

"I can stay here more."

"Good." He takes her hand and leads her back to his bedroom.

Thirteen

SYDNEY, AUSTRALIA

It took much longer than expected to find a place to set up their workshop and clean room, which is necessary to provide a contamination-free climate for manufacturing James' design utilizing microchips.

The venture capitalists come to visit. Clay is disappointed to learn his project has been pushed to the side for now, as the investors want to direct all funding to James' invention. They are concerned that Clay's idea of carbon capture on a moving vehicle is too challenging.

On the positive side, the entrepreneurs received the additional funds needed. Clay acknowledges it will take all their effort to produce the first full-sized transformer unit and have it ready for the pilot program's target start date. A local residential community has agreed to be the test subject.

Even though they are extremely busy, Clay and James, who grew up on the same street where their families still live, attend an engagement party for a mate from their suburb. Many of their own family members and friends are present. Until the party, they had both been tight-lipped regarding their business.

When Clay gives the news about the company and how they want to work towards improving energy efficiency and also capturing emissions, he realizes that many people do not have a clear understanding of net-zero goals.

"It is about reaching a balance between emissions of greenhouse gases due to human activities and the removal of these gases, of which carbon dioxide is the biggest part," he explains.

James observes several confused looks and tries to help out. "Of course, carbon moves around naturally between the atmosphere, ocean, plants, and rocks. Humans are changing nature's carbon cycle by burning fossil fuels and sending more carbon in the form of carbon dioxide into the atmosphere, which is causing the Earth to warm. Some of this CO2 makes its way out of the atmosphere through the carbon cycle, such as plants absorbing it, but because we emit so much, it keeps increasing in the air. Also, when trees are cut down, they release much of the carbon they store. Because of deforestation, some tropical forests emit more carbon than they capture."

Despite noticing how only a few people are still listening, James continues. "While inventors are developing ways to capture carbon at the source, such as at power plants, and also extract it from the atmosphere, these processes are slow and expensive so far. We want to develop products to facilitate achieving net-zero."

Clay and James get a nod or two and a "Good work, boys" from their friend's grandfather. The subject changes to the latest footy match as the group moves to the lounge room. James's 15-year-old nephew remains behind, wanting to know more and full of questions for his uncle.

It is time for Simon and Sam to return to school. Colin drops them off, and the boys surprisingly do not put up too much of a fight. Once home, he pulls Hannah away from the kitchen, suggesting they get back in bed to take advantage of this last day before his routine begins.

Afterward, with arms wrapped around each other, he remembers catching her singing the previous day. Interrupted by his sons, he didn't have the chance to find out more.

"By the way, what were you singing yesterday? I didn't know you sang."

"I don't. I mean, I'm not good at it, but I've listened to these John Denver songs so many times that I can match my voice to his fairly well, and a song of his was stuck in my head."

"John Denver, huh?"

She laughs. "Yeah. I like his music, and I thought a lot of him for his environmental efforts. The song you overheard was 'Poems, Prayers and Promises.' It is a little eerie since he was singing about looking forward to growing old, and little did he know that he would die a premature death at 53."

"A plane crash, right?"

"Right. Do you want me to play a few of his songs on my laptop?"

"Sure."

They listen to "Follow Me" and "Shanghai Breezes." Running his hand up and down her arm, Colin admires the softness of her skin. He holds her petite, smooth hand, as if examining it, and puts his fingers through hers.

Closing his eyes for the last selection, "Annie's Song," he takes the love song's lyrics to heart. When the tune comes to an end, he gives her a kiss and whispers in her ear, "Listening to all of this could be dangerous."

She gives him a half-smile. "Well, it sounds sweet and all, but he and Annie got divorced."

"This moment has been ruined!" he teases.

The next two weeks go by quickly. Colin becomes absorbed in work once again. Hannah is overjoyed to have time to continue working on her novel.

One night, after Simon and Sam go to bed, Colin is texting, and she is on her computer, focused on her writing and not paying any attention to what he is doing. He looks over. "Why are things so easy with you?"

"What do you mean?"

"Usually, girlfriends become irritated about my texting and emailing for work at all hours. They get suspicious and think I'm messaging other women. I get a lot of complaints."

"I have nothing to complain about, and I don't have a problem with you working or being friends with other women. If you ever wanted to move on, I could be an adult and be friends, and I would still watch the boys. I'm not the 15-year-old who took a pair of scissors to her boyfriend's letterman's jacket."

He laughs out loud. "What was *that* about?"

"David was Mormon, and his family moved back to Utah. He left me his jacket and said he wanted to have a long-distance relationship, but then broke up with me. Since we were in high school, breaking up made perfect sense, but I got upset and got out the scissors."

He stares at her.

"Stop looking at me like I'm crazy! He didn't need the jacket. He was at a new school and could get one there. I was angry for one day and then moved on to the next boy. I promise, I'm not the stalker type."

With a big grin on his face, he asks, "So, there were a lot of boys, huh?"

"Yes, but there wasn't any sex going on if that's what you are thinking. I thought high school was too young for that."

"I know. You were a good girl. And I'm relieved to hear that I don't have to worry about you going mad, but I do want you to care, to be passionate about me."

"Believe me, I am. I would think you can tell."

"Oh, I can." He crosses the living room to lean over and kiss her. "You are absolutely what I want. I have never gotten on so well with a woman."

He takes a seat beside her. "You must have been popular in college, too."

"I was in band in high school, a clarinet player, definitely *not* part of the school's popular crowd, but I always had a boyfriend in the band, usually a different one each semester. David's letter jacket was for band, not sports. Riding on the bus back from Friday night football games in the fall was where many a relationship started with people in band. Being asked to sit with a boy you liked in the dark was a big deal."

Trying not to laugh, he bites his lip. She continues. "Then in the spring, we would go to competitions and ride buses to other cities and even states. I was used to receiving a lot of attention from boys, but when I went to college, no one asked me out the entire first semester."

"Poor baby."

She rolls her eyes. "I took matters into my own hands, and over Christmas break, I wrote to a boy in the dorm who I had only talked to one time. There was an address book of students' home addresses. Of course, this was before the days of social media and texting. He wrote back, and we began dating with the new semester. We were together for two years, and then I met my husband."

"Did you break that poor college kid's heart?"

With a look of sincerity and regret, "You know, I think I did."

Kiera is at the local high school to student teach for her last semester. The teenagers are being rowdy. Mrs. McMullen announces, "Class, hush. Miss Donnelly is ready to give her lesson."

The class does not quiet down, but Kiera begins anyway. "Today, we are learning about cell structures." She displays a slide of a cell diagram on the large screen at the front of the room.

"The center of a cell is the nucleus, and inside is the nucleolus, which has the primary function of ribosomal RNA synthesis and ribosome biogenesis."

The students continue to chatter and ignore her. One boy shakes his head and pulls out a phone from his pocket.

She turns to Mrs. McMullen, who shrugs her shoulders.

By the end of the day, Kiera finds herself questioning if she should be a teacher. To her surprise, she went through the entire semester break, including the two weeks before and after, without having an asthmatic episode. While it would have been wise to tell Ryan about her condition in case something happened, she was fine on their trip. However, after only three hours with these high school kids, she had to excuse herself and use her inhaler in the teacher's lounge.

The first two weeks of the semester had been hectic, and she was doing a good job of putting Ryan out of her mind. At the same time, she is extremely disappointed that he has not reached out since their Great Barrier Reef trip. That night, she decides to call him.

"I'm a terrible teacher. The kids won't listen to me."

"What is the regular teacher doing about the students' behavior?"

"My mentor teacher had a family emergency, so there is a substitute, but the students don't want to listen to either of us. I don't know how to make Biology interesting. I'm not sure why I am telling you this, but for some reason, I thought you could help."

"You know, I think I can. I well remember high school Biology being boring as crap. In college, when it was specific to marine life, even though the same concepts applied, it kept my interest. What specifically are you trying to teach right now?"

"About cells, cell structures, cellular processes."

"Why don't you combine your passion for marine life and make it part of the regular biology lessons?"

"OK. I guess I can do that."

"Do the students know how you became interested in ocean science and about rescuing sea turtles?"

"No."

"Share your experiences with them and your special projects in college, such as the nurdle cleanups. Let them get to know you. And you should know their names to call on them individually. Make them be involved. Maybe divide them into teams on Fridays and create a game from what you have been teaching during the week for extra credit."

She still feels stressed and unsure.

Ryan keeps trying. While feeding his new aquarium critters, he tells her about his research in graduate school on cellular immunity. "Cells have the ability to rid themselves of infection. This was first recognized in starfish."

He goes on to explain how studying squids led to the discovery of the way nerve cells communicate. Another interesting fact he shares is that marine snails have been used to understand the cellular processes responsible for learning and memory.

"I can go on and on. I still have the research paper. Do you want me to email it to you?"

Sounding hopeful, she replies, "That would be great, thanks."

"I even have some snails you can take to class with you. If you feed them, they will come out of their shells to eat. I think the students would like that."

"Why do you have snails?"

"I finally got a saltwater aquarium last week with fish, sea urchins, and snails." He takes a picture of the aquarium, along with his favorite sea urchin, and sends it to her.

"This is Max. He is an awesome tuxedo urchin. By eating any algae or debris he comes across, Max keeps the tank clean while moving around at night. It would be too stressful for him to go with you to school, and he wouldn't move since it is daytime."

"You are starting to remind me why I studied biology and ocean science." Smiling at the blue ball-like creature with bands of soft pink spikes similar to hair, it doesn't look like something really alive.

"Why don't you come over in the morning before school and pick up the snails?"

"OK. Naomi is also a student teacher, and she drives us. We will be there at 6:15, though. High school starts early, remember?"

Rolling his eyes at the bad memories, he responds, "Yes. I remember."

Ryan hangs up, feeling good about encouraging Kiera. He had planned to give her space for a few months, knowing it would be her busiest semester ever before graduating the first weekend of December. Now, he can't wait to see her.

Hannah learns it is Father's Day in two days from a TV commercial. This is almost three months later than the U.S. recognizes it. She gets a white piece of poster board and writes *Happy Father's Day* in the middle. Simon and Sam color the poster and draw pictures.

When they get up on Sunday morning, the boys bring their creation into the kitchen. Colin is having coffee, and she is making pancakes. "We Love You, Dad," his sons yell at the top of their voices, showing him what they made.

"Hugs all around," announces Hannah, giving the twins a hug. "Now give your dad a hug." She has noticed how he isn't very affectionate with them. Not wanting to tell him what to do, she plans to find ways to encourage more tenderness among the three.

That night, he asks her to spend the night. After the reef trip, she began spending Friday and Saturday nights with him. She says "Yes" to a third night in a row. While he would like her to do this even more, she prefers being alone. It is hard to resist the urge to sneak back to her own place when she has trouble sleeping.

They stay up later than usual as he is feeling talkative and not the least bit tired.

"I was thinking about how I don't know much about your childhood or even what town you grew up in."

"I didn't grow up in a town. I grew up in a special-purpose district."

"What is *that*? Sounds like a sci-fi movie set in the future where the government divides people up into districts."

She laughs. "No, it's not the future. This started in the 1970s. It is called The Woodlands and is governed by a Board of Directors, so there is no mayor or city council. The planned community is about 30 miles north of Houston in a pine tree forest. It was founded by George Mitchell, who owned an oil & gas company before becoming a residential developer. He went out of his way to save the trees during development and focused on sustainability."

"Interesting. Go on."

"I lived in a subdivision that was the land of the Bidai, a Native American tribe. Their artifacts were discovered during development. We had a house built in 1984 when there were around 18,000 residents in The Woodlands and now there are over 120,000. I remember driving there every weekend from Houston to see the progress on the house."

"I pictured you growing up in the country wearing cowgirl boots and riding horses."

"Ha. Horses don't like me, and I've never worn cowgirl boots in my life."

"Now that I think about it, you don't have a Texas accent at all."

"I've never thought so. My parents were from Chicago. My friends were from the East Coast. Houston was booming in the 80s, and The Woodlands was and is an attractive place to live."

"And after that?" he asks, remembering she lived near Dallas.

"Then I went to the University of North Texas and stayed in the Dallas/Fort Worth area for over 25 years. My husband and I moved to the hill country when our son left for college. We loved having property, but I would not have wanted to raise him there."

"Why not?"

"Because the schools were excellent in Fort Worth, and there were endless activities like museums, zoos, aquariums, martial arts and exercise classes, indoor and outdoor playgrounds, and water parks."

"You're a good mum."

She grins, partly at the word "mum," which still sounds funny to her. "Let's get some sleep!"

"One more thing. Why don't horses like you?"

"We went horseback riding on several vacations, and my horse was always the uncooperative one. I'm sure it was me doing something wrong, but I always felt they didn't like me."

He gives her a kiss goodnight.

She falls right to sleep, but he wakes her up a few minutes later by asking, "When is your birthday? I can't believe I haven't asked this before."

"It was last week."

"What? Why didn't you tell me?"

"I didn't feel like celebrating the fact that I turned 50."

"How can you not celebrate your birthday?"

"Well, I did. I told you I was having dinner with my son. I picked up food and brought it to his apartment, along with some cupcakes. That was my birthday celebration. I wanted to hear all about the work he is doing."

Colin doesn't respond.

"I'm sorry. I am a little sensitive with you about my age, and I wanted to keep it to myself."

"That is silly."

"I know. Are you mad?"

"Yes, I am, but only a little." And he gives her another goodnight kiss, this time for real.

Kiera has a successful day at school and cannot wait to tell Ryan about it. She brings the snails to his university office just before 5 pm. Her heart sinks when she sees the beautiful blonde girl sitting beside him. One of the professors is leading a meeting. Setting the glass bowl on the first table, she tries to be quiet, but the sound makes everyone turn to her.

"Sorry. I am just dropping this off for Ryan."

His wave goes unseen as she exits in a hurry.

Two days later, Ryan is on a research vessel with two marine biology professors, three master's students, including Kim, and two PhD students. Michael, who tried to save Professor Taylor's life, is one of them. There will be no scuba diving on this outing. The discussion Kiera walked in on concerned the one-day whale expedition and the importance of monitoring their migration to protect them as climate change affects their food supply.

"This is the sonobuoy you will collect your data from," Professor Spiner explains. "I know you are already analyzing this type of data, but now it will be in real-time."

Ryan examines the cylindrical device, which is about as long as his arm.

Professor Davis motions to Michael. "Do you want to do the honors of throwing it overboard?"

Observing how Kim keeps watching Ryan and seems distracted, Dr. Spiner shakes his head at the thought of another department romance. After seeing them go badly over the last 25 years, he believes dating someone you work with is never a good way to go. The drama has led to two divorces, people resigning, and a lawsuit for harassment.

To keep her busy, the professor hands Kim a gadget for measuring distance. "We need to stay over 100 meters from the whales. You can be in charge of this." He shows her how to use the device.

Dr. Davis points as he speaks. "Ryan, you have been analyzing data from the recorded sounds of the hydrophone at the ocean's bottom in that area. I can't wait for you to share with everyone at the next department meeting about the algorithm you created to determine the presence of whale acoustics by whale type from the underwater recordings."

A whale in the distance launches itself up in the air and crashes back into the water with a huge splash. Before this day, the young man had never heard in person the sound of whales blowing air through their blowholes or the slap of their fins. The rubber smell is distinct.

Kim sits beside him. He looks down at his laptop. The screen shows something being detected from the newly dropped sonobuoy.

She leans in closer. "Can you turn up the volume so we can hear?"

"We need to wait for it to record. Then, I will speed up the recording, enabling us to hear. In real-time, the human ear cannot detect all of the sounds because large whales communicate in part at very low frequencies. The long wavelengths allow communication from hundreds of kilometers away. But, of course, you know this."

"Actually, whales are not my specialty," she tells him. "I have focused more on corals and marine plant life."

Still staring at his computer screen, he says, "Now listen." Sounds begin to come through. Loud, energetic blasts range from whistles and screeches to grunts and growls. The screen changes to display the whale acoustics as circles with different colors.

"What is that?" Kim asks.

"This is a spectrogram. It is used to help us see and hear patterns in the whales' vocalizations. The spectrograms are converted to numbers for analysis later."

He describes the different sounds they make and the songs they sing. "The humpback's song is probably the most complex in the animal kingdom, with repeated themes lasting up to 30 minutes. Some humpbacks sing for hours at a time."

The group is out on the water for several hours. Ryan spends the following two weeks analyzing data for the professors and PhD candidates to meet a publishing deadline. For the most part, he thinks of nothing else and has never put in so much overtime before. The thought finally occurs to him to text Kiera and ask how the student teaching is going. *Much better*, she replies.

Fourteen

Simon and Sam's autistic school has parent-teacher conferences today. Colin asks Hannah to go with him, knowing she will find the insights useful. They both take the boys to school, pretend to drop them off, but then park and chat for a while before the meeting. He chose the first time slot of the day.

The conference is in a front office room. The school does not want the children to discover their parents are in the building because some find it unsettling to know a parent is there when they cannot be with them.

Their teacher, Mrs. Burris, explains that, in her opinion, the twins should be in separate classrooms because of the differences in their abilities. However, they will not cooperate with being apart.

"A few times, I have insisted that Simon spend part of the day with the more advanced group, but he won't participate. He isn't being challenged the way he should. I think he likes being the star of the group, further behind. Also, he knows it upsets Sam to not be in the same room. While Simon is delayed for his age, he has the capacity to read and do work well beyond what he is doing now."

Hannah does not respond, thinking Colin will, but he is quiet.

Mrs. Burris looks back and forth between the two of them. "What is their home situation? Are the two of you living together?"

"No!" Hannah practically yells and then lowers her voice. "I live in their garage apartment. Colin moved into Marci's home because he felt that was where the boys were most comfortable and where they wanted to be."

She feels like guilt is written all over her face, even though it shouldn't be, since he and Marci were not a couple.

When Hannah first began picking Simon and Sam up from school, she told the music teacher for their last class how she watches them every afternoon. Taken aback by the question regarding their living arrangement, she regains her composure, returning the conversation to the subject of education.

"For now, why don't we leave the boys in the same group, and we will talk about it with them over the next few weeks to prepare for a change."

"Sounds like a plan," Mrs. Burris confirms, turning her head to Colin.

"I agree," he acknowledges.

On the drive home, they do not discuss the meeting. To him, it was a reminder of his sons' uncertain future. At first, Hannah is annoyed that the teacher seems to have a negative attitude about what Sam is capable of. But then she becomes determined to encourage them academically and prove her wrong. Both boys possess the ability to achieve. She is on a mission now, but keeps these thoughts to herself. He drops her off at the house and goes on to the university.

That afternoon, instead of solely reading to the boys, she insists they read. Sam will only repeat a few words in each story. Simon can read but does not enjoy it, nor does he speak with clarity.

She gets the idea to use the recorder on her laptop for story time. The first book they do this for is *Dooly and the Snortsnoot* by Jack Kent, published in 1972. Hannah's mother read it to her, and she read it to her son. In addition to being one of her earliest memories, she kept it because of the handwritten note from her mom on the title page.

Simon is given the part of the narrator, while she speaks for the mom and dad in the story. Sam is willing to participate because he wants the part of Dooly, the boy who starts out small like children his age, but has giants for parents. He gets to repeatedly yell, "Fee Fi Fo Fum!"

After replaying the recording, Simon complains, "I sound terrible."

"That's not true, but you do need to pronounce the words more clearly for the microphone to pick up what you are saying. Let's do it again."

They do this many times before the child is satisfied with how he sounds, and Sam has his parts down.

Colin gets home from work. "We have a surprise for you, Dad," shouts Simon as he walks through the door.

They play the audio for him while Simon turns the corresponding pages of the book. "That's great, boys," he tells them.

The brothers chase each other through the house, screaming, "Fee Fi Fo Fum!"

He moves closer to her. "Was Sam really reading, or did he have his part memorized?"

"It was from memory, but the point is that he is finding his voice and becoming interested in books."

The next day after school, Hannah brings the boys and their toy dragons into the backyard. "Tell me what kind of adventures the dragons go on."

Simon reveals a tale of a young dragon who gets lost and must find his way back home to the cave where his family lives.

"Why don't we go inside and make our own book of dragon adventures?"

The three of them sit on the couch, and she opens a software program for transcribing voices. "Now state loudly and clearly what your story is about."

Simon speaks, amazed to see the words he is saying appear on the screen.

Sam decides to give it a try. He talks into the microphone but vocalizes too quickly and does not enunciate enough.

Hannah slowly repeats what he said, pointing to each word. Sam begins to sound them out to ensure they are correct. She is not surprised the boy knows much more than he demonstrates at school.

The twins are finally content with their performances after working on the short story for over an hour. "I can't wait for Dad to get home," shares Simon.

When their father walks through the door, both boys are all over him, speaking simultaneously, so he doesn't understand.

"Your sons wrote their own story and want you to read it. Come over here. It is on my computer."

He reads aloud their imaginative tale. "You boys really did this?"

"Yes!" They shout triumphantly and run off to another room.

She restarts the dictation program. "Tell me how wonderful I am."

Colin laughs as the words appear on the screen. "You *are* wonderful, aren't you?"

Hannah continues with her mission of having the boys read each day. Once a week, they record themselves to create their own stories.

Since dragons are a favorite topic, she gets every dragon-related book the library has to check out. After Simon does his reading, she lets him play video games and somehow gets Sam to stay and read with her. Before, he always wanted to be side by side with his brother, but more and more, Sam is willing to do things without him. He reads a short early reader book all on his own for his dad. She watches as Colin fights back tears.

After the twins go to bed, she is working on her novel, and he has papers to grade. Thinking about the difference in his sons, he is unable to concentrate. "You are amazing. It seems you missed your calling to be a teacher, but it isn't too late."

She shakes her head. "No way. I can't handle children in large numbers, not more than two at a time. I took over as Cub Scout den leader for six months because our leader fell ill, and those boys wouldn't listen to a word I said."

"Your son must have listened to you."

"Yeah, with a lot of begging and bribing," she laughs.

While not wanting to get into this topic with him now, she has been doing some research on autism and its possible causes. She was shocked to read about a link between exposure to air pollution and increased risk of autism. Since climate change worsens air pollution, she decided to subscribe to the *Climate Council.* The Australian group is a nonprofit that supports climate policies and solutions. She made a donation and will receive newsletters on the latest in climate news, research, and ways to contribute to the cause.

The following Sunday, Colin is busy with work. He has mountains of papers all over his home office. The twins are being loud, so Hannah takes them to her place.

After two and a half hours, he decides to see how things are going. While climbing the stairs, Hannah, Simon, and Sam can be heard cheering. He enters to see the three fixated on a Dallas Cowboys football game. His sons have never been willing to watch any sports with him.

She finally acknowledges his presence once the extra point is made.

"I can't believe you are turning my boys into American football fans. Come down when the game is over."

A few days later, when Colin gets home from the university, he finds them all in the kitchen wearing Cowboys jerseys. "No Way. I forbid this. Those are coming off!" He chases Simon and Sam around the house, acting as if he is going to take off the shirts. Finally, the brothers crawl under their beds to get away from him. Deciding against dragging them out, he moves to the living room, quietly whispering to Hannah, "Yours is coming off later."

SYDNEY, AUSTRALIA

Clay, James, and Theresa are nervous. Their electric transformer device will begin testing today in the pilot program community. Theresa handled countless interactions between the power company and the city. They can only hope for no outages or problems. The investors want to make a big deal of it, inviting local media. The young innovators do not like this attention before having a proven product.

The ribbon-cutting ceremony is short. Thankfully, the vice president of the venture capital company spoke on their behalf. James especially feared he would be asked to speak. The green ribbon around the unit is cut, and the power is switched over to the transformer with a drum roll. The group will be on pins and needles until this testing phase is complete. The plan is to constantly monitor the system's functioning from their lab, with each person taking a shift.

James has kept it to himself that he experienced an electric shock twice while building the test unit. He became sloppy out of fatigue and desperation to finish on schedule and did not follow safety protocols. Theresa saw the burn on his finger. He dismissed it as a cooking incident at home. The second time, the shock caused muscle spasms in his hand, going up part of his arm. Later, he felt numbness and tingling, which went away within 24 hours, to his relief.

This last incident was a wake-up call to slow down and be more careful. Even though he and Clay have always been close, James does not feel he can be honest about these occurrences or how he believes his mind is faltering.

Ryan receives a text from Kiera. *I know you are at work, but I was wondering if you can talk.*

He immediately calls.

"My dad had a heart attack. He is at the hospital. I just found out."

"Are you at your dorm?"

"Yes."

"I will come get you."

He would never share this with her, but hospitals make him anxious. His grandmother developed an infection after an inpatient stay, which led to sepsis, and she died.

They find her dad's room. He looks weak but manages to give his daughter a slight smile.

"Dad, this is Ryan."

"Hi. I have heard a lot about you."

The young man nods, unsure of what to say.

"The doctor told me I need heart bypass surgery. I have three arteries that are over eighty percent blocked. I agreed to it."

Seeing tears well up in her eyes, Ryan speaks. "I have known several people who have had heart surgery and went on to live for many more years. My mom said that six weeks after her Uncle Peter's heart bypass surgery, he was hiking up a mountain in Utah, where he lived. You will be good to go in no time."

Her father begins a reply, but then winces in pain.

"We will let you rest now, Dad."

Stepping out in the hallway, she tells Ryan, "I want to wait for the nurse. I have some questions. You have no idea how relieved I am to hear my dad is willing to have this surgery."

"It makes sense that he is agreeable and wants to get better."

"You don't understand. Dad has always avoided doctors. And it didn't help that Mum's treatment did not save her life."

He wants to reach out and hold her hand, but doesn't. "I think he wants to live and be here for you and your brothers."

"I agree."

The nurse approaches and introduces herself. She gives the details of the procedure and how it will be performed in four days, with a five-day hospital stay post-surgery.

Walking towards the hospital exit, Kiera begins coughing uncontrollably and feels her chest tighten.

The look on her face scares him. "What's wrong?"

Reaching inside her purse, she pulls out the inhaler, shakes it, takes a long puff, and then another.

"Let's sit down." He puts his arm around her, leading them to the nearest waiting area.

"I'm sorry."

"There is nothing to be sorry about. I'm glad you are OK."

"I should have told you that I have asthma. I can go for weeks without having an attack, but I never know when it will hit."

"At least you had the inhaler."

"Yes. I learned my lesson years ago to never go anywhere without it."

"Someday, they will have a way to prevent attacks, so you don't have to worry about this."

She gazes into his eyes, trying to be positive.

He makes an effort to be comforting on the drive back. Ryan tells her that her dad will be fine and explains in more detail about his great-uncle, leaving out how Peter is his longest-living relative on his mother's side. Almost everyone else died prematurely from heart disease.

"It was a good thing he made such a great recovery because he had four children to raise. Everyone called him 'Popeye' because he sang 'I'm Popeye the Sailor Man' to his kids when they were little."

She cheers up and laughs. "Growing up, our doctor had the *Popeye* cartoons playing in the waiting room. My little brother Kevin began eating spinach because he thought it would make him stronger. He was always trying to prove his strength by lifting things around the house and trying to lift me and Kian, which, of course, he couldn't do."

"Sounds like your doctor was successful with Kevin on the goal of having that cartoon on, to get kids to eat their vegetables. Not me. I would rather lift weights for hours a day than eat spinach. And I'm not good about vegetables in general, except for potatoes, of course."

He pulls up next to the building closest to her dorm.

"I have something for you." From the glove compartment, he retrieves a *Best Teacher Ever* coffee mug and hands it to her.

"I love it. Thank you!"

"I saw it at the store and thought of you."

Feeling unusually brave, she decides to say exactly what is on her mind. "Sometimes I'm confused. Are we just friends?"

It had been easy all year to keep Kiera in the friend zone. Ryan thought it was best for both of them, but when asked this direct question, he had to be honest with her and himself.

"I don't want to just be friends. I think you are beautiful, and I am crazy about you." He says these words while staring straight ahead, but then turns to her.

Leaning over, she gives him a quick kiss on the lips.
He looks at her with surprise.
She smiles and gets out of the car.

Fifteen

SYDNEY, AUSTRALIA

Clay covers the night shift to monitor the pilot project. It was hard to get James to take a break and not be there all the time. "I will text you if something happens. Go home."

Three hours later, the red light comes on. "Crap!" yells Clay out loud to himself. He texts James to meet him at the site where the unit is located.

At the time they arrive, the power had been off for 30 minutes. They try their best but cannot figure out what is wrong. After two hours, they abandon the test, and the neighborhood goes back to its regular setup.

James is terribly upset. "Everything is ruined!"

"We will figure it out," assures Clay.

"It's too late. The investors will drop us."

"No, they won't. They will give us another chance."

James is clearly not listening. Clay is concerned. His mate appears to be at his breaking point. He tries one more time to get through to him.

"Everyone wants this to work. Now, let's get busy and figure out why the power went off."

When Colin returns home from work, Hannah is sitting on the living room couch with her laptop. He hears the joyful sounds of his sons playing a video game in their room.

As he leans over to kiss her forehead, he sees cartoon teeth images on the computer screen. "What are you doing?"

"Setting up a dentist appointment online for Ryan."

"Shouldn't he do that for himself?"

"Are you seriously saying that to me?"

He bursts out laughing. "No, I'm only kidding. I wanted to see what you would say. I would never tell you how to parent. Your son has already proven he can survive in the adult world. He is doing excellent work at the university. I saw the marine science article in the school paper that mentioned him."

She has a proud, satisfied look on her face.

Turning anxious, he decides to broach a new subject he has been putting off discussing. "We have a fundraising dinner Thursday night for a museum in Brisbane, OK?"

Her expression tells him the answer is *No*.

"You have to go. You are my girlfriend now."

"I think you are better off going by yourself. You need to understand, I am not a good social partner."

"And why is this?"

"I wouldn't know what to say to people."

"Right, as if you have ever been at a loss for words," he chuckles.

"I'm not joking."

"Really? You won't go with me?"

She is quiet. Then, with a big sigh, "Fine, I'll go."

He bites his lip, trying not to give away too big of a smile. "Can you ask your son and Kiera to watch the boys?"

"Sure."

Hannah texts Ryan this request. He finally lets her know that Kiera's father is having heart surgery on Friday morning. Even so, she wants to come over and welcomes the distraction. They will both be there.

She sends him messages to relay to Kiera about how she will be praying for her dad and to not hesitate to ask if there is anything they need.

Thinking about Kiera's father's surgery brings back painful memories of her own parents dying from heart disease. She is worried for the girl.

In the middle of the night, Hannah wakes with a jolt, realizing that Thursday is the anniversary of her husband's shooting.

How could she not have thought about this before now? She had been doing too good of a job of putting the past behind her and moving on with a new life. An overwhelming sense of sadness comes over her. Sleep escapes her for the rest of the night. She is thankful to be alone in the apartment and not with Colin.

The next morning, she watches from her window as he leaves for the day, taking the boys to school. *What is she doing? This isn't the life she was meant to have.*

She begins to feel differently about everything. Originally, she believed reaching the one-year mark would allow her to feel better, but now it is the opposite. Getting back in bed, she has a good cry before managing to lift herself up and move on with her day, exercising, writing, and picking up the twins from class.

The time spent with Simon and Sam, assisting with homework and taking turns reading stories, does give her a tremendous sense of purpose. The following afternoon, Sam gives her an unexpected hug before going off to play.

He had just done an outstanding job reading a new book. She finds it hard to fight back the tears.

During the night, she sees a grown-up Sam in her dreams. He is a teacher, reading to his young students. Then clouds form around her so that she cannot see. A break in the clouds exposes Allison and Ryan up ahead on a mountain trail, the same trail they were on in New Mexico many years ago. She tries to catch up to them, but they disappear.

At the trail's end, she sits on the rock formation where they rested that day as a family. She remembers it well because they were above the clouds. She had never looked down at clouds before, except from an airplane. They watched them rise. Jack was the last one to get up, and she took a picture of him surrounded by the white billowing mass.

She hears her late husband's voice. "How can you do this to us? I thought we were soulmates. How can we be soulmates now?"

Her eyes open. It does not take long for the tears to flow.

Memories return of her father insisting that her mother would come to him in dreams. He also swore the light turned on spontaneously for the bookshelf: the one that shined on her mom's Hummel figurines.

Is Jack trying to communicate with her?

Thursday evening arrives. Kiera and Ryan come up the sidewalk holding hands.

"I don't believe my eyes!" exclaims Hannah, feeling pure joy as she witnesses this from her position on the couch.

"What?" asks Colin.

"They are finally a couple. Look!" She goes over and opens the door.

The young man had seen his mother peering out the window and knew what she was thinking. Watching her try her best not to say anything, he lets her off the hook.

"Yes, Mom. We are together now."

With a giant grin, she hugs them both and then grabs her purse and phone. "Text me if there are any problems. It will probably be 11 before we get back."

"Later than that," Colin lets them know.

She takes a deep breath, not looking forward to the evening. While wishing they didn't have this dinner event, she does feel better about things. Ryan moving on with his life is a blessing. And like his father, her son is not one for dates. She is certain he has no idea that Jack was killed one year ago today.

On the drive, Colin suggests that he take Ryan to a rugby game.

"He wouldn't like it," she blurts out.

"O...K.. Sorry, I mentioned it."

"I didn't mean to be rude, but he has no interest in sports at all. I know that is out of the ordinary to you, but it is true. He used to question why we watched football. I guarantee he doesn't even know what rugby is exactly. It would not be fun for him."

He doesn't respond.

Maybe she should have offered up another activity for her son and the man in her life. The truth is, she isn't comfortable with the idea of them getting to know each other better and does not feel it is necessary.

As they enter the venue, Hannah immediately feels like a Plain Jane with all the beautiful women popping out of their low-cut dresses. She forced herself the day before to buy a dress for the occasion, one with long sleeves as she gets cold easily, and a long length to cover up her legs.

Before the sit-down dinner, there is a cocktail hour. Making their way to the bar, she notices a gorgeous younger woman eyeing Colin. She is definitely hot, an adjective that no one would ever use to describe herself. Pretty has been mentioned several times, and one or two referred to her as beautiful, which seemed a bit of a stretch. Colin has never commented on the subject, but knowing he would find this other woman very attractive, she begins to wonder if she is enough for him.

After getting their drinks, he observes her hand shaking as she tries to hold a wine glass steady. He takes the glass and pulls her aside.

"Are you OK?"

"I warned you that I am not good at this kind of thing, didn't I?"

"You are being silly. It will be fine."

She nods and tells him what he wants to hear, "Yes, it will be fine."

Once her hands are settled, they carry their drinks over to a couple he knows. Colin makes the introductions. She zones out and misses their names, catching only the end of how the wife owns some type of store two streets over.

The woman asks Hannah what she does, a perfectly normal question, one would think, but she is caught off guard and doesn't know what to say. Something keeps her from explaining her role as a caregiver for the boys. Instead, she proceeds to ramble on in the most awkward way about her previous jobs, concluding with the current project of writing a fiction novel, an activity she had not planned to share with anyone there. When asked what the story is about, she replies, "a romance," and changes the subject to a topic Colin can talk about to take over the conversation.

He goes on to discuss his latest research. She could feel his embarrassment during her exchange with the couple. It was a mistake to accompany him here.

Finally, the longest happy hour that was anything but ends, and it is announced for everyone to take their seats at the long tables. Hannah and Colin sit side-by-side. He becomes engrossed in a discussion with the men next to and opposite him. Another man is across from her. Thankfully, he is listening intently to the others.

The woman to her left and two more women on the other side of the table try to converse with her over the appetizer. One asks if she practices yoga and meditation, to which she shakes her head, "No." The ladies discuss their mental well-being and how the classes have given them mental clarity, calmness, and increased body awareness.

Hannah giggles. "I am too hyper to meditate. I like to keep moving, so walking is my preferred exercise." The others do not find this humorous. She should have demonstrated an interest in the subject rather than dismissing the idea.

Overhearing her laughter, Colin is relieved. Under the impression that things are finally going well, he returns to his exchange with the men.

When the main course is served, he wraps up the latest series of dialogue to ask how she likes her dinner. Only because people are listening, she replies, "It's delicious." However, the salmon with lemon sauce is something she can barely tolerate. He has completely forgotten she does not eat fish. When the subject came up months before, he did say she had just not tried dishes prepared the right way. Apparently, he was wrong.

He briefly beams at her, feeling like this night is a success, while she is miserable.

Clearly in his element, he continues to socialize and have the best time ever.

This isn't an occasional thing for him, she thinks to herself. Until recently, parties and events had been a regular occurrence in his life.

Hannah is relieved when her plate is taken away without anyone commenting on how little she ate. The women gave up talking to her, which she was fine with, and this went unnoticed by Colin.

Her mind is occupied with thoughts about her husband and their lack of a social life. They liked living in the middle of nowhere, perfectly content to hang out with each other and not need anyone else. For the 20 years they lived in the Fort Worth area, she was thankful his job did not require dinners and social events. One company he worked for years ago did have an annual barbecue with everyone in jeans and a petting zoo of farm animals for the kids. That was her kind of function.

While dessert is being served, she checks her phone, gasping at the sight of five texts.

He turns to her. "Is everything OK?"

She doesn't answer until reading all the messages.

"Sounds like Ryan and Kiera have their hands full. Jane's oldest son fell onto the corner of a coffee table, requiring stitches above his eye. She brought her three younger boys to your house since her daughter wasn't home. Jane texted three times to fill me in, and Ryan texted twice to let me know how crazy they are all acting."

"Do you think we need to leave?"

"No. They can handle it. Jane is on her way home, anyway."

Lamington cake is something she had never heard of. It is wonderful, and coffee at nice restaurants always tastes so good. She smiles at the thought of her son dealing with a house full of wild children. *Payback time.*

After a post-dinner presentation that lasts for over an hour, it is time to leave.

Colin takes her hand. "You must see the view from up here."

The fundraiser is on the top floor of the tallest building in town. They step out onto the balcony to see Brisbane at night with all its lights.

He pulls her close and kisses her. "I love you."

Silence.

Between the moonlight and the brightness coming from inside, her face can be seen fairly well. It is undeniable. She does not welcome these words. Thinking they were both at the same point in their relationship, he is shocked.

Looking away, Hannah reveals in a wavering voice, "I'm not ready to say that yet. I hope you understand."

Dropping his arms from around her waist, he moves towards the railing. They both stare out at the city.

"Today marks one year since I lost my husband. I am having trouble dealing with that."

"Oh, OK. I didn't realize."

While feeling better about why she isn't ready to reciprocate her love for him, he still questions if they are right for one another.

It is an uncomfortable ride home.

"Are you going to spend the night with me?" he asks, turning into the driveway.

"If you want me to."

"Of course I do."

"I will say 'Goodbye' to Kiera and Ryan and then go up and get my things." She steps towards him, planting a quick kiss on his lips.

Kiera sits in the hospital waiting room with her brothers. Kevin keeps crying. "He will be fine. Don't worry," she says, holding his hand.

Ryan arrives following a morning meeting at work, surprised to find her in such good spirits. "I'm proud of you for being so brave and positive." He puts his arm around her.

"I had a dream about my dad fishing at his favorite spot on his birthday many years from now, and I feel confident he has a future."

What she doesn't tell him is that she does not believe it is only a dream. To her, it is a precognition that will absolutely come true. She has never shared these concepts but has read books on the subject. The readings explain how a premonition is a feeling of something bad happening. Precognition relates to the future, good or bad.

In the vision, her dad was fishing with his grandson. She has no idea if it is her son or one of her brothers' sons. Someday, she will learn that her dad has taken his grandson fishing, and the event will have "broken the dream" she experienced all these years before. What she desires is for the boy to be her and Ryan's son.

She keeps looking at him, wondering what their future holds. *Do they have a future together?* The fact that she and Ryan have not really kissed except for a few pecks on the lips and cheeks is bothering her.

He becomes aware of her glances. "Is there something you want to talk about?"

"No. Just sitting here with you is comforting. Thanks for being here."

"Of course." Leaning his head back against the wall, he closes his eyes.

She stares at his lips while his eyes are shut. Her father is in there with his life on the line, and all she can think about is when and where she and Ryan will passionately kiss. *Should she make the first move?* If she waits for him, there is no telling when that could be. She begins to make a plan.

SYDNEY, AUSTRALIA

Clay wants his friend to speak with a psychologist. James is troubled to the point of being unable to function and proceed with their plans. After working up the nerve to broach the subject, he is met with a glare.

The thought occurs to him to trick James and make an appointment for both of them to meet with a therapist. Then, he comes across a local inventor who had many failures before becoming successful. Clay contacts Mr. Shields, and the fellow microengineering major agrees to view their project.

As they go through every step of the process with this man who asks all the right questions, James has a lightbulb moment and realizes what went wrong.

A few days after being released from the hospital, Kiera and Ryan visit her father at home. He is recovering nicely and feeling fairly well. Friends who also work at the resort are helping out and providing meals.

During the water taxi ride to the island, he remembers that she does not like boats much.

"So, being on this boat bothers you?"

"I'm not crazy about it, even though I do this all the time." She keeps her lifelong issues with motion sickness to herself. While the condition only results in mild nausea, it is embarrassing to admit. Medication only works about half the time.

"I love it."

As he surveys the water, she studies him. "It is good to see you."

"Yes, I know. I'm sorry I have been so busy this week, but I know you have also."

She nods in agreement.

A cab service van follows a back road to the house at the far end of the resort property.

While coming up the steps of the porch, a gray-brown bird lands.

"I've never seen a bird like this," he remarks.

The creature proceeds to produce the longest, craziest laugh.

"It's a kookaburra," she explains.

"A song just popped into my head from childhood."

"Yes. It was written over 90 years ago."

They sing the first few verses before stepping inside.

Ryan brought a basket of food that his mother had assembled. Kiera's brothers act as if they do not want him there, but Mr. Donnelly seems genuinely happy to see him. The three sit at the kitchen table and chat for a while. When it is time to leave, she gives her dad a big hug and a promise to return the following weekend.

They walk to the water taxi because she mentions there are places to see along the way. "Does your dad know we are more than friends now?" he asks.

"Yes, I told him. He was pleased."

As Ryan thinks back to their discussion at the museum months before about the idea of losing both parents, he puts his arm around her. "I'm glad he is OK."

Taking him on a tour, she tells him about a spot in the woods where she often went growing up. It is popular with neighborhood kids, but she is hopeful no one else will be there. Kiera has a plan that this is where they will truly kiss for the first time. She sat there as a young person, wondering what her life would be like. Who would she marry? Would she marry? Would she ever fall in love? Would anyone ever fall in love with her?

They hold hands and follow a trail. "Wow," he exclaims.

There is no need to announce they have arrived at their destination. Massive tree limbs twist and turn under and over each other to create a natural jungle gym. He tries to follow the limbs, but it is hard to tell which limb belongs to which tree.

"These are smooth-barked apple gum trees, or some call them Sydney red gums." She touches one of the twigs covered in green leaves and creamy white flowers. "The flowers bloom only this time of year."

The tree in the middle has wooden planks nailed to the trunk that go up about 10 feet to where a large limb extends out, leading to many others.

"My brothers loved to climb these trees, and I would sit on this bench someone built and let them play."

Ryan examines the smooth pinkish-brown bark of the middle tree. He begins to ascend the planks.

"What are you doing?"

"I'm only going to the first limb. Don't worry, I'm not going to keep climbing and fall and break an arm in front of you."

"Believe me, that is precisely what has happened before. I did see a boy fall and break his leg. At least two others have broken arms. Those are just the kids I know of."

He reaches the branch and takes a seat. "Are you going to join me?"

"I guess so." This wasn't her plan. Sitting on the bench was the plan.

Climbing up, she does her best to not look down. He moves over, giving her the spot closest to the trunk. The slant of the branch has him gravitating towards her.

Because they are so close, Ryan naturally leans in and kisses her. This time, it is not only a peck. He opens his mouth and so does she, and they engage in a long, deep kiss for the first time in their lives. It is a good thing her back is firmly planted against the tree, or she might have fallen out.

Incredible is how she is feeling right now. Kiera fixes her eyes on him, trying to hold onto the moment.

Sixteen

For a couple of weeks after the fundraising dinner, things felt different with Colin. Now, it appears they are interacting as they had been, for the most part. She knows he is a little hurt.

One morning, Hannah hears yelling and crying from downstairs. She makes her way to the main house to find the boys being uncooperative about getting ready for school.

"The only reason to stay home is if you are sick. If you don't go, you will have to spend the day in bed, and no video games for a week," she lets them know.

Simon and Sam stare at her in disbelief.

"Why don't you get ready, so we can play games when you return?"

They both say "OK" and run to collect backpacks and lunch boxes.

"Thanks, you always know what to do," their dad expresses in a frustrated voice.

"I don't want to overstep, but it seemed like a good solution."

"You aren't overstepping. Please intervene whenever you see fit."

"They are losing motivation, and their initial enthusiasm for us all reading together has worn off. I need to come up with an incentive plan."

That night, she reads the twins a bedtime story before joining Colin in the living room.

"I have something to talk to you about," he informs her. "I have this annual trip with my rock-climbing group to go bouldering and camping next weekend on Magnetic Island. Should I cancel?"

"No, that's fine. You should go, but what is bouldering?"

"Bouldering is climbing without ropes and harnesses."

"That's crazy."

"The rock formations on Magnetic Island are not high, and we place a pad on the ground if anyone were to fall, but no one has fallen yet."

"Well, have fun. Where is this island?"

"It is over 1100 kilometers from here. There is a man in our group who is a pilot and owns a small plane, so he is flying us."

"Sounds like a death wish, a small plane, and climbing without ropes."

"I will be fine. I promise."

"You better be. I'm not going to tell you what to do, but it isn't very responsible of you to take risks this way with being a father."

He is surprised by her response.

She continues. "My husband loved motorcycles, but he sold his last one before we had our son. We stopped riding because we didn't want to leave our son as an orphan."

"*You* on a motorcycle?"

"Yes. Back in the day, it was quite a thrill to wrap my arms around Jack and go for a ride."

"You say you aren't telling me what to do, but you are."

"No, I'm not. It is your call. I won't say another word…" With a big sigh, "I didn't mean the part about being irresponsible. You should do what you enjoy."

"I wish it were something we could both do."

Hannah laughs. "Well, in addition to hating small planes and the idea of rock climbing, I also hate camping. Sorry, but none of this is for me."

"How can you hate camping?"

"When my son was in Cub Scouts, I didn't get a wink of sleep during one of their campouts. I got so excited because I thought the sun was coming up and the night was over, but the brightness turned out to be the moon. And I learned that birds can chirp at nighttime, not just in the morning. It was the longest night of my life."

"There is nothing like camping at the beach and sleeping to the sound of the ocean."

"If you say so."

"There are women in the group. Don't you want to come and keep them away from me?" he teases.

"Right, women in short shorts and tank tops above you, climbing. You can ogle their asses all you want."

"I'd rather eye your arse."

With a skeptical look, she takes his hand as he leads her back to the bedroom.

Halloween is a few days before Colin's trip. Jane's mother, Mimi, is a seamstress and makes costumes for her grandchildren. Hannah paid her to make Pikmin clothing for Simon and Sam. Their dad joked that after all the trouble of creating the outfits, his sons would probably change their minds and want to be something else.

"Oh no, they won't! Like it or not, they are going to be Pikmin. Mimi spent hours on this."

The twins did not change their minds.

Simon proudly slips into his red costume. The covering for his head has no ears, a pointy nose, and a red stem on top with a green leaf.

Sam is covered in yellow, with giant ears, no nose, and a white flower.

Neither character is supposed to have a mouth, the boys point out.

"You have to be able to breathe!" is the response.

Hannah and Jane take all the kids trick-or-treating. Her husband has two jobs, so he is at work. Their three youngest are dinosaurs, compliments of Grandma Mimi, and brother Danny is in his soccer uniform. The daughter stays home to hand out candy. Colin has no problem remaining behind.

Kiera finally checks the time. She didn't mean to still be at the library past dark, but the windowless building did not allow her to see the sun setting. Walking back to the dorm, she believes someone is following her. *Or do they just happen to be going in the same direction?*

She cannot shake the idea of being in harm's way and begins to run. Using her card key to enter the building, she is safe but hurries up the stairs anyway.

Coming down the hall on her floor, she stops and slides down along the wall, unable to breathe.

Naomi opens the door to see her friend sitting in the hallway.

"What's going on?"

"Just another asthma attack."

"Why aren't you using your inhaler?"

When retrieving it from her purse, chills set in, along with trembling hands that feel numb. There is none of the usual coughing. The inhaler does not work.

"This isn't asthma. This is something else," states Naomi, helping Kiera up.

Standing on the steps with a large backpack that Friday afternoon, Colin exhales deeply.

"You don't need to worry about us or feel guilty," she promises him. "Go. Have fun."

He suggested Kiera come over, but Hannah insisted it was not necessary. She and the boys would have a good weekend.

After a goodbye hug, she puts the dog in the laundry room and goes upstairs to bring Rosie into the main house for the first time. Usually, she leaves her alone on Friday and Saturday nights.

The ordinarily skittish cat struts around, curious about this new territory. Hannah hears the brothers arguing and makes her way to their room. Then Bailey begins to bark. When she returns to the living room, the tabby is nowhere to be found. Calling out for help, Simon locates her under his dad's bed, but she is beyond reach. They leave some treats and wait.

Finally, Rosie comes out from hiding. She eats and explores some more until her cat mom escorts her to the couch. Sam is instructed to let Bailey out. The dog immediately finds them and places his nose on the unfamiliar animal. The cat bats at his face but doesn't seem scared.

"I think she likes him!" yells Simon.

Hannah decides there is nothing to worry about as her sweetie quickly gets used to the new environment with a dog and two loud children. She and the boys have dinner and watch a movie. Sam falls asleep halfway through and then goes to bed without a fuss. Simon stays up a little longer, feeling as if he is getting away with something.

The following morning, Sam wakes up with a fever. She takes his temperature. The result is not high enough to warrant a trip to the emergency clinic. He has no appetite but understands the importance of drinking fluids.

Simon does not eat much for lunch, so she isn't surprised when, by the afternoon, he also has a fever and willingly climbs into bed. The brothers sleep for the rest of the day, managing a small amount of soup for dinner. She had to try four different kinds before finding one that they would each eat.

Because the boys went to bed early and had slept so much during the day, she expected one or both to wake up during the night, but they slept through. She went into their room and checked on them several times, feeling their foreheads, which didn't feel nearly as hot as earlier. Bailey slumbered at the foot of Simon's bed while Rosie spent the night on Sam's pillow, a sight that touched her heart.

Sunrise brings a barking dog and his new feline sidekick into the kitchen for breakfast, but not two little boys. She starts a movie in their room while encouraging the twins to eat yogurt. They go back and forth between watching and sleeping. By the third movie of the day, she begins to feel bad.

When Colin arrives home that evening, there is a note on the door.

Don't come in. Call me.

He immediately pulls out his phone. "What is going on?"

"The boys are sick, and now I have symptoms. I think you should stay in the apartment." She opens the door, placing some of his belongings on the porch and her beer turkey chili for him to have for dinner.

"I'm sorry you guys are ill."

"We will get well soon. No reason for you to risk getting it. I didn't text you on your trip because I wanted you to enjoy yourself. Their fevers weren't dangerous or anything."

"Thanks for taking care of them, Hannah."

"No problem, and on the bright side, I got a lot of writing done."

"Great. When are you going to tell me what your book is about?"

"Someday." With that, she shuts the door.

Hannah does not want to reveal any information about her book until she has finished it. She decided that because her character, Professor Alex Biggio, writes historical fiction novels, the other main character, Karen, is already a fan of his when she relocates to Australia from the United States.

Karen moves with her daughter Emily after her husband dies from cancer. The newly single mother is a high school Math teacher and has no problem getting a job in Melbourne. Emily is 18 and ready to start college. She enrolls at the University of Melbourne, and Dr. Biggio is her English professor. Karen learns of a community lecture the professor is giving and attends. This is where they meet.

While different enough from her life, she wonders what Colin will think.

She has enjoyed researching the Gold Rush era in Melbourne during the 1850s and 60s, which led to many wealthy people becoming involved in the city's expansion during the 1870s and 80s. Her made-up protagonist and professor wrote a fictional story set in 1861. He followed with a sequel in the next decade, centered around a prominent architect and the woman he loves.

Hannah read how Melbourne was settled by people from Tasmania, without authority from the British. She did not know about the rivalry between Melbourne and Sydney, another interesting fact. Impressed with the Royal Exhibition Building, the location is included in a scene for her story. She still hopes to visit Marvellous Melbourne, a nickname for the city she had never heard of.

Colin settles into the suite. He had not been in Hannah's bedroom in the daytime, only visiting her there at night for short rendezvous while the boys slept, and she wanted the lights off.

There is a *Best Cat Dad Ever* coffee mug with a cartoon drawing of a man's hand doing a fist bump with a black-and-white cat. Beside the mug is a picture of her husband with a real black-and-white cat. The second picture is of father and son at Ryan's high school graduation.

It sinks in more how her heart is not free to love him. He clings to the hope that this will change, but the notion of being in competition with a dead man enters his mind.

Late at night, a woman from the rock-climbing trip texts him with an invitation to a party on Friday. He lets her know he is seeing someone. She is about 15 years his junior. And gorgeous. The invitation is flattering since he felt old over the weekend. Climbing was noticeably more challenging because he had not worked out much over the last eight months. His muscles have lost some of their tone, and he has gained some weight. The last two days completely exhausted him, instead of leaving him feeling exhilarated as in the past. He falls right back to sleep.

After three nights by himself, he admits that the peace and quiet were enjoyable. Sam had begun waking up with nightmares two or three times a week on school nights, often ending up in his bed.

Before, Colin thought Hannah would move into the main house at some point. Now understanding the need for solitude, he decides not to pester her anymore about only being in his bed on weekends for the most part.

With everyone well, it is time to return to the house and let her have the apartment back. They make the switch and say their goodnights.

About 40 minutes later, she knocks on the door and hands him the cat.

"Rosie doesn't want me. She keeps meowing at my door to leave and come be with the boys, so I guess she is your cat now."

Pointing down to bowls, food, and a litter box, "Here are her things. I will bring the rest in the morning."

She walks away.

"Rosie still loves you," he calls out.

Without turning around, she responds with a wave of her hand.

Naomi convinced Kiera to get help. Initially, her friend refused. Also stressed, the soon-to-be college graduate and English teacher made a virtual appointment with a therapist, timing it so she would have 30 minutes alone first. Earlier in the day, she asked Kiera to come to her room at 7:30 pm to discuss something.

"This is Linda. I was telling her about my anxiety and worries for life after university. Now it is your turn. I will be back in 30 minutes."

Naomi leaves.

Not wanting to be rude to this friendly face on the screen, she quietly says, "Hello."

The next few weeks fly by. Colin is heads down with research and preparing for finals. The sisters who provide the meal service have a family emergency, so Hannah finds herself in the role of cook. She makes chicken noodle casserole with baked cinnamon apples, a favorite of hers. The boys won't touch it. Colin says he likes it, but she knows he is just being nice.

Simon and Sam become even more uncooperative about doing their homework and working on their reading. Hannah remembers how she used to bribe her son with *Pokémon* trading cards. She orders some *Pokémon* shows on DVD and watches with them. They were not familiar with the show but got hooked in no time. She lets them know that, going forward, homework and reading need to be done first before watching any more episodes. This works like a charm.

A few days later, the boys are once again putting up a fight about going to school. Hannah comes down the stairs. Their dad had gotten them ready and out of the house, but they were in the front yard stalling about getting in the car. She tells them that they need to be good about going to school every day, and then on Fridays, they each get five *Pokémon* trading cards. This changes their attitude, and they hop in the backseat.

"*Pokémon?*" inquires Colin.

"Yes. They had never seen it, but now love it. I think I can keep them going for years with this because there are 25 years of *Pokémon* TV episodes, plus movies, video games, toys, and endless trading cards. I told you I needed a new plan to motivate them, and now I found one."

"You are a genius." He gives her a kiss on the cheek.

When Colin gets home on Friday, the twins show him their trading cards. They are excited beyond belief. She fed them an early dinner and started a movie. The two adults enjoy a quiet meal.

"I'm glad you are OK with me bribing your sons," she laughs.

"Was your son into *Pokémon?*"

"Yes. I bribed him to learn to read with the trading cards."

"Does he still have them?"

"They are in storage in Texas."

"How old was he?"

"Almost six."

She knows he is wondering if his boys will always be behind. "I did some research, and children with autism often improve with age. Look at how far Sam has come over the last two months."

"You are right." Lowering his voice to almost a whisper, he adds, "I just wonder if they will ever be on track with others their age."

"I believe it is absolutely possible. Those two have all kinds of potential."

He nods, appreciating her positivity.

"A family I know bought property, built a house for themselves, and brought in a mobile home for their autistic son. He works at a warehouse and drives. Their daughter does not have autism, but she flunked out of college. Unable to support herself, they purchased a second mobile home for her. Many people face a failure to launch with their children."

She continues. "I don't think you should worry about the future. I predict the boys will live together independently, with Simon watching out for his brother. I think they both will find careers they enjoy."

He reaches over, placing his hand on hers.

SYDNEY, AUSTRALIA

The neighborhood agrees to give the testing another go. After all, they were only without power for a few hours. Clay, James, and Theresa drive to the unit and turn it on from the site. This time, it is only the three of them. No public. Not even the investors.

A week goes by. And another. No issues develop.

Deciding it is safe to celebrate, they agree to go out. Theresa receives a last-minute text from her latest boyfriend and changes her mind. Clay and James go to a local restaurant for beer and pizza.

"Thanks for coming to my rescue when I was down," James acknowledges.

"Of course, mate. What are friends for? And believe me, I was not happy either."

"Right, but you didn't let it affect you."

"Not true. Maybe not outwardly, but I was a disaster during that time, making weird mistakes on all kinds of things. And if you recall, I couldn't figure out what went wrong. It was all you. You saved us."

"It took all of us and your idea of having Stan Shields come visit."

The two young men clink glasses and take a big sip. They decide that no matter what happens with their current investors, they will proceed with their company, one way or another. James lets Clay know he has been thinking about his process for carbon capture on vehicles and wants this to be their next priority.

Kiera makes it a point to practice the breathing techniques the therapist taught her three times a day. It has helped. At first, the topics included graduating, teaching, and her father. Today is different.

"Is there anyone new in your life?"

"No."

Linda expands her inquiry.

"We have known each other for months. Now we are together. Everything is good."

It takes a few sessions, but deeper emotions are finally revealed about relationship anxiety and fears over whether things will work out with Ryan or not.

Counselor and client examine techniques to combat negative thought patterns: an exercise Kiera finds incredibly challenging.

Hannah has not heard from Ryan in several weeks. She sees Kiera often. Thankfully, the girl agreed to watch Simon and Sam on Saturday nights. Then every Thursday evening, she rescues Jane by babysitting her two youngest boys. The exhausted mother has her hands full with activities for the three other children.

"Two boys are better than three and a whole lot better than five," Hannah teases Kiera, dropping off dinner for all of them.

It is time to plan a graduation celebration, so she gives her son a call.

After hanging up with him, she interrupts the boys' game. "Are you both sure you want to see Kiera graduate? I have to warn you that graduation ceremonies are long and boring."

"We do!" confirms Simon enthusiastically, with Sam smiling beside his brother.

"Are *you* certain about this?" Colin asks her.

"I am bringing handheld video games in my purse if needed."

"OK. Good idea. I will be participating in the commencement, so you are on your own."

When Kiera's name is announced, Ryan, Hannah, Simon, and Sam, along with the graduate's dad and brothers, do their best to scream as loudly as they can.

Colin and Hannah host a party at his house. Kiera's friend Naomi arrives, accompanied by her parents, brother, and grandmother, who all flew in from Melbourne. Naomi will teach English at the same high school where Kiera will teach Biology. All celebrations and congratulations are directed towards both girls.

Ryan pulls his mom aside. "There is something I need to tell you. I am going to propose tonight."

She stares at him, speechless.

"I thought you would be beside yourself with joy."

"I...am. I think I am. I am concerned, though. Don't you think you should date for a year first?"

"We have known each other for most of the year. Being friends first counts."

There is a moment of silence, and then he speaks. "I'm confused. I thought you would be happy for me."

"I'm sorry. Of course, I am. I just feel like I'm supposed to encourage you to be cautious, take your time."

"I know she is the one."

"Yes. I can see that." She gives him a big hug.

The party ends, and everyone leaves, including her son and Kiera.

Hannah informs Colin of this latest development, finishing with, "What if she says 'No'? He will be devastated."

"She won't say 'No.'"

"How do you know?"

"Trust me. She will say 'Yes.'"

Ryan calls an hour later. "She said, 'YES!'"

Seventeen

Kiera and Ryan are sitting on his couch the following night. While excited about being engaged, she woke up that morning thinking about how he had yet to say the words, *I Love You*. And he hasn't kissed her again, at least not the way he did in the tree. He certainly has not suggested anything else. Maybe he thinks she wants to wait until they marry, but she doesn't know how to broach the subject.

It was his idea to get married so soon, the first weekend of February. He must love her and want to be with her in every way. But something is nagging at her: the possibility that he sees her as a life partner and true romantic love is missing on his part. Taking a deep breath, she is determined to push through these thoughts and enjoy spending time together. *It is all in my mind.*

She picks up a photo album from the coffee table that his mom had recently made. After viewing pictures of him growing up and of his sister and friends, she has a proposition.

"Why don't we go to the States so I can meet your friends and your sister. It only seems right to meet these important people in your life." He had mentioned his Scottish friends Lewis and Leo many times. She knows they play games online every weekend.

"We can do that."

"Really?"

"We should go right after New Year's."

Colin has dinner with friends. Upon returning, he notices how Hannah seems down. She gives him a quick hug and retreats upstairs to be alone. After putting the boys to bed, he knocks on her door. She is drinking a glass of wine with the bottle on the table.

"Are you OK?"

"I am just sitting here thinking about things I have never thought of before."

He sits down beside her. "And what would that be?"

"Until today, I had never given much consideration to the pressures on a man of having a wife and children. The excitement of my son becoming engaged has turned to worry about the future. Of course, for a long time, the money aspect has not been all on the man, but still, life is so expensive."

She explains her situation growing up.

"I had never thought about it from my dad's perspective, but in retrospect, I know he was stressed supporting us and helping out his own parents. Money must have been tight. They did not discuss such things in front of me, but I remember my mom bounced a couple of checks to my music teacher for private lessons. My dad would never have said, 'No, we can't afford that.' I learned after I finished college that they had a lot of credit card debt."

Taking another sip of wine, she continues. "I never thought about it from my husband's perspective either. We always had enough money to pay our bills, but he must have felt pressured to have a career. I know he hated business trips as much as my dad did. I could have worked full-time if needed, but I felt working part-time was in the best interest of our family. And in the later years, he became fully remote, no trips at all."

Colin begins to feel uncomfortable with the subject of her spouse.

"And I was always the person who did all the meals, shopping, cleaning, and housework. I worry my son thinks this is how it should be. I need to straighten him out for Kiera's sake."

He leans in and kisses her cheek. "Ryan and his wife will be just fine."

She proceeds to communicate every thought that comes into her mind.

"The only time my husband did the dishes was on Christmas one year, and I watched in horror as he took the bloody plate of a roast and dumped it in the soapy water to clean the dishes. I did not say a word. I just made a note of what I needed to rewash."

Finally realizing she has talked long enough, she tells him, "You should get back downstairs in case the boys wake up."

"I should." He stands up, eyeing the bottle of wine.

"I am putting it away. You do not need to worry about me. I promise."

"OK. See you tomorrow."

Ryan is at the seashore. He looks older and bigger as he runs up onto a sand dune chasing a beach ball. Every time he bends down to pick up the ball, the wind blows it away. Children are laughing in the background. A little boy scampers towards him. "I want it, Daddy." He hands the ball to the youngster, who is around six or seven years old and has on *SpongeBob* swim trunks.

Kiera comes into view. She has a bright, cheerful smile on her face. A girl about half the boy's size, wearing a swimsuit covered in pineapples, reaches out to her brother, trying to take the ball away.

"Be nice," their mother says. "Let's keep playing." The family of four kicks the ball around to each other.

The sound of the neighbor's dog barking wakes Hannah up. She closes her eyes, attempting to fall back to sleep and resume the marvelous dream, but she can't. It is time to start her day anyway.

Back at his apartment after a busy day at work, Ryan is beginning to worry about this trip. He has never traveled without his parents planning everything, so he calls his mom.

"Kiera wants to go to Texas and meet Leo and Lewis, cousin Tiffany, Aunt Tracy, and Uncle Alex, and then go to Oregon to meet Allison."

"That sounds fun, right?"

"Right, but I have not been on my own vacation, not like this."

"Don't worry. I will help you make arrangements and get you organized to know what to do. How long of a trip are you thinking?"

"A week, not including travel time."

"How about two nights in Fort Worth, stopping in Waco just for the afternoon, and continuing on to Galveston for two nights, and then flying from Houston to Oregon to spend three nights there. Sound good?"

"Yes."

"Do you want to make sure that you each have your own room?" she delicately asks.

"Yes."

"Do we need to have a talk about the birds and the bees?"

"Mom, give me a break."

"Let me do some research, and I will get back to you about a plan for the trip."

She calls him back about two hours later. "First, you will fly into DFW and stay at the historic Fort Worth Stockyards Hotel, showing Kiera our old house and neighborhood, and meet your cousin. Unfortunately, your aunt and uncle will already be back in Washington, D.C. by then."

Hannah continues. "After Fort Worth, you can drive to Waco to visit Leo at the technical school and then head to Galveston to visit Lewis at his university. I found a small house near the beach to rent. You can check the rental car in at the Houston airport and fly to Portland, Oregon. Allison says the bus next to hers is a vacation rental. It has a bed in the back and bunk beds in the middle. OK?"

"Yes. Thanks, Mom. It will be nice to see Leo and Lewis. Of course, I play games with them, but I haven't seen Lewis in two years and Leo in longer than that."

They proceed to reminisce about how the brothers left Texas for Scotland, speaking in American accents but returning with thick Scottish ones. She wondered if it was intentional on their part to fit in over there. And it did not take long for an American way of talking to resurface. Hannah and Ryan discuss the idea of whether living in Australia will change their speech over time.

After hanging up, she thinks about how his friends were such a big part of her life. She was always taking them places to have fun. Their own mother had two younger daughters to take care of as well.

Leo and Lewis's parents divorced when they were in high school. The dad moved back to Scotland, and their mom stayed in Texas with the kids. The boys took the breakup hard. In Scotland, the government covers the cost of college. Since the brothers were Scottish citizens, they both went overseas to attend university after their respective high school graduations, one year apart.

However, it did not work out for either one of them. They dropped out, coming back to the States together and working odd jobs for a couple of years before discovering their career interests.

Once learning of Lewis's passion for cleaning up the oceans and holding companies responsible for pollution, Hannah told him about the program at Texas A&M Galveston, where he could study Marine Environmental Law. She hopes he will either get a job with a nonprofit or go to law school. Remembering how good he was at arguing his point, even as a young boy, she smiles at the thought of Lewis J. Mackenzie, Esquire.

Leo was in the Robotics Club during high school and brought over an impressive robot he had built. While not feeling up to a university engineering program, he is thriving at the state technical school. The goal is to work as a robotics technician alongside engineers.

Since it is three weeks before Christmas, Hannah has been buying gifts to send to family and friends in the States. The idea of summer break being in December, January, and February takes some getting used to. She is thankful that the autistic school has afternoon camps three days a week this time of year.

Colin is busy teaching a summer course to make it up to the professor who covered for him during the filming of Hongi Hika. She has noticed how unusually tired he seems lately.

One afternoon, he returns home with news that his genealogy contact found her great-grandfather's brother, Tom Ryan, who immigrated to Australia from Ireland. He worked in the mines. His son, William, became a lawyer, and his grandson, William Jr., pursued a law career, as well. William Jr. had two sons and a daughter in the 1970s. Brayden committed suicide in his 20s. Cara's whereabouts are unknown. She has an arrest record for drugs. The younger son, Patrick, is a physician in Sydney. He is 54.

"You should contact Patrick. I have the phone number and address of his medical practice."

"I will mail him a letter. That way, if he does not want to communicate, he doesn't have to."

She writes, giving her phone number and email address. Surprisingly, Patrick emails three days later, stating that he would love to meet and asking if it is possible this Saturday.

Colin grins. "Perfect. We can go to Sydney for the weekend. Kiera can watch the boys, and we can go back to the hotel you liked so much. This time, we can do it right, if you know what I mean."

"We could have done it right the first time, but you never came to my room," she teases.

"I desperately wanted to come to your room during our weeks of filming, but I thought you might slap me."

"I would never slap you."

"I promised myself that I wouldn't put the moves on you while we were working together, and I couldn't risk any hard feelings between us. My concentration levels would have been shot, wanting to get back into bed with you each day."

Moving near, he kisses her ear and whispers, "Were you really lying there, hoping I would come to you?"

"Dad," yell Simon and Sam in unison as the clomping of dirty feet comes from down the hall. The boys had just walked in from playing in the backyard.

"Saved by the bell," he jests.

Kiera agrees to be in charge of the kids for the weekend so Hannah and Colin can go to Sydney. Ryan will join her part of the time.

The night before, Ryan accepted his mom's invitation to dinner. He brings a toy Christmas train to set up for the boys in their room, keeping them entertained while she prepares dinner.

Colin is at the kitchen table with a beer. "Your son will make a good dad someday."

"I agree, but I hope Kiera doesn't get pregnant right away. I should have a talk with them."

"I think they can figure it out for themselves."

"You don't even want to know what I bought for them."

"What did you do?"

She sits down and speaks softly. "I bought a newlywed's book that also includes sex tips and drawings about positions."

"You didn't."

"I did. On Christmas, I will put it in a bag under the presents he takes back to his place in case it would be helpful on their pre-wedding trip."

"I want to see it."

"Later!"

She stands up, and he gives her a playful pat on the bum, saying, "We don't need a book to tell us what to do anyway."

"I agree, we have it covered. Although there are a couple of positions I have never thought of."

He studies her with immense curiosity and the biggest smile on his face. When "later" arrives, however, his interest dwindles as fatigue sets in, and he goes to bed early.

They take an afternoon flight to Sydney because Colin had an important morning meeting. Settling into their hotel room around 4 pm, it is enjoyable to spend time together, with no chance of being interrupted by two short people who shall remain nameless.

In the downstairs restaurant, the hostess leads them to a table overlooking the harbor, bridge, and opera house. The food is delicious. Passengers from a cruise ship disembark, reminding Hannah of the cruise she went on with her parents. The vessels have become much more elaborate and taller over the last few decades.

Staying up late to watch movies is something the pair has never been able to do.

After ordering room service the next morning and getting back in bed for a while, it is time to meet Patrick and his wife, Cathy, for lunch at the Portside Sydney restaurant inside the Sydney Opera House.

Colin and Hannah arrive first. When Patrick enters, it is immediately obvious to her who he is, as his resemblance to her Uncle Peter is remarkable.

Patrick and Cathy have two sons and a daughter. Cathy explains that their firstborn, Clay, has a master's in engineering. He recently began a start-up alternative energy and carbon capture company to address climate change issues with two other grads. Daughter Dru is a second-year medical student, and son Glenn is a first-year medical student.

"They are Irish twins, only 11 months apart."

"Wow, you had your hands full, didn't you?" laughs Hannah.

Cathy admits her children are completely stressed out, and so is she. "I thought I'd have it made once the last one finished high school, but I guess not."

"The worry never ends. Hang in there. They will get through it."

The ladies have a few laughs over their adult children. Glenn is the first one to fall victim to their fodder. He graduated with "honours" from university but could not figure out how to use the oven in his new flat. Texting his mother a picture of the control panel, he requested assistance in turning the appliance on. The future doctor also didn't realize the need to clean the lint tray on the dryer since he had always used a community laundry facility. When home for Christmas holiday, Cathy discovered his bag was full of clean but damp clothes.

Patrick is a neurologist, specializing in Alzheimer's disease and dementia. Colin tells him about his mother's early-onset Alzheimer's and how his grandmother probably had it, too, but they didn't know what it was back then. "Everyone just thought she was crazy."

"You should have genetic testing done," Patrick suggests. "There is medication you can take to delay the onset if needed. Dr. Hauser in Brisbane is at the top of our field."

The two couples say their goodbyes after a wonderful lunch. Nothing is said about meeting another time. Hannah likes them but has the feeling that their family will never be the extended family she imagined for Ryan when first seeking out relatives. Now that he is marrying Kiera, this no longer concerns her. She is filled with joy over her son having someone in his life and a second family.

After lunch, Colin and Hannah stroll around the harbor for a while. From a distance, they see a group climbing up the bridge. She read how the climb takes three hours. "Let me guess, that is what you want to do."

"Not today. I have no energy."

Once back at the hotel, he falls fast asleep. She finally wakes him at 5 pm. "It's almost time to leave for our dinner cruise."

"Why did you let me sleep so long?"

"Because you were tired. It is fine. I worked on my novel, enjoying the view of the waterfront."

He is quiet on the outing, but they take pleasure in the scenery and scrumptious dishes.

Upon returning from their weekend, it becomes apparent that Colin isn't himself. He has been fatigued lately, but this is different.

"I feel like the Alzheimer's discussion got to you," Hannah tells him.

"It did. It brought back bad memories about what Mum went through, and John. I called Dr. Hauser's office and made an appointment for the first week of January."

She gives him a hug, but does not get much of one back.

Eighteen

Hannah has trouble getting into the Christmas spirit, between Colin being in a low mood and it being so warm. She associates Christmas with colder weather, although a warm holiday season is not foreign to her. From growing up in the Houston area, she well remembers several 80-degree Christmas days.

Colin returns from the university late one afternoon to find her and his sons putting up a Christmas tree.

"You said to go ahead without you."

"I know. Believe me, it's fine." He rolls his eyes but then moves closer.

"What is this? This is a real tree. Marci has an artificial one somewhere."

"The boys wanted to pick out a real one, and so did I."

He stares at her as she continues.

"People think a real Christmas tree is bad for the environment, but I read this isn't true. It takes a few years for a good-sized evergreen like this to grow, during which time it gives off much-needed oxygen for the planet. Then, in its place, another will be grown. Buying real ones keeps tree farms in business, allowing them to plant even more for wildlife that don't get cut down. The production and shipping of artificial trees result in higher carbon emissions. Real trees can be recycled into mulch and compost for people to buy for their yards and properties."

Without responding to her knowledge of the benefits of live trees, he goes to his room to change clothes.

It was a hard day for him because the department head pointed out during a meeting that it had been over three and a half years since his last published work. He did not appreciate being singled out and put on the spot for a lack of fresh ideas on research topics. The satisfaction on some of his associates' faces was evident.

After the tree is complete, Hannah enters his office. "Do you have a lot of work to do?"

"Yes. This summer class isn't one I usually teach, so it is a tremendous amount of work for me."

She doesn't have a reply.

"Is there something else you wanted?"

"No." She leaves the room, wishing she could go upstairs, but knows it is necessary to heat meals from the service and keep Simon and Sam from bothering him. Colin eats while he works.

Later in the evening, when he joins her in the living room, she brings up the subject of Christmas. "It would be nice if we could enjoy the season. Do you have something against Christmas?"

He shrugs.

"Don't you think it is fun to see the boys so excited and to buy them gifts?"

"Marci always had them on Christmas, and my gifts never seemed to measure up to what she already got them."

Hannah perks up. "I have some great gift ideas."

She shows him her Amazon shopping cart on her phone.

"They will like those. Thanks for doing that."

"I wish you would be more excited about the holidays. Is there anything you like about it?"

"I enjoy eating Pavlova."

"What's that?"

"It's a meringue dessert."

"That sounds familiar, like lemon meringue pie?"

"Kind of, but Pavlova has a crunchy outer part and is soft in the middle with fruit on top. It is named after a Russian ballerina, Anna Pavlova, who toured Australia and New Zealand in the 1920s. The Kiwis say they created the dessert in her honor, but it was us."

She smiles, trying to embrace this Australian tradition. "Is there a specific recipe?"

"Well, Marci probably had it in the kitchen somewhere. She used my sister's recipe that we grew up eating. It was nice of her to give me one each year. I think it was her way of saying 'Thank You' for not interfering with her wish to spend every Christmas with our sons."

"OK. I'll find it."

"You don't have to."

"I want to. I mean, I'd like to try to make it."

"What are your holiday traditions?"

"Going to church on Christmas Eve and then coming back to sit by a small campfire in the backyard and make s'mores. Instead of real wood, we began using artificial logs made of renewable materials that produce less greenhouse gas emissions. Ryan wanted to put an end to our fires altogether for the sake of the environment until I came up with the alternative wood idea and convinced him we only do one fire a year."

Colin is quiet, thinking about all of her Christmases with Jack.

"But I want to start new traditions."

He nods. "So, what do you want for Christmas?"

"You and I don't need to exchange gifts."

"Ha! I think I know enough about women to know they don't mean it when they say things like that."

"Santa already has presents for us."

"Right. Santa. This means you are getting something for me, and I have nothing for you."

"We both have gifts from Santa. That is good enough for me."

Giving her a look that says he isn't buying it, he begins to think of what to get her.

Kiera and Ryan make a decision for her to spend Christmas and the few days before with her family, and he with his mom. They will see each other on the 26th. Kiera and her brother, Kian, five years apart, share a birthday on December 23rd. Kevin is 1½ years younger than his older brother. The December birthday has always been a big celebration for them with friends on the island. Kian makes a comment to his sister. "Ryan won't be here, will he?"

Ryan wasn't sure at first about spending Christmas with Colin. He does have fun watching Simon and Sam madly tear off wrapping paper. Their reactions to the gifts are amusing. Assembling toys and keeping the boys busy playing with them all day is an enormous help to their dad.

Colin gives Hannah a box of liquor-filled chocolates and some scented candles.

"Santa" brought him a book by Dr. Rangihiroa Panoho called *Māori Art: History, Architecture, Landscape & Theory*, with over 300 illustrations and many images never published before by renowned New Zealand photographers. She searched his home office high and low, but was happy to learn he did not already have the book at the university.

He also receives many different snacks to have with his beer, all of which he appreciates. Colin makes a funny face when opening a box filled with new socks. Without saying anything, Hannah moves over to stick her finger in the hole on the bottom of his left sock.

"Oh, OK. I get it."

The boys laugh hysterically. Their dad wads up each pair into a ball to throw at them, which they return, and this goes on for a while.

She is pleased to see his spirits lifted, at least for now.

He then unwraps his last present, pulling out a navy-blue cap with a matching Texas star outlined in white.

"You will *never* turn me into a Dallas Cowboys football fan," he proclaims.

"We shall see," she states with a mischievous grin.

Hannah got creative with ways to gift money to her son, hiding it in various objects, such as rolling Australian fifty-dollar notes and placing them inside environmentally friendly, reusable, washable drinking straws.

She tells him about their relatives over Christmas dinner. Ryan is fascinated by Clay Ryan's company, the energy-saving transformer units, and the idea of carbon capture on vehicles, a concept he has never heard of before. He explains how concrete, plastics, fuel, and carbonated drinks are made from captured carbon.

"People will drink it?"

"Yes, Mom. They already do. That is what carbonation is. It is carbon dioxide. Now, soda companies can capture their own emissions, filter it, and put it in their products."

Observing the confused expression on her face, he asks, "What did you think carbonation was?"

"Never thought about it."

"Since only so much can be reused for products, a lot of captured carbon is injected deep underground in reservoirs, which is controversial. Australia is the perfect place for doing this with its immense availability of geologically stable land. Other countries could send their captured carbon here for storage to increase the chances of the world meeting the 2050 goal of net-zero emissions."

She knows nothing about the subject, and Colin, who usually has something to say about every topic, is quiet for the entire meal.

"I wish I could talk with Clay about this."

"You can."

After sending a *Merry Christmas* text to Patrick with a request for his son's contact information, she hears back straight away.

Ryan decides to contact Clay in a few weeks.

Hugging him goodbye, she mentions an idea about Kiera. "Tell her she is welcome to stay at the garage apartment until the two of you marry."

"That would be good. Thanks."

In conversation, it came out that her friend Naomi is moving into a flat soon with another teacher. Kiera was invited there, but has reservations about doing so because it will be crowded, and she doesn't know this other girl.

Hannah does not understand why he wouldn't have his fiancée be with him, but she isn't going to touch that topic with a ten-foot pole. His apartment is small, though. The couple will be moving into a much bigger place after their wedding.

The following day, Ryan takes the water taxi to the island and a van to the Donnelly family home. After greeting everyone, he hands out small presents from his mother to Kiera's dad and brothers. The boys get up to leave, uninterested in it all, but he stops them.

"There is something in this other bag from me that I think you two will like."

Kian rips off the paper to find the latest video game console, including a generous gift card for downloading games. The brothers scream.

"I could almost hug you," says Kevin to his future brother-in-law.

In the third bag are science experiment kits and books for Kiera to use during the Environmental Science Club meetings she will lead as a teacher. One kit demonstrates how to make seawater drinkable by extracting the salt, which, unfortunately, requires a lot of energy for real-world use, as he explains. "For this reason, only a handful of countries, mainly in the Middle East, employ this method."

Returning to the mainland a few hours later, they drive to his complex. A new car with a big green bow on top is in the parking lot.

"I guess someone got a car for Christmas. What a gift!" she exclaims.

The pair walks over to the shiny red electric vehicle.

"It sure is nice," Kiera comments. "I like this shade of red."

"It is called passion red."

She scrunches up her forehead and gives him an adorable, questioning look. "How do you know?"

He reaches into his pocket, taking out a keyless device to hand her.

"It's yours. Merry Christmas and Happy Birthday!"

"You're kidding."

"I'm not."

"You got me a car?"

"I did."

"That is crazy."

"Why? You don't have a car. You need one, and we are getting married. Aren't you happy?"

"Of course, I am. Thank you." She stands stiffly, trying to make sense of her discomfort.

"Let's go for a drive."

Becoming noticeably upset, her voice wavers. "I don't have a license."

"Why don't we go inside and talk? Then, I will take you for a drive."

Sitting on the couch, there is silence for only a minute or two, but it feels like much longer to Ryan.

"Are you having second thoughts about marrying me?" he asks.

"No! Not at all." She throws her arms around him. "I'm so sorry. I didn't mean for you to think something like that. It's just now I realize for the first time how you come from money, and I don't."

"I don't come from money. That isn't true."

"What you don't understand is that a lack of money has been a concern my whole life. My dad and great-uncle basically shared a salary for years, and then came the expenses from Mum's illness."

He isn't sure what to say.

She continues. "My scholarships are only partial. I will be paying back student loans for years. I guess these are things we should discuss before we get married."

"Can I ask how much?"

"$45,000"

"That's nothing."

"Nothing?" She can't believe her ears.

"Not nothing, but it isn't an issue at all."

"It makes me feel like we come from different worlds even more for you to see that as nothing."

"I told you, I didn't mean nothing, but we will have that paid off within our first year of marriage with both of us working. And the money for your car and mine came from a small inheritance my grandfather left me. It is funny, actually, how the majority of his money has now gone to purchase electric vehicles. He hated that idea."

"Why?"

"I don't know. His career was in the oil and gas industry. He liked big trucks and suburbans. To him, the subcompact car I drove wasn't even a real automobile, let alone something electric."

"What is a suburban?"

"It's like an SUV but bigger. And, by the way, this car is for both of us. I don't want to have to drop you off for work at the high school at 6:30 in the morning."

With a laugh, he proceeds to state his case. "Also, I can't pick you up at three in the afternoon, and you aren't going to want to wait until 5:30. You will be running out of that place!"

She makes a fake frown, pretending to be offended. "I plan to be thoroughly involved with after-school tutoring and clubs, thank you very much. I won't be running out of there."

"Seriously, though, Kiera. Don't misunderstand. Life costs more and more these days, and buying a house is crazy expensive. It isn't like we will have tons of money to do whatever we want. We will always need to live modestly."

"I understand. Believe me, I don't have extravagant tastes, and I don't care about a fancy house or clothes."

"I'm the same way. And I drove my old car for seven years with paint chipping off because it was already 14 years old when my parents got it for me. I went to public schools and a state university. We lived in a small house in a regular neighborhood. I was required to work during the summers but not during the school year until graduate school. Then I worked year-round as a research assistant."

"I know. You are a hard worker." She puts her hand on his.

"So yes, I recognize that I have been fortunate in my life, but I didn't get whatever I wanted."

"You know, when I asked to meet your friends and sister, I wasn't even thinking about how much it would cost."

"Again, not to sound like money is no object, but if it is important to you, we should go on the trip. You don't need to worry about the money," he assures her and then grins. "My mom already told me that she will pay for most of it as an engagement gift. She thinks your idea is great."

Kiera arrives at Colin's. First, she spends time with the boys. They show her all of their presents from Santa. Her future mother-in-law accompanies her upstairs later. "If you need anything, just come down or text me, OK?"

Hannah enjoys seeing the bride-to-be each day. She was interested to hear that the young couple embraced the season the week before by visiting a holiday market, playing Christmas mini golf, and going to the square for Christmas carols around an enormous tree with laser displays. Ryan mentioned none of this. These are activities she had always wanted to do this time of year, but could not get her husband or son to agree.

Naomi lets her friend know that the other teacher was proposed to on Christmas Day and is now moving to Sydney. New plans are made for Kiera to stay with Naomi after the trip. Hannah understands, but had hoped to bond more with the girl.

Following a successful clothes shopping outing with Kiera, Hannah takes Rosie to the veterinarian for a checkup. When first adopting the cat many months ago, she was surprised to learn that rabies does not exist in Australia. Of course, a yearly rabies vaccine is required in the US, which is an important subject for pet owners and anyone bitten by an unknown dog, as she was years ago.

While in the vet's waiting room, she flips through a magazine, *Business View Oceania*, with an article about a historic hotel called the InterContinental Melbourne The Rialto. The intriguing building is tan and red with columns, arches, and steeples. Built in 1891, this was the height of Melbourne's boom-time gold rush, when it was the richest city in the world. The other structures surrounding the hotel were demolished in the 1970s and replaced with modern glass buildings.

Filled with excitement once again about Melbourne, the trip she never got to go on, Hannah suggests to Colin at dinner that the two of them get away for a long weekend there. He indicates a lack of interest, so she drops the subject, hoping to bring it back up another time.

During the night, she has a dream that they actually do go to Melbourne. After having lunch in the hotel's atrium restaurant, the couple ventures over to the Block Arcade, a historical shopping area. He teases her about wearing blue jeans and a T-shirt and not being up on fashion.

While making their way back along Collins Street, he tells her how people used to dress up and come here to the north side for the shops and cafes. "They would walk from one end to the other in hopes of being seen by other wealthy people."

As the hotel comes into view, Hannah sees someone rushing towards them who resembles her husband. He runs up and wraps his arms around her.

"I've been searching all over for you. What are you still doing with this man?"

It *is* Jack.

Nineteen

It is New Year's Eve. The plan is to attend a carnival and fireworks display. Hannah is thrilled that Ryan and Kiera are coming as well, so they can go on the rides with Simon and Sam. Her body isn't what it used to be, and she now has lightheadedness and vertigo issues, something she has not shared with anyone. The next day, the soon-to-be Mr. & Mrs. Laren will leave for their trip, landing in Texas on January 2nd.

At the last minute, Colin mentions he is not feeling well.

"Should I take the boys anyway, or should we stay home?"

"It would be great if you could go ahead. I have to warn you about fireworks. Sam, in the past, has become very upset by the sound of them."

"Ryan and I can drive separately, and I will give Sam the choice."

They leave with Colin lying on his bed. He gets up soon after because he isn't sick but desperately wants time alone and can't shake this fatigue.

Deeply disappointed to learn the day before that there would be no movie premiere for his Hongi Hika film, the news was like a punch in the gut. Instead of a theatrical release, as he imagined, a streaming service purchased the rights to add it to the lineup in March. There is not much of a marketing plan in place either. All of this is beyond his control and for the production company to manage. He can only hope his hard work doesn't get dropped for underperformance and become forgotten.

Hannah and the boys walk in the door around 10:30. It turned out the town had a drone show of lights instead of the usual fireworks. Sam loved it. She puts them to bed and sleeps on the couch since Colin is in his room with the door shut. Kiera is in the garage apartment for the last time.

The following morning, she drives to pick up her son. They will come back to get Kiera, who was panicking about not being ready and sleeping in too late.

Ryan needed to give his mom instructions on feeding the aquarium critters anyway.

She hands him a small bag to put with his carry-on items. "It is only one and a half hours to Sydney, but the flight from Sydney to Dallas is over 15 hours. And then it is 22 hours from Portland, Oregon, to Brisbane. You need entertainment. This mini-DVD player will connect to your laptop."

He flips through the DVD case. She knows he has never been one for mainstream movies that would be available on the airline's selection, and there were many technical difficulties on the flight over anyway, when she tried to watch.

"Kiera will love *Turtle: The Incredible Journey*. It is about the loggerhead turtle's 25-year journey from Florida to the North Atlantic, Africa, the Caribbean, and then back to Florida to lay eggs. Only one in 10,000 turtles completes the entire journey."

"Thanks, Mom."

"There are 9 ½ hours of *Jacques Cousteau - Pacific Explorations*, including five episodes in Australia and three in New Zealand. I watched it earlier in the year. Cousteau made it a point to have many interactions with Aboriginal Australians and the Māori, which I liked."

"Great."

Opening a second bag, she pulls out two books. "I also got you Tim Winton's latest book, *Juice*, and his book *Shallows* for Kiera, about a young woman who joins an anti-whaling group, upsetting her family and community. Then there are granola bars, cookies, and other snacks, and look at this..."

She unfolds a small, navy-blue blanket with a sea turtle. "I read that airplane blankets are sometimes not washed for 30 days. Not what you want to curl up with."

He shakes his head at the thought and then says, "We'd better get going."

"Right." During the process of collecting his things, Hannah thinks of something else. "You know that being there will bring back a lot of memories. Your dad would want you to remember the good times with him, be happy, and live your best life. Don't forget that."

She gives him a quick, partial hug since their hands are filled with bags.

They arrive at the airport. Driving away from the drop-off area, she hopes the couple will have a great trip. Her husband used to say, "You don't really know someone until you travel with them."

After dating for a few months, she and Jack drove nine hours to Big Bend National Park for a rafting trip, spending two nights along the river, camping out. Jack knew she was the one for him upon returning from a successful vacation.

She could not believe the rafting trip did not include accommodations with bathroom facilities. It was a shock when learning that the group planned to stay along the river wherever they happened to stop, sleeping on the ground without tents. She remembers feeling dirtier instead of cleaner from trying to bathe and wash her hair in the Rio Grande. Hannah did not complain. Apparently, if she had, there may never have been a marriage or a Ryan Philip Laren.

Ryan and Kiera board their second flight of the day to Dallas. They watch the loggerhead movie, taking a long nap under the turtle blanket afterwards.

She wakes up before he does and uses the laptop to explore facts about the destinations related to their trip.

Later, they read their respective Tim Winton books, followed by an episode of Jacques Cousteau. While at the airport earlier, they listened to the John Denver song "Calypso," which is a tribute to Cousteau and his research ship by that name. Ryan explained that John had the privilege to go on an outing with the oceanographer.

After an hour of viewing scuba divers in the depths of the ocean surrounded by astonishing things, she feels hopeful that someday her asthma will be controlled and not prevent her from doing whatever she wants to do.

Ryan falls asleep, but she keeps the DVD playing.

When the second Cousteau show ends, Kiera puts the laptop away, managing to do so without waking him up. Unable to resist taking a peek at the night sky, she opens the window shade, which does rouse him.

"Sorry, but check this out. The Milky Way is visible from where we are right now. Isn't it amazing?"

He leans over to peer out the window.

The night sky is lit up with stars, and in the middle are long billows of dust in a faint band of light.

"Can we visit the Space Center in Houston?"

Groggily, he replies, "Sure, we can do that."

"My dad loves to talk about space and the planets. Do you know much about Astronomy?"

"No, I don't."

"Dad got me interested when he pointed up to the sky one night, and a planet looked like it was moving backward."

"That sounds familiar."

"It is called apparent retrograde motion. Since Earth has a faster orbit, we witnessed Jupiter appearing to zigzag and move backward as Earth caught up to the slower-moving planet. That has always been a favorite memory of mine. And this was out at the beach without a telescope."

"Cool. I do recall when Pluto was no longer considered a planet. My mom didn't like that. Not sure why she cared, except she grew up being taught there were nine planets. And I remember a school moon project when I was probably eight or nine. She and I went outside at night for a month to draw the moon in all of its phases. It was a nice thing to do before bed."

"I love sitting outside, gazing at the moon. Well, I'm sorry I woke you. We should sleep some more now." Kiera shuts the shade, brings the blanket over them, and they close their eyes.

A minute later, she asks, "Did you know sky brightness at night has been increasing significantly every year?"

"No."

"Of course, it isn't just about being able to see the stars. The brightness is a sign of energy being used inefficiently, resulting in more carbon dioxide emissions. I joined *DarkSky International,* an organization with a mission to educate people on how excessive artificial light can harm wildlife, humans, and our climate. They work with communities to install lighting that reduces light pollution. In April, there is an event called International Dark Sky Week. Telescopes will be available. The purpose is to encourage everyone to use lights only when necessary and at the lowest levels, with warm colors such as orange and yellow, which are the least disruptive to wildlife. We should go."

"We will."

They both drift off to sleep.

Arriving in Texas mid-morning, they rent a car. Kiera is terrified of the Dallas/Fort Worth traffic. Ryan sees her holding onto the passenger door armrest. "I know it is a little scary with everyone going so fast, and sometimes you will have a wall on one side and an 18-wheeler on the other. I have done this many times. Don't worry."

She does not respond, so he changes the subject. "After we check into the hotel, there is a good steakhouse for lunch, and then we can go on a carriage ride through the Stockyards."

"I don't eat beef, remember?" she says, still anxious as a motorcycle speeds past, cutting over in front of them.

"Actually, I don't eat steak either. I grew up going there with my parents. I always get roasted chicken and a baked potato."

"Sounds good."

They reach the Stockyards Hotel, a historic brick building. To Kiera, the lobby is like something out of the classic Western movies she watched with her dad. A carpeted staircase with wooden banisters is front and center. The maroon walls are covered in paintings of horses, cattle, and cowboys. A wood-paneled check-in counter extends above their heads, similar to an old-time bank or train station.

After walking upstairs, they enter her room first. It has the biggest bed she has ever seen, with pillows decorated in yellow roses and the state flag of Texas. The wooden headboard has a star carved into it. A blanket over the back of the couch has a map of the state.

She sits in the rocking chair, admiring a painting of a bluebonnet field. "This is so nice."

The lamp by her has a miniature saddle in the middle. A bronze statue of cowboys on horses rounding up cattle is on the coffee table. Every piece of furniture is solid wood, even the toilet seat.

A little while later, the couple descends the stairs to the H3 Ranch restaurant. It is busy, so they are shown to a booth across from the bar. Kiera sees deer heads on the wall and saddles for bar stools. Above the bar is the backside of an animal with its rear end and tail. The sign says Buffalo Butt Beer.

"My mom loves that beer," he shares.

"Do you hunt?"

"No. My dad took me quail hunting when I was little. When he shot one, I cried and said, 'Why do you hate birds?' He bought some quail from a breeder and built a huge cage for them in the backyard to show me that he didn't hate birds. They lived for a long time. It was down to one male and one female for the last two years, and when the female died, the male was so upset that he was hurting himself trying to get out. With companionship, he was fine, but not when alone. We took him to the woods and let him go. Somehow, he flew away, even though he had been in an enclosure for years, only able to flutter short distances."

Ryan tells her some history of the Stockyards, once the largest livestock-trading center in the southwest, and the hotel. "Bonnie & Clyde stayed here in 1933 while on the run. Tomorrow morning, we can see the cattle drive. You haven't lived until you see one," he laughs.

"I feel like you are making fun of it."

"No, I'm just being silly, but I'm not a cowboy or western person. I don't like country music. I have never worn western wear, not even cowboy boots. We did go horseback riding on a few of our vacations. I would much rather be at a beach."

The pair enjoys a nice lunch. "That was so good," she comments after finishing the last bite of pecan pie.

"Time for a carriage ride," he announces.

As they step outside, a Fort Worth police officer is standing under the awning. She spots the panther on his police badge. When the man's eyes meet hers, Kiera says, "I was looking at your badge and the panther on top. On the trip here, I read about the history of Fort Worth and the story behind the panther."

Smiling, he asks, "Where are you from?"

"Australia."

"Enjoy your stay."

"Thank you."

After going down the sidewalk, Ryan inquires, "What is this about the panther?"

"I thought you would know."

"I don't."

"In the 1870s, an economic crisis and terrible winter storms made things so slow in Fort Worth that a panther was seen asleep by the courthouse because no one was around to chase it away. Residents adopted the name Panther City, and the panther is on the Fort Worth police badges, among other places." She continues with other facts and information.

"It seems like you know more about where I grew up than I do."

At the carriage ride location, she is surprised to see such enormous horses. They take a seat inside, and the driver places a blanket over them. It is cold but not unpleasant. Kiera thought Ryan's mom was so sweet to buy her some new shirts and a jacket for the trip when they went shopping. She had no idea ice and snow are often an issue in winter here. Hannah told her it could be 80 degrees or 20. "You just never know." An internet search translated this to 26 or minus 6 in Celsius.

Hannah and Colin had not spent much time together the last few days. She knows he is buried in papers for the summer course and has been out of sorts and a little under the weather.

When entering the living room to get something, he sees her checking her phone. "Are you expecting to hear from someone?"

"No. I don't want to see any messages. I want Ryan to be safe, enjoying his trip, and not thinking about his mother. Believe me."

"So, you are worried about him?" he asks, sitting down on the couch.

"I always worry. They could be in a car accident or get attacked. The possibilities are endless in my mind. Ever since he left home at 18, if I don't hear from him for a while, I am not entirely convinced he is still alive. So no, I don't want to hear from him because he is with Kiera, but on the other hand, it would be nice if he could send a *having a great time* text, or something.

He gives her an understanding smile. Hannah holds his gaze, deciding, at that moment, she is ready to tell him she loves him. The following night, they have a play in Brisbane and an after-party to attend, so she will tell him then.

She had not fully acknowledged how hurt he must have been when not reciprocating his *I Love You* three months before. He probably feels as if she will never get to the same place, and this is what has been bothering him.

How could she not have recognized this?

Rosie comes into the room and jumps up into Colin's lap. The cat had never done this before. *Maybe they both realize they love him.*

SYDNEY, AUSTRALIA

The enterprisers receive the update they have been waiting for. The investors are funding them to move on with their operation, relocate to a large warehouse, and begin producing units for wider distribution. First, they need to hire people to assist with production. Theresa tells them the best bet is to hire undergrad engineering students all on a part-time basis.

Interviewing students who are just like they were a few years back is a fun activity. Clay especially likes a red-headed girl named Amy. Theresa secretly gives the thumbs down on her after noticing his attraction. She does not want anything distracting Clay, which isn't fair, but they agreed it had to be unanimous for each candidate hired. Clay has no idea that it was Theresa who did not select Amy, or the reason why. They all privately typed in their rankings of the candidates, so there was no discussion among the three.

In the morning, Ryan and Kiera exit the Fort Worth hotel to witness the cattle drive. Before long, they hear the clomping of hooves, the sound of a bell worn by the lead longhorn, and see men dressed in cowboy attire riding horses while shouting cattle calls. It is a slow procession. Kiera had imagined before that the longhorns would be running past them. It was definitely a sight she had never seen.

Some of the animals and cowboys remain behind to entertain with rope tricks. She declines the offer to sit on a longhorn and have her picture taken.

"Can we go to the John Wayne Museum now? I saw the brochure in the lobby."

"Sure. I didn't know you were a fan."

"One time, my dad and I watched six hours of his movies back-to-back. It was a nice day to be with him, without my brothers around."

On the route to the museum, they pass by a mechanical bull.

She turns to him, "Are you going to ride it?"

"No way!"

He enjoys seeing Kiera interested in the museum. Afterwards, they stop at a petting zoo to feed the goats before it is time to visit his cousin.

"We could go on a Ghost Tour tonight with stories about local paranormal activity," he suggests.

"No ghosts!"

"Because you believe they exist?"

"Yes!"

Nodding his head in agreement, "OK. No ghosts."

On the drive to see his cousin, Tiffany, he explains that she and her husband, Dale, live in the house he grew up in. His parents gave them a good deal on it when he went to college, and they moved to the hill country. The couple has a 10-month-old baby girl. And Sammie the cat is there too.

"My dad said Sammie communicated to him somehow that she wanted to stay. So, if you believe the cat is a reincarnation, it makes sense my grandmother wanted to be part of her granddaughter Tiffany's life."

"It does make perfect sense. Have you talked to your aunt lately?"

"No. I feel bad because she will call and leave a message, and I will text instead of calling back. I find it hard to speak to her because all I can think about is the shooting. And also, I don't like to talk on the phone. Except to you, of course."

"Of course," she jests. "But your aunt must be very busy with being a Congresswoman."

"Yes. I thought she would drop out of the election after the shooting, but she didn't. I don't understand why anyone wants the job, but it is good that some do. I hate politics myself with the whole Democrat vs. Republican thing. I wish all politicians had to run as individuals without all this party nonsense, but that will never happen."

He turns onto his old street. "See, this is just a normal neighborhood of small homes. Nothing fancy. Some call them starter homes or cookie-cutter homes because they are similar. It is nicer on the inside. My dad put in a lot of upgrades."

After pointing out the houses of his childhood friends, they park in the driveway. A tall, thin woman with long, dark brown hair, the same shade as Ryan's but with golden highlights, opens the door. While his cousin is preparing some snacks in the kitchen and Dale is on the phone, he gives her a tour of the house.

"This was my room growing up. They decided to keep my old bunk beds. For some reason, they are already planning on having four children."

"Do you think four is too many?"

"Yes, I do. I wouldn't want to be outnumbered. Two is enough, don't you think?"

"I suppose so," she says with a grin.

"My sister's old room is the baby's room." Baby Ashley is napping and has been sick, so they do their best to speak softly. Sammie is in there with her.

Ryan leads her to the backyard. "And this is the tree fort my dad built for me."

They climb up the wooden planks nailed to the tree and sit down inside.

"This is where Savannah broke my heart. I was six or seven. We were boyfriend/girlfriend for maybe a week, and then she told me she didn't like me anymore and had a new boyfriend."

"I thought you never had a girlfriend before."

He laughs. "I don't think a week in the first-grade counts. We probably barely talked to one another."

"I told you that I never had a boyfriend before, but I had never even been on a date until you."

"Why do I find that hard to believe?"

"It's true."

She wants to tell him she loves him. She wants to give him a big, long kiss. But she doesn't.

Instead, she changes the subject. "You know, we don't have any pictures of us together."

"You are right. I guess we don't. Do you want me to ask them to take pictures?"

"No, we can ask your sister."

"Good idea. I don't use social media much. I never post pictures or think about taking pictures other than of marine life, but I absolutely want pictures of us."

With a nod of agreement and a realization that nothing is going to happen in this tree, she suggests they go back inside to visit.

As Kiera sits in the living room with Tiffany and Dale, she is uneasy and quiet for a while. Then she asks about their little girl, and Tiffany is delighted to show her all the baby pictures they have taken. She also brings out photos from her high school and college cheerleading days. There is an album of herself in every different dance costume and cheerleading outfit she has worn since the age of six.

They depart, and Ryan is relieved that the subject of his dad or the shooting never came up.

Along the way back to the hotel, she observes his phone flashing on for a second and sees the name Kim, but doesn't say anything. His phone is set to one ring before going to voicemail and is on silent, so he is unaware of the call coming through. This greatly bothers her. He had mentioned Kim several times regarding work projects they were involved in last semester. Is this why she is calling when it is still holiday break for his department, or is it something else?

Twenty

On the night of the play, Simon and Sam go to Jane's house for her daughter to earn money by babysitting.

Hannah falls asleep during the performance. Colin gives her a nudge, along with an irritated glance.

At the after-party are actors and actresses he has known for years, including his friend, Donald, who wrote the play.

"Glad you could make it, mate." The man gives him a hearty handshake.

"This is Hannah."

They are interrupted by other people Donald hasn't seen in a while, so he moves on to socialize elsewhere.

A woman enters wearing the sexiest red dress. Tall and gorgeous, probably early 30s, her brunette hair with highlights flows just past her shoulders. Hannah sees him staring and then realizes the familiar woman is staring back. Now, she is headed in their direction.

"Colin, so good to see you."

Overcome with emotion, he isn't thinking straight and forgets to make introductions.

"And who is this?"

He stammers. "This. This is Hannah. Hannah, this is Monique."

The ladies acknowledge one another with a nod as Hannah suddenly recognizes her from the pictures she first found of Colin on the internet, close to a year ago.

In an odd voice, he asks, "How long have you been in town?"

"I moved back last month after deciding to give up acting on the show. I missed my family. My sister had triplets, if you can believe that. And a year later, her husband left her. She needs me. Also, my mother has not been in good health."

Falling silent, he is shocked to learn his former lover has returned.

"Wow, triplets. That is incredible. Your sister will be thankful for your help, and so will your mother," remarks Hannah, attempting to make things less awkward as he is clearly affected by seeing her again.

Someone else comes up to greet Monique, and the two go off together.

Hannah puts her arm around him, but he makes an uncomfortable face. They have uneasy exchanges with a few more people and leave the party early.

At first, neither one speaks on the drive home. Although she had seen coverage of their relationship on the internet, she did not want to admit to looking up the details of his love life online. She finally asks the question, knowing full well the answer.

"Did you and Monique use to date?"

"Yes."

"Were you in love with her?"

"Yes."

Nothing else is said. She abandons her plan to tell Colin she loves him that night.

Kiera and Ryan have breakfast in Fort Worth before leaving for Waco, a 90-minute drive away, where Leo attends the technical school's robotics program.

She can see he is unhappy. "Is everything OK?

"Yes."

With a deep breath, he decides to share what is on his mind. "Being at my old house has me a little down about my dad. My mom warned me I might feel this way. She said he would want me to focus on the good memories. Easier said than done."

"I know all about that. I'm sorry."

In the car, they listen to his favorite DFW radio station until the signal is lost. Upon reaching the city, he points out some Waco landmarks.

"After lunch, we can go to the river and walk across the Waco Suspension Bridge. This was the only good way to cross the Brazos River in the late 1800s to continue to Fort Worth, especially with cattle. The toll was five cents per cow. People were also charged. Finally, the county bought the bridge, ending the tolls. To avoid paying, some floated their herds down the river."

"I didn't know cows could swim," laughs Kiera.

"They can naturally float and tread water."

Their first stop is the Mammoth National Monument, since they have over an hour before it is time to meet Leo for lunch.

"Australia never had mammoths, but I learned about them in school. They weighed over 9,000 kilos."

"You know I have no idea what that means," he reminds her.

"Pounds would be over twice that. So, closer to 20,000 pounds."

They examine mammoth fossils, read about them in displays, and walk along a wooded trail. It is much warmer today and doesn't feel like winter at all.

"I just remembered why my mom suggested we come here. She read how scientists want to clone living elephant cells containing mammoth DNA to bring mammoth-like creatures back to life on the Arctic tundra. The tundra's permafrost contains extreme amounts of carbon that, once thawed, will go into the atmosphere and raise global temperatures. By having giant animals continually uprooting trees and shrubs, scientists think this will allow natural grasses and herbs to grow, keeping the ground frozen."

"Do you think it could work?"

"I don't know, but in large numbers, they would trample the snow cover to keep snow from insulating the ground and allow the permafrost to feel the bitter cold."

As Ryan speaks, a bright red cardinal goes flying past them.

"Look at him," Kiera points. "Just beautiful." She pulls out her phone to get some pictures.

"Native Americans believe that if you spot a cardinal, you will have good luck within 12 days of the sighting, so we will see what our luck brings," he smiles, remembering how his grandmother was a bird-watching enthusiast.

They get back in the car to meet for lunch. "Here we are. This is Crickets, my favorite restaurant. I used to come here with my parents. I recommend the shrimp tacos. My dad and I would play pool and foosball here."

"I know what foosball is, but what do you mean by pool?"

"I believe the British and Australian term is billiards." Ryan teases her on their many word differences as they walk across the parking lot.

Leo and his girlfriend Felicia are waiting in a booth. Felicia is warm and friendly. She tells Kiera about moving to Texas with her mom and two brothers after their home was destroyed when Hurricane Katrina hit New Orleans. The family moved in with relatives in Houston. Now, she lives in Waco, studying to become a nurse.

Kiera proceeds to give a lecture on how climate change leads to storms with higher rainfall and flooding. Aware of going on too long, she changes the topic, telling this new acquaintance about life on the island, growing up with two brothers, and how her dad just had surgery. Felicia's mother is in poor health, and she never knew her father.

Grabbing Kiera's hand, she decides to lighten the mood. "Let me see this gorgeous engagement ring." Leo rolls his eyes, worried his significant other is getting ideas.

"How is school going?" Ryan asks his long-time friend.

"Good. We recently completed a project working on the coolest robot for the police department. It can go into places and provide video to officers before they go inside and put their lives at risk."

Felicia becomes annoyed. "Why didn't you tell me about this?"

"You have told me how you don't like robots and believe I am contributing to people losing their jobs."

She explains her position. "My uncle lost his job at a warehouse after they brought in robots. It was a scary time. We came close to being kicked out of the rental house and had to get food from community food pantries until he found another job. My mom did not make much at the grocery store."

Giving her boyfriend a dirty look, she adds, "Of course, I recognize the value of using robots to save human lives."

"What does your uncle do now?" inquires Ryan.

"Pest control. Turns out, he likes driving around and going to different places instead of being at a warehouse all day."

"That's good."

"And there will never be a shortage of bugs," Kiera remarks. "They are multiplying even faster with climate change."

Their food arrives, and the group continues to talk about various subjects. Felicia asks where they are staying in Galveston.

"We rented a small house by the water," Ryan replies.

An excited expression comes across Leo's face. "Awesome, a whole house. Can we come?"

He slowly answers, "Of course," eyeing his fiancée, who indicates the situation is all right with her. "We are meeting your brother tomorrow night for dinner. Lewis is busy with a project during the day, even though he is on winter break."

"Sounds like a plan," his friend confirms.

Kiera excitedly talks about how they will visit Moody Gardens the following morning. She mentions the Coral Reef Rescue Project.

"Their aquarium lab received corals from Florida to keep them sheltered from disease. Later, the offspring from this coral will be sent back to restore the reef. Of course, coral is facing more diseases from warmer waters caused by climate change."

Felicia knows her boyfriend is not interested. "I think the two of you should just go. We will go to The Pier and then The Strand."

"What's that?"

"The Strand is a cool place with shops, restaurants, and bars in an area where the buildings are well over 100 years old," she explains.

"And The Pier has carnival rides and a roller coaster." Pointing to Ryan, Leo continues, "This guy doesn't like rides. Can you believe that? I can't wait to ride the Iron Shark roller coaster."

"I've never been on a roller coaster, and I am fine keeping it that way. Are you going before or after you drink a bunch of beer?"

"Before. I have learned my lesson about that."

Ryan picks up the tab for lunch.

"Thanks, Dude."

"No problem. You are a student, after all."

"Oh, one more thing," Kiera remembers as the four walk to the parking lot. "We are stopping at the Space Center on the way. You can join us."

"That's OK," says Leo. "We won't leave for a couple of hours, so we will probably get to Galveston about the same time."

At Space Center Houston, Kiera leads them to the Moon Exhibit first. "This is all about Artemis. I have been following it."

He shakes his head. "I don't know anything about it."

Surprised to hear this, she shares what she knows.

"Artemis I involved NASA launching an unmanned spacecraft to orbit the moon. Artemis II will have a crew of astronauts aboard for a flyby test past the moon. On the third mission, they will land on the moon. Artemis IV has the crew constructing the first lunar space station."

Moving on to the next exhibit, she tells him how technology developed by NASA for space travel combats climate change with new ways to trap greenhouse gases and test for emissions. Ryan is intrigued.

She could spend hours here, but decides to cut it short since there isn't enough time for everything. "Well, let's get going to Galveston."

"We can stay longer," he insists.

"It's fine. I am ready to get to the shore."

They are quiet on the drive until turning beside the ocean, where Kiera notices the road is a good distance above the beach. She sees a wall built up along the edge of the sand. "That is a tall wall."

"Yes. The seawall is there to prevent destruction from hurricanes. Years ago, Galveston was a busy port city. The Strand was known as the Wall Street of the South. When the hurricane hit in 1900, the community was devastated. Thousands were killed. The seawall was constructed, but the area was never the same. Houston became the go-to port city. We saw a movie about the topic when I visited with my parents."

The small beachfront rental is in an area where the homes are modest but well-kept. The house is white with gray shutters on all of the windows. It sits about eight feet above the ground on gray-painted beams. A large porch covers the entire front, wrapping around halfway to the left side with stairs on the right. There are three rocking chairs and a porch swing. Underneath is a picnic table and a metal table with four matching chairs and a grill.

"I guess we can do a cookout," she suggests as they walk up the steps.

He makes an uncertain face. "I have never used a grill, have you?"

"No."

Their friends are waiting on the swing. They had parked in back.

Once inside, Leo claims one of the bedrooms. "We'll take this room if that's OK," he says with a big grin. The couple had been apart for the holidays and school break. They both share dorm rooms with other people.

Ryan and Kiera inspect the other two options. "Which one do you want?" he asks.

She chooses the room with a seashell comforter and curtains. The last one has a surfboard hanging above the bed.

They decide to go to the grocery store. Ryan walks down the hall to ask their guests if staying in for dinner is an agreeable plan, but realizes he can't because they are otherwise occupied.

Felicia and Leo have shut the door to their room and are making no effort to be quiet. This makes their hosts uncomfortable.

Not a word is spoken on the way to the store. Ryan knows they should discuss the topic since he has no idea how she feels. He tries to find the words but can't.

Later, the couples eat pizza while streaming a military movie. Leo and Ryan have spent countless hours playing jet-flying games over the years. The two are blown away by the cinematography that makes them feel like they are in the cockpit. After an intense fighting segment, the young men turn to their significant others and notice both ladies are asleep.

"I guess I should have asked what movie they wanted to see," confesses Ryan.

Leo shrugs his shoulders, and they keep watching, engrossed until the end.

Hannah and Colin wake up pretending as if nothing happened the evening before, at least giving the appearance of this to one another. She spent the night with him as was usual on Fridays.

When he is in the shower, she googles Monique and re-visits the posts about them. They were quite the couple, photographed many times around Australia promoting the play based on historical figures from his book about colonial New South Wales. Donald wrote the screenplay and directed the drama. Monique was one of the lead actresses. *Could he still be in love with her?*

As the day progresses, Colin finds it more difficult to be in the same house with Hannah. He had wanted her in his bed, but in his imagination, she was Monique.

After checking emails, he reads the report about testing negative for a specific gene associated with Alzheimer's disease. While relieved, he knows this does not mean dementia is not in his future, and he has been consumed with thoughts of aging ever since meeting her relatives. The bloodwork did reveal a Vitamin D deficiency, so a high-dose supplement was prescribed. Hopefully, this condition is the reason for his fatigue, mood changes, and sleep problems.

In case these test results mean he is all of a sudden supposed to be cheerful, he decides not to share the findings with Hannah yet. Being with her but obsessing over Monique makes him anything but content.

Four years ago, he was completely in love with Monique, and it hurt deeply when she ended their relationship. He used to go crazy seeing pictures of her with the young man she left him for. The soap opera co-stars' onscreen romance promptly turned into a real-life one. It took over a year for him to feel like he was over her, but now, it is as if no time has passed. The feelings have all come back, and he is engulfed in them.

Colin reminisces about the exciting times they shared when the play based on his book became a hit in Brisbane. Book sales skyrocketed. He received invitations from several universities to present his research at on-campus seminars. This was coordinated with the play's tour locations. The production moved on to Sydney, Melbourne, and Adelaide. He cherished the time spent traveling with Monique and was mesmerized watching her on stage. So were others, as she received glowing reviews.

The positive critiques led to Monique being contacted by a soap opera in Sydney to join their cast as soon as the play ended. They began a long-distance relationship, at least that is how he saw it. However, she set about making excuses as to why it was never a good time to visit.

With being so busy learning her lines and developing her character, she suggested they wait to see each other for her birthday. He bought her a diamond necklace and planned a special dinner where he would tell her that he loved her. The day before his trip, she texted and told him not to come. She had met someone else.

He was devastated. Over time, he began dating casually, not being serious about anyone. Setting eyes on Monique at the party was equivalent to a light switch turning off his feelings for Hannah and placing his heart back in time.

Twenty-One

Ryan and Kiera drive to Moody Gardens the following morning. He tells her about their reservation for a penguin encounter.

She gasps with enthusiasm. "That is so neat! I don't understand why your friends were not interested in coming with us."

"Not everyone cares as much about wildlife and nature. Like they said, they would rather ride rollercoasters and drink beer. Leo knows I don't drink. I could see the disappointment on his face when we didn't bring back any alcohol from the store last night," he snickers.

Once they turn onto the road for the gardens, large glass pyramids are visible in the distance. The parking lot is lined with palm trees, and the grounds are still covered in Christmas decorations. In the lobby, a tree-shaped arrangement of poinsettias stands that must be at least 20 feet high.

The first stop is the aquarium pyramid. The penguin encounter is in 30 minutes. As they walk through a tunnel with 360 degrees of glass, marine life swims above their heads, below their feet, and on either side, including sting rays, nurse sharks, and fish of all kinds.

They reach the jellyfish gallery. This brings back memories for Ryan of his first trip to Corpus Christi, years before he found the blue dragon.

"Were you stung?"

"Yes! And then the day after, we went up on an aircraft carrier and saw countless jellyfish in the water where I was swimming."

Arriving at the penguin habitat right on time, they are led back into a room with eight others, where a biologist greets the group. The tour begins with a demonstration of how penguin food is prepared. Their leader takes them to various areas while discussing the care, training, and conservation of these aquatic flightless birds. Afterward, they are guided to another room, and a staff member brings out a penguin to interact with the guests.

The small, young male waddles around. It goes over to Ryan first, turning his head up at him. The group is told not to touch "Myron" as only his caregivers can do this.

At the end of the tour, the bird steps in different colored paint and walks across a canvas for a piece of penguin art. Everyone draws a number from a jar, and Kiera wins the prized art.

The couple returns to the habitat to watch the 15 penguins move around the rocks. She gets tears in her eyes when remembering a lecture where the professor shared how thousands of baby emperor penguins died when the ice they were living on melted in the Antarctic. The decline in sea ice due to climate change is putting most of the penguin population in jeopardy.

Ryan tries to point out how, at least, these penguins are well taken care of.

Their last stop before leaving the aquarium pyramid is in a dark room called Deep Sea Adventure, where creatures from the deep ocean are showcased that have developed bioluminescence, or the ability to produce light.

They move on to the rainforest pyramid filled with vibrant green plants, Giant Amazon River Otters, Komodo dragons, monkeys, and sloths, not to mention many different birds and fish. A green bird with a yellow top beak and black bottom beak lands right beside Kiera, mouth wide open.

"I wish we could feed them," she comments.

The final activity before leaving for the day is a 4D movie about sharks. They pick up their 4D glasses and take a seat in the theater.

She turns to him. "I have heard of 3D, but not 4D!"

"I know. I didn't realize it existed, but the seats move, twist, shake, and even tickle you and push out air to make you feel like you are part of the action."

The show is thrilling. She grabs onto his arm several times when the sharks on the screen appear to be coming directly at them.

After the gardens, he receives a text from Leo to meet for a late lunch on The Strand, so they head that way.

Kiera observes a campground from the car window. "We should go camping sometime."

"I'm not a camper," he confesses.

"Not fancy enough for you?" she teases.

"Very funny. It's just that I could never get a decent night's sleep."

"Well, I always enjoyed camping with my family. We haven't done that in years." She sighs at the good memories.

"I am willing to give it a try again for you."

Upon returning to the beach house after a delicious meal, their guests spend the afternoon behind closed doors while Ryan and Kiera go for a walk along the shore. At one point, they sit and listen to the waves and sounds of nature, feeling no need to talk at all.

That evening, the group drives to Gaido's for dinner. This was a favorite restaurant of Ryan's mom and her own parents. Growing up, she ate there every year, and then brought her son and husband several times.

"The shrimp and grits are terrific here," he lets Kiera know.

Lewis shows up late. Leo and Felicia had just ordered their second round of drinks. Ryan tries not to see dollar signs in his head, wondering what the bill will be.

Everyone listens as the marine environmental law student speaks about his Ocean Conservation Club and their projects to encourage companies to use biodegradable products instead of plastics that end up in the water.

His brother changes the subject, addressing the elephant in the room, Ryan's dad. Leo does this in a way that brings back funny memories for all of them. "Remember when your dad made us wash our feet in the bathtub whenever we came to your house barefoot?"

Ryan laughs. "Yes. He was a stickler for being neat and tidy. He couldn't stand the idea of *your* dirty feet running around on our clean carpet."

"I remember running across your house, and he yelled, 'No Running! This isn't a gymnasium.' He scared me a little when I was very young, but I know he was a nice man," Lewis recalls.

"Right. He didn't like it if we moved too fast or talked too loudly. I guess that is why they didn't have more kids, so I wouldn't have anyone to run wild with on a daily basis. He often said, 'You're a good boy, Ryan,' but I know it was my quietness he liked."

Leo thinks back to other events. "I'll never forget how he took me to the emergency room when I fell off my bike and broke my arm while my parents were out shopping. Then he fixed my bike. He also found our dog when it was lost."

"Your mom was so nice to take us on fun outings all the time," remarks Lewis.

"She will be happy to hear that you remember."

Colin is trying to resist the urge to reach out to his old flame. Then that evening, while Hannah is making dinner for the two of them, Monique sends him a text. *Can't stop thinking about you. Want to meet somewhere soon?*

He is out of his mind with longing and doesn't know what to do.

Simon and Sam had just left for the neighbor's house to celebrate Ned's birthday with pizza, cake, and ice cream. He feels sick to his stomach with thoughts of hurting Hannah, but wanting Monique.

After putting dinner in the oven, she comes into the living room to do some cleaning. The boys and Bailey made a mess earlier. Kneeling to clean a spot on the carpet, her knees make sounds when getting back up.

"I am getting old," she says with a laugh, but his face appears serious.

"What? Are you worried about me getting old?"

Silence.

"You are, aren't you? You are wondering, what *are* you going to do with me when I am an old lady?"

There is no response.

With a glare, she states, "Maybe you *should* be with someone younger."

Lowering his head, he stares down at the floor.

Hormonal changes have been taking a toll on her. Thankfully, the night sweats have only happened in her apartment, not in Colin's bed. She has kept her irritability in check so far. However, between already having issues and feeling like he is still in love with Monique, she cannot contain her emotions.

"You want to be with Monique, don't you?" she shouts.

His inability to even look at her confirms what she is thinking.

"Well, you just go for it. Be with someone 20 years younger and see how that works out. You may look good through your 50s, but your 60s will be here before you know it, and believe me, things will change for you. Muscle atrophy will set in, and you will get flabby. Your skin will turn all dry and scratchy like a lizard. Can you imagine losing that signature head of hair of yours? I can tell it is thinning. I love how men talk about women and menopause as if they don't go through hormonal changes and declining testosterone. So, you go be with Monique before everything goes to hell!" Her voice is practically screaming by the end of her tirade.

He doesn't say a word.

"It is over between us. This will not affect my taking care of the boys while you are at work, but we are done here. Take the lasagna out of the oven when the timer goes off. I have lost my appetite." She gathers up her things, and Colin doesn't stop her. He sits there and lets her walk out the door.

Once back at her apartment, she tries to convince herself this is for the best. I mean, what did she think would happen? That they would grow old together?

In the middle of the night, Hannah wakes up crying. It takes over an hour to get back to sleep. When the sun rises, she gets out of bed feeling oddly indifferent.

While dressing, she hears a thud against the bathroom window. A bird similar to a parrot lies on the shingles. Opening the window to get a better view, the bird is still breathing and might only be stunned. She reaches out to bring the creature inside for an internet search on what to do.

Discovering the best way to help a feathered friend is to bring it to a wildlife rehabilitator, she locates one only 30 minutes away. There is a good chance it has internal injuries and will die if not treated. The bird is a crimson rosella, a parrot native to the area. An unofficial determination based on a few articles is that this is a girl parrot. After a short phone call, they are on the way.

Nearing their destination, the parrot flutters a few times in the paper bag, the suggested form of transportation for a small, injured bird.

"Hang on, Patty. We are almost there."

The rehabbers greet them at the door, inviting her in.

When removed from the bag, Patty does not fly away, only moving her wings a little.

"I think she has a concussion. We will give her a full evaluation and release her when ready. Thanks for making the trip."

Satisfied about helping the bird, she is also thankful there was no sight of Colin or the boys as she left and returned.

The twins have been wearing her out, and their school's mini camps don't start up again until next week. Time to herself is priceless. Her book is a priority. She makes significant progress with varying the language used in her story by eliminating the excessive reuse of words after "noticing" the characters were doing too much noticing, realizing, smiling, etc.

The afternoon flies by. She has not checked the phone for many hours. Pretending not to care if Colin messages her, Hannah breathes deeply as she grabs her purse.

Ryan texted only minutes before. He let her know the trip was going well and ended with how lucky he is to have her as a mom.

Wow, he must be in one great mood, she thinks to herself. *His happiness is what's important. I am fine by myself.*

Twenty-Two

Kiera and Ryan fly to Oregon to see Allison. From Portland, it is less than an hour's drive to Salem. He explains how his sister lives in a school bus, and the bus next to hers is rented out by the owner to vacationers.

"It is so pretty here. So many trees."

"Yes, and everything is green, even in winter. It is nice to see trees and not building after building, as in Dallas/Fort Worth."

They pull up to the bus home. Allison comes outside, and Ryan introduces his fiancée. The ladies embrace.

"I was sorry to hear you were sick. I'm glad you are well now." Kiera knew his sister was ill all of November and part of December with a parasite most likely contracted by swallowing contaminated water during a kayaking trip.

"Yes, having beaver fever was scary, but I'm fine. I should have gone to the doctor sooner. I thought I could fight it off and was trying to avoid antibiotics, but that is what I needed. It was great to get back to work. We had a terrible forest fire season last summer. I have been replanting trees and native grasses."

"Fires are so scary. We had a bushfire on my island a few years ago. It took a week to put out the fire."

"We have forest fires that can go on for a month here. This is becoming more common with climate change. And the warmer river water makes it more likely people will get sick like I did."

The group is still standing on the front porch. Just as he is about to suggest they go inside, Allison explains, "I'd give you a tour of my bus, but I haven't cleaned up yet. Why don't we do that later and check out your bus."

Ryan bites his lip, trying not to smile as he remembers how messy his sister was when she came to visit growing up. Her room and the kitchen would become a disaster in nothing flat. One time, he saw her spill a drink on the carpet and promptly told his parents. Having someone to tell on was a rare opportunity. He also recalls sharing the bathroom and seeing her hair everywhere, beauty products filling the counter, and towels and clothes on the floor.

Of course, he was only neat as a child because his mom was there to insist that he be that way. When left to his own devices in college, he became very untidy. He has been much better about keeping a cleaner place since moving to Australia.

Allison escorts them to the rental bus. The owner left her the key. It is painted a light shade of blue and has a shingled roof, similar to what would be on a house. The roof extends out over a porch with an outdoor table, chairs, and grill, all surrounded by lights along the railings and posts. A back door leads from the porch's far side to an extra room. She unlocks this entrance, revealing the nice-sized space where Kiera will sleep. The impressive bathroom connects to the back of the bus through another door. The actual bus part has bunk beds, a couch, and a modern kitchen area. They unpack their suitcases.

After his sister grills chicken and vegetables for an early dinner on the porch, which the neighbors allow her to use frequently, she mentions the plan for the following day. "We should leave around 9 am for the ninety-minute drive to the Valley of the Giants for a hike. The trail is only 1.3 miles. It is supposed to be around 58 degrees tomorrow, warmer than usual, so it should be nice. Many of the trees are 20 feet in circumference, 200 feet tall, and hundreds of years old. It is amazing there."

"Sounds good," he confirms.

"I have to warn you though, the drive through the mountains can be a little scary. We need to be quiet and listen for the sound of trucks coming from the other direction. There are a lot of logging trucks in the area. Passenger vehicles sometimes have to find a place to pull over because the trucks need more room to pass. I have driven it many times and only had to get out of the way once."

"So," Allison says, as her face turns from serious to amused, "Do you trust me?"

Ryan glances at Kiera, who nods her head. "We do."

That night, the bedding for the built-on room cannot be found. The couple, who have never slept in the same room, use the bunk beds. He takes the top bunk. They chat for hours, giggling like children up past their bedtime.

Allison knocks on the door at 8 am. Her brother, visibly groggy, opens it. "You guys are still sleeping? We have a big day planned. I brought ingredients for omelets. I will get them started here while you two get dressed. My stovetop isn't working."

Kiera gets ready first. Ryan notices his sister checking her phone as she did a few times the night before. He knows her boyfriend is on a trip with others from the forest department for a climate change conference in Washington, D.C. "Have you heard from Brandt?"

"No. I am trying to resist the urge to text him. I don't want to seem needy."

"I think it is fine to text at the end of the day and ask how his day went. That's not being clingy."

"I can't believe you are getting married before I do."

Unsure of a response, he shrugs his shoulders. Girlfriend/boyfriend matters have never been a topic of conversation for them. He did hear from his parents about cheating boyfriends and other drama.

"I wish Brandt was here so we could meet," he finally says.

"Me too. My mother does not like him. She came here and stayed on this rental bus when I was sick. Brandt tried to be nice to her, but she ended up being rude and basically blamed him for my illness since he introduced me to kayaking and said he should have warned me about contracting the disease from the water."

In an effort to cheer her up, he comments, "I'm sure she will come around."

The first part of the drive is a regular highway where they can talk. "I read that Oregon has the most polluted waters in the country. What's up with that?" Ryan asks.

"We have many more miles of rivers than the other states, except for Alaska. But yes, there is a big problem with the water being warmer than it used to be, leading to less oxygen and more bacteria. And the lakes are a problem also."

She continues. "I am taking a course on forest management and clean water next month and another on climate-smart forestry. We must support the forests and their ability to adapt to climate change. Of course, our forests pull carbon dioxide from the air, but did you know that a fully grown tree can release hundreds of gallons of water as water vapor to help cool its surroundings in warm weather?"

He is amused by her lecture. Allison is as passionate about the forests as he is about the oceans. With a response on the tip of his tongue, she does not give him time to answer.

"Before trees can purify our air and contribute to the water cycle for clouds and rain to be created, they need water. The department manages the forests in the best way to promote reliable water sources and a healthy watershed or drainage basin. When we allow prescribed fires to burn, timber companies to cut down trees, and roads and hiking trails to be built, we do this in a way that helps water resources, not negatively impacting them."

"So awesome that you can continue to learn this way after college," he remarks.

"Because I was sick, I missed the class on monitoring the forests for insect damage and tree diseases, but my supervisor gave me the information. Insects and disease are on the rise with global warming."

The trio turns quiet for the rest of the drive. To their relief, they never encounter any trucks, arriving at the trailhead safely.

They begin their forest journey, and the only sounds heard are the breezes through the trees and the many different types of birds. It is a workout with the steep terrain.

"I said to be quiet on the mountain road. You guys can talk now."

"We are just taking it all in and enjoying everything, right?" Ryan turns to Kiera.

"Yes, it is stunning, and I love these hiking shoes your mom got for me."

His sister stops beside a green bush. "I remember your mom always took elderberry gummies to fight off colds. She gave me some when I first went to college. This is elderberry, but the berries don't grow until August."

She points to the ferns growing all around. "And this is sword fern. Now, you two stand by that Western Hemlock so I can take your picture."

The couple positions themselves in front of the giant tree. He puts his arm around her.

Kiera requests a few retakes until she is satisfied with the photo.

Allison uses this opportunity to share more knowledge.

"The Western Hemlock is the State Tree of Washington. These trees here are over 500 years old. There are recordings of some at 1200 years. The needles can be chewed or used to make tea. They are rich in vitamin C. The cambium layer below the bark is the part of the tree that grows and is edible. The bark was used for medicine years ago."

She examines the tree, always on the lookout now for damage and disease.

"Close to the trail's end is Big Guy, a fallen Douglas fir knocked down by a storm years ago. It is estimated to be around 600 years old when it fell. It has a diameter of seven feet, so it is huge. We will take more pictures there."

After the hike, they sit at the picnic table area. Allison brought sandwiches and apples. Ryan pulls out some familiar snacks from his backpack. His sister grins. "I remember those granola bars and peanut butter cookies. When you were little, they said you pretty much lived on them. They couldn't get you to eat much else."

He rolls his eyes, and she changes the subject. "When we are done eating, let's return to the trail. There is something that I want to show you a little off the path."

A small olive-colored bird lands on the table.

Kiera watches it peck at some leftover crumbs from the people before them. "He is cute."

"Yes, this is an American goldfinch. In winter, males are olive, but in summer, they are bright yellow."

They finish lunch and follow Allison, climbing over a large fallen tree and then down a slope. Suddenly, their leader slips, hitting the ground and crying out in pain while rolling partway down the hill.

"Stay here," Ryan says to Kiera, carefully descending to where his sister is holding her right ankle and wincing. Her face is bleeding from a branch that scratched it.

"My ankle. I think it is sprained."

"Do you have a first aid kit in the car?" he asks.

"No. I should, but I don't. I always ride with a partner for work in his truck."

"Let's get you up. Try to lean on me as best as you can."

Kiera meets them at the car, bringing wet paper towels from the restroom for Allison's face.

Ryan helps her into the front passenger seat, allowing for the most leg room, and gets behind the wheel, making adjustments for his height.

He drives cautiously for about ten minutes and then hears a rumbling sound. In an alarmed voice, he tells the others, "I think a truck is coming."

Kiera becomes worried. "I hear it too. What are we going to do? There is nothing but sheer rock to our right."

Allison calmly states, "You must cross to the other side of the road. See, there is a place to pull over, up there on the left."

"Cross over? That is so dangerous!" Panic takes over him.

"We have no choice."

He rapidly veers to the left and goes up onto a flat surface.

The logging truck passes by, taking up both lanes to go around the curve. Their car would have been in its direct path.

Staying put for a few minutes, everyone is silent.

"It is safe now," his sister assures them.

Ryan takes a deep breath, backs up, and then gets on the road.

No one speaks all the way to town, even after reaching the main highway. A quick stop at the drugstore is made to purchase an ankle wrap. They also pick up antibiotic cream, bandages, and an ice pack. A visit to a medical clinic is declined.

"This isn't the first time I've done this to my ankle. And I already have crutches."

After arriving back at the bus community, he assists Allison up the steps of her home, treating the swollen ankle and still bleeding face. "We will bring over dinner later, OK?"

"OK. Thanks."

Once in the rental bus, he sits on the couch with his eyes shut.

"What's wrong?" asks Kiera.

"I feel like we risked our lives today because of the logging truck. It makes me mad."

"We should be thankful to have returned safely, and walking the trail will always be a good memory, right?"

"You're right. Sorry. I'm fine."

She puts her head on his shoulder.

They knock on Allison's door around 6 pm after taking a nap in the bunk beds.

"Come in."

"I thought we would go and pick up some tacos. Does that sound good to you?"

"Yes, it does. Thanks."

Over dinner, his sister announces, "You two are going to the Columbia River Gorge tomorrow to see the waterfalls and awesome overlooks."

"Why don't we do something you can do with us, like a movie?" Ryan suggests.

"I don't want you to miss the gorge, but we can see about a movie when you get back."

"OK. Good."

"I'm sorry about earlier. I know it was scary."

"Why do they allow so much logging anyway? I understand wood is needed for building materials, but it doesn't seem like we need paper as much as we used to, right?"

"True. Demand is down, but not as much as you would think. Oregon is the largest softwood lumber producer in the country. Logging is done in about a third of the state's forests. We work with state and private landowners to ensure they follow responsible management practices to keep the forests healthy and replant trees. Of course, harvesting timber is important anyway to make room for younger trees to grow. Leftover wood pieces are used for biofuel, and local buildings have woody biomass as their energy source. So, there are benefits."

Skepticism is written all over his face.

Convincing himself that things never would have worked out in the long run with Hannah, she had not been out the door for long when Colin texted Monique and asked her to dinner.

As usual, she cares for Simon and Sam on Monday afternoon, plotting a quick escape once Colin returns from the university. He walks in and tells the boys to get ready for gymnastics night, avoiding any eye contact with her. It is obvious he has plans for the evening.

In the morning, she sees pictures on the internet of Colin and Monique leaving a downtown restaurant. He has his arm wrapped around her waist, smiling that big, gorgeous smile. The thought of the two of them in bed together makes her ill.

Despite what was said previously, she doesn't know how this will work, living right there above him and caring for his sons. Getting out of this situation seems necessary, but she will wait until after the wedding before making a change.

For their last day in Oregon, Ryan and Kiera arrive at Multnomah Falls.

"Wow! No wonder this is the highest waterfall in the state. I have always loved waterfalls," she says excitedly.

The group ahead of them takes pictures of each other with their heads back and mouths wide open. She realizes what they are doing, but Ryan isn't paying attention.

When they get to that spot, Kiera tells him to take a picture as she tilts her head back and opens her mouth.

"What are you doing?"

"Trying to make it appear like the falls are going into my mouth."

"OK. Cool. Hadn't thought of that one."

He takes the picture. The pair laughs about how it really does look that way.

Upon returning from their adventure, Allison admits she is too tired to go to the movie theater but is up for streaming one instead. They let her choose, and she selects a horror/sci-fi film called *A Quiet Place*. The lack of dialogue takes a little getting used to, as the characters will be killed by aliens if they are heard, but it turns out to be suspenseful.

The three say their goodbyes because it requires a very early start to the day to get to the airport. Since his sister cannot attend the wedding after missing so much work due to her illness, she hands him a small plaque. It is made from local wood and has the words "*Wishing You a Lifetime of Happiness - Allison*" carved into it. She made it herself.

He gives her a big hug, and so does Kiera.

The couple ends up talking for hours from their separate bunk beds as they did their first night, something they will regret the next day. But Kiera is pleased the trip was a success and is glad she suggested it.

On the plane ride back, they sleep for the longest time. She wakes with a start, following another nightmare. Ryan asks what is wrong, but she claims nothing.

Kiera has no intention of ever sharing with him her belief that she is the reincarnation of a woman from the early 1900s who was abducted but able to escape and make it back to her family. The woman became pregnant by her assailant but went on to lose the baby during childbirth.

Almost everyone would say they are only dreams, but she has had the same visions or nightmares for years now. She knows this woman, feeling what she felt, and seeing what she saw. In these repetitive dreams, the woman later marries but loses their baby too, and another one, this time dying in childbirth herself.

She is quiet, lost in her own thoughts.

He finally speaks. "Are you in the mood to read a thesis paper?"

"What do you mean?"

"Kim contacted me for help with her paper. She emailed what she has so far. Do you want to both read it and let her know what we think?"

Kiera bites her lip, trying not to smile too much about how happy she is to hear that this was the reason for Kim's call. "Yeah, sure."

Twenty-Three

Naomi moved while Kiera was on her trip. It worked well for Hannah that her future daughter-in-law could be with her friend until the wedding after all. Ryan and Kiera know nothing about the situation between her and Colin.

The young ladies enjoy some free time before their teaching careers start. Naomi enrolled in a night class to work towards her master's in English. While the course does not begin until the following month, she is already working on a paper after contacting the professor and getting the syllabus early. She is committed to going to the library at least twice a week for research.

Ryan has been back at work for a week and is heavily involved in new assignments. At first, many in the department were still on vacation, but Kim and the rest of the staff returned that day. They all attend a meeting about goals for the upcoming semester. Professor Spiner explains the latest projects they plan to begin soon.

Kim is distracted and can't take her eyes off Ryan. *He is engaged,* she tells herself. *It is now or never to make a move.*

After the meeting, he goes back to his office. Kim leaves but texts him later. *Can I come to your place tonight? I can't make sense of these statistical models for my research.*

No. Let's meet at the library at 6:45. He needs to put in an extra hour of work and wants time to grab something to eat.

Once there, Kim leads him to a secluded part of the library instead of sitting at the tables in the middle. He explains the variables, coefficients, and different parts of the model. She isn't even trying to understand, going back and forth on the best way to tell him how she feels.

After a while, he realizes the information is not sinking in and types up the explanations on her laptop.

"Now you have what you need to review this tomorrow." He stands up, suggests it is time to leave, and escorts her through the dark parking lot.

They reach her car. "Thanks for helping me," she remarks, moving in for a hug.

Standing stiffly with arms straight, he does not reciprocate the action. "You're welcome," he replies, uneasy about her affections.

Almost his height when wearing platform shoes, she pulls her head back slowly, placing her lips on his. He doesn't pull away. She opens her mouth, and so does he.

Naomi is on her way to the library and witnesses this scene. She changes her route so there is no chance of Ryan seeing her.

He allows the kiss to end naturally and then steps backward. "See you tomorrow," he mumbles, not knowing what else to say, and immediately walks away.

Kim wants to go after him, but decides against it.

Back at his apartment, Ryan doesn't know what to do. He wishes he could speak to his dad. Since that isn't an option, there is only one person he knows who can sort through this. He makes the call.

"I kissed another girl. How can I get married now? What should I do?"

Hannah has him explain about Kim, who she is, and how he knows her.

"Do you want to date Kim and spend time with her?"

"No. Absolutely not."

"Do you love Kiera and want to spend your life with her?"

"Yes!" he proclaims.

"Then, there is your answer. It was just a kiss. It doesn't mean anything."

"I feel guilty that I let it happen."

"It sounds like you were caught off guard and didn't know how to react. Maybe you were curious. It is OK if you liked the kiss. If there is any part of you that wants to spend time with Kim to decide how you feel about her, then do that. But if you know this isn't what you want, forget about it."

"I know I am not interested in Kim, but shouldn't I tell Kiera what happened?"

"My advice is not to."

He hangs up and texts Kiera to ask about her day. She suggests they chat on the phone, but he lets her know that he is tired.

Naomi cannot concentrate on her research. She decides to return home and pass on what she saw.

Kiera cries and cries. Naomi has no words of comfort other than to say she is sorry. She gives the troubled girl several hugs throughout the evening.

The former bride-to-be feels that everything is ruined. There will be no wedding day.

Ryan arrives at work a little later than usual. Kim is not there. She is off meeting local biologists with one of the professors. He texts Kiera his usual morning greeting, but she does not reply.

It isn't until three in the afternoon that he begins to worry about not hearing from her all day. He finds it almost impossible to focus on his assignment when calls go straight to her voicemail. The minute the clock displays 5:00, he tries one more time to text and then drives to Naomi's.

Kiera opens the door but stands in the doorway, not letting him in. He can tell she has been crying. She gives him back the ring.

"What's this?"

"Naomi told me she saw you and Kim in the library parking lot. It's over." With that, she shuts the door.

"Kiera. Let's talk about this."

"There is nothing to talk about," she says through the closed door.

Two girls who live in the unit on the corner come down the hallway. He doesn't want to cause a scene, so he leaves.

For an hour, he tries to call, text, and even email, but no response.

Next, he calls his mom.

"Did you tell her how Kim kissed you and that you have no interest in her?" says Hannah, trying to be calm but feeling her heart race.

"Yes. Well, I texted and emailed that, but I don't know if she read my messages."

"Where is this apartment she is at?"

"You can't go there!" he practically yells, outraged at the idea.

"Yes, I can, and I am."

Ryan finds this embarrassing, but he does think Kiera will listen to his mother over him. He gives her the address, but first, they discuss the situation for a while longer. Speaking this way about relationships and matters of the heart is new for them.

Once the heart-to-heart ends, he does something he has never done before. He says a prayer that his mom can get through to Kiera.

She knocks on the door, but there is no answer. "Kiera, it is Hannah."

Deciding not to ignore this woman who has been so good to her, she opens it but walks away to sit on the couch. Naomi is at the library since she got nothing done the night before.

Hannah enters to see her eyes all red and swollen.

She takes a seat and embraces the girl with every fiber of her being. This wonderful person, whom she so badly wants to be her daughter-in-law, grabs onto her, and the tears start again. Anxious to end the bad feelings and plead her son's case, she waits.

Finally, Kiera stands up for a tissue and begins to calm down.

"Ryan loves you. He has no interest in Kim. *She* kissed him."

"Naomi says he was kissing her back."

"He was taken off guard. The bottom line is that he does *not* have feelings for her and has no interest in spending time with her or dating her. He absolutely wants to marry you."

With sadness turning to anger, "I feel like he lied to me. He didn't tell me."

"I…Well, I'm afraid I told him not to."

The shock in the air can almost be felt.

"I'm sorry. He told me what happened. I asked him some questions and came to the conclusion that the kiss meant nothing. He thought he should tell you, but I didn't see the point in upsetting you."

Finding it hard to breathe, she continues. "Are you going to be able to forgive him and put this behind you?"

Kiera is quiet.

"Did you read his email?"

Shaking her head, she pulls up the message on her phone.

Hannah encouraged Ryan to send a second email, expressing his love for his fiancée and communicating the reasons they are right for one another. After her son revealed that he had never said "I Love You," she could not believe her ears.

Kiera's heart softens upon reading these words. She reads it one more time. "I forgive him."

"Good. Are you going to put him out of his misery and let him know?"

"Yes. I will call him."

"OK. I am leaving then. I will call you in the morning. We need to talk more about the wedding and plan your shower."

The two women step forward for a big hug.

As Hannah drives back to her place, she questions why she is encouraging them to get married at such a young age. Evidently, her son is a complete knucklehead, as most men are.

Also, getting married two weeks after starting a new job as a teacher seems like too many life changes at once. It would make more sense to wait until Kiera is on a school break, but she would never say this to them. In her opinion, living together for a year first would be ideal. Apparently, this type of arrangement goes against his beliefs.

The following day is Colin's birthday. Hannah did not think of this until he left for work. The boys must recognize their father.

"What do you want to get him?" she asks.

"A poster," yells Simon.

"OK, let's make a poster." They enjoy drawing various characters, and this keeps them busy for a while, which is always good for her.

Rosie prances into the kitchen, patiently allowing her former owner to pet her but really wanting a second breakfast. The cat must spend eighty percent of her time in the twins' room, taking over their bean bag chair.

Hannah, Simon, and Sam go shopping to buy a cake, balloons, and other accessories. She seeks out the loudest noisemakers she can find. They stop at the sporting goods store to pick out a rock-climbing T-shirt.

After putting up the decorations, she tells them, "I need to leave when your dad gets home. Wait until I am gone, and then get the present and poster, and say 'Happy Birthday.' Don't forget to give him a hug."

They do not question this.

When the birthday boy arrives, she makes a quick exit.

The brothers give their dad a celebration, hugs included.

Colin texts her. *Thank you for organizing my birthday. Do you want to come down and have tacos with us?* He is hoping they can be friends, but that is probably asking too much.

No thanks, is the reply.

His plans for Monique to drop by after his sons went to bed are thwarted when a pounding headache sets in, brought on by the sounds of party horns, balloons popping, and boys screaming.

Being reunited with Ryan brings Kiera peace and a stronger relationship. She decides it is time for complete openness and confides in him about seeing a therapist.

He shares his two months of therapy visits, one summer in college, when dealing with thoughts of hopelessness over the state of the Earth and climate change. It was affecting his day-to-day functioning.

She takes the quest for honesty one step further, telling him about the woman in her dreams. This leads to a discussion on the concept of reincarnation.

Never guessing Ryan would believe in the possibility, he even proposes an interesting suggestion. "Professor Ryan found my relatives. Why don't we ask him about researching women on the island years ago who meet the description and life experiences you described?"

Hannah throws the bridal shower at a local restaurant. On the drive over, she thinks about what kind of mother-in-law she should be. She wants Kiera to know she is there for her and can talk to her about things, but does not want to be seen as annoying or overly involved in their lives.

Everyone invited can attend. Kiera receives towels, candles, a *Bride* tote bag, wine glasses (when neither drinks), *Mr. Right/Mrs. Always Right* travel mugs, a blanket, and a picnic basket. The final gift is a pillow with the word *Tonight* on one side and *Not Tonight* on the other. The married women all giggle.

As Hannah settles up with the host, she overhears the ladies teasing the bride about her wedding night. Kiera is visibly embarrassed.

On the way home, she realizes no one gave her daughter-in-law-to-be a negligee. At her own bridal shower, Hannah's friends gave her several negligees, which she wore for a couple of years. At some point, it became more practical to just get naked.

Deciding to stop at the mall, she picks out two nightgowns/negligees, one conservative and one more revealing, for Kiera to take on the honeymoon. If the girl does not like them, she does not have to wear them.

While out, she receives a text from Colin. *Jane is bringing her kids to the wedding because Kiera knows them all. Now Simon and Sam think they are going. Is it OK for me to be there and bring them?*

OK. Yes. Hannah had not thought of this issue with everything else on her mind. Jane is the only one who knows about the breakup. She is waiting until after the wedding to tell Ryan.

Twenty-Four

WEDDING DAY

Kiera and Ryan are getting married on Swaggerty Island at the beach. Unlike Hannah's dream, the event is during the day, and releasing baby sea turtles is not on the agenda. The ceremony is at 11:00 am on a Saturday, with a wedding reception to follow in a grassy area near the beach under giant tents. Hors d'oeuvres will be served, along with finger sandwiches, and many different types of fruits and desserts, in addition to the wedding cake.

The cake is a traditional white cake with three tiers. Instead of bride and groom figurines on top, there are seashell designs in a circle with a turtle and a blue dragon, all made of icing. Just as she dreamed, the wedding decorations say: *Olive and the Blue Dragon, Ryan and Kiera.*

After the reception, a helicopter will fly the couple off the island to Brisbane for a 3:30 plane ride to Port Douglas, where they will take a second helicopter to spend their first night together in an underwater room on a pontoon, surrounded by sea creatures visible through a wall of windows. Hannah discovered this months before and thought to herself, *what a place for a honeymoon!*

Dinner will be catered for them, and all the daytime guests who came to snorkel, scuba dive, etc., will be gone. The following night is at a resort, returning late Monday to get back to work on Tuesday.

The evening before the big day, they all gather on the island for a rehearsal and dinner. Jess from the first-year residential hall is a bridesmaid, along with Naomi. Kiera's brothers are the groomsmen.

The rehearsal is not at the beach but in an area beside the restaurant. The group goes over the sequence of events, including how the ladies will arrive right before the ceremony. The groomsmen and the bride's father will meet them as they exit the van.

Once everyone has their parts down, they go into a private room for dinner. Hannah is impressed watching her son converse with his new family members, and there is no hint of wedding jitters.

The groom and his mother stay at a local resort, and so do Naomi and Jess. Kiera wanted to spend one last night at her family's home. Everyone else who does not live on the island will come by water taxi in the morning.

The big day is here. It was hard to sleep, but Hannah is excited, not tired. She and Ryan meet Naomi and Jess for breakfast, and before they know it, it is time to prepare for the wedding.

While Hannah has worn dresses from time to time over the years, she normally feels uncomfortable in one. Now, she is actually eager to do so for the first time since her own wedding. The dress she chose is a light-rose color with lace beginning at her collarbone and going down to her knees, followed by three layers of smooth ruffles. It is sleeveless, not something she normally chooses, but they will be outside at the beach, not in a cold, overly air-conditioned room. It would have been nice to wear something like this to the dinner or play with Colin, although those rooms were freezing cold.

Ryan did not go to the prom and had never worn a tuxedo. Helping him put on his jacket and bow tie is a treat, and seeing him this happy and handsome is priceless.

They make it to the beach location early to ensure it is all set up correctly.

Mother and son go over some things. From a distance, Hannah sees Colin arriving with the boys...and Monique. Her jaw drops.

"What's wrong?" Ryan looks over his shoulder but does not detect what is causing her reaction.

"Nothing's wrong. Everything is fine. There is something I didn't tell you." She speaks too slowly, not coming right out with it, so he turns around again and spots Colin holding hands with another woman.

His face becomes red, and he rushes in their direction.

"Wait. It is fine. Come back."

Colin sees the angry young man heading towards him and leaves the others to meet halfway.

"What are you doing to my mom?" he demands with piercing eyes.

Hannah, out of breath, catches up. "Ryan, it is fine. We broke up a few weeks ago. I decided to wait until after the wedding to tell you. It isn't a big deal. It's not like we were in love with each other or anything."

It's not like we were in love with each other. The words resonate in Colin's ears and sink deep into his mind, heart, and soul.

The groom continues to stare fiercely.

"Look at me." His mother reaches up to turn his face to hers. "It's all good, OK? This is *your* day. We are all thrilled for you and Kiera. We are here to support you. Including Colin."

As she speaks, tears form, which her son notices, but Colin is wrapped up in his own thoughts.

"You have tears in your eyes," Ryan softly says into her ear.

"Because I am upset that you are upset. It has nothing to do with…*him*." She motions towards her ex with a rising voice.

They move away.

Colin is left standing there, and for a minute, has trouble breathing as he thinks about her words, dismissing what they had together and hearing the disdain as she referred to "*him*." Watching her walk off, his feelings of adoration and attraction come rushing back.

He soon becomes aware of being away from Monique for too long and hopes no one has been observing this interaction. After making his way to where people from the university are gathered, he finds Monique chatting it up with two professors.

Finally deciding his mom has the situation under control, the groom circulates to visit with guests.

Jane marches over. "I can't believe he would bring her here."

"I know," Hannah agrees. She cannot wait to have some wine at the reception.

While Ryan is wrapping up a discussion with Professor Spiner, a guy not much older than himself approaches, who has his same thick dark hair and green eyes, and also his height and build. The girl at his side has red hair.

"Hi, Ryan. I am Clay Ryan."

"What? You are? I didn't know you were coming."

Ryan called his distant cousin the week before, speaking with him for over an hour, mostly about his company, but he had never seen a picture. The two of them tried to figure out what they are to one another. They came up with fifth cousins but are not entirely sure.

The young lady with Clay introduces herself. "I am Amy. Kiera and I used to spend summers on the island with our church group."

"OK. Yes. Nice to meet you. I remember now. She did mention you. I'm sorry. I am just surprised."

She smiles. "I told Clay I was coming back to the island for a wedding, and it was discovered through conversation about you and him being related. Small world, huh?"

"It sure is. My mom will enjoy meeting you both after the ceremony."

As he speaks, Kiera's dad signals him to come up front.

An announcement is made for everyone to be seated. The wedding party gets into position. The van pulls up, and the bridesmaids exit, followed by the bride.

Hannah beams at the sight of the wedding dress she and Kiera picked out. They had to search high and low for the right gown.

The bride-to-be did not like the first 25 to 30 garments they saw. Her soon-to-be mother-in-law knew all too well the feeling of being self-conscious in an outfit. She understood the girl did not want something too puffy, too showy with a long train, or too revealing with a plunging neckline, or backless, or where one leg is exposed all the way to the upper thigh, as another young lady in the store had chosen.

The two women were ecstatic when they finally found the right one. The fit is perfect, not too slim or too full. The short sleeves are designed with leaves in see-through lace. The rest of the dress has a lining under the lace so that it is not see-through, and the lace turns from a leaf design into flowers as it goes down to the ground, but without a train.

Kiera takes her dad's arm as the music begins. The bridesmaids, escorted by the groomsmen, complete the walk down the aisle to take their places. Father and daughter look at one another. He gives her a broad smile, one she hasn't seen in years, and they follow the runner lined with flowers to the altar.

When she sees the way Ryan is gazing at her, Kiera's heart skips a beat. It is a reminder of the feeling she had a little over one year ago on the day she first laid eyes on him at the university.

After the officiant announces they are husband and wife, Simon gives a loud shout of "Whoo Hoo!" The newlyweds turn to each other and laugh, along with most of their guests.

The wedding celebration moves up the beach to the tents, where everyone gets food and drinks. Wine, beer, and punch are served, and later, champagne will be brought out for a toast.

Simon and Sam begin to run around with Jane's boys.

Jane tries to get them all to have punch and sandwiches and settle down. This lasts about five minutes. Then Ned touches Sam, says "You're it!" and runs away. Sam, still holding his drink, takes off running, and the red punch comes flying out of the glass and lands on Monique's ivory dress.

The woman screams, causing Sam to stop and turn around.

"My dress. It's ruined. You creep! Look what you have done."

The boy bursts out crying.

"Don't speak to my son that way," exclaims Colin.

"You just let them run wild. You allowed them to practically yell in the car the whole way to the water taxi and then run around on the boat."

He tries to pull her away. "Let's discuss this over here."

"There's nothing to discuss," Monique shouts. "I don't want any part of this. I'm leaving."

Colin follows, trying to talk to her, but gives up and lets her leave. He returns to the group to find Hannah hugging Sam and kissing his cheek. She tickles him, making him laugh. "You go have fun. Today is a day for celebrating. Don't worry about that silly woman, OK?"

"OK!" Sam enthusiastically sprints ahead to catch up with the other boys.

Hannah stands up, her eyes meeting Colin's. Biting her lip hard in an attempt not to smile, she moves away quickly, going over to Jane. The two ladies howl with laughter.

Colin apologizes to the guests around him for the scene. He spends the rest of the party conversing with the other professors.

Clay and Amy introduce themselves to Hannah.

"Wow, you look so much like my side of the family," she remarks.

Amy laughs. "I know. People would think Ryan and Clay are brothers."

"Tell me, how did you two meet?"

"Well, after Clay wouldn't hire me at his company, he called to apologize."

"Now wait a second. I wanted to hire you. It wasn't my fault."

"Anyway, he came up with an excuse about how he wanted to pick my engineering brain instead of just asking me out."

"This is true. I am a chook."

"We are in a getting-to-know-you phase."

The young people glance at one another. Clay has been slow in his approach, but he is determined not to leave the island without kissing Amy.

Ryan and Kiera catch their flight to Port Douglas. They sleep most of the time. After landing, a limousine waits to transport them to the heliport for the ride to the activity pontoon. Hannah felt that everyone should ride in a limo at least once in their lives. The driver points to the open bottle of champagne sitting on ice in the back.

While performing their wedding toast with fruit punch at the reception, standing firm with a personal no-alcohol policy, they waver and decide it is acceptable to have a little champagne. It is their wedding day after all. They both turn silly very quickly, giggling and kissing the entire ride.

It is different being on the pontoon with no other guests. A staff member shows the bride and groom to their room and lets them know dinner will be served on deck in 20 minutes. They both eye the bed, feeling nervous about what will happen later. He sits at the foot of it, taking in the ocean view. Kiera joins him. Placing his hand on hers, he kisses her cheek. "We did it."

As the sun sets, dinner includes a flavorful barramundi dish for her and basil pesto pasta for him, along with a delectable coconut vanilla dessert. There is an option to sleep on deck outside in a "reefbed," but that is not something honeymooners would want to do. For a while, they sit on the deck bed, consisting of a mattress in a giant basket with a canopy. They lie down, pushing the canopy away to see the stars while listening to the ocean. Ryan begins to feel sleepy and realizes it is time to get to their accommodations.

The glass wall of the underwater room makes for a romantic space as the soft light outside keeps it dim but allows you to see the water and creatures at night.

Kiera changes into the negligee and comes out of the bathroom. The expression on his face is priceless, and it fills her with joy. She has a sense of being truly desired for the first time in her life. He tells her how beautiful she is and kisses her intensely before removing his clothes and then her gown.

They make love, feeling relieved afterwards that it was not something to worry about, like they had both been doing. It was quite good, actually.

With bodies intertwined, they watch the fish swim past, followed by a dugong. "Look!" she shouts. To get a better view, they rush to the glass wall, standing there naked.

"I guess it is good we weren't distracted by marine life a little while ago," he teases, but then his face turns serious. "You don't think that is your mom, do you?"

She laughs hysterically and pulls him back to bed.

Twenty-Five

Colin tosses and turns. Around midnight, what he had missed earlier, before the wedding ceremony began, comes to him.

Hannah did have tears in her eyes because of me. It was painful for her to see me with Monique because she loves me. I know she does.

Finally drifting off to sleep, he later squints his eyes at the bright sunshine of midday and hears the goose-like honking sounds of white-bellied sea eagles. He joins Hannah for lunch on the patio of their beachfront home.

They are in their early 60s, laughing up a storm about her grandchildren's exploits. The conversation moves on to another favorite topic, his sons. Simon is a children's storybook writer, and Sam works at a toy store. The twins share a small house with a pool in the backyard. They are not completely living independently, financially or otherwise, but close to it.

This seaside scene fades, and the sidewalk where he lives now appears. Hannah is walking away from him. He calls out, but she won't turn around.

"I love you. Come back," he repeatedly says, and then wakes up.

I have to win her back. The clock displays 4:32. He begins to devise possible plans to redeem himself in her eyes.

Later in the morning, the boys are busy with a video game. This is his opportunity to straighten things out. As he ascends the stairs to her suite, she opens the door to leave.

"Hi."

"Hi," she replies. "Is there something you wanted?"

"I want." He stops and starts again, "I want. I mean, I wanted to say I'm sorry for bringing Monique to the wedding. She found out we were going and invited herself. I should have told her no."

With a shrug, "Well, it was good for a laugh."

He stares at her.

"Anything else?"

Colin slowly inhales and closes his eyes, knowing what her response will be.

"I want another chance."

He opens his eyes to find her looking at him as if he were crazy.

"Let me get this straight. You dumped me for another woman, had sex with her for a few weeks, and now you want me back? I don't think so."

Hannah moves towards him, saying, "Excuse me," to get him out of the way.

He watches her march down the stairs. When she reaches the last step, he calls out, "Technically, you broke up with me, you know?"

She does not turn around.

After returning to his place and slumping on the couch, he sits for a while before deciding to send a text.

I love you and want to spend my life with you. I will tell you this every day until you come back to me.

Kiera is sad to leave the pontoon that morning until the shuttle bus pulls up at their resort, and she catches sight of the lagoon-style pool surrounding the entire property. "It just goes on and on."

Her new husband opens the door to the fanciest hotel room she has ever seen. The couple gets into bed, deserving of their honeymoon suite.

Later, they locate the reserved poolside cabana, where lunch and snacks are served. Staying for four hours, Ryan never thought he would want to lounge by a pool for so long, only swimming for about 30 minutes.

"I guess I am a grown-up after all," he laughs.

They have an early dinner and then stroll along the beach afterwards as the sun sets.

Hannah does not hear Colin's text come through. She is on the way to Ryan's old apartment to move him into the couple's new one.

Arrangements were already in place for someone from the pet store to transport the aquarium. There is no furniture to relocate since it all came with the accommodations, leaving only personal items she can handle.

Her son did a pretty good job of packing things up before the wedding. The goal is to ensure the couple has everything they need for their return. This includes the delivery of furniture she and Kiera shopped for. The groom said he would be fine with whatever his bride chose. Smart man.

It was a fairly simple move, but there is always more to do than you first think. Hannah wished she had hired someone to perform the move-out cleanup, which was made more difficult by Ryan's lack of cleaning skills, even though he is better than he used to be.

As she pulls into the driveway, eager to pour herself a glass of wine after a long day, she is proud of herself for barely thinking about Colin. It was easy to push him out of her mind while focused on the task at hand, and the idea of them reuniting is ridiculous and not worth considering.

She takes a few sips and removes her cell from her purse. It was unusual to go all day without checking it. The pet store guy and furniture delivery people were on time, so a phone was never needed.

Her heart pounds as she reads Colin's text. The words *"spend my life with you"* hit hard. She begins to cry.

Why am I crying? Do I want to get back with him? Do I honestly love him enough?

Hannah wakes up at first light with the attitude that Colin is saying these things but does not mean them, and in a few weeks, he will move on to someone else. She will do her best to ignore any declarations of love or longing looks from him. While true, she dreams about him almost every night, this does not mean they should be together.

The newlyweds return and enter their new home. Ryan tells his wife he likes the furniture and texts his mom, *Thanks for doing everything.* Kiera calls her mother-in-law to say thanks and tell her about their honeymoon, minus the sex parts, of course. He smiles to himself, never comprehending until now how much his mother will enjoy having Kiera in her life as well.

The new semester is about to begin at the university, and Colin has a lot to do to prepare. One afternoon, he comes back earlier than usual. As he passes the window before reaching the front door, he peers in. Hannah and the boys are dancing in his living room to music.

When he first saw the trio spinning around almost a year ago, it pushed him over the edge to fall for her. This time, the song is "Jump" by Van Halen, so the twins keep jumping as high as they can and drop to the floor half the time.

The scene doesn't last long before she sees him standing there and stops. He has never danced with her, but his sons have. Overcome with emotion, he has to compose himself before entering the house.

Trying to be funny and lighten the mood between them, he asks, "Is this what goes on when I'm not here?"

She gives him a half-smile, lets Simon and Sam finish the song without her, and then turns off the music, leaving right away.

The next day, when Colin gets home, Hannah is gathering her belongings for a quick exit when she sees him wince in pain and put his hand to his jaw.

"When did this jaw pain start?" she inquires.

"About two weeks ago."

Moving over to him, she places her finger on the joint where the jawbone connects to the skull beside his left ear and pushes in. "Open your mouth."

"Ouch!" he yells.

"You have temporomandibular joint disorder or TMJ. Two to three times a day, you should open your mouth really wide and close it. Then, with mouth only slightly open, wiggle your jaw from side to side."

"Go ahead." She does the exercise with him.

"Do you hear popping and other sounds?"

"Yes."

"This exercise might prevent TMJ from becoming serious for you."

"I didn't know you went to medical school."

"I am aware of this because I have the same problem, but it isn't a problem because I do the exercises."

She stares at him for a moment. "And I just realized that you haven't gone surfing in a long time. You told me once what it does for you, keeping stress and anxiety at bay. You need to get back to that."

As he nods in agreement, she says, "See you tomorrow."

Watching her go fills him with regret once more for hurting her. The comments on surfing are spot on. He never should have stopped the activity that grounds him.

On the morning of the boys' birthday, which happens to be a Saturday, Hannah goes downstairs. Simon answers the door and jumps up and down as she holds a large bag of presents. He starts to tear the wrapping.

"Wait for your brother," his dad says.

Colin brings her some coffee, and once Sam finishes dressing and comes into the room, he gives the go-ahead. "Now you can open them."

Simon rips off the paper to discover an airplane made of foam with a launching device where you pull a trigger to send it up in the air. Sam notices he has a box in the same shape and cheers. The second gift is a light-up toy for their room that displays various dinosaurs on the walls and ceiling when the lights are off. The last one is matching T-shirts with the words Double Digits and the number 10, which they care nothing about, but Hannah likes them and thinks turning 10 is a big deal.

She shows the twins how to load the planes. Simon sends his flying through the air. Colin is distracted, not watching the miniature aircraft as it circles back and hits him directly in the head. His sons dramatically fall down laughing.

"Thanks, Hannah," he remarks, pretending to give her a hard time about the gift choice while holding his head.

"Did that hurt?" she teases, knowing it didn't since she did her research before buying them.

While they play with the airplanes, he turns to her. "Their birthday wish is for Jane's three youngest boys to spend the night tonight. They decided not to have a party. Grandpa Phil is coming next month to spend time with them instead."

"A sleepover. Fun. I'm sure I will hear all kinds of screaming and carrying on."

"Are you really going to leave me alone to deal with this?"

Laughing, she confirms what he already knows. "Yes! If I were you, I would drive them to McDonald's, and let them eat and play on the jungle gym until they are worn out before bringing them home."

"You mean Macca's."

"What?"

"In Australia, McDonald's is called Macca's."

"Right. I forgot."

"But, good idea, I will do that."

"Well, see you guys later."

Trying one more time to bring her back into his life in some semblance of how it used to be, he asks, "We are going to the beach. Do you want to go?"

"No thanks, but don't stay too long. If you wear them out and the other three are full of energy, that will be a recipe for disaster."

He sighs, thinking about what is ahead for him later.

Giving Simon and Sam a big hug, she tells them again, "Happy Birthday!"

Wishing he were included in the hug, his feelings of loss grow worse every day. He continues to text nightly messages professing his love, never receiving a reply.

That evening, he reaches out.

I took your advice. We are at Macca's. They are having a blast.

The phone is beside her as she works on her book, but she believes it is best not to engage.

Wish you were here.

She ignores him.

Continuing to stare at his phone, he beats himself up. What was he thinking? Why did he let her walk out the door that night?

Analyzing the situation, he acknowledges how he got carried away with the idea of Monique wanting him back. However, he is convinced his belief that Hannah could never love him played a role. It is more than a factor. It was the reason. He has to keep trying to reconnect with her.

I know you can never love me the way you loved your husband, and I accept that now. If you love me even a little, that is enough for me.

No reply.

If you won't give me a second chance, can you at least forgive me for what I did?

Hannah isn't sure she should answer. She does think she forgives him but does not understand why. If her husband had carried on with another woman, it would have been inexcusable. Why does she want to let Colin off the hook? Is it because she doesn't feel strongly enough about him to be deeply hurt?

One thing is clear. She is not ready to communicate with him about this, and consequently, his pleas go unanswered.

Unlike Colin, she has a great night's sleep. In the morning, squeaky chirping sounds can be heard. Outside the bathroom window, a crimson rosella is building a nest in the tree hollow just above the roof line. He is a Paul, not a Patty, as his crimson red is much brighter. A second parrot lands on the rooftop. This one is a girl similar to Patty. The two work on building their nest.

As hunger sets in, she moves away to make breakfast. Hearing footsteps coming up the stairs, she opens the door to find Colin bent over, placing an envelope partway under the mat.

"What's this?"

"Just read it, please," he quietly says and leaves.

While eating, she reviews his list of positive traits he sees in her. He explains that she is the only person he has ever shared his family history with and how he has never in his life been able to talk with someone the way he talks to her. The last three paragraphs describe in great detail their lives growing old together. And he tells her she is beautiful.

Returning to the other room to brush her teeth, she again watches the birds. Paul seems to notice her and comes closer. Pressing her nose to the window, she sees a heart-shaped twig in his beak.

Kiera settles into her new home with Ryan. Several weeks have passed without visions of the woman from long ago. She begins to dream about being a mother and having a healthy baby, and then another, and one more. Her dreams are good ones about her own life.

Twelve days after their wedding, it is Valentine's Day. The couple has reservations at a fancy restaurant. Hannah reminds her son to buy his new bride roses and chocolates. Dinner isn't enough, she advises him.

It pleases her to know the young people can enjoy the holiday.

The neighbor calls to see if Simon and Sam want to come over and make Valentine's cookies. She escorts them across the street. The two women visit, but Jane is distracted and keeps checking her phone, finally stating mid-conversation, "The boys can stay until their dad gets home. You can go."

Hannah, content to have a quiet afternoon and evening, returns to the house to collect her things. She opens the door, surprised to see Colin standing there when his car was not in the driveway.

He picks up a bouquet of roses from the coffee table to hand her. She smells the sweet fragrance before placing them back.

"I have one request. Will you dance with me? We have never danced. Just one time."

She does not say anything.

After selecting a song, he guides her to the middle of the room.

They slow dance to "Follow Me." Colin sings the parts he believes apply to them. Lying in bed together, listening to John Denver's tunes, seems like weeks ago, not months.

While starting with about a foot between them, they are now up against one another. With her head on his shoulder, tears run down her face.

"I do love you, Hannah."

"I love you, too."

She only lasted two weeks, not even two, but she can't help it. She loves him.

He pulls out a piece of paper from his pocket. It is a receipt for two tickets to Melbourne.

Twenty-Six

TWO YEARS LATER

Hannah hears a message come through on her phone. *It's time*, Ryan's text reads. She quickly finishes lunch and drives to the hospital. The parents-to-be had been there since 3 am. Their baby is finally ready to be welcomed into the world.

Colin and the boys arrive later that afternoon. Hannah leads them to Kiera's room.

"This is Logan Aidan Laren," she tells them.

Ryan and Kiera were determined not to ask the sex of their baby until birth, even though they were tempted at every doctor's visit. Their last name is Laren because it was shortened from McLaren, the Scottish surname of Ryan's dad's ancestors. Logan means "little hollow" in Scottish Gaelic. It is also the name of a river in Queensland. Since Kiera credits Great Uncle Aidan with saving her family from certain disaster in Ireland, honoring his memory has a special place in her heart. The couple learned of the pregnancy while on a trip to the Emerald Isle. Kiera's dream of visiting there finally came true.

The 12-year-old twins move to get a closer look at the baby boy.

Standing away from everyone, Hannah whispers to Colin, "I can't believe I'm a grandma. I am thrilled for them, but it makes me feel old."

He kisses her forehead. "It will be fun. We can babysit."

"Right, like that is what you want to do."

"I do, and Simon and Sam will like it too. You know I am turning into a homebody."

She puts her arm around him. He watches his sons interact with the young family, thinking back to the devastating news when they were diagnosed with autism at two years old. Now the boys attend regular school. While special accommodations are made for them, they can mostly keep up with the others. He is optimistic about their futures.

The expectant parents moved into a small house before the baby was born. It was a fixer-upper, which Hannah helped fund and coordinate. They have solar power, all new appliances, the most energy-efficient ones on the market, and a two-car garage for charging their electric cars.

With the hectic schedule of a move and a baby being born, she keeps forgetting to mention to her son how blue dragons are turning up in large numbers all over the Texas Gulf Coast. They are warning people not to touch the sea slugs. Scientists believe that climate change is responsible for this development as warmer waters change ocean currents. Years ago, finding one was rare and a big deal to their family.

Colin, Hannah, Ryan, and Kiera visited Swaggerty Island two years before to review the island's archives, searching for the woman Kiera had dreamt about for so long. Even though the dreams ceased prior to the outing, she still wanted information. They read about a woman named Mary Laura Davenport who worked at the asylum and died during childbirth. The facts were limited, yet they brought her closure.

Ryan now works for his cousin Clay's company, deciding to do so for a period of time and then get back to marine science. His role is to provide the data analytics needed to support their mission. From the comfort of his own home, he assists by delivering video presentations to persuade community leaders, local governments, and businesses to purchase the transformer units. They are also in negotiations with shipping industry leaders for carbon capture on ships. Next, they will tackle cars. It was a hard decision to leave the university. However, Ryan is passionate about being part of the effort to reach net-zero emissions by 2050.

Unfortunately, they were unable to attend Clay and Amy's wedding in Sydney because it took place too close to Kiera's due date. Amy and Kiera have been conspiring to bring Naomi and James together. Neither one dates nor is agreeable to a blind date. The ladies will have to get creative about bringing the pair to the same location, where they will, perhaps, be forced to communicate with one another, possibly at a dinner or some event. Naomi completed her master's degree and continues to teach at the high school. While James needs to remain in Sydney for the business, there is no reason Naomi couldn't relocate and teach at a new school, should they actually hit it off.

Kiera began taking a new asthma medication over a year ago and has not had a single asthmatic attack. She and Ryan finally went ocean walking, also called helmet diving or sea walking. Later in life, they have a pact to face their fears, enroll in a scuba class, and go for a dive.

For now, they found the most intriguing place off of Green Island in the Great Barrier Reef Marine Park to walk on the actual sea floor, aided by the heavy weight of the helmet, which you do not feel underwater.

Tapping into the artistic side she had as a child, Kiera made sketches of their ocean walking adventures and all the sea critters they encountered. She is turning them into a children's book. Parrotfish are her favorite to draw with their protruding teeth and hilarious "grinning" faces. On one helmet dive, they saw a dugong, an olive ridley, and a green humphead parrotfish that must have weighed well over 100 pounds. The couple has an idea for an ocean science app they plan to develop, but are keeping it a secret.

Since the baby was due one month into the high school's first term, she decided to take the year off from teaching and work part-time from home, tutoring students over video calls. Every Thursday, she will continue leading the Environmental Science Club meetings in person.

Allison and her fiancé, Brandt, finally made it to Australia for a visit last year. Kiera and her sister-in-law often text and message one another. Allison gives her great ideas for club activities since she also volunteers with Oregon high school students in addition to her position with the forest department. The newly engaged couple recently decided on a private ceremony in June for just the two of them in Hawaii, standing near a volcano, followed by a week of hiking and camping. Hannah does not get the volcano or such an outdoorsy honeymoon, but she is happy for her stepdaughter.

Two days after Hannah's grandson is born, she receives a call from Susan, Allison's mother, who is devastated as she has been planning her daughter's wedding since the age of fourteen. She has kept wedding ideas in a binder all of these years. The two women had never talked on the phone for any length of time and had not seen each other since Allison's college graduation. Jack's first wife was on an around-the-world cruise at the time of his funeral service.

Susan rants for the first twenty minutes about their desire to marry in Hawaii without her. She then goes on for another twenty with a tirade on how Brandt is not the right man.

Hannah tries her best to defend Brandt and point out positive traits. She isn't about to let on how Allison revealed their plan to never have children and retire by 45 to travel the world. Her parting words to her husband's ex are that, as parents, they can offer advice, but in the end, they must accept their children's decisions and wish them the best.

That weekend, Colin and Hannah have dinner out. Jane's oldest daughter is now old enough to come over and watch the boys.

On the drive to eat, she directs him to make a stop. "I have something I want to show you."

They pull up in front of a bookstore. "Look," she points.

A display of her novel is in the window. The title is *Il Mio Amore Texano, A Love Story*. She chose the title, which translates to "My Texas Love," because the character of Professor Biggio is Italian and speaks the language. He says these words to Karen after professing his love for her. A happy ending, of course.

"Well, look at that. I am so proud of you." Colin leans over and kisses her cheek. He knew her work was being published, but did not know copies had been received by the local store the day before.

His new book should be in print soon. Hannah piqued his interest in the subject of Italians coming to Australia during the Victorian Gold Rush from the small amount of research she did. He decided to delve deeper, discovering several noteworthy Italian families and writing about their adventures and accomplishments.

The Hongi Hika film is still reaching new viewers each week. The streaming service renewed the rights for a third year. Soon after it became available almost two years ago, the university surprised him with a special event to show the film to an auditorium of students and award him Professor of the Year.

They enter the restaurant and take a seat by the window. As the waiter brings them each a glass of wine, Colin, facing the front door, develops a surprised expression.

"Uh oh."

"What?" She turns her head to witness a very pregnant Monique standing at the hostess station with a handsome man in his 30s.

Monique spots them as well and comes over to their table.

Hannah greets her first. "Congratulations! When are you due?"

"In two weeks."

"Wow!"

"I know. It is our first wedding anniversary, so we wanted to go out. This is my husband Matt." Turning to him, she continues with the introduction. "And this is Colin and Hannah. Colin was involved in a play I did."

Matt nods, giving no indication he is aware of any romantic history.

"Congratulations on your anniversary, also." Hannah smiles at the couple.

Colin finally speaks. "Yes. Congratulations."

His former lover replies, "Thank you. It was nice to see you both," and pulls her spouse away by the arm.

Their eyes meet.

"Does it bother you to see her?" she asks.

"It does not bother me at all. I am happy for her. This is how it should be."

"I agree." She feels confident he is telling the truth.

They have a delightful meal and take a stroll on a lighted trail behind the restaurant. Beautiful peacocks can be seen along the way. He explains how the peacock originated in India and was brought to Australia by the British in colonial times.

When near the end of the trail, Colin steps in front of Hannah and holds her hands.

Getting down on one knee and removing a velvet box from his coat pocket, he presents her with a beautiful diamond ring.

Without delay, before he might chicken out, he lovingly asks, "Will you marry me?"

Tears fill her eyes. "Yes."

He stands up and hugs her tightly. The last two years had been the best in his life. This time, he would never let her go.

Epilogue

The year 2045.
Australia becomes the first country to achieve net-zero emissions, but other countries are coming close and reaching milestones. There is hope that the 2050 goal will be met.

Bibliography

"Adopt A Koala," World Wildlife Fund Australia, WWF-Australia 2018. https://wwf.org.au/adopt/adopt-a-koala/ (Accessed June 28, 2025)

"Adopt A Penguin," World Wildlife Fund Australia, WWF-Australia 2018. https://wwf.org.au/adopt/adopt-an-international-species/adopt-a-penguin/ (Accessed June 28, 2025)

"Adopt A Platypus," World Wildlife Fund Australia, WWF-Australia 2018. https://wwf.org.au/adopt/adopt-a-platypus/ (Accessed June 28, 2025)

"Adopt A Turtle," World Wildlife Fund Australia, WWF-Australia 2018. https://wwf.org.au/adopt/adopt-a-turtle/ (Accessed June 28, 2025)

"Air pollution linked to autism in new study." UR Medicine. June 11, 2014. YouTube video, 4:01. https://www.youtube.com/watch?v=mI1xtqsKjCg

"Artemis Exhibit: We Are Going Back to the Moon to Stay," Space Center Houston 2024. https://spacecenter.org/exhibits-and-experiences/artemis-exhibit/ (Accessed July 4, 2025)

Armstrong, Martin. "ENVIRONMENT. Where the Ocean's Microplastics Come From." August 11, 2022. 2025 Statista. https://www.statista.com/chart/17957/where-th-oceans-microplastics-come-from/ (Accessed June 17, 2025)

"Australia's Energy Commodity Resources 2024: Carbon capture and storage," Australian Government | Geoscience Australia, Last Updated July 15, 2024. https://www.ga.gov.au/aecr2024/carbon-capture-and-storage

Baumhardt, Alex. "Oregon has most miles of polluted or 'impaired' waterways nationwide, new analysis says." Oregon Capital Chronicle 2025. March 23, 2022. https://oregoncapitalchronicle.com/2022/03/23/oregon-high-among-states-with-most-polluted-waterways-according-to-new-analysis/ (Accessed July 4, 2025)

BBC Earth. "Why Female Turtles are Taking Over Raine Island | Planet Earth III Behind The Scenes | BBC Earth." October 16, 2023. YouTube video, 3:08, https://youtube.com/watch?v=BRlbSji4w2c

"Be a Reefer. Help Save Our Coral Reefs: Moody Gardens Coral Reef Lab." 2025 Moody Gardens. https://www.moodygardens.com/attractions/coral-reef-lab. (Accessed July 4, 2025)

"Bioenergy in Oregon." Oregon Department of Energy. 2025 Oregon.gov. https://www.oregon.gov/energy/energy-oregon/Pages/Bioenergy.aspx. (Accessed July 4, 2025)

"Blue Dragon Sea Slug: The Prettiest Poison," U.S. Department of the Interior | Bureau of Ocean Energy Management, March 19, 2024, https://www.boem.gov/newsroom/ocean-science-news/blue-dragon-sea-slug (Accessed July 4, 2025)

Bowers, Vicki, "Panther City," March 23, 2019, YouTube video, 3:03, https://www.youtube.com/watch?v=MfiPJ0sj71w

"Campus Tours." 2025 Texas A&M University Corpus Christi. Virtual Tours/Campus Tour Video. https://www.tamucc.edu/admissions/tour/campus-tours.php. (Accessed July 5, 2025)

"Climate Change," 2025 Great Barrier Reef Foundation. https://www.barrierreef.org/the-reef/threats/climate-change (Accessed June 27, 2025).

Codger, Kiwi. "Episode 57; Hongi's Rotorua Campaign-Part 2." Kiwi Codger, June 16, 2022, YouTube video, 21:53, https://www.youtube.com/watch?v=t1oqlBlWiE8

Codger, Kiwi. "Episode 71; Hongi's Journey to Death." Kiwi Codger, May 18, 2023, YouTube video, 14:27, https://www.youtube.com/watch?v=gC1vBDa2qzc&t=550s

Codger, Kiwi. "Hongi Goes to England: Episode 26, Musket Wars #8." Kiwi Codger. December 24, 2019. YouTube video, 10:16. https://www.youtube.com/watch?v=d7VeRL7a0x4.

"Conservation Efforts on the Great Barrier Reef," 2025 Sailing Whitsundays. https://sailing-whitsundays.com/article/conservation-efforts-on-the-great-barrier-reef (Accessed June 27, 2025)

Cox, Nicholas P., "The Great Storm (The Galveston Hurricane of 1900), Fort Bend County Libraries Adult Programs, September 28, 2020, YouTube video, 19:18, https://www.youtube.com/watch?v=2v1wYk2Efwg

Diary of a RollerCoaster Girl, "Iron Shark – 4K On-Ride POV | us Galveston Island Historic Pleasure Pier," August 22, 2024, https://www.youtube.com/watch?v=R8oFU1JuJBA

"Don't know anything about Pikmin? Start here!" 2025 Nintendo. August 2, 2023. https://www.nintendo.com/us/whatsnew/dont-know-anything-about-pikmin-start-here/ (Accessed June 17, 2025)

"Downtown." 2025 Galveston.Com & Company, Inc., https://www.galveston.com/trip-planning/areas/downtown/ (Accessed July 4, 2025)

"Facts: The Blue Sea Dragon." Deep Marine Scenes. June 23, 2020. YouTube video, 1:54. https://www.youtube.com/watch?v=7idnv4X9mjs.

"Fast Track to Net Zero by 2050." Bipartisan Policy Center. March 3, 2022. YouTube video, 2:28. https://www.youtube.com/watch?v=rddM601-06o

"First People's history & languages." Cairns Regional Council. https://www.cairns.qld.gov.au/experience-cairns/facts-figures-history/first-peoples-history (Accessed June 28, 2025)

Flintoff, Brian. "Māori musical instruments – taonga puoro – Melodic instruments – the family of Rangi," Te Ara – the Encyclopedia of New Zealand, http://www.TeAra.govt.nz/en/photograph/42158/tutanekai-playing-his-flute (Accessed June 20, 2025)

"Forest Basics. Western Hemlock." 2025 Oregon Forest Resources Institute. https://oregonforests.org/forest-types-tree-guide/tree-variety/western-hemlock. (Accessed July 4, 2025)

"Galveston Island Historic Pleasure Pier," 2025 Galveston.Com & Company, Inc, https://www.galveston.com/whattodo/attractions/pleasurepier/

"Great Barrier Reef Full Day Adventure," 2025 Journey Beyond. Cruise Whitsundays. https://www.cruisewhitsundays.com/experiences/great-barrier-reef-full-day-adventure/ (Accessed June 27, 2025)

Hamacher, Duane. "The First Astronomers: How Indigenous Elders read the stars." Astronomical Society of Victoria. April 13, 2022. YouTube video, 1:21:24. https://www.youtube.com/live/ZCW4OiyIrHE?si=BP0RJSLJPG3CKTY8 (Accessed June 18, 2025)

"History of The Woodlands." 2025 Visit The Woodlands, Texas, https://www.visitthewoodlands.com/about/history/. (Accessed June 30, 2025)

"Hongi Hika." Blog: NZShortWalks. https://walkinnz.home.blog/hongi-hika/ (Accessed June 26, 2025)

"Honoring the Past," 2025 Stockyards Heritage Development Co. https://fortworthstockyards.com/our-story/ (Accessed July 3, 2025)

"How Do Microplastics Get into Blood?" June 2, 2024. Avoid Microplastics. https://avoidmicroplastics.com/microplastics-blood/ (Accessed June 18, 2025)

"Iandra Castle," 2025 Iandra Castle. https://iandracastle.com.au (Accessed June 25, 2025).

"INTERCONTINENTAL MELBOURNE THE RIALTO – A PASSION FOR THE PAST." 2020 Business View Publishing, September 29, 2020. https://businessviewoceania.com/intercontinental-melbourne-the-rialto-a-passion-for-the-past/. (Accessed July 3, 2025)

James, Tyler. "Multnomah Falls: A Must-See Destination on Your Oregon Itinerary." 2024 That Oregon Life LLC, January 4, 2022. https://thatoregonlife.com/2022/01/multnomah-falls/. (Accessed July 4, 2025)

"John Denver talks about Jacques Cousteau and Sings Calypso."
@JohnDenver. Official Site of the John Denver Archives, operated by John
Denver's Estate. June 25, 2014. YouTube video, 6:22.
https://www.youtube.com/watch?v=VU4rKlXTI4U

Kennedy, Kelsey. "24 Best Restaurants in Waco Texas." 2025 The Waco
Things, December 12, 2024. https://thewacothings.com/best-restaurants-in-
waco-texas/. (Accessed July 3, 2025)

Kennedy, Kelsey. "A Guide To Visiting The Waco Mammoth National
Monument." 2025 The Waco Things, May 22, 2024.
https://thewacothings.com/waco-mammoth-national-monument/.
(Accessed July 3, 2025)

Kennedy, Kelsey. "FREE In Waco: Waco Suspension Bridge." 2025 The
Waco Things, December 30, 2024. https://thewacothings.com/waco-
suspension-bridge/ (Accessed July 3, 2025)

Kent, Jack. *Dooly and the Snortsnoot.* G.P. Putnam's Sons, 1972.

"Kerikeri History," Kerikeri Community Website.
https://netlist.co.nz/communities/kerikeri_new/History.cfm
(Accessed June 18, 2025)

Kitch, Troy. "Dealing with Dead Zones: hypoxia in the Ocean." Produced by
National Ocean Service/NOAA/ Department of Commerce, February 22,
2018. NOAA Ocean Podcast: Episode 13, 18:40.
https://oceanservice.noaa.gov/podcast/feb18/nop13-hypoxia.html
(Accessed July 6, 2025).

"Kookaburra | Sing-Along Video with Lyrics for Kids [SONG]." Singing
Bell. April 24, 2024. YouTube video, 1:58.
https://www.youtube.com/watch?v=KEsKV91yJiw

"Kuranda Koala Gardens," Kuranda Village in the Rainforest. Kuranda 2025.
https://www.kuranda.org/listing/kuranda-koala-gardens (Accessed June 27,
2025)

"Kuranda Scenic Railway," Kuranda Village in the Rainforest. Kuranda 2025.
https://www.kuranda.org/listing/kuranda-scenic-railway (Accessed June 27,
2025)

Lambert, Tim. "A History of Melbourne." Local Histories. March 14, 2021. https://localhistories.org/a-history-of-melbourne/ (Accessed June 30, 2025)

Lemmin-Woolfrey, Ulrike, "Sydney vs Melbourne: 7 Key Differences To Know Before You Visit." Travel Awaits, November 12, 2023. https://www.travelawaits.com/2755415/sydney-vs-melbourne-key-differences-to-know-before-visiting/ (Accessed June 30, 2025)

"Living History: Our Story." 2024 InterContinental Melbourne The Rialto. https://www.melbourne.intercontinental.com/hotel/history/ (Accessed July 11, 2025)

"Māori Wrasse: The Friendly Giant of the Great Barrier Reef," 2025 Great Barrier Reef Tours. https://greatbarrierreeftours.com/great-barrier-reef/great-barrier-reef-animals/maori-wrasse/

McKinnon, Malcolm. "Volcanic Plateau places - Lake Rotoiti to Lake Rotomā", Te Ara - the Encyclopedia of New Zealand, http://www.TeAra.govt.nz/en/photograph/15019/wishing-tree-te-ara-o-hinehopu (Accessed June 22, 2025)

"Melbourne, Australia: The Untold Story Behind the World's Most Livable City." Couch To Culture: Explore the World Remotely. June 19, 2025. YouTube video, 12:21. https://www.youtube.com/watch?v=PB6aYoRaGt8

"Moody Gardens Attractions: Aquarium Pyramid, Rainforest Pyramid, 3D & 4D Theaters, Animal Encounters." 2025 Moody Gardens. https://moodygardens.com/attractions. (Accessed July 4, 2025)

Morales, Jonathan. "Climate change puts coastal crabs in survival mode, study finds." SF State News. November, 2014. https://news.sfsu.edu/archive/climate-change-puts-coastal-crabs-survival-mode-study-finds.html (Accessed June 18, 2025).

"Mt Coot-tha precinct." Brisbane City Council 2025. https://www.brisbane.qld.gov.au/libraries-venues-and-facilities/malls-and-precincts/mt-coot-tha-precinct. (Accessed June 18, 2025)

"Old West at Its Best. Bonnie and Clyde Junior Suite." 2025 Stockyards Hotel, LLC. https://www.stockyardshotel.com. (Accessed July 3, 2025)

"Oregon Department of Forestry: Fire, State forests, Forest resources, Forest benefits," https://www.oregon.gov/odf/Pages/index.aspx (Accessed July 4, 2025)

"Oregon is number one." November 8, 2016. 2025 Oregon Forest Resources Institute. https://oregonforests.org/blog/oregon-number-one. (Accessed July 4, 2025)

"Our Vibrant Indigenous Culture," Kuranda Village in the Rainforest. Kuranda 2025. https://www.kuranda.org/about/indigenous-culture (Accessed June 27, 2025)

"Perfect Pavlova Recipe." Preppy Kitchen. May 2, 2024. YouTube video, 12:01. https://www.youtube.com/watch?v=mW-XF7tLDMQ

Perrine, Milena. "Saison Turkey Chili (and Charred Corn Tortillas)," 2025 Craft Beering. https://www.craftbeering.com/best-beer-turkey-chili-recipe/ (Accessed June 23, 2025).

"Photos." 2025 Stockyards Hotel, LLC. https://www.stockyardshotel.com/gallery/. (Accessed July 3, 2025)

"Picture Gallery," 2025 H3 Ranch. https://www.h3ranch.com/pics (Accessed July 3, 2025)

Pig & Whistle Historic Pub. Pub Classics, Steak, Ale & Mushroom Pot Pie. https://www.pigandwhistle.co.nz/menu (Accessed June 22, 2025)

Poppie, Tammy. "Cardinal Meaning & Symbolism: The Ultimate Guide." 2025 On The Feeder, Updated November 9, 2023. https://onthefeeder.com/cardinal-meaning-symbolism/. (Accessed July 3, 2025).

"Quicksilver Port Douglas (Port Douglas, Queensland)," 2025 Great Barrier Reef Tours. https://greatbarrierreeftours.com/tours/great-barrier-reef/quicksilver-port-douglas/

"Raine Island Recovery Project," 2025 Great Barrier Reef Foundation https://www.barrierreef.org/what-we-do/projects/raine-island-recovery-project (Accessed June 27, 2025).

Rasmussen, Carol. "Study Projects a Surge in Coastal Flooding, Starting in 2030s." NASA. Jet Propulsion Laboratory. Jane J. Lee / Ian J. O'Neill, July 7, 2021. https://www.nasa.gov/centers-and-facilities/jpl/study-projects-a-surge-in-coastal-flooding-starting-in-2030s/ (Accessed June 19, 2025)

Ray, William (host). "S1 E4: Warrior Chief: The Story of Hongi Hika – Black Sheep." RNZ Podcasts. Black Sheep. October 20, 2022. YouTube video, 21:21. https://www.youtube.com/watch?v=KUQwgD8siLs

"Reefsleep." 2025 Journey Beyond. Cruise Whitsundays. https://www.cruisewhitsundays.com/experiences/reefsleep/ (Accessed July 4, 2025)

"Reefsuites: Australia's First Underwater Accommodation on the Great Barrier Reef," 2025 Journey Beyond. Cruise Whitsundays. https://www.cruisewhitsundays.com/experiences/reefsuites/ (Accessed June 27, 2025)

Reid, Richard. "Not Just Ned: A True History of the Irish in Australia: Irish in Australia background." The National Museum of Australia. https://www.nma.gov.au/exhibitions/not-just-ned/background. (Accessed December 15, 2024).

Reid, Richard. "Not Just Ned: A True History of the Irish in Australia: Irish convicts." The National Museum of Australia. https://www.nma.gov.au/exhibitions/not-just-ned/family-history/irish/convicts. (Accessed December 15, 2024).

"S2 E8: The Musket Wars – RNZ." The Aotearoa History Show. August 21, 2022. YouTube video, 26:28. https://www.youtube.com/watch?v=85aX8Byl3OM

Salmons, Matthew. "Hongi, our national greeting," September 16, 2017. 2025 Stuff Digital Limited. https://www.stuff.co.nz/the-press/news/96504348/hongi-our-national-greeting (Accessed June 19, 2025)

"Sample Menu for Reefworld." Sailing Whitsundays, Updated September 13, 2022, https://sailing-whitsundays.com/article/Sample-Menu-for-Reefworld (Accessed July 4, 2025)

Scorzafava, Lauren. "New study highlights the need for urgent action to reverse runaway light pollution." 2025 DarkSky International, January 19, 2023. https://darksky.org/new/new-study-highlights-the-need-for-urgent-action-to-reverse-runaway-light-pollution/. (Accessed July 3, 2025)

"SEA FEVER EXPLAINED | The Parasitic Cnidarian Infection | Why Jelly Fish are a Blight on our Earth." Roanoke Gaming. April 8, 2022. YouTube video, 33:28. https://youtu.be/lXY8aw_8rKs?si=LBLBpT-IX538o_Hk

"Seize the Decade." Climate Council. https://www.climatecouncil.org.au/our-work/. (Accessed June 30, 2025)

Shavit, Joseph. "Scientists reprogram elephant stem cells to revive the woolly mammoth." 2025 Microsoft, December 18, 2024. https://www.msn.com/en-us/science/biology/scientist-reprogram-elephant-ste-cells-to-revive-the-woolly-mammoth/ar-AA1w5GEJ. (Accessed July 3, 2025)

"Sir Thomas Brisbane Planetarium." Brisbane City Council 2025. https://www.brisbane.qld.gov.au/libraries-venues-and-facilities/venue-and-places/sir-thomas-brisbane-planetarium (Accessed June 18, 2025)

"Space for Everyone," Space Center Houston 2024. https://spacecenter.org (Accessed July 4, 2025)

Tapsell, Paora. "Te Arawa – European impact," Te Ara – the Encyclopedia of New Zealand, http://www.TeAra.govt.nz/en/te-arawa/page-4 (Accessed June 20, 2025)

Tapsell, Paora. "Te Arawa – Warfare and marriages." Te Ara – the Encyclopedia of New Zealand, http://www.TeAra.govt.nz/en/interactive/35247/roadside-stories-island-romance-in-lake-rotorua (Accessed June 19, 2025)

"The beautiful Hinehopu/Hongi trail – over 400 years of HISTORY," EverFIT, January 1, 2023, YouTube video, 7:25, https://youtu.be/RAtWr3_VIfQ?si=w-0W9cXCGJL0xXLI

The History Guy. "History of The New Zealand Musket Wars." The History Guy: History Deserves to Be Remembered. May 23, 2017. YouTube video, 7:04. https://www.youtube.com/watch?v=GeVXAz6MGBA&t=282s

"The Myth of the Rainbow Serpent," The Archaeologist, March 4, 2025.
https://www.thearchaeologist.org/blog/the-myth-of-the-rainbow-serpent
(Accessed June 28, 2025)

"The Village of Indian Springs - The Woodlands, TX."
TheWoodlandsTX.com. Online Community.
https://www.thewoodlandstx.com/indiansprings/. (Accessed June 30, 2025)

"The Whitsundays Sustainability Hub," 2025 Tourism Whitsundays Ltd.,
https://www.tourismwhitsundays.com.au/sustainability-environment/
(Accessed June 27, 2025)

"Things To Do." 2025 Fort Worth Stockyards.
https://www.fortworthstockyards.org/home/things-to-do#categories.
(Accessed July 3, 2025)

"Things to do in Rotorua," 2025 RotoruaNZ.
https://www.rotoruanz.com/things-to-do, (Accessed June 23, 2025)

"Thriving Oceans Membership" and "The Trade Up," 2025 Surfers For
Climate Org Powered by Shopify.
https://surfersforclimate.org.au (Accessed August 26, 2025)

"Timeless Elegance in the Heart of Melbourne." 2024 InterContinental
Melbourne The Rialto. https://www.melbourne.intercontinental.com
(Accessed July 11, 2025)

Tomlinson, Jessica. "Valley Of The Giants Is A Must See in Oregon." 2024
That Oregon Life LLC, November 5, 2018.
https://thatoregonlife.com/2018/11/valley-of-the-giants/. (Accessed July 4,
2025)

"Tracing the Legacy of Great Hunger Trauma with Oonagh Walsh, PhD."
Irish American Heritage Museum. December 6, 2022. YouTube video,
1:29:02. https://www.youtube.com/watch?v=fYpmXsdAFPw

"We Slept UNDERWATER on the Great Barrier Reef! | Reefsuite |
Whitsundays | Unique Hotels," Life in HD, April 20, 2024.
https://www.youtube.com/watch?v=rXzAQbLX-FI (Accessed July 4, 2025)

Weeden, Meaghan, "Real vs. Fake Christmas Trees: Which is Better for the Environment?" 2025 One Tree Planted, December 3, 2024. https://onetreeplanted.org/blogs/stories/real-vs-artificial-christmas-trees. (Accessed June 30, 2025)

"Welcome to Kerikeri," Kerikeri Community Website. https://netlist.co.nz/communities/kerikeri_new/Index.cfm (Accessed June 18, 2025)

"Welcome to Seawalker Green Island," 2025 Seawalker Green Island|Part of the Quicksilver Group, https://seawalker.com.au (Accessed August 3, 2025)

"What are nurdles? The plastic pellets threatening marine life." Fauna & Flora. June 20, 2022. YouTube video, 2:08. https://www.youtube.com/watch?v=7qsc82ErMB8.

"What is the sculpture at the entrance to TAMU-CC?" 2025 Texas A&M University Corpus Christi. 2017 Mary and Jeff Bell Library. https://help.library.tamucc.edu/faq/153284. (Accessed July 5, 2025)

"What We Do." 2025 DarkSky International. https://darksky.org/what-we-do/. (Accessed July 3 5, 2025)

"Why Do Kangaroos Flex Their Muscles?#shorts." A2JCREATIONZ. YouTube video, 0:33. https://youtube.com/shorts/W-agM7Xppt0?si=s-o-Y3DuB3RI5BfA

"Why Male Dolphins Gift Sea Sponges?! #animalfacts." Interesting How's. YouTube video, 0:41. https://youtube.com/shorts/dSYCGcsqj5U?si=-zmuo9bTSdm3MPr-

Wikipedia contributors, "Haka," *Wikipedia, The Free Encyclopedia,* https://en.wikipedia.org/w/index.php?title=Haka&oldid=1278944466 (Accessed March 9, 2025).

Wikipedia contributors, "Māori people," *Wikipedia, The FreeEncyclopedia,* https://en.wikipedia.org/w/index.php?title=M%C4%81ori_people&oldid=1295255984 (Accessed June 13, 2025).

Wikipedia contributors, "Mokoia Island," *Wikipedia, The FreeEncyclopedia,* https://en.wikipedia.org/w/index.php?title=Mokoia_Island&oldid=1257438274 (Accessed November 24, 2024).

Wikipedia contributors, "Pikmin," *Wikipedia, The Free Encyclopedia*, https://en.wikipedia.org/w/index.php?title=Pikmin&oldid=1259066656 (Accessed November 24, 2024).

Winter, Marcus. "The Love Story of Hinemoa & Tutanekai (in Sand)." Marcus Winter The Sandman. June 15, 2020. YouTube video, 3:45. https://www.youtube.com/watch?v=XlMHqdFdO7U

Wood, Johnny. "CLIMATE ACTION: What does net-zero emissions mean and how can we get there?" 2025 World Economic Forum, November 9, 2021. https://www.weforum.org/stories/2021/11/net-zero-emissions-cop26-climate-change/ (Accessed July 8, 2025)

Zombor, Luke, "Carbon Capture in Australia: A Sustainable Future Ahead," 2023 Green Energy Watch, September 13, 2023, https://www.greenenergywatch.com.au/carbon-capture-in-australia-a-sustainable-future-ahead/ (Accessed July 13, 2025)

Extended Author's Notes

Chapter One

Swaggerty Island is a fictitious island.

For the Laren family, the description of Texas A&M Corpus Christi campus is from their website listed below and also from a personal visit by the author. See: "Campus Tours." https://www.tamucc.edu

The Texas A&M Corpus Christi library online has a document explaining the *"Momentum"* sculpture created by Robert Roesch and its meaning. See: "What is the sculpture at the entrance to TAMU-CC?" https://help.library.tamucc.edu/faq/153284

Professor Mark Clarke is a fictional character, as are all characters in the story.

There are many different sources that describe the blue dragon sea slug and various YouTube videos about the creature. See: "Facts: The Blue Sea Dragon" by Deep Marine Scenes and their list of references and helpful links. https://www.youtube.com/watch?v=7idnv4X9mjs.

Chapter Two

MacDermid University is a fictitious university in the made-up town of Kirkdam.

Kiera's professor gives a lecture on Nurdles: There are many difference internet sources and YouTube videos about nurdles. See: "What are nurdles?

The plastic pellets threatening marine life" by Fauna & Flora:
https://www.youtube.com/watch?v=7qsc82ErMB8.

In the information section below the "What are nurdles?" video, it says: "Find out more and take action," at https://www.fauna-flora.org/nurdles/

To learn more about how you can support the fight against ocean pollution or participate in nurdle cleanups, search Nurdle Cleanups in your area or go to https://oceanblueproject.org or https://www.seashepherd.org.au/latest-news/.

Professor Ryan's lecture is from multiple sources.

He tells the class, "Today, about 20% of all Māori, over 170,000, now live in Australia." This is from Wikipedia, among other sources. See: Wikipedia contributors, "Māori people." https://en.wikipedia.org/wiki/Māori_people

Information from the rest of his lecture can be found in the following podcast (but the same info is found in multiple sources on the internet). See: Ray, "S1 E4: Warrior Chief: The Story of Hongi Hika – Black Sheep," https://www.youtube.com/watch?v=KUQwgD8siLs

See Also: Codger, "Hongi Goes to England: Episode 26, Musket Wars #8," https://www.youtube.com/watch?v=d7VeRL7a0x4.

The History Guy on YouTube is a good resource as well. See: "History of The New Zealand Musket Wars," https://www.youtube.com/watch?v=GeVXAz6MGBA&t=282s

The following is a blog called NZShortWalks with a section on Hong Hika and places to see and walk in New Zealand: https://walkinnz.home.blog/hongi-hika/. The NZShortWalks blog lists Wikipedia as a source and suggests watching Kiwi Codger's YouTube videos to learn more. https://www.youtube.com/@kiwicodger

Another source for the reader to learn more about New Zealand history is the Te Ara Encyclopedia of New Zealand found online: https://teara.govt.nz/en

Chapter Three

Details on *Pikmin* are from Wikipedia and also personal experience as the author has seen her own son play the game many times. See: Wikipedia contributors, "Pikmin."

Visit the Nintendo website (https://www.nintendo.com/us/) for Pikmin games and an article titled "Don't know anything about Pikmin? Start here!"

Article:
https://www.nintendo.com/us/whatsnew/dont-know-anything-about-pikmin-start-here/

Available Games:
https://www.nintendo.com/us/search/#q=Pikmin&p=1&cat=all&sort=df

An internet search of "Irish potato famine and mental health" results in many different sources discussing what Colin tells Hannah: "Your son's disposition is probably the curse of being Irish and from the starvation by our ancestors during the potato famine which affected our genes, making us more likely to be depressed." See: "Tracing the Legacy of Great Hunger Trauma with Oonagh Walsh, PhD." At URL:
https://www.youtube.com/watch?v=fYpmXsdAFPw

The Ryans Down Under is a fictional title, and Colin's book is not based on a real book.

Regarding Hannah's children's books, there is a book called *Walter and the Magic Carrot*, written by the author, and available to read for free at the following URL:
https://www.storyjumper.com/book/read/173228751/Walter-and-the-Magic-Carrot

Hannah's other children's book, *The Blue Dragon,* is a fictional title not based on a real book.

At work, Ryan learns: "A significant amount of this plastic debris in our oceans comes from the simple act of machine-washing clothes made of polyester, acrylic, and nylon. Most of what he wears is quick-drying athletic clothing. These items are exactly what the problem is about. He has always made it a point to use as little plastic as possible but overlooked the fact his clothes *are* a form of plastic." See: Armstrong, "ENVIRONMENT. Where the Ocean's Microplastics Come From."
https://www.statista.com/chart/17957/where-th-oceans-microplastics-come-from/

"Another alarming piece of information is described. Microplastics are in our blood and organs and could damage veins and cells. *Absolutely frightening,* thinks Ryan." Again, there are many sources on the internet regarding this subject.

See: "How Do Microplastics Get into Blood?"
https://avoidmicroplastics.com/microplastics-blood/

To learn more about how to help the Earth and reduce your impact, visit:
https://earth911.com

To learn how to reduce your exposure to microplastics visit:
https://earth911.com/health/reduce-microplastic-exposure/

Chapter Four

Information on Hannah and Ryan's visit to Mount Coot-tha and the Sir Thomas Brisbane Planetarium with the Skylore exhibit and Cosmic Skydome is from the Brisbane City Council website. See: "Sir Thomas Brisbane Planetarium" and "Mt Coot-tha precinct."

URLs below:

https://www.brisbane.qld.gov.au/libraries-venues-and-facilities/venue-and-places/sir-thomas-brisbane-planetarium

https://www.brisbane.qld.gov.au/libraries-venues-and-facilities/malls-and-precincts/mt-coot-tha-precinct

For what Ryan reads on the Skylore exhibit and to learn more, See: Hamacher, "The First Astronomers: How Indigenous Elders read the stars" by the Astronomical Society of Victoria." Their YouTube video URL is below. The Skylore exhibit's curator is Dr. Duane Hamacher, and the information is based on his book by the same name as the video.
https://www.youtube.com/live/ZCW4OiyIrHE?si=BP0RJSLJPG3CKTY8

Colin explains to Hannah about his love of surfing and a real-life charity he is involved with that promotes climate action. "And I am a member of an organization called Surfers for Climate. I donate and volunteer at sessions with a contractor mate of mine to educate local tradespeople on greener building, and I help promote environmental campaigns throughout the year."
https://surfersforclimate.org.au/pages/about

Chapter Five

In 2011, Dr. Richard Reid was the Senior Curator of the National Museum of Australia's Irish in Australia exhibit "Not Just Ned." The museum's website contains an essay by Dr. Reid from which Professor Ryan briefly mentions the subjects of Irish Catholics in Australia and Irish acceptance of Aboriginals in his lecture. See: Reid, "Not Just Ned," and the URLs below for more information:
www.nma.gov.au/exhibitions/not-just-ned/background
www.nma.gov.au/exhibitions/not-just-ned/family-history/irish/convicts

Chapter Six

Ryan mentions to the kayaking group about an article he read from a San Francisco State University study finding that "porcelain crabs can go into survival mode to adapt to lower ocean water pH and warmer temperatures due to climate change, but this leaves them with less energy to grow and reproduce." See: Morales, "Climate change puts coastal crabs in survival mode, study finds." URL: https://news.sfsu.edu/archive/climate-change-puts-coastal-crabs-survival-mode-study-finds.html. The article mentions the following citation as a primary source:
Paganini, Adam W., Nathan A. Miller, and Jonathon H. Stillman. "Temperature and acidification variability reduce physiological performance in the intertidal zone porcelain crab Petrolisthes cinctipes," *Journal of Experimental Biology* (November 12, 2014).

Chapter Seven

For information on the history of Kerikeri, what to do, where to stay, and where to eat, See: "Kerikeri History" and "Welcome to Kerikeri." URLs below:

https://netlist.co.nz/communities/kerikeri_new/History.cfm
https://netlist.co.nz/communities/kerikeri_new/Index.cfm

"I have given entire lectures about potatoes." The History Guy discusses what Colin mentions about potatoes and the Musket Wars. See: "History of The New Zealand Musket Wars,"
https://www.youtube.com/watch?v=GeVXAz6MGBA&t=282s

The Aotearoa History Show discusses the same topic. See: "S2 E8: The Musket Wars – RNZ."
https://www.youtube.com/watch?v=85aX8Byl3OM

The engineering entrepreneurs and Net-Zero: "They are all anxious about failing in this endeavor and letting their investors down. Overriding this fear is the motivation to contribute to Australia reaching a balance between the amount of greenhouse gas produced and the amount that is removed from the atmosphere. Net-zero emissions by 2050 is a world-wide goal, but the trio hopes to help achieve this even sooner." There are many sources on the internet from which to learn about net-zero and the 2050 goal. See: Wood, "CLIMATE ACTION: What does net-zero emissions mean and how can we get there?" at URL: https://www.weforum.org/stories/2021/11/net-zero-emissions-cop26-climate-change/

There are many YouTube videos on the subject of Net-Zero also: See: "Fast Track to Net Zero by 2050," by the Bipartisan Policy Center. The video lists the following website to learn more: https://www.decarbamerica.org

The film production shoots footage of the villagers starting their day by singing and praying as the sun rises. Then a group performs a *Haka,* or traditional war dance, involving facial expressions of fear and sticking out their tongues while chanting loudly and stamping their feet. See: Wikipedia contributors, "Haka." To learn more:
https://en.wikipedia.org/w/index.php?title=Haka&oldid=1278944466

"Rawiri moves closer and begins to lean his face into hers. Her reaction is to step back. Colin laughs. "He wants to give you a *hongi.* It is the Māori greeting of touching noses and sometimes foreheads, too. It is their way of showing unity by exchanging the breath of life, called the *ha.*"
See: Salmons, "Hongi, our national greeting." To learn more:
https://www.stuff.co.nz/the-press/news/96504348/hongi-our-national-greeting

"I let him know how the angle of the moon's orbit will alter in the 2030s, leading to significant increases in high tide flooding when combined with the sea level rise. Of course, this means it is all the more important to plan ahead," See Rasmussen, "Study Projects a Surge in Coastal Flooding, Starting in 2030s." The information is from an article on NASA's website from their Jet Propulsion Laboratory. https://www.nasa.gov/centers-and-facilities/jpl/study-projects-a-surge-in-coastal-flooding-starting-in-2030s/

"Hannah sits up. 'You told me to remind you to check the script for the Australia scenes and make sure it was revised to emphasize how Hongi Hika's motivation in developing good relations with missionaries was to have more opportunities for trade and acquiring muskets. It was about personal goals of power and revenge, not religion.'" See: "Hongi Hika" NZShortWalks Blog: https://walkinnz.home.blog/hongi-hika/

Colin's fictional film scenes depicting the end of Hongi's life are from the following: See: Codger, "Episode 71; Hongi's Journey to Death."
https://www.youtube.com/watch?v=gC1vBDa2qzc&t=550s
Kiwi Codger's video lists the following references:
Augustus Earle's account, page 62;
http://www.enzb.auckland.ac.nz/docume...
Captain Peter Dillon's Account, Page 331:
http://www.enzb.auckland.ac.nz/docume...
Richard Cruise's account, P19; http://www.enzb.auckland.ac.nz/docume...
Wakahuia Series on Hongi Hika...Mahoe 29:15;
WAKA HUIA - HŌNGI HIKA FULL EPISODE

Chapter Eight

"They have a late dinner at the Pig & Whistle Historic Pub. 'I highly recommend the Steak, Ale & Mushroom Pot Pie,' suggests Colin." See: "Pig & Whistle Historic Pub"
The restaurant's website and menu: http://www.pigandwhistle.co.nz

Hannah mentions making turkey beer chili. "I will eat any food with beer in it," she laughs. "I don't like to cook much, but I do make beer turkey chili a few times a year." For a recipe, See: "Perrine/Craft Beering."
https://www.craftbeering.com/best-beer-turkey-chili-recipe/

While having dinner in Rotorua, Colin says: "A group of us will go to the (Mokoia) island ahead of them on a boat. Tikitere is also called Hell's Gate because it is the most active geothermal spot in this area. It has acidic lakes, mud pools, a small mud volcano, and a hot waterfall called Kakahi Falls." For information on Rotorua, Hell's Gate, Kakahi Falls, etc., See: "Things to do in Rotorua," https://www.rotoruanz.com/things-to-do.

"He (Colin) goes on to speak of the forbidden love story between a young man named Tūtānekai, who lived on Mokoia Island, and his sweetheart, Hinemoa. The girl's father forbade her to marry him, ordering his daughter not to canoe over to the island. She decided to swim instead, listening to the sound of Tūtānekai playing the flute to direct her where to go." See: Flintoff,

Wikipedia contributor, "Mokoia Island," Tapsell, "Te Arawa – Warfare and marriages," and Winter, "The Love Story" video on YouTube. URL: https://www.youtube.com/watch?v=XlMHqdFdO7U

For the Te Arawa battle with Ngāpuhi on Mokoia island. See: Tapsell, "Te Arawa – European impact." The URL below describes how the Te Arawa lacked firearms and retreated to Mokoia Island with all the area's canoes, but their enemy assisted the Ngāpuhi and Hongi Hika with providing canoes. http://www.TeAra.govt.nz/en/te-arawa/page-4

For more about the battle and Hongi being hit in the helmet, See: Codger, "Episode 57: Hongi's Rotorua Campaign-Part 2." https://www.youtube.com/watch?v=t1oqlBlWiE8

Hinehopu/Hongi Trail and The Wishing Tree. For a great video of the trail that makes you feel as if you are there and includes history of the area, along with information on Hinehopu and The Wishing Tree, See: "The beautiful Hinehopu/Hongi trail" from EverFIT at the following URL: https://youtu.be/RAtWr3_VIfQ?si=w-0W9cXCGJL0xXLI

For information on visiting the trail, See the URL below for the Department of Conservation (NZ). Hinehopu/Hongi's Track: https://www.doc.govt.nz/parks-and-recreation/places-to-go/bay-of-plenty/places/lake-rotoiti-and-lake-rotoma-scenic-reserves/things-to-do/hinehopu-hongis-track/

For a picture of the tree and information, See: McKinnon, "Volcanic Plateau places - Lake Rotoiti to Lake Rotomā," URL: http://www.TeAra.govt.nz/en/photograph/15019/wishing-tree-te-ara-o-hinehopu

"Finally, it is her turn. She moves to the podium. 'My presentation is on low-oxygen areas called dead zones in our oceans where most marine life cannot survive.'" For Information on Kiera's presentation, See: Kitch, "Dealing with Dead Zones: hypoxia in the Ocean." URL below: https://oceanservice.noaa.gov/podcast/feb18/nop13-hypoxia.html

Chapter Nine

"The next morning is an early start for the drive to Iandra Castle." Iandra is a heritage-listed homestead that looks like a castle. Completed in 1911, this was the home of George Henry Greene of Ireland. It is located near the town of Greenethorpe named after Mr. Greene. Iandra Castle has open house days each year to visit the homestead, gardens, and other buildings on the property. See "Iandra Castle." https://iandracastle.com.au

Chapter Ten

When Ryan invites Kiera to the Great Barrier Reef, he says, "Some of the money from tourism goes towards conservation efforts for the reef. The tour guides preserve the reef by teaching others how to protect it." See: "Conservation Efforts on the Great Barrier Reef," https://sailing-whitsundays.com/article/conservation-efforts-on-the-great-barrier-reef

and See: "The Whitsundays Sustainability Hub," https://www.tourismwhitsundays.com.au/sustainability-environment/

Ryan tells Kiera, "Climate change is the biggest threat to the Great Barrier Reef, not the people visiting there." See: "Climate Change," 2025 Great Barrier Reef Foundation. https://www.barrierreef.org/the-reef/threats/climate-change

They discuss Raine Island. See: "Raine Island Recovery Project," https://www.barrierreef.org/what-we-do/projects/raine-island-recovery-project

Ryan also says, "If you want, we can join these reef protection groups." To learn more about the Great Barrier Reef Foundation and how to donate: https://www.barrierreef.org

"Speaking of Raine Island, did you know that 99% of the baby sea turtles hatching there are female because the area is the hardest hit by climate change and warmer temperatures which females can withstand more than males?" See: "BBC Earth," https://youtube.com/watch?v=BRlbSji4w2c

Chapter Eleven

Hannah and Colin's conversation on kangaroos and dolphins:

"Boys can be over-the-top competitive," he laughs. "Even male kangaroos like to show off their forearm size, and of course, the bigger stronger ones in nature get the females." Hannah rolls her eyes. "It is all a little obsessive if you ask me."

See the following video: "Why Do Kangaroos Flex Their Muscles?"
https://youtube.com/shorts/W-agM7Xppt0?si=s-o-Y3DuB3RI5BfA

Hannah says, "male dolphins will dive into the water and bring back sea sponges to the females they are interested in. Leave it to a dolphin to realize that being sweet is what works. They are so smart." "Aren't *I* sweet?" he asks. See: "Why Male Dolphins Gift Sea Sponges,"
https://youtube.com/shorts/dSYCGcsqj5U?si=-zmuo9bTSdm3MPr-

For Ryan and Kiera's experience on a pontoon at the Reef, See: "Quicksilver Port Douglas," https://greatbarrierreeftours.com/tours/great-barrier-reef/quicksilver-port-douglas/

"The funniest fish Hannah has ever seen appears in front of the window closest to her. It is huge with a large blue-grey face and the biggest lips." See: "Māori Wrasse,"
https://greatbarrierreeftours.com/great-barrier-reef/great-barrier-reef-animals/maori-wrasse/

Ryan and Kiera watch "Sea Fever." The following YouTube video explains about the movie, the red hair theory, and the eyes popping out. See: "SEA FEVER EXPLAINED," https://youtu.be/lXY8aw_8rKs?si=LBLBpT-IX538o_Hk

Chapter Twelve

The characters visit Kuranda Village. Information on the Kuranda Scenic Railway, Kuranda Village, Kuranda Koala Gardens (wildlife park), and some history of the Diabugay people is from the following website: https://www.kuranda.org. See: "Kuranda Scenic Railway," "Our Vibrant Indigenous Culture," and "Kuranda Koala Gardens."

When Colin tells Hannah about the Rainbow Serpent, this information is from the following two websites: See: "The Myth of the Rainbow Serpent," The Archaeologist.
https://www.thearchaeologist.org/blog/the-myth-of-the-rainbow-serpent
and "First People's history & languages," Cairns Regional Council.
https://www.cairns.qld.gov.au/experience-cairns/facts-figures-history/first-peoples-history

"Hannah geta an idea. She pulls up the website for the World Wildlife Fund Australia to show the twins a list of animals they can 'symbolically' adopt to help save them." See: "Adopt A Platypus," "Adopt A Koala," "Adopt A Penguin," and "Adopt A Turtle." The website URL is: https://wwf.org.au.

Chapter Thirteen

Hannah talks about where she grew up. The information on The Woodlands and its founder, George Mitchell, is from The Woodlands Convention & Visitors Bureau's website. See "History of The Woodlands." https://www.visitthewoodlands.com/about/history/

Hannah discusses growing up in a subdivision where the Bidai tribe lived, and their artifacts were discovered during development." See "The Village of Indian Springs - The Woodlands, TX." https://www.thewoodlandstx.com/indiansprings/.

Chapter Fourteen

Hannah, Simon, and Sam record themselves reading a favorite childhood book of the author's. See: Kent, *Dooly and the Snortsnoot.*

"While she did not want to get into this topic with Colin, she has been doing some research about autism and possible causes. She was shocked to read on the internet about a link between exposure to air pollution and increased risk of autism." There are many different sources on the internet discussing a link between exposure to air pollution and increased risk of autism. See: "Air pollution linked to autism in new study" by UR Medicine at the following URL: https://www.youtube.com/watch?v=mI1xtqsKjCg

"Since climate change worsens air pollution, she (Hannah) decides to subscribe to the Climate Council." The Australian group is a nonprofit that supports climate policies and solutions. She makes a donation and will receive newsletters on the latest in climate news, research, and ways to contribute to the cause. See: "Seize the Decade." Check out their website: https://www.climatecouncil.org.au/our-work/.

Chapter Fifteen

Excerpt:

> While coming up the steps of the porch, a gray-brown bird lands.
> "I've never seen a bird like this," he remarks.
> The creature proceeds to produce the longest, craziest laugh.
> "It's a kookaburra."

"A song just popped into my head from childhood."
"Yes. It was written over 90 years ago."
They sing the first few verses before stepping inside.

See: "Kookaburra | Sing-Along Video with Lyrics for Kids [SONG]."
URL: https://www.youtube.com/watch?v=KEsKV91yJiw

Chapter Sixteen

Hannah read how Melbourne was settled by people from Tasmania without authority from the British and also learns about the rivalry between Melbourne and Sydney. There are many sources which discuss the rivalry. For one, See: Lemmin-Woolfrey, "Sydney vs Melbourne." https://www.travelawaits.com/2755415/sydney-vs-melbourne-key-differences-to-know-before-visiting/

To learn more about the History of Melbourne, See: Lambert, "A History of Melbourne." https://localhistories.org/a-history-of-melbourne/

And see the YouTube video "Melbourne, Australia: The Untold Story Behind the World's Most Livable City" by Couch To Culture: Explore the World Remotely. https://www.youtube.com/watch?v=PB6aYoRaGt8

Chapter Seventeen

No references

Chapter Eighteen

When Hannah talks about the benefits of real Christmas trees, there are many sources on the internet discussing this topic, See: Weeden, "Real vs. Fake Christmas Trees: Which is Better for the Environment?" https://onetreeplanted.org/blogs/stories/real-vs-artificial-christmas-trees

One Tree Planted plants trees around the world in areas that need it the most. To learn what they are about and support their reforestation work, see their website: https://onetreeplanted.org

Colins tells Hannah about his favorite Christmas dessert, Pavlova. There are many different recipes on the internet and YouTube. For a YouTube video, See: "Perfect Pavlova Recipe" by Preppy Kitchen. https://www.youtube.com/watch?v=mW-XF7tLDMQ

The video mentions what Colin says about the dessert being "named after a Russian ballerina, Anna Pavlova."

Ryan tries to explain carbon capture to his mother. "Since only so much can be reused for products, a lot of captured carbon is injected deep underground in reservoirs, which is controversial, but Australia is the perfect place for doing that with its immense availability of geologically stable land. Other countries could send their captured carbon here for storage to increase the chances of the world meeting the 2050 goal of net-zero emissions."

There are many sources on the interest explaining this concept. See: Zombor, "Carbon Capture in Australia: A Sustainable Future Ahead" and the Green Energy Watch website:
https://www.greenenergywatch.com.au/carbon-capture-in-australia-a-sustainable-future-ahead/

Also see the Geoscience Australia website on this subject:
https://www.ga.gov.au/aecr2024/carbon-capture-and-storage

Hannah mentions a hotel called the InterContinental Melbourne and the magazine she learned about it from. The magazine is a real article cited below. However, there are many sources on the internet discussing the history of the hotel and of Melbourne. See: "InterContinental Melbourne The Rialto," https://businessviewoceania.com/intercontinental-melbourne-the-rialto-a-passion-for-the-past/.

Also, go to the hotel's website for photos, information on rooms, dining & amenities, and some history: See: "Timeless Elegance in the Heart of Melbourne." https://www.melbourne.intercontinental.com

And "Living History: Our Story."
https://www.melbourne.intercontinental.com/hotel/history/

Chapter Nineteen

"While waiting at the airport earlier, they listened to the John Denver song 'Calypso,' which is a tribute to Cousteau and his research ship by that name. Ryan explained that John had the privilege to go on an outing with the oceanographer." See: "John Denver talks about Jacques Cousteau and Sings Calypso." https://www.youtube.com/watch?v=VU4rKlXTI4U.

Kiera tells Ryan about sky brightness at night increasing significantly every year and how DarkSky International educates people and works with

communities. To learn more about the organization, See: "What We Do."
https://darksky.org/what-we-do/.

Also See: Scorzafava. "New study highlights the need for urgent action to
reverse runaway light pollution." https://darksky.org/new/new-study-
highlights-the-need-for-urgent-action-to-reverse-runaway-light-pollution/.

The description and history of the Stockyards Hotel in Fort Worth is from the
author visiting the hotel personally and also looking at their website. See:
"Photos." https://www.stockyardshotel.com/gallery/.

Also See: "OLD WEST AT ITS BEST. BONNIE AND CLYDE JUNIOR
SUITE." 2025 Stockyards Hotel, LLC. https://www.stockyardshotel.com.

The description of the Fort Worth Stockyards and activities is from the author
visiting the area many times and from looking at their website. See" "Thing to
Do." https://www.fortworthstockyards.org/home/things-to-do#categories.

"A little while later, the couple descends the stairs to the H3 Ranch
restaurant." See: "Picture Gallery," https://www.h3ranch.com/pics

Ryan tells her some history of the Stockyards, "once the largest livestock-
trading center in the southwest," and the hotel. See: "Honoring the Past,"
https://fortworthstockyards.com/our-story/

The website above also explains about the cattle drive under "The Herd," and
lists shops, bars, restaurants, tours, and other attractions. In the "Tours"
section is the Ghost Tour that Ryan mentions to Kiera, but she declines.

Kiera tells Ryan about why the city he grew up in is called Panther City, a fact
he never knew. See: Bowers, "Panther City."
https://www.youtube.com/watch?v=MfiPJ0sj71w
The YouTube video above mentions the Dallas Morning News as a primary
source. The link to their news article is below:
https://www.dallasnews.com/news/curious-texas/2018/06/06/why-is-fort-
worth-called-panther-city-curious-texas-investigates-a-regional-rivalry/

Chapter Twenty

When Ryan and Kiera visit Waco, they talk about the Waco Suspension
Bridge, visit the Waco Mammoth National Monument, and have lunch at
Crickets. All of these places are mentioned in a website called The Waco
Things: https://thewacothings.com

Ryan and Kiera discuss the topic of scientists cloning elephants to bring back mammoths. There are many different sources on the internet that discuss this topic. See: Shavit, Joseph. "Scientists reprogram elephant stem cells to revive the woolly mammoth.". https://www.msn.com/en-us/science/biology/scientist-reprogram-elephant-ste-cells-to-revive-the-woolly-mammoth/ar-AA1w5GEJ.

Ryan says to Kiera: "Native Americans believe that if you spot a cardinal, you will have good luck within 12 days of the sighting, so we will see what our luck brings." See: Poppie, "Cardinal Meaning & Symbolism: The Ultimate Guide." https://onthefeeder.com/cardinal-meaning-symbolism/..

Ryan's friend Leo says, "We recently completed a project working on the coolest robot for the police department. It can go into places and provide video to officers before they go inside and put their lives at risk." There are many articles on the internet about police around the country utilizing robots.

Kiera discusses the Moody Gardens Coral Reef Project at lunch. See: "Be a Reefer. Help Save Our Coral Reefs," https://www.moodygardens.com/attractions/coral-reef-lab
The link above describes the project, provides a link to donate to the cause, and explains that by visiting Moody Gardens, your ticket purchase helps with ocean conservation and other causes.

"The Strand (in Galveston, Texas) is a cool place with shops, restaurants, and bars in an area where the buildings are well over 100 years old," Felicia explains. See: "Downtown," https://www.galveston.com/trip-planning/areas/downtown/

"The Pier has carnival rides and a roller coaster." Pointing to Ryan, Leo continues, "And this guy doesn't like rides. Can you believe that? I can't wait to ride the Iron Shark roller coaster."

For a video of what it is like to ride the Iron Shark, see the following YouTube video posted by Diary of a RollerCoaster Girl, https://www.youtube.com/watch?v=R8oFU1JuJBA

For more information about The Pier, See: "Galveston Island Historic Pleasure Pier," https://www.galveston.com/whattodo/attractions/pleasurepier/

Ryan and Kiera visit the Houston Space Center. https://spacecenter.org

Kiera tells Ryan about the Artemis missions. See: "Artemis Exhibit: We Are Going Back to the Moon to Stay," https://spacecenter.org/exhibits-and-experiences/artemis-exhibit/

Ryan mentions The Galveston Hurricane of 1900. See: Cox, "The Great Storm." This YouTube video presented by Dr. Cox provides in-depth information by about the hurricane and long-term consequences. https://www.youtube.com/watch?v=2v1wYk2Efwg

Chapter Twenty-One

For their adventures at Moody Gardens in Galveston, Texas, See: "Moody Gardens Attractions: Aquarium Pyramid. Rainforest Pyramid. 3D & 4D Theaters. Animal Encounters." https://moodygardens.com/attractions.

Gaidos is a real restaurant in Galveston, Texas that the author has been to a number of times. The food is excellent! https://www.gaidos.com

Chapter Twenty-Two

It is never said exactly where Allison works. Character discussions regarding the forests in Oregon, fires, forest resources, replanting of trees, helping landowners, and duties and coursework for Allison's position are based on information from the following website:
https://www.oregon.gov/odf/Pages/index.aspx

"The first part of the drive is a regular highway where they can talk. 'I read that Oregon has the most polluted waters in the country. What's up with that?' Ryan asks." See: Baumhardt," "Oregon has most miles of polluted or 'impaired' waterways nationwide, new analysis says."
https://oregoncapitalchronicle.com/2022/03/23/oregon-high-among-states-with-most-polluted-waterways-according-to-new-analysis/

Ryan, Kiera, and Allison's adventure at the Valley of the Giants in Oregon is inspired from the following: See: Tomlinson, "Valley of The Giants Is a Must See in Oregon." https://thatoregonlife.com/2018/11/valley-of-the-giants/.

There are many sources that discuss the Western Hemlock. The Oregon Forest Resources Institute is one of them. See: "Forest Basics. Western Hemlock." https://oregonforests.org/forest-types-tree-guide/tree-variety/western-hemlock.

Ryan and his sister Allison have a discussion about the logging industry in Oregon and the use of biofuel. This conversation is based on information from the following: See: "Bioenergy in Oregon." https://www.oregon.gov/energy/energy-oregon/Pages/Bioenergy.aspx. AND See: "Oregon is number one." https://oregonforests.org/blog/oregon-number-one.

Kiera and Ryan's outing to Multnomah Falls was inspired by another *That Oregon Life* article. See: James, "Multnomah Falls: A Must-See Destination on Your Oregon Itinerary." https://thatoregonlife.com/2022/01/multnomah-falls/.

Chapter Twenty-Three

"Everyone invited can attend. Kiera receives towels, candles, a *Bride* tote bag, wine glasses (when neither drinks), *Mr. Right/Mrs. Always Right* travel mugs, a blanket, and a picnic basket. The final gift is a pillow with the word *Tonight* on one side and *Not Tonight on the other*. The married women all giggle." These items can all be found on Amazon: https://www.amazon.com

Chapter Twenty-Four

Ryan and Kiera's honeymoon in a Cruise Whitsundays Reefsuite. See: Life in HD, "We Slept UNDERWATER," https://www.youtube.com/watch?v=rXzAQbLX-FI The video references: https://www.cruisewhitsundays.com/experiences/reefsuites/

The newlyweds mention their wedding night dinner: See: "Sample Menu," https://sailing-whitsundays.com/article/Sample-Menu-for-Reefworld

Before they retire to their "Reefsuite," the couple lies on a "Reefbed" on deck. See: https://www.cruisewhitsundays.com/experiences/reefsleep/

Chapter Twenty-Five

Laughing, she confirms what he already knows. "Yes! If I were you, I would drive them to McDonald's, and let them eat and play on the jungle gym until they are worn out before bringing them home."
"You mean Macca's."
"What?"
"In Australia, McDonald's is called Macca's."
"Right. I forgot."   See: https://mcdonalds.com.au

Chapter Twenty-Six

"With the hectic schedule of a move and a baby being born, she (Hannah) keeps forgetting to mention to her son how blue dragons are turning up in large numbers all over the Texas Gulf Coast. They are warning people not to touch the sea slugs. Scientists believe that climate change is responsible for this development as warmer waters change ocean currents. Years ago, finding one was rare and a big deal to their family." See: "Blue Dragon," and the website for the Bureau of Ocean Energy Management: https://www.boem.gov/newsroom/ocean-science-news/blue-dragon-sea-slug

"For now, they (Ryan and Kiera) found the most intriguing place off of Green Island in the Great Barrier Reef Marine Park to walk on the actual sea floor, aided by the heavy weight of the helmet, which you do not feel underwater." See: "Welcome to Seawalker Green Island." https://seawalker.com.au

BOOK CLUB Group Discussion Questions

QUESTION 1: How long should someone wait after the loss of a spouse before dating?

It has been eight months since she lost Jack. She begins to feel guilty about her physical relationship with Colin. The idea of one year being the appropriate amount of time to be in mourning hangs over her, but she does not know where that concept comes from.

QUESTION 2: After the death of a spouse, how common do you think it is for a new partner to feel as if they will always be in second place?

After a few drinks, Tim makes a comment he probably shouldn't have. "Her husband will always be the love of her life."

It sinks in more how Hannah's heart is not free to love him. He clings to the hope this will change, but the notion of being in competition with a dead man enters his mind.

QUESTION 3: Is young love or first love really that different from love in older age?

"You don't have to worry about him hurting me. If it doesn't work out, I will be fine either way. It is different for younger people. I think you have been afraid to be in a relationship because the idea of it not working out feels devastating to you, but it isn't the same for me."

QUESTION 4: How can dreams and nightmares impact our waking lives?

Hannah is running across a dark street. The man with a gun is chasing her again. He is going to catch up. She turns down an alley, and out of the corner of her eye, sees a porch light turn on. The sound of his boots hitting the ground stops for a few seconds, allowing her to run farther, climbing over a short chain link fence and into a backyard to hide behind a doghouse...

QUESTION 5: Do you believe in reincarnation?

> She awakens with a smile on her face. This is her favorite recurring dream, one of many she believes connect her to a woman who lived on the island over 100 years ago. Most of what Kiera encounters in these visions reveals a painful past.

QUESTION 6: What would you say to someone if they revealed a belief that they are the reincarnation of someone else?

> She takes the quest for honesty one step further, telling him about the woman in her dreams. This leads to a discussion on the concept of reincarnation. Never guessing Ryan would believe in the possibility, he even proposes an interesting suggestion: "Professor Ryan found my relatives. Why don't we ask him about researching women on the island years ago who meet the description and life experiences you described?"

QUESTION 7: Do you believe in soulmates?

> She hears her late husband's voice. *"How can you do this to us? I thought we were soulmates. How can we be soulmates now?"*

QUESTION 8: Do you believe a loved one can send signs after they are gone, such as a bird or a light?

> The bird stares at her as he holds a heart-shaped twig.

> Memories return of her own father insisting that her mother came to him in dreams. He also swore the light would turn on spontaneously for the bookshelf: the one that shone on her mom's Hummel figurines. *Is Jack trying to communicate with her?*

QUESTION 9: How involved should parents be in their adult children's lives? Do you ever worry about leading them in the wrong direction?

> Back at the condo, Hannah hopes she is steering her son in the right direction. While not wanting to squash his dreams, she has read about the extreme rigors of a PhD program and how one can get all the way to the end, only to have their dissertation rejected. Writing and research have not been his strongest qualities.

QUESTION 10: Do you think younger generations are more likely to allow climate change to affect their emotions and outlook?

> He shares his two months of therapy visits one summer in college when dealing with thoughts of hopelessness over the state of the Earth and climate change. It was affecting his day-to-day functioning.

QUESTION 11: What measures should someone take to get a friend or loved one the help they need when suffering from anxiety or depression?

> Clay wants his friend to speak with a psychologist. James is troubled to the point of being unable to function and proceed with their plans. After working up the nerve to broach the subject, he is met with a glare. The thought occurs to him to trick James and make an appointment for both of them to meet with a therapist. Then, he comes across a local inventor who had many failures before becoming successful. Clay contacts Mr. Shields, and the fellow microengineering major agrees to view their project.

> Naomi convinced Kiera to get help. Initially, her friend refused. Also stressed, the soon-to-be college graduate and English teacher made a virtual appointment with a therapist, timing it so she would have 30 minutes alone first. Earlier in the day, she asked Kiera to come to her room at 7:30 to discuss something. "This is Linda. I was telling her about my anxiety and worries for life after university. Now it is your turn. I will be back in 30 minutes."

QUESTION 12: Do you think Hannah worries excessively about her son and needs professional help, or is that part of having grown children, and the concern never ends?

> "I always worry. They could be in a car accident or get attacked. The possibilities are endless in my mind. Ever since he left home at 18, if I don't hear from him for a while, I am not entirely convinced he is still alive."

QUESTION 13: Why do you think it can be so difficult for adult children to accept a new partner in a parent's life?

> "I still don't trust him."

www.ingramcontent.com/pod-product-compliance
Lightning Source LLC
Chambersburg PA
CBHW061736310726
48969CB00002BA/573